*Soho Square* is the fourth volume in
*The Performers*, a compelling sequence
of historical novels which trace the
changing fortunes of two families from
the beginning of the nineteenth
century into the twentieth. The
background is set in the different
worlds of the development of medicine
and the theatre, both professions in
which the families of Abel and Lilith,
who began life as urchins in the gutters
of Seven Dials, become inextricably
intertwined. Through the pages of
*Gower Street*, *The Haymarket*,
*Paddington Green* and now *Soho Square*
Claire Rayner follows the turbulent
lives of Abel, Lilith, and their
successors, paints a vivid portrait of
these two storm-tossed families, and
evokes the social changes and attitudes
of the last century.

Also in Arrow by Claire Rayner

THE RUNNING YEARS
GOWER STREET
THE HAYMARKET
PADDINGTON GREEN

# Soho Square
## *Book IV of*
# The Performers

Claire Rayner

Arrow Books

Arrow Books Limited
17–21 Conway Street, London W1P 6JD

An imprint of the Hutchinson Publishing Group

London Melbourne Sydney Auckland
Johannesburg and agencies throughout
the world

First published in Great Britain by Cassell & Co. Ltd 1976
Corgi edition 1977
Reprinted 1980
Weidenfeld & Nicolson edition 1982
Arrow edition 1985
© Claire Rayner 1976

Printed and bound in Great Britain by
Cox & Wyman Ltd, Reading

ISBN 0 09 938010 2

*For Peter Schwed*
*With affection*

# ACKNOWLEDGMENTS

The author is grateful for the assistance given with research by the Library of the Royal Society of Medicine, London; The Burroughs Wellcome Medical History Library and Museum; Macarthy's Ltd, Surgical Instrument Manufacturers; The London Library; The London Museum; The Victoria and Albert Museum; Westminster City Library; Leichner Stage Make-up Ltd; Raymond Mander and Joe Mitchenson, theatrical historians; Miss Geraldine Stephenson, choreographer and dance historian; The London Fire Brigade; The Metropolitan Police, New Scotland Yard; The Abortion Law Reform Association; and other sources too numerous to mention.

Claire Rayner

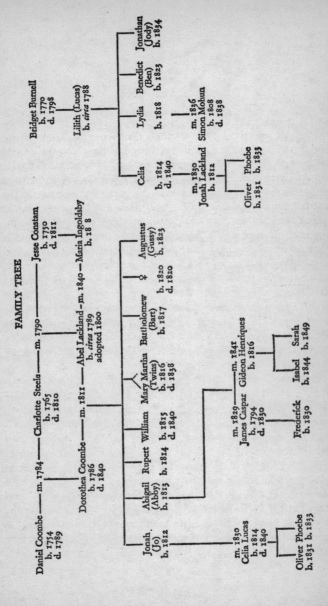

FAMILY TREE

Daniel Coombe
b. 1754
d. 1789
— m. 1784 —
Charlotte Steele
b. 1765
d. 1810

Jesse Constam
b. 1750
d. 1811
— m. 1790 —

Bridget Burnell
b. 1770
d. 1798

Lilith (Lucas)
b. circa 1788

Abel Lackland — m. 1840 — Maria Ingoldsby
b. circa 1789                b. 18  8
adopted 1800

Dorothea Coombe
b. 1786
d. 1840
— m. 1811 —

Celia
b. 1814
d. 1840
m. 1830
Jonah Lackland
b. 1812

Lydia
b. 1818
m. 1836
Simon Mohun
b. 1808
d. 1838

Benedict
(Ben)
b. 1823

Jonathan
(Jody)
b. 1834

Oliver            Phoebe
b. 1831          b. 1833

Abigail
(Abby)
b. 1813

Rupert William
b. 1814
d. 1840

Mary   Martha
(Twins)
b. 1816
d. 1838

Bartholomew
(Bart)
b. 1817

♀
b. 1820
d. 1820

Augustus
(Gussy)
b. 1823

Jonah
(Jo)
b. 1812
m. 1830
Celia Lucas
b. 1814
d. 1840

m. 1829
James Caspar
b. 1794
d. 1830

Gideon Henriques
b. 1816
m. 1841

Oliver      Phoebe
b. 1831    b. 1833

Frederick
b. 1830

Isabel
b. 1844

Sarah
b. 1849

# CHAPTER ONE

THE pigeon sitting on Charles the Second's head in the middle of the Square sank its own head further into the ruff of feathers round its neck as another icy gust of wind came bursting up Carlisle Street to send last year's dead leaves and scraps of gutter rubbish whirling about the grass at the base of the statue's plinth. Looking at it, Jonah felt a sympathetic shiver and pushed his hands more deeply into the pockets of his heavy overcoat. It was much too windy to be standing here on a blustery street corner; and anyway he had business that needed to be attended to on this busy March morning, matters of some moment which required his immediate attention. To loiter here so was to bring himself down to the level of the capering urchins getting in the way of the swearing sweating men unloading the huge Pickford's fly wagon across the Square, was almost to make himself as stupid and lazy as the gossiping staring housemaids leaning on their brooms on neighbouring doorsteps.

But whatever animadversions he cast upon himself it made no difference; still he stood there with his shoulders hunched a little against the wind and his hat, a well-brushed silk one with a curly brim (for he had never lost his boyhood interest in and taste for elegant clothes) set forward to shield his face. Not that he really expected anyone would see him and recognize him, nor even would care much if they did; it was more that he felt an obscure need for something behind which to hide, and his own hat was all that was available. And so he stood and stared at the fly wagon slowly disgorging its contents on to the pavement and steps in front of number twenty-two, as interested as any of the other onlookers in this unexpected new arrival.

Unexpected because it had been a long time since Soho Square had had any pretensions to fashion. The streets that ran into it, Greek Street and Frith Street and Bateman's Buildings, were narrow and mean and far from salubrious. Some of the most wicked people in all London – thieves and whoremongers and murderers and worse – were known to make their habitation there, and this had inevitably removed from the Square, reasonably handsome though it was with its elegant flat-fronted houses, its green central garden, and lofty regal statue, any attraction for the respectable and well-to-do. There had been a time when such people had made their home here, but now the Square was undoubtedly a place of commerce and confusion. Artists' colourmen jostled the manufacturers of blacklead and the purveyors of billiard balls, glass-makers worked cheek by jowl with furniture factors, booksellers and publishers, while the Hospital for Women glowered across the sooty grass at the House of Charity which not only gave succour to such beggars of good repute as it could find but also furnished the hospital with many of its most needy patients. Father O'Leary's chapel on the corner of Sutton Row offered what solace it could to the devout, as did the French church to the many foreigners who lived near the Square, while doctors and lawyers of all shades of respectability from the somewhat dubious to the downright disreputable filled in what space was left.

Yet here was arriving furniture which was quite obviously the property of a person of the first stare of fashion. Sideboards of the most marvellously carved mahogany embellished with mirrored shelves; chairs so thick in upholstery, so deep in buttoning, so twirled in leg and so gleaming in velvet as to leave onlookers breathless; beds positively a-drip with tassels and fringing, alive with carved rosewood scrolls and inset tapestry in their half-testers so that it was not possible to imagine anything as prosaic as sleep taking place beneath them; tables and footstools and brass rails and bamboo screens – all went up the shallow steps to be hauled through the black-painted door under its elegant curve of fanlight while the onlookers crept ever nearer in an attempt to see inside the house, for perhaps the owner of all this richness would be visible, and must surely be a person of considerable importance.

When the piano with the pink silk fronts and the fretted candleholders went in, the housemaids said it must be the home of an opera singer. When a loveseat padded in the most gleaming of yellow silk and with a pair of matching footstools appeared the knowing urchins reckoned it was just another whorehouse, and when a huge and most beautiful French bathtub with gilded decorations and a vast marble base was carried up the steps by all six of the men together someone opined it must be a duke at the very least 'or 'is fancy piece' as one of the smallest and most sharp-eyed of the urchins shouted. Altogether, the delivery of the contents of number twenty-two provided as enjoyable a morning's entertainment as the Square had known all week.

The sight of all this richness both encouraged Jonah and cast him down. He was comforted to see that at least she intended to live in some sort of style. She might have chosen to live in a strange part of the town, but she did mean to live well. She would not, clearly, be likely to seek any sort of pecuniary aid from him. And although no one could call Jonah Lackland parsimonious, he did have many calls upon his purse, and would not relish being involved in any other person's need. Whoever that person might be. But simultaneously he was depressed by the very elegance and fashionableness of it all. This lady was no retiring creature, that much was certain. Her possessions displayed a degree of showiness that reminded him all too painfully of persons and places he did not wish to recall. A particular person who had lived in just such elegance, who had been just as showy.

He shivered again as once more the wind sent icy fingers down his collar and round his ankles. It was ridiculous that it should be so cold so late in March. There should be a smell of spring in the air, even here in the middle of London. And then he had to admit that though windy it wasn't so *very* cold, and indeed the sky did show a most tender blue above the chimney-pots that was very springlike, and in Frith Street there were barrows of early flowers being sold, primroses and violets and even some daffodils. No, his shivers were of apprehension and he could not deny it. So many of the anxieties of his younger years had been stirred up again by the information that there was to be this new arrival at twenty-two Soho Square, so many disagreeable memories had jostled in his mind this past few weeks that he was quite cast down in his health by it all. He could not remember when he had last felt so low.

He turned then to go, intending to strike down Carlisle Street to Dean Street, where there was a music publisher who had promised him the first refusal of a new batch of songs 'that'll double yer takin's in a week, or I don't know the difference betwixt a jew's 'arp and a mandolin,' he had assured Jonah. Jonah had known perfectly well when he had been invited to hear the songs that the man was a rogue, that he was peddling the same melodies to half a dozen others with the self-same promises of exclusiveness, but he had agreed to visit him just the same. That to go there would mean going through Soho Square on the very day *she* was to arrive had not, he assured himself, had anything to do with it. That was just a coincidence that he had not realized until he was actually in the Square. But Jonah was a bad liar at the best of times, and he certainly could not convincingly lie to himself. 'Oh, damn it all to hell and back,' he whispered miserably into his collar, and again hunched his shoulders as if to shut out the disturbance that so filled him.

But before he could reach the corner of Carlisle Street there came a sudden increase of hubbub behind him. He turned his head and saw a most elegant town equipage come spanking round the corner of Soho Street. It was a high-wheeled pair-phaeton painted in a rich blue, with a seat behind on which was perched a diminutive groom, and with the leather hood folded down in spite of the wind.

Sitting up on the driver's seat was a woman; she did not appear, from this distance, to be particularly tall, yet somehow she gave the impression of being a person of considerable stature and importance as she sat there in a mantle of blue that precisely matched the paint on her phaeton, the reins held with apparent negligence in her left hand, and the whip in her right.

But she was clearly in firm control of her vehicle, for as it reached the corner she cracked the whip with a casual twist of her wrist that was most graceful to see and the perfectly matched grey ponies wheeled and curvetted and came to a perfect stop behind the fly wagon.

The heavy dray horses standing lethargically in front of it stamped and snorted at the sound, looking back over their huge shoulders at the new arrivals, and one of the ponies on the phaeton whinnied loudly and tried to rear, but with a sharp pull on the reins and an accurately placed flick of her whip the driver brought him into control again. And then laughed and without looking back even for a moment tossed the whip and reins to the little tiger who caught them both as he came leaping off the phaeton behind her.

Everyone around gawped in silence as the woman stood there on the pavement looking up at the house, slowly pulling her gloves from her fingers, seemingly quite unaware of the interest she had aroused, although Jonah for one was quite sure that she was extremely conscious of her audience and was relishing it enormously. For a moment he even thought she knew that he was there, standing across the Square and staring at her from beneath his black silk hat brim, but then dismissed that. She could not know – would probably not even recognize him if she looked directly at him. But he recognized her, and his belly seemed to tighten as he looked at her.

It had been more than twenty years since he had seen her, and she had been just a child then – well, perhaps a little more than a child, at thirteen – but she was easily recognizable. Her hair then had been unruly black curls, and it was still curly, but now done in a most fashionable style with bunches of ringlets over her ears and peeping out modishly under her expensive silk-lined bonnet. Her face then had been round and soft and dimpled, and now it was, he could see, still dimpled – for she suddenly smiled at one of the cheekier of the urchins who had ventured close enough to hold out his hands to beg – but more shapely, with pleasing shadows beneath the cheekbones, and a firm jawline that melted into her long neck with the smoothest of curves. Her eyes, as he remembered, had been very dark brown, so dark as to look black sometimes, but he could not see those from here, not fully. All he could see was that she had grown up to be a very handsome woman indeed, as handsome as her mother before her had been.

And now he did turn to go. He had seen her, and his worst fears had been realized. He had hoped with an absurd hopefulness that she would be just like any other woman who had lived three and thirty years, had been wed and widowed and had, furthermore, spent many years in provincial living. He had hoped he would see her as ordinary, one he could dismiss from his mind as no possible disturber of his peace. And now he knew his hopes had been quite ridiculous. This woman, even seen from the far side of Soho Square, was clearly one of great character and magnetism. It showed in every line of her body as she went up the steps of her house, in the tilt of her head, in the easy way she moved. It showed in the fascinated stares of the people around, all clearly bedazzled by her style, her handsomeness, her sheer presence, and it showed, above all, in the way Jonah himself was filled with such foreboding at the sight of her. Lydia Mohun, like her mother before her, was trouble looking for somewhere to happen. And Jonah made up his mind to it, as he went striding up Carlisle Street, that wherever that somewhere was, it would not be on *his* doorstep. Not if he could help it.

Westwards from Soho Square the streets are as un-fashionable as the Square itself; narrow, noisy, reeking of rotting vegetables, burned fat from the cookhouses, horses and overcrowded humanity. But then, where the roads widen and the gutters become almost clean carrying away only the sooty rainwater that falls on the smooth cobbles, style begins to show itself. Wide porticoes with scrubbed white stone steps leading up to them, black-painted iron railings and creamy stucco show the habitations of the rich and the powerful. In Grosvenor Square, where the richest and most powerful of the Town could be seen on any day of the week, the houses were particularly big, particularly lavishly furnished, and for at least one of the inhabitants on this March morning particularly claustrophobic.

'I wish you would not demand that I sit in the dark, Mamma, simply because *you* choose to,' Jody said, and twisting in his seat swung his legs up so that his knees were hooked over the delicate arm of the gilt chair, which creaked under the assault.

'Please, take care,' she said. 'These chairs were very costly.' But the remonstrance was almost automatic, and Jody ignored it, as indeed he would have done had her tone been twice as waspish. 'I prefer the softer light,' she said then, 'and it is not kind in you to complain. Knowing as you do how much it distresses me—'

'Oh, Mamma! As if it matters one whit whether we have the curtains open or closed! You wear so thick a curtain about you, and sit so determinedly kitty-cornered, it would take a man with a telescope to see more than the end of your nose. You do it just to plague me. I hate sitting in this mausoleum! Especially when you are in such ill sorts.'

'I am not in ill sorts, and you must not say I am! I asked only that you give me a little of your company, and give me news of the town. It is not so much to ask, surely, my dear one, when I am so lonely, and so shut away from all as I am—'

'Oh, Mamma, you do prose on so! There is nothing I can tell you. The people go about the streets, the gutters stink and the river flows. What more is there? When I talk of my own interests you complain, and—'

'That is not fair! Did I not just pull you out of such a scrape as would have caused you great trouble, if I had not? You shall not say I am unkind to you, simply because I ask you to talk to me!'

And they were off again, wrangling in the same dismal way, round and round in circles, with Jody alternately sulking and then suddenly sparkling at her and coaxing her, and then flouncing away in sulks again. But she could bear his sulks, could bear the sound of irritation, even boredom, in his voice; she could bear anything as long as he was with her. For Lilith the greatest of hell was to sit through the long afternoons and even longer evenings when he was out of doors about his own affairs, leaving her in her ill-lit room with her face veiled even when there were none about to see her. When he was here, she could forget her cruelly scarred face, her loneliness, her desperate boredom. Just to see him and hear him and feel the warmth of him near her was enough to push all her misery to one side.

And she had discovered, painfully, that there was but one way she could keep him there with her and that was by being captious. If he wanted money – and when did he not? – much as she ached to pour it into his lap, she played the game of being hard put to find enough to meet his needs. She made him sit there while she counted up her assets and computed her own needs, to see what she had left over for him. He knew as well as she did that it was all a hum; that she could and would at any time give him all he asked. And he also knew that she played this game with him in order to keep his company.

There had been times when he had tried to break her of this habit of pretence of whining parsimony by coming to see her and sit with her when he did not want money from her; but that resolve soon failed. She was so cloying in her sweetness to him, so clinging and so greedy for him that he felt sometimes that if he spent more time with her than he must he would be engulfed, digested, quite absorbed by her.

Today he was more than usually irritable at the masquerading. He had to separate her from some two hundred pounds, a sum large enough to give even him pause, but he could not help it. He had begun by winning quite heavily and the losses, when they had started, had seemed small, not enough to dent his pocket at all. Until the end of the evening when, flushed with a full bottle of brandy – and he had not meant to swallow quite so much – he had added up his score, and been shocked almost into sobriety by it. To owe so much and to the same men who had brought him so close to disaster last time, several months ago now – it was all very alarming.

Last time they had threatened to carve him into butcher's meat, had painted such a word picture of the damage that they could and would do to his seventeen-year-old face and body that he had been downright nauseated; and he had sat there and heaved and retched and they had laughed at him, but with no humour in it. They had meant every word they said.

That time his Mamma had been genuinely troubled to find it, for it had been a sum in four figures; so much so that she had sold several of her shares in the Haymarket theatre to John Buckstone, the manager. That had meant she relinquished all control over the place, and that had hurt her, he knew. She had always had a special feeling for the old Haymarket theatre, and had gained much pleasure from perusing the lists of plays and players selected to appear there, and sending imperious messages that such and such a one was not to be employed on any account, and that such and such a playwright was never to have his work selected.

He had, indeed, shared some of her pleasure in her power there, and had used it to pay off some of his own scores, just as she did. There had been that little dancer who had laughed at him after his first attempt to bed her, and left him sore with rage and fear for his prowess. Well, his Mamma had seen to it that she was thrown out of her place at the Haymarket in the very next production. So, he had to admit it was sad that the only way she had been able to raise the money he had needed was by selling out of the Haymarket, but what else was there? To sell a larger parcel of property would not be good money sense; to sell actual jewels – and she had many – would mean to lose considerably, for a forced sale never realized full worth. The Haymarket shares it had to be.

And now he had to do it again. Somehow he had to part her from a sizeable sum. He sighed sharply, and swung his legs back to the floor. This bickering way was getting him nowhere, and besides he had a mind to be out tonight, to see the new performance at Drury Lane. She must be brought to the point. . . .

It took him a good deal over an hour, some seventy-five minutes of wheedling and coaxing and teasing and laughing, but it was well worth it, for she gave him at length a Bill against her lawyers for two hundred and fifty pounds with little more than a *moue* of disapproval, and he hugged her and kissed her with real warmth when at last she handed it to him.

'You are the dearest Mamma in the world!' he said and stood up to brush the knees of his fashionable spongebag check trousers and then to fold the precious Bill and set it snugly in his pocket. So great was his sense of real gratitude this time – for he had been very frightened last night when they had threatened yet again to take their knives to him – that he even cast about in his mind for some extra reward for her, and at last dug out a scrap of theatrical gossip of the sort she dearly loved. It was all the poor old creature had left of her past, after all, he told himself, and grinned down at her carelessly, his head on one side as she looked up at him adoringly, the glint of her eyes shining even through the folds of her cream lace veil.

'I have news of the next Haymarket production, Mamma,' he said. 'I daresay you will not hear as you used to of all that goes forward there? Well, there is to be yet another revival of *Ivanhoe.*'

'So soon?' She was all eagerness. 'I did not think they did so well with it last year! It was a sorry burlesque, I was told. And it did not run above seventy performances, as I recall—'

He had moved away from her now to stand peering into the shadowy mirror above the fireplace, trying to set his cravat more to rights. 'Well, success or not, it is to be done again with Richard O'Hare playing Ivanhoe—'

'Oh, that is no surprise!' she said, and settled back in her chair, nodding a little. 'He has a most romantic way with him, I'm told, though I believe he is not an actor of any real stature—'

'And Rowena is Mrs. Plunkett again, and they have a new performer for the Lady Rebecca, quite unknown, I believe. In London at any rate.'

'Oh?' She was all attention. She had herself played the Noble Jewess in an enormously successful production. Once. Long ago. 'An unknown, in so important a part? Surely not!'

'Oh, I believe she is far from being a tyro.' He turned from the mirror, and smiled at her. 'No, indeed! They promise great things for her, those who have seen her performance. In this very part, as well – she had huge success, I'm told, in Edinburgh.'

She was suddenly very still. 'Edinburgh? A new actress from Edinburgh?'

He peered down at her, puzzled by the note in her voice. 'Aye. She is, I believe a most popular performer there, but has just lately come to live in London. Lydia – Mohun, I believe it is. Aye, that is it. It is said Moon, but spelt in the Cornish manner. Do you know her?'

# CHAPTER TWO

THE sun slanting along the Oxford Road, past the Marble Arch newly erected at Hyde Park Corner to stare haughtily up the Edgware Road, sent fingers of shadows under the trees in the park and decorated the breakfast-room floor at number three Stanhope Terrace in a most agreeable way. Gideon stood at the door for a moment looking at the way they were all framed in the morning light, not thinking anything in particular but just enjoying the sight of them.

Especially Abby. She sat at the top of the table with Isabel pinafored against the splash of her bread and milk on one side of her and, on the other side, Sarah perched high in her wicker baby chair and banging her hands on the front of it. In Ellie's eyes the removal of such babies as these two from the nursery at breakfast time was little short of heathenish, but Abby knew how to handle Ellie. She had been housemaid and cook general at Abby's other house in Paddington Green before being promoted to head nursemaid here at Stanhope Terrace, and though she had the privileges of the long-time servant she rarely, if ever, enjoyed any licence. Not with the capable Abby in charge of the household, Gideon thought, and smiled a little as his eyes moved to Freddy sitting, as ever, with his head buried in the Pall Mall Gazette as he stuffed his breakfast into his mouth at breakneck speed.

His red hair, well brushed and neatly arranged above his workmanlike black suit and spotless collar, positively shone; not for Freddy the deliberate look of grubby shabbiness so assiduously cultivated by so many of his fellow students; he was far above that sort of childishness, he had told Gideon loftily once when his stepfather had gently teased him about the perfection of his dress. But for all his punctiliousness about his personal habits, he was no dull prude, not Freddy; and he looked up now and caught Gideon's eye and winked at him, and with an exaggerated sigh folded the newspaper carefully and held it out as Gideon came to take his own place at the foot of the table.

'There's no other answer for it,' Gideon said. 'I shall have to order two copies to be left each day, if I am to be able to read the day's news through the crumbs and the creases you create! How many times must I tell you? You are twice welcome to it, wretched boy – when I have finished!'

'Yes, sir!' Freddy said cheerfully. 'I'll try to remember. But you need not be too put about today, for I took special care not to leave so much as a fingermark on the money market news or the share lists! And that is all you read, after all!'

'Oh, I am not all the money-grubber you choose to think me!' Gideon said cheerfully, immediately opening the paper to the money market page. 'Or not entirely! Abby, my love, Sarah is about to commit some mayhem with her pap—'

Abby, looking round from wiping Isabel's chin in time to catch the bowl Sarah was lifting above her head, laughed. 'Then you come and feed her, do, while I pour your coffee – she's as villainous this morning as seven twice her size. Young vixen!'

'I shall deal with her, Mamma,' Freddy said cheerfully. 'Eat your breakfast, do. You know you will be late if you do not. Gideon—' He looked over his shoulder at Gideon helping himself to eggs at the sideboard. 'Gideon, I would be grateful if you could spare me some time this afternoon, when I come back from Nellie's. I am in need of some financial advice—'

'Freddy! What for?' Abby looked up sharply. 'You have only just had this quarter's allowance, surely! You are not getting into debt, are you?'

'Oh, hark at her! Such an assumption to make! Every inch the trustful parent, are you not? No, my dear foolish Mamma, I do not have my pockets to let! I have never yet been such a one, so I shall hardly start now. It is something quite other, I do assure you. I will talk to you about it, when I am ready. As always! This is to be a matter between Gideon and me for the present.' And he smiled at her with so disarming a friendliness that she was abashed.

'Aye, well, I should know better, I daresay.' She said and smiled back. 'Clearly there are matters that men discuss that we poor women could never understand!'

'Which coming from you is doing it up a bit too brown!' Gideon said and came back to the table. 'With twice the money head on her shoulders than I'll ever have, you'd be wiser to talk to your Mamma and that's a fact, Freddy. Although my time is yours of course, if you wish it.'

'I do,' said Freddy easily, then expertly mopped Sarah's face, and made her laugh by sticking out his tongue at her and crossing his eyes. 'Mamma shall know my affairs when I am ready – but I prefer to talk to you first. Today will be most suitable for me, if you can spare the time.'

'So be it,' Gideon said equably. 'At a little before six then?'

'Splendid!' Freddy stood up to brush his coat into smooth perfection again and Abby looked up at him and marvelled, as she so often did, that she could have produced so very large a young man, for he stood a full two inches above six feet in his stockings, quite dwarfing his mother who had always regarded her own five feet four as a respectable enough height, but now doubted it.

'I shall leave now, I think, instead of waiting for the half past eight omnibus,' he said. 'It is a lovely morning, and I shall walk. I can take the cross paths through the Park, and see how they are getting along with the glazing of Mr. Paxton's Palace. It should be near on finished by now, for they say the first exhibits will be coming in very shortly.'

'Oh, take me, Freddy, take me!' Isabel cried shrilly, and tried to scramble down from her chair. 'Do, Freddy, please—'

'So, I shall, my little love, but not today,' Freddy said. 'Not until there is more for you to see! And I must be away to the hospital, and would not be able to fetch you back – and then what would happen? Imagine Ellie coming to hunt for you among all those workmen! She'd be as cross as two sticks—'

And Isabel pouted, and then laughed, for she was a sunny-tempered child. Freddy bent and kissed her and then his mother and the baby, and went round the table to touch Gideon's shoulder in farewell as he went by.

But before he could reach the door it burst open – not too strong a word for the flurry that caused it – and Phoebe was in the room in a great sussuration of skirts, with Ellie following hard behind her and scolding at the top of her voice.

'If I've told you once, I've told you 'arf a dozen times, it's not for the mornings as crinolines that size is meant! There's yer aunt, as elegant a lady as any would wish, and you don't see 'er peacocking about in such an 'uge skirt so early in the day! You wear the gowns as I put out for you, and you can put on that one this afternoon, to pay yer mornin' calls. But to come to the breakfast parlour in it is downright ridiculous, and I ain't afraid to tell yer so, if any others is!' And she frowned at Freddy with great ferocity, for Phoebe had gone slipping away from her to stand behind him and set her hands about his waist in a mock imploring hug.

'Oh, do protect me, Freddy!' she said, and giggled at the way Ellie snorted in response. 'Indeed, I am quite, quite terrified! All I did was put on this pretty gown for all of you to admire and Ellie carries on as though I were the world's worst. Indeed, you must protect me, or she'll tear it from my back!'

Freddy, stepping neatly sideways, turned and stood looking down at his cousin – for she was small, not much above five feet and a couple of inches – and examined her judicially. She was wearing a most charming gown of lemon gauze trimmed with tiny stuff rosebuds in darker yellow, with matching ribbons tying the bunches of dark ringlets above her ears. The great bell of the skirt was very light, so light indeed that it seemed to move a little with her every breath, rising and falling in the sunshine, and she stood there with her hands clasped gently in front of her, her head on one side and looking up at Freddy with her lips set in a half smile that clearly displayed a very pretty dimple at each corner of her mouth. She looked entirely delectable, and it was apparent to all of them that she was even more aware of the fact than they were.

'Well, there is no question that you look most handsomely set out,' Freddy said after a moment, 'and would grace any drawing-room. No question. However, is this suitable garb for the breakfast parlour, one wonders? Ellie thinks not, while you disagree. But how can I be expected to take any part in so desperately important a decision? How can I, a poor bedazzled male set almost speechless by the glory of your appearance – and the size of your crinoline – be asked to offer any—'

'Oh, do stop!' Phoebe said, and produced a pout as pretty as her smile had been. And just as well considered. 'You shall not tease me, but you shall tell Ellie that—'

'—she is absolutely right! It is not a garment for the breakfast table!' Abby said equably. 'And having made precisely the effect you wished, little monkey, you shall change immediately. Good-bye, Freddy. You won't have time for your walk if you don't set out at once. We shall see you at dinner. Early, remember, because of the party—'

'Yes, I must go. Good-bye, Phoebe. You look quite perfect! Is this the dress for tonight, then? I shall look forward to it all with even more pleasure, now – good-bye.' And he kissed her forehead and hugged her with the vigorous hug he had always been accustomed to give her, and she smiled up at him, without any artfulness this time but in her usual pleasant way, and kissed his cheek, and went away with Ellie to change her gown.

As usual, Phoebe had started the day with a little excitement, and all of them set about the morning's business feeling that little bit more lively in consequence. Even if that March morning had not been bright with spring sunshine the Henriques household would have been content; because they usually were. It was a contentment born of that which existed between Abby and Gideon, and had done throughout the eight years of their marriage, percolating through to all of them and making the pair of cousins feel as much Gideon's children as were his own two small daughters, and making Phoebe accept her aunt's maternal authority in a way she had never accepted her own mother's.

Not, thought Gideon, as he exchanged an amused glance with his wife behind Phoebe's departing back, that it was likely that Phoebe even remembered her mother. They never talked of the past in the Henriques household; the present was too busy and too agreeable, and the past, so much of it, had been so very distressful that none of them wanted to think about it, let alone talk of it.

There were times, of course, when Gideon had to step back into that past, when he went to visit his mother. Each Friday morning, with punctilious care, he took the omnibus to the city to spend two hours sitting with Leah, as vigorous and as black-haired as ever, for all her sixtieth birthday was so far behind her. His father was never there in the room with her, however, and Gideon, although he always started his visit by asking after Nahum's health, accepted his absence as inevitable.

When Gideon had married Abby after two years of determined pressure on his part, and almost equally determined resistance on hers – although at last it had crumbled – he had turned his back on his co-religionists, though not on his religion, for he could never do that, and also on his father, dearly as he had always loved him. If this was the price he had to pay for his marriage to Abby, then pay it he would, he had told his parents, and his mother had accepted the inevitable, though his father had not and never would. He mourned his son as dead, for to him any son of the congregation who married a Gentile was beyond the pale.

And Gideon too mourned – for his father's unhappiness, and wished it could have been otherwise. Sometimes – very rarely – he would look at Abby and his daughters, at the happiness of his stepson and his wife's niece with whom he shared his home and his care and would ask himself if he had any right to enjoy such felicity, when doing so caused so much agony to his own father; but he could never find it in his heart to blame himself, for he knew he had not been totally selfish in so following the dictates of his own desires. He had made himself happy in marrying Abby, he knew – but he knew equally well that he had created a lot of happiness for others. And no man could ever be castigated for that.

He often gave thanks to his God for his happiness. He would go at regular intervals to the Saturday morning services at

Bevis Marks Synagogue, sitting at the back in one of the unreserved pews, to pray quietly yet fervently – and alone. The other men, even though many of them had watched him grow up, ignored him totally, behaving as though he were not there. And at the end of the service he would quietly fold his prayer shawl and set it in its velvet bag emblazoned with gilt Hebrew letters, and walk back again to Stanhope Terrace where Abby would smile at him and welcome him to the tranquillity of home and never speak a word about where he had been and why.

She too mourned the tragedy of her husband's exclusion from family and friends, and much more keenly because of her sense of guilt; it had been for her sake he had parted with his past, for her love he had jettisoned the love of his father. But in eight years she had learned to contain her guilt within her and not burden him with it. She could smile at him, and touch his hand and say nothing on those days when he chose to fast, could accept his demands for strange rules about his meat and how it was prepared in the kitchens, and never made any comment.

Today being Friday, Gideon had a spare half hour before he need leave the house; he would go straight to his mother's home and return to the counting-house of the factory in Irongate Wharf Road in the early afternoon.

Not that his visit to his mother was entirely a social one; he would discuss with her the affairs of his parents' banking business and offer such advice as he could. Just how she managed to persuade her husband to accept that advice he did not know, but somehow she did, for the bank flourished, in spite of the loss of Gideon who had been its main prop and stay in the days before his marriage. Now he gave all his energies to Caspar's, the business that he had taken over when he married Abby, and in the eight years they had been together it too had flourished exceedingly. The arrival of the railways had been a great spur, for their factory was situated so marvellously conveniently for the terminus of the Great Western Railway; they had, therefore, been able to undercut many of the other manufacturing apothecaries with whom they were in competition. From selling entirely in the London area in the early days, now

26

they sent their pills and potions and ready-made plasters and concoctions of all sorts as far west as Exeter. In the past year they had become even more ambitious, as the railways spread their steely tentacles into every corner of the country, and had branch offices in Runcorn and Norwich, and even as far north as York now where Oliver, Phoebe's solemn and very efficient brother, sat in command of the work of Caspar's and accrued more and more profit to the company's coffers.

Gideon, smiling at his wife and daughters across his breakfast table on this shiny March morning, had much indeed to be happy about. Domestic felicity and money as well – what more could a modern man want? Gideon felt himself to be so totally in tune with the spirit of the age that had he been superstitious he would have been almost afraid to contemplate his own good fortune. But he was not superstitious; indeed, with his firm views of religious morality it would have been positively sinful to fear some malign fate. When a man behaved, as Gideon did, with all duty he could to his God and his fellows, he had nothing to fear.

Thinking of his duty to his fellows reminded him of his promise to Jonah, and he said, 'Abby, my love, have you talked with your brother lately?'

'Not since last week, on Sunday as usual,' she said. 'Why do you ask?'

'He sent a message yesterday. Wanting me to come to see him at the supper rooms today. Difficult – there is the meeting with Sydenham at one o'clock and now Freddy wanting to talk to me at six – I shall be hard put to it to be ready for Phoebe's party tonight at this rate. It might be easier to see Jonah after dinner, perhaps. Will Phoebe notice, do you suppose, if I am absent from her little entertainment?'

'Notice? My dear, she would be mortified! And never call it "little" in her hearing, I do beg you! We have heard nothing but tableaux, tableaux, tableaux this past month! She will most certainly miss any member of her audience who dares be absent, I promise you – and anyway, Jonah will be here tonight himself. You do not think she would fail to insist on *his* presence, do you?'

'Oh. Perhaps he will be willing to tell me what it is he wished to consult me on here, then? Does he dine?'

'No, he cannot leave the supper rooms until after the first show there, he says. He will not be here until close on half past ten, in time for Phoebe's performances. There will be no chance to talk of any business matters here, Gigi, I am sure. You had better go to King Street, if it is so important it cannot wait until Sunday.'

'He said it was important,' Gideon said, and stood up as Phoebe at last came back into the room seeking her breakfast, and now wearing a neat green morning dress.

'So, Phoebe! Is all ready for your great entertainment tonight? From all your aunt says, I am under the impression it is to rival the Exhibition itself!'

'Of course!' Phoebe said airily. 'For the Exhibition is no more than a huge tangle of workmen and glass in the park, while my tableaux are ready now! Oh, Gideon, you will enjoy it all, I promise you! I have four different costumes, and the most delicious scenery arranged and—'

'No, tell me none of it! Let it be a surprise,' Gideon said hastily. 'You will spoil my anticipation if you give too much information. Abby, I shall have to go to Covent Garden this afternoon then, between the meeting with Sydenham and six o'clock. Can you manage in my absence?'

Abby smiled at him, and then stood up too, scooping up Sarah as she did so. 'I daresay! I am not quite helpless, I believe! And there is nothing that cannot wait until tomorrow, anyway. Henry will be there all day today, so he will oversee where necessary. Good-bye, my dear – and as ever, I hope all is well in the City,' and they exchanged a kiss and parted amiably at the foot of the stairs, leaving Phoebe, as always, to finish her breakfast alone, for Phoebe alone among them had no special daily tasks with which to busy herself.

Not that she was not capable of rushing about in great flurries of activity; with her morning gossips with her many friends culled from the large houses hereabouts, and her hectic rounds of calls, sitting elegantly in the pretty little carriage which had been her father's eighteenth birthday present, her

28

daily rides in Rotten Row accompanied by a little coterie of elegant young men who were the brothers of her friends (and fortunate the young men of the district who had sisters of an age to be friends of the much admired and sought after Miss Lackland), and her parties and balls and entertainments galore, Phoebe was a busy young lady. But not at breakfast time, when she would sit in luxurious comfort eating hot toast and drinking tea and thinking of her day's costumes.

Freddy, by now marching at great speed across the park, thought of her sitting there with her elbows on the table and her cup held between her two hands (for she was never quite so elegant at home as when she was abroad) and smiled a little at the thought of her. Such a silly, empty-headed little wretch that she was! To apply her undoubtedly sharp little mind to the sort of frippery affairs she did was so wasteful – but so very endearing. And she is very young, after all, thought Freddy, with all the wisdom of his own almost twenty-one years. In time she would become less giddy, and would settle her mind to more important things than parties and the tableaux *vivants* she so adored.

She had been told about this form of drawing-room entertainment by the mother of one of her friends, in whose youth thirty years ago such things had been fashionable, since when she had started quite a craze for them in the district. She spent hours reading books on Greek myths and historical events, planning arrangements and costumes and pretty effects for them, and Freddy had to admit that she had become very gifted with them.

He would sit and look at her being Queen Boadicea in a chariot made of a kitchen table upended, encouraging her troops with noble gestures, or Helen swathed in yards of white satin and yearning over Troy, and feel the spell she could weave over him – had always woven from the time he first set eyes on her when he was a raw ten-year-old and she a wide-eyed seven in white frills and pinafores.

His steps lengthened and his speed increased as he thought about that spell now. Quite when he had realized that the way he felt about his cousin Phoebe was not mere childish affection, but a real, mature and very adult love, he did not know. Sometimes it seemed to him that he had loved Phoebe all his life. The time before she had appeared now seemed to be shadowy, unlived time. There had been his mother and Ellie and himself and the seven elms of Paddington Green and their little house and that was all, an all which was very pleasant no doubt, but not precisely *exciting*.

And then there had been Phoebe, and all the colours had brightened and the days had become longer and more promising, the fireside evenings more cosy, the games on the Green more dramatic, the work at school harder, the holidays more idyllic. *Everything* had been increased in value.

His mother's wedding to Gideon had been an important event, but not because of the wedding so much as because Phoebe had torn her dress, specially made for the occasion (quiet wedding though it had been), and in trying to staunch her bitter tears Freddy had kissed her, and for the first time discovered that being a boy of thirteen kissing a girl of ten was a very grown-up thing to be, and created very grown-up feelings.

The birth of his first half-sister had been a great event too, and again not because of that squalling red-faced scrap who was Isabel but because Phoebe had chosen to be very dramatic about it all, and cried bitterly 'for fear' she had wept, 'Aunt Abby and Uncle Gideon won't want me to stay here any more,' and had needed many hugs and kisses from him (kisses she appeared to enjoy a great deal) to be reassured that it would be over his dead body that she would be removed from the family.

Looking back on it all now, he knew perfectly well she had not been at all afraid, really. From the time she had come to live with her aunt 'temporarily' after her mother's dreadful death, while her father 'organized matters better' it had been clear that this was to become a permanent arrangement. They had none of them intended it that way at the time, he was sure, but with hindsight it was obvious that it had been inevitable. His Uncle Jonah was not the man to be able to take the sort of care of a girl that was needful. The best thing that had ever happened to Phoebe was coming to live with her aunt, Freddy told himself, as he went striding on down the sunny path towards the glitter of Paxton's huge Exhibition building.

And for me, a secret little voice whispered in his ear, and for a moment he grinned to himself. Indeed, and for him. Life without Phoebe to see every day would be insupportable. Poor Uncle Jonah, having only Sunday to share with her!

Uncle Jonah. His face sobered as he thought of him. How would he take the matter? There would be no problem about money, he was sure of that. He knew that his patrimony was considerable; Gideon had told him, on his eighteenth birthday, that half the income from the Caspar business was his, as befitted the only son of the founder of it, and though he had protested, realizing full well that a large part of the business's success was due to the effort and acumen Gideon had brought to it to add to his mother's good business head, his stepfather had been adamant.

'There is more than enough for us in half the profits, Freddy,' he had said. 'And indeed, you are a very rich young man, for the business will grow, that I promise you! And always, half of it is yours, so do not argue with me now or ever. That is the way it is to be.'

No, there would be no problems about money. He would have enough and more to support a wife handsomely, to provide her with all the fripperies and clothes and parties and fun any young bride could want. And to fill a nursery with toys and joys of all sorts – and for a moment he let his mind drift into its favourite fantasy, seeing himself as a paterfamilias to a crew of little Isabels and Sarahs, with Phoebe sitting beautiful and loving among them all. And then pulled his mind back to the matter in hand.

Jonah.

How would Jonah react when he was told, as Freddy now fully intended to tell him, once he had obtained the details of his financial position from his stepfather tonight, that he wished to marry his only daughter?

Freddy just did not know. And for all his good sense – and he knew himself to be a practical sort of young man, and not one given to nonsensical anxieties – he simply could not foretell the answer. He would just have to wait and hope that there would be no objections from that direction.

He left the park at the Grosvenor Gate, and hailed a hansom cab in Park Lane, still thinking about his Uncle Jonah and what he might say. It never occurred to him, however, to wonder what anyone else might have to say — Gideon and Abby or even Phoebe herself. As far as Freddy was concerned that March morning, the only unknown quantity in his plans was Jonah.

# CHAPTER THREE

By the time Freddy reached Nellie's, having urged his driver to make even more haste than usual (and like all cab drivers this one was far from averse to earning a larger tip than the usual fourpence from indulging his own delight in hurling his vehicle through the crowded streets to the intense risk of every person or object that stood in his way), he was late, and his heart sank a little. He was not precisely frightened of his grandfather, as were most of the other students, but he knew enough of his temper to take his displeasure very seriously. Abel Lackland could be exceedingly sharp with any young man who was in the least dilatory; and Freddy ran up the steps of the hospital, pushing his way through the crowds already waiting for the doors to the outpatient department to open, he pulled his watch from his waistcoat pocket and grimaced. That walk through the park had been a most foolish piece of self-indulgence.

But all was well, and as he looked swiftly round the crowded entrance hall, he breathed again. There was not as yet any sign of his grandfather standing with his hands thrust into his pockets and glaring pointedly at the huge clock which adorned the wall opposite the entrance; only the usual handful of lounging students who greeted him noisily and produced their familiar ribald jokes about people who had been so busy lechering about the town the night before that they could not keep their morning appointments. And he joined in as he usually did, knowing as well as they that the noisiness and vulgarity of their talk did not in any way bespeak true coarseness of nature, but was a protective shield against the pain of the day's work; the sights that students saw and the diseases that were displayed to their inexperienced eyes could make the most stolid of young men weep if he had not learned to feign unconcern. And taproom jokes were the easiest way to do it.

The morning was a busy one, once Abel did arrive, for he swept them all up and hurried them along to the surgical wards to do the day's dressings and study the effects of the operations performed during the previous week, almost without giving them time to catch their breaths.

Freddy, his street coat carefully hung up and replaced with the rather shabby but not yet bloodstained one that would mark a senior student who had started to perform operations himself, was more than once grateful for that half hour walk in the park that had started his day. As he dealt with one suppurating wound after another, the reek of the pus and the sour dressings that had to be removed was enough to make anyone's gorge rise, and he fixed his mind on the memory of the scent of grass and young trees and morning air whenever the miasma threatened to become too much for him.

And succeeded well, for the nurse who had been standing beside him as he worked grinned at him when he had finished the last – a particularly rotting wound left after an amputation below the knee – and told him he'd done well to hold his breakfast within him. And he had reddened a little, for this was praise indeed from one of these hardbitten females. The nurses were better than those at some of London's hospitals – with Mrs. Bartlett as the Matron in charge it could not be otherwise – but they were still women of low class and little sensitivity, quite incapable of the sort of feminine delicacy that naturally made true ladies (such as Phoebe for example) shrink from the work that had to be done in hospitals like Queen Eleanor's. Not for the first time Freddy marvelled at the fact that any woman at all could perform the sort of tasks that these women did.

He was supposed to be spending the afternoon in the dissecting rooms in the hospital basement, studying anatomy by carving up a human arm, and he was not particularly looking forward to that. He had decided to become a surgeon once he left school not because he had any high academic interest in the discipline, but because he could think of nothing else he par-

34

ticularly wanted to do. The chance of working for Caspar's had of course been there, but his mother had told him firmly that this was not demanded of him, half-owner though he was, and, indeed, she felt it would be better for him if he chose some other area of activity.

'For,' she had said earnestly, 'I believe it would be a mistake for you to work too closely with Gideon. I love you both dearly, but I know you both well. Gideon is a man of very strong will and character, as are you, my dear boy, and I could not bear it if you worked together and found yourselves disagreeing. As it is, the affection between you both gives me much joy. Had your own father lived, you could not, I am sure you will admit, have had more fatherly love and concern than you receive from Gideon' – with which Freddy had agreed most fervently – 'and although there is no obvious reason to suggest you *would* fall out if you shared work in our counting-house there is always that risk. So some other profession, I think—'

It had not occurred to either of them that Freddy should do as did so many of the well-endowed young men of their acquaintance – nothing; for Freddy was not made of the stuff of a dilettante. He had to do something with his life; and in casting about for that something his eyes had fallen upon his grandfather. He had learned to admire Abel, once he had the chance to get to know him, although he could not ever imagine himself loving him, for he was so very remote a man as well as so very important; but he could respect him. And therefore his occupation.

Which was why he now found himself in the second gruelling year of his studies, and often a little cast down by them. Anatomy was one aspect of the work that he did most profoundly dislike. The bodies they had to work on were so very dead, so exceedingly unpleasant in their effects on all his senses – not least the olfactory – that there were many times he was tempted to go to his mother and grandfather and beg their pardons for discommoding them, but please could he enter an Inn of Court and be a lawyer? Anything rather than spend one more hour in the basement dissecting rooms at Nellie's.

But then there would come an aspect of the work of a student that made him feel that what he was learning to do really was tolerable after all, was as much concerned with the easing of human pain as the cool academic digging into the human structure that so fascinated his grandfather, and so repelled him. There had been such an occasion early in his second year of study, when he had been at lowest ebb, and as close as damn it to throwing in his hand.

Abel had arranged a special demonstration of the new anaesthetic method, bringing the entire student population of the hospital crowding into one small operating theatre to watch Dr. John Snow, a close friend of his from St. George's Hospital. Freddy had been at the front of the mob, not because he particularly wanted to be, but because the others had managed to outshuffle him, remaining firmly at the back. So he had had a particularly clear view of all that went forward.

'I am here to show you the answer to a hundred centuries of men's prayers.' Snow, a man of medium height and receding dark hair above a commonplace face, had a faintly Yorkshire accent and a dry way of speaking that made the high-flown emotion of his opening words sound positively ludicrous, and a few of the young men listening to him giggled.

'Aye, ye may laugh, gentlemen,' Snow said coolly. 'It is easy to laugh if you never had the need of an operation, if you have never had to be tied to an operating table with leather straps cutting into your wrists and ankles, and a huge market porter lying across your chest to hold you down while a surgeon sets a knife to your mangled leg and slices through the muscle and then takes a saw to your exposed bones – aye, that makes you go white, does it not, gentlemen? You've seen enough of surgery surely to know what hell it is – for the surgeon as well as the patient. Well, now, we have searched a long time – many, many centuries, as I say, for a manner in which we can control the pain our knives inflict. The Bible speaks of such a method but it was only God who was able to use it. Ye'll recall, I am sure, that He set Adam into a deep sleep before he removed the rib that he fashioned into Eve. Well, since then, we surgeons have sought the same God-given skill. We found it a short time ago. And here it is.'

He held up a small green glass bottle and the students craned and gawped and were disappointed, for as the answer to a prayer it looked feeble enough. He seemed to sense their reaction, and laughed suddenly, a crack of sound that made Freddy blink.

'Ye don't believe me! Now, well, why should you? Come – you–' and he seized the student standing next to Freddy and tugged him by the arm until the boy was sitting on the narrow operating table. 'Lie you down – aye, down, man!' and he shoved at the boy who lay down, unable to resist, but looked very afraid, and Snow stood behind his head and curved one hand under his chin, while the student rolled his eyes at his watching friends, who grinned heartlessly back.

'You,' Snow said then, looking up and catching Freddy's eye, 'Come and stand here behind me so that you can see over my shoulder – aye, that's it. Now watch, and tell your fellows what it is you see.'

He took a handkerchief from his pocket, and then set it over the nose and mouth of the boy on the table. Immediately his eyes widened into even greater alarm, and he tried to struggle to sit up, but Snow, his muscles hard and powerful despite his far from strong appearance, pushed him down again with insulting ease. With one smooth gesture he lifted the green bottle to his mouth and seizing the cork between his teeth twisted it open, and then began, very slowly, to drip the contents on to his handkerchief.

'Well, boy, start your talking!' he said, his voice muffled through the cork still held in his teeth and Freddy swallowed and said, 'Er – yes – well. Dr. Snow has wetted the handkerchief with some of the contents of the bottle he displayed. It has made the cloth look a little grey – and it seems to be a very volatile material, for already the damp patch is shrinking—'

'Well observed, lad,' Snow grunted.

'—and the stuff smells strange – sweet— Oh!' The note of surprise in his voice made the other students cluster even nearer, and they could all see how the way the boy on the table had started to writhe, the way his eyes had glazed over yet remained open so that it seemed as though he was staring up at Snow in great ferocity.

'Keep talking,' Snow said peremptorily. 'And do not breathe too deep yourself, or you will be affected by the stuff.'

'Well, he seems to be behaving very strange – not like Peter at all,' Freddy said, and again someone giggled. 'For he is fighting Dr. Snow – who is putting more of the liquid on to the handkerchief – Peter is breathing very deep and heavy, and seems to be – he is asleep! He is not fighting at all, now, and – Dr. Snow has removed the handkerchief and the mouth is quite lax and open and he is snoring a little – he's not in a coma, is he, Dr. Snow?'

'D'ye fear I have killed your fellow, young man?' Snow laughed again. 'No, lad, medical students are not so easy to dispose of. I often wish they were—' Again, the soft titter from the watchers. 'But I have set him asleep. But it is a very special sleep. Now, you—' and he jerked his head at another student, a tall and heavy man with broad shoulders who looked more like one of the hospital porters than a would-be medical man. 'Come and do some damage to your friend here. Imagine he has kissed your sister – aye, hurt him! This is a demonstration, not a game of catch as catch can!'

Gingerly at first and then with some enthusiasm the student pinched the boy on the table, and then, as he got no response, pinched again, and then punched him in the arm. And still the soft snoring went on as Snow dripped more of the contents of the green bottle and the students watched, and whispered to each other.

'Well, that is enough. He only kissed her, after all.' Snow said and again earned the students' approving response. 'Take a look at his arm closely gentlemen. Do I see a bruise forming? Indeed, I do. There is no doubt in my mind the lad suffered real injury. But did he flinch? Did he show any sign of his pain? I ask you, did he?'

'None at all,' Freddy said wonderingly, and put out his hand and gently touched the one staring eye, feeling the smooth dampness of the eyeball under his fingers, and Peter did not blink or move, still lying there snoring peacefully. 'Do you see that?' he said. 'He did not blink! And there is no manner in which a conscious feeling man can avoid blinking when his cornea is touched!'

Snow looked over his shoulder at him, his eyes very bright. 'Ye're an observant and intelligent lad,' he said, in a low voice as the other students crowded closer to repeat the touching experiments. 'If ye've an interest in the subject of anaesthetic treatment there could be a considerable future for you in learning about it—'

Freddy reddened and bobbed his head a little awkwardly. 'I don't know, sir,' he said. 'I have not thought about the matter of the future. Though I must say, this is better than anatomy—'

Snow grinned at that, and briskly recorked the bottle in his hand and put it back in his pocket. 'Well, anatomy and dissection have lost more surgeons to the craft than owt else, to my knowledge. 'tis a pity ye've no taste for it, for it is a great study, a very great study. The proper study, it has been said. But there – it turns the stomach and well I know it – hold him, now!'

His voice had sharpened as Peter, on the table, began to writhe and fight, much as he had when the handkerchief with its damp patches had started to work its effects, and for the next few minutes they were occupied in holding him down, and reassuring him that all was well as he woke, retching and then shouting, and at last settled to a slightly puzzled and barely awake state as the students asked him questions, showing him the bruises on the arm. But he shook his head a little stupidly and denied any memory of any of it. And Freddy, together with the rest of them spent the next half hour talking, questioning and listening to Snow, discussing the new magic. They heard of the American dentists and their early experiments with nitrous oxide, the laughing gas, and then with ether, and also heard how Snow himself had been so enamoured of the idea of easing pain in this way that he had tried it in the outpatient rooms at his own hospital of St. George's on patients needing teeth removed, and then for an amputation by Robert Liston at University College Hospital in Gower Street.

'And now I'm working with chloroform, gentlemen, which you have just seen me give our young friend here. It is better than nitrous oxide, which is weak and hard to control, more effective than powdered opium, or chloride of hydrocarbon or acetone, all of which I tried, and it is also much better than ether which is strong and causes severe irritation of the bronchial tubes and other chest apparatus and has claimed a death or two. Mind you, so has chloroform. There was a great fuss and noise about a case in Newcastle-upon-Tyne a year or two back. A rough country practitioner with more courage than wit, I'm afraid, gave a farm woman – a great fat creature with poor breathing, ye understand – chloroform for the removal of a toe she had injured. He gave her too great a dose, and did not ensure, as I hope you observed I did, that he removed the pad from the face from time to time to allow the entry of clear air. It set us back a little, that case – but now I have great hopes of chloroform, great hopes indeed. It is a good and useful medicine. I shall go on using it in any matter I can, with safety, learning as I go, especially in childbirth, which the women say is a greater pain even than surgery. You must all of you do the same when your time to practise alone comes to you. It is not enough to destroy the patient's diseases with your knife. Always remember that you must also avoid destroying the patient with your pain and using this material in this manner will protect you from that hazard. And your patients, of course. They need protection from us, God knows.'

Again the snigger, and again Snow quirked his eyebrows at them. 'Well, I can understand your laughter, I suppose. There is little to do *but* laugh at some of the miracles we see in medicine today, for we are Christian men and not given to falling on our faces on the ground to worship as savages do when they see the unbelievable. Go away, all of you, and remember what you have learned here today. It is not magic but good medicine. Real medicine, indeed. I am willing to foretell that some of you will be making investigation with your knives on living human bodies in a way that hitherto has been only possible on cadavers. Some of you, because of chloroform, will be cutting into guts, and chests, and one day, perhaps into hearts and brains. Aye, hearts and brains! There are problems yet to solve – particularly the matter of the pus that forms after the knife has made its journey, and the fever that accompanies it, and kills our patients, but we will solve them. And then we shall see what we shall see. Meanwhile, gentlemen, back to your anatomy! For, anaesthesia or not, until a man knows his way around the architecture of his patient, from basement to attic, he cannot be of use as owt but a street butcher. Good afternoon!'

And after that afternoon Freddy did indeed return to his anatomy classes with a deeper understanding of the need for them, though he could never, he knew, develop a real enjoyment of the work. To be able to look after people without hurting them would be a gratifying experience, however, and for that reason he applied himself more than he had hitherto to the learning of the names of bones and muscles, nerves and joints and arteries. There seemed more value in it now.

But for all that, he was still grateful when a chance arose to miss one of the hated classes, and today when his grandfather beckoned him aside after luncheon and told him gruffly that he required his company elsewhere that afternoon, he was delighted, even without knowing the reason.

He followed Abel into his own sanctum, a room so cluttered with books and papers and anatomical drawings that there was barely room for a person to sit down; but Abel cleared some space on the old sofa that stood against one wall, and indicated Freddy should seat himself, and then took a decanter and a pair of glasses from a corner cupboard and poured brimming measures of Madeira for them both.

'I show you no favour as a student on the wards, Frederick,' he said gruffly, 'but damn it all, it's a poor situation if a man cannot give his own flesh and blood an occasional special notice without being regarded as too partial! Your health!'

Solemnly they drank, Freddy looking a little covertly at the old man above the rim of his glass. He was a splendid-looking fellow, it could not be denied, and Freddy felt himself redden a little even as he thought it, for there was somehow a smack of vanity about it; he had been told often enough, heaven knew how alike they were and in so many ways. Not in colouring though. His grandfather had thick white hair now, but Freddy knew it had been very dark, quite unlike his own red thatch which he had inherited from his father, James. And Freddy was sandy and freckled while his grandfather was very pale. However, they had the same sort of eyes, narrow, startlingly green and direct in their glances.

'So? What are you staring at, my boy?' Abel said sharply, and now Freddy really did flush.

'I am sorry, sir. I – I was comparing us, if you will forgive me. I am told we are much alike in appearance.'

Abel cocked his head a little and stared at him and then drew a sharp breath. 'Aye. We are alike, I daresay. There is much of your father in you, however. Much.'

Freddy tightened his lips. He knew little of the details of his father's history, but enough to know there had been bad blood between his father and his mother's family and even though he had no memory at all of his dead father, he strongly resented any slur upon him. 'No doubt, sir,' he said now, his voice very crisp. 'It is proper indeed that it should be so, and I for one am most glad of it. *Most*.'

Abel looked back at him for a long moment and then smiled. 'Aye, well. You are right, of course, to feel so. All sons should feel such partiality for their fathers. None o'mine did, I can tell you.'

'Indeed, sir?' Freddy said politely, and stifled a sudden wave of irritation. Bad as an afternoon spent in the anatomy room would be, one spent listening to a lot of old family talk that did not interest him in the least would be even worse. The old man, admirable as he was in so many ways (and Freddy yielded to none in his respect for him as a surgeon: he had too watched those hands moving so fast as to be a blur as they performed an amputation to feel otherwise) was showing his years, getting reminiscent and dull.

'Aye. *Indeed*. But I will not bore you with what is clearly not a matter of interest to you. The time no doubt will come when you will want to quiz me about your uncles. However—'

Freddy had the grace to look abashed, and now Abel smiled much more widely, so that his hard-edged face softened and showed blurred lines over the jaw and round the tight mouth. 'However,' he went on, 'I am going to have to bore you a little with ancient matters. There is an old woman of my acquaintance who is very anxious to meet you. She has wanted to do so for many years and I have always resisted her. However, she is now about to die—'

'I am sorry to hear it, sir,' Freddy said at once, for he was well-mannered enough, Abby having reared him most carefully to be so.

'Why should you be? You do not know her! And she is indeed very old. Past eighty, though she claims to be far more—' Abel grinned suddenly, a rather lopsided grin. 'She is an incredible old besom, Frederick! She befriended me when I was about half your age, a gutter boy caked thick with the dirt of years, gave me my first bath and my first real clothes. And the first real concern anyone had ever shown me, that I knew of.' His eyes had gone a little blank suddenly, as though he were looking inside himself and not at all at Freddy, and the young man stared at him with real interest.

Abel blinked at the directness of his gaze, and then grinned again. 'Now you would like to know more, would you not? Well, want shall be your master, for I shall not tell you. One day, perhaps, but not now. All I will say is that she is my very good friend, has long been so, and wishes to see you before she dies. I am inclined to allow her this – with your permission, of course.' And he looked sardonic, raising his eyebrows questioningly.

'By all means, sir,' Freddy said hastily, and got to his feet as Abel stood up and put down his glass. 'Is she in the hospital now?'

'Here? Good God, no! To bring her here would take half the Queen's guard and more beside. Past eighty she may be, but she's a formidable old wretch. I shall miss her sorely when she's gone—' and he stood very still for a moment, staring out of the window.

'Er – shall I require my street coat, then, sir?' Freddy ventured after a moment.

'Eh? Oh, yes, street coat, by all means,' and he turned to look for his own. 'You will, by the way, not tell your mother of this visit, Freddy.' Abel looked at him fiercely. 'Not because I have any wish to deceive her but because she will not fully

43

understand. And I really do not wish to be bothered explaining it all to her.'

'Yes, sir,' Freddy said, more mystified than ever and Abel laughed, and pulled the door open. 'Go and fetch your coat, boy! And make yourself spruce, for it is to a whorehouse we go on this visit, and you might as well know it now as later!'

Freddy stood at the foot of the huge bed and blinked and swallowed and tried to look as nonchalant as he felt was expected of him. From the moment they had entered this house he felt as though he were in some sort of a dream world. The street outside had been so *ordinary* – as grey and noisy and traffic-infested and cluttered as any other London street – and then they had rung the bell of this ordinary-looking house, and been ushered into – what? Freddy had never seen anything like it, a place so draped with silk curtains, so mirrored about the walls, so heaped with velvet cushions, so heated and scented and above all so extraordinarily populated.

At first the lighting had so bewildered him that he could not at all make out the people who were in the big room they entered; there were red-shaded gaslights, and blue and green shaded gaslights, and pools of shadow as well as great swathes of brilliance, but after a while his eyes became accustomed to the contrasts, and then he felt himself positively blush at what he could see.

The room contained little furniture apart from cushions strewn on the floor and sofas – a great many of them – all heavily upholstered in golden yellow velvet; and lying about on these were young women, dressed as Freddy had never seen women dressed before.

One in particular, the first he noticed as being unusually garbed, had semed to be wearing a perfectly ordinary gown, a large crinoline under a tight bodice – until he had realized that it was made of almost totally transparent gauze, and the lady was wearing nothing whatsoever underneath. Bare female flesh was far from being unfamiliar to him, for he could hardly be in the second year of his studies without having been exposed to human nudity in both sexes, but the nudity he had learned to

44

become accustomed to was of dead bodies, or very sick ones. It certainly was not the rounded, rosy and thoroughly voluptuous nudity that was being displayed to him here.

He looked away from the lady in the transparent gown in some haste (considerably to her amusement) but found no respite, for beside her was another wearing a pair of frilled drawers and nothing else at all, apart from a great deal of rouge outlining her nipples, while beyond her on a sofa lay a girl who wore her hair over her shoulders, like a schoolroom miss, but displayed her legs – and more – in a most unschoolgirlish manner.

But what amazed him most of all was the way his grandfather seemed so at home in these extraordinary surroundings. He stood there in the middle of the room, his hat in his hand and nodding affably at the company in general said, 'I am here to see Lucy. Is Nancy above stairs with her? I told her I would come today.'

'She is that Mr. Lackland!' The girl with the unbound hair scrambled to her feet (much to Freddy's relief, for her skirts now fell in some decency about her legs, atlhough she was still displaying far more of her breasts than seemed proper to him). 'I'll tell 'er you're 'ere – she said as you was comin'. 'Ere, Mr. Lackland, sir, I wants to talk to you before you slings yer 'ook. You will, won't you? It's important, see, and I got to talk to yer—'

Abel looked down at her. 'You're new. I have no recollection of seeing you here before.'

'What if I am? The others say you're the one I should talk to an'—'

There was a sound from the doorway, and Freddy turned his head and peered into the shadows, and was startled enough to take a step backwards, for coming towards him was the bulky figure of Mrs. Bartlett, the woman who ruled Nellie's nurses so ferociously. And although she looked very incongruous here, with her dark print dress and clean white apron and bare reddened arms – for her sleeves were rolled up like a kitchen maid's – she seemed to have the same powerful effect, for the girls who had been clustering round Abel disappeared

45

back into the shadowy corners of the big room, even the little one who had been holding on to his sleeve and being so importunate.

'Glad to see you're 'ere,' Nancy said sharply to Abel. 'If you'd left it much longer she'd be gorn. Come on—' and she turned on her heel and marched to the door, but not so fast that Freddy did not have time to see that her eyes and nose were reddened as though she had been weeping.

This was indeed a new vision of Mrs. Bartlett and, bemused, he followed her and his grandfather from the room and up the stairs (which were lined with paintings which made him blink, so explicit were they in the scenes they depicted) almost ready for anything to happen on this very surprising afternoon.

And now he stood at the foot of the bed holding his hat in both hands and turning it nervously between his fingers, and staring. His grandfather was sitting on the edge of the bed, holding the hand of the occupant between both of his, and looking down at her with an expression on his face that was so tender and so concerned that it quite transformed him. Freddy had seen him show concern for his patients many, many times, but he had never seen him look like this.

And for whom? For a perfectly hideous old woman who was quite the hugest Freddy had ever seen. Even lying here in bed he could see that she was grotesquely fat, the bedclothes lifting absurdly with the bulk beneath them. Her face seemed to be made of circle after circle of yellowish glistening flesh, from the middle of which a pair of very small and very bright eyes stared out, the whole surmounted by a lace-trimmed cap which even Freddy, uninterested as he was in female fashion, could see was in the mode of at least fifty years before. Altogether she was the most extraordinary sight he had ever seen, and that she could evoke in his stern grandfather such a degree of concern was even more extraordinary.

On the other side of the bed stood Nancy Bartlett, her hands folded on her apron and her head thrust forwards ferociously as she stared down at the occupant of the bed. And to pile even more amazement on to Freddy, she was weeping, making no attempt to mop away the tears that trickled down her grooved cheeks, only sniffing heavily from time to time.

46

There was a silence, and then a thin voice came from the figure in the bed.

'Shut yer noise, yer lump o' gutter meat,' it said. 'If yer can't let me die decent wivaht all that bleedin' din, yer can bugger orf. Is that 'im?'

'Yes, Lucy,' Abel said softly. 'This is Frederick. He is Abigail's son.'

'Come 'ere,' the thin voice said, and Abel looked up at Freddy, his eyebrows raised, and Freddy swallowed, and came a little uneasily round the bed to stand beside his grandfather.

He felt the sharp little eyes on him and could not bring himself to actually meet their gaze, but then, ashamed of himself, he lifted his head and looked back at her. And as he stood there in that overheated room, its huge coal fire and tight-closed curtains giving it an almost overwhelming stuffiness, he saw that this woman was not as repellent as he had at first thought. Those eyes, bright, very knowing, had a life that was all their own; there was even now a gaiety about them, a sort of courage, and a great deal of – was it laughter? He blinked and stared back and quite suddenly grinned. He couldn't help it.

'How d'ye do, ma'am,' he said, and his voice sounded outrageously loud in this cluttered room, where even the sounds from the street came muffled through the heavy curtains. 'I am glad to make your acquaintance.'

The huge face quivered, the lips moved in a tetchy way, and the eyes seemed to narrow, and he realized after a moment that she was smiling too; and he smiled even more widely himself. And then looked up and saw that Nancy on the other side of the bed was producing a curious stretched grimace of her own, while tears still streamed down her face, and he turned his head and looked at his grandfather, and he too was smiling.

The room sank back into a silence broken only by the sound of the fire hissing and crackling gently in the grate, and the little eyes closed, and then opened again and the cracked voice said, ' 'E's my likely lad. My likely lad. Good boy, Abel. Mind yer ways, now—' And then the eyes closed again, and after a moment Abel bent and smoothed the forehead of the vast face with one hand, and gently extricated himself from the grip of the old woman's pudgy fingers.

'I must return to the hospital, Lucy,' he said softly. 'I must bid you good-bye sometime, and as bad now as later. You're an old besom to get to this state, you know that?'

'Likely lad,' she said again, and once more that spasm of movement crossed her face, and now Freddy knew it immediately for a smile, and suddenly, amazingly, although he did not know this woman, knew nothing of her history, her character, or even her full name, his throat tightened with unshed tears. Whatever there was or had been between his grandfather and this heap of dying flesh in its ludicrous satin heaped bed, it had the stuff of tragedy in it. He wanted to weep for them both.

They left Nancy at the bedside, going quietly from the room, and Abel stopped for one brief moment to look back before closing the door. And then went swiftly down the stairs, gesturing at Freddy to follow him with a jerk of his head.

They were almost at the front door when the little girl with the unbound hair reached them and clung urgently to Abel's sleeve.

'I told yer – I got to talk to yer—' she said, and Abel looked down at her, and then pulled his watch from his waistcoat pocket.

'Well, be fast about it. I haven't all day to stand here.'

'What abaht 'im? This is private.' She looked over her shoulder at Freddy, and he turned at once to move away, but Abel shook his head quickly.

'He is a surgeon as well, and I imagine this is a surgical matter,' he said, and Freddy blushed; and did not know whether it was gratification at being described as a surgeon while still but a student, or with embarrassment.

The girl still hesitated, and Abel looked down at her shrewdly and said, 'Well, you might as well be out with it! Have you brought the pox with you, or are you increasing? If it's the pox I'll tell you now there are no easy answers. I'll take you to the hospital and treat you but never think I'll keep it a secret from Lucy—' he stopped then and frowned and shook his head almost like a dog shaking off an importunate fly, '—or whoever takes charge for her. Because I won't. She has always kept a good house, and always will. You need not be afraid that she –

that anyone will throw you out if it is the pox. This is a *good* house with good people in it. They will not let you work till you're well, but they'll keep you—'

' 'Tain't the pox.' The girl was still holding Abel's sleeve, but she was not looking up at him now. Her head was bent and she watched her own fingers pleating the cloth of his coat.

'Oh, increasing, are you? Well, you need not fear that either.' Abel said. 'I know most houses would throw you out for that, but not Lucy's. I shall take care of you when your time comes, and if you wish it, your babe will be found care as well. There is help available.'

She was still silent and Abel put out a hand and lifted her chin so that she had to look at him. He spoke more gently now. 'You need not fear,' he said again. 'The London Ladies will take care of your baby. They have done so for many, I do promise you. My wife and my daughter Martha are themselves concerned in the proper placing of such infants by the Society and I can promise you that many of them have better homes than ever their poor mothers had! You can rest easy, I do promise you—'

'I ain't 'avin' no baby, not no'ow,' she said, and her voice was sulky. 'They said if I tol' you, you'd 'elp me, but I ain't 'avin' no baby—'

He frowned. 'If it isn't the pox, and you are not increasing, then I don't see that—'

She shook her head away from his hand. 'I never said I wasn't increasin', did I? I said I wasn't 'avin' no baby, not no'ow. Tried to talk to ol' Nancy, didn't I? But she's so set about with that old 'un up there she ain't got no time for nuthin' – an' not for the likes o' me anyway, as 'asn't bin 'ere more'n a few days. So I ask the girls an' they says as 'ow you was a surgeon, an' I should tell yer—'

'What did you say?' Abel's voice was suddenly so harsh that even Freddy jumped, and the girl took an involuntary step backwards. But she was not frightened for long.

'I tol' you,' she said stubbornly. 'I ain't 'avin' no baby. You can do it, can't yer? Yer a surgeon, ain't yer? I'll pay yer all right – they say there's lots o' crinkle goin' 'ere, so I reçkon it'd be a good job for you. Only it better be quick. It's bin four times I ain't seen, now, and that's too bloody long for anyone—'

He took her shoulders in his hands, pulling her round so that her face was lit properly, for she had moved back a little into the shadows, and his voice came very hard and crisp.

'Listen to me, you – you – listen to me! I am a surgeon. I take care of the sick, I treat the pox, I look after women in their time. I am not a back-street butcher, you hear me? I do not procure abortions, and never ever dare you put such a proposition to me again, do you hear me? Whoever told you that I could be asked such a thing lied in her teeth, and God help you if ever you tell anyone that I would do such a thing for you, or anyone else. You understand me? *Never.*' He almost shook her, had been told of the punishments that could be heaped on any hand out, momentarily alarmed; and as much for Abel as for the girl, for the old man's face was so suffused with rage that for a moment he really feared he would fall into an apoplexy.

'You heard this piece of gutter meat? You heard her? She asked me – *me* – to procure an abortion for her. With Lucy above stairs in such a— The – she asked *me*—' and he shook his head, almost choking with his rage.

Freddy set one hand on his grandfather's shoulder, and with the other reached for the front door. 'We had better go, sir,' he said, keeping his voice as calm as he could. It was not easy, for the old man's reaction had frightened him, and he jerked his head at the girl who slid away into the shadows, obviously as alarmed as Freddy was himself. After a moment Abel took a deep breath and turned and let Freddy lead him out on to the noisy street and stand there with his head up for a moment breathing in the normality of it all.

And Freddy too was grateful to escape from what had been a most extraordinary afternoon; and not the least surprising had been his grandfather's intense reaction to the girl's request. Freddy knew perfectly well that of all medical sins, the procurement of abortion was considered by all decent practitioners to be the most abominable. At their very first lecture at Nellie's as raw youths about to become medical students, they had been told of the punishments that could be heaped on any medical man venial enough – or stupid enough – to be cozened into such an act. Transportation or years in prison, and no chance ever to practise again; it had not been all that long, after all, since a surgeon could be legally hanged for doing such a thing, they had been told. But even allowing for that, his grandfather's fury had been more than he would have expected. Surely, a man who practised his profession not only among the gutters of Seven Dials but also in such places as this house in Panton Street, must be accustomed to receiving such pleas? It was all very puzzling, Freddy thought, as they at last made their way towards the Haymarket in search of a hansom cab to take them back to the hospital.

# CHAPTER FOUR

GIDEON decided to walk to the Supper Rooms; quite apart from the fact that a hansom cab would be hard put to find a way through the tangle of costers' carts, drays, pedlars, street musicians and the rest of the hubbub that filled the narrow streets of Covent Garden, he felt the need of some exercise. The morning hours spent with his mother in her brazier-heated drawing-room in Lombard Street always left him feeling starved of air and action and today he felt more pent up even than usual.

Looking back on the young years he had spent living in that self-same atmosphere he marvelled a little now; how was it he had never recognized the narrowness of it all then, the constriction of the long money-busy days and parent-centred evenings? He had loved them both too well, perhaps had been so zealous on their behalf that he had been unaware of his own deprivation. Thinking now, as he so often did, of the richness and satisfaction of his life in Stanhope Terrace he once more thanked God for His goodness, grateful for the way his lines had fallen. He was so very well bestowed a man!

He paused for a moment when he reached the end of King Street to stand and look at his brother-in-law's establishment with a critical eye. Jonah had recently had the front repainted and embellished, and indeed it looked most elegant, tricked out in gilt paint and crimson trimmings; a most welcoming – indeed beckoning – sight in the middle of the greyness of the London street. Clever Jonah, Gideon thought, to cozen his customers so even before they crossed the threshold! Any passer-by who saw the place must feel the attraction of it, and have his hand in his pocket looking for money to spend even before he had realized he had decided to enter the swinging glass doors.

Pushing through the door himself, and ducking under the

crimson velvet curtain that created a second portal just inside, Gideon took a deep breath, smelling the welcome in the air. There had been a time when the Celia Rooms had been very low class indeed, reeking of cheap beer and boiled cabbage and over-ripe game pies, but in the past ten years or so Jonah had done much to change that. His customers had gradually come from the better parts of the town, had changed from being market porters bent on getting drunk amid their work-mates to glossy-hatted citizens looking for a not-too-naughty night of comfortable pleasure away not only from the watchful eyes of careful wives but even from the stuffy punctiliousness of their clubs. Here at the Celia Rooms a man could relax after a day in counting-house or office or shop with a glass of good Madeira in one hand, a well-made cigar in the other and an agreeable companion across the table. The food was good – plenty of well roasted mutton, beefsteak pies and oysters – and smelled attractive, and Gideon felt a sudden pang of hunger as he took off his hat and coat and dropped them on a table just beyond the curtain.

There were no customers in, not at this time of the afternoon, for it lacked a few minutes to four, but the place was far from empty. The little stage at the far end was brightly lit, with its curtains looped back, and in the middle of it two girls in spangles and tights were turning a series of complicated somersaults in perfect synchronization and in rhythm with the sprightly music being produced by three musicians in the small pit below the stage. The pianist, sitting at the keyboard with his overcoat on in spite of the warmth, his hat on the back of his head and a cigar clamped between his teeth, was singing round it in a coarse cracked voice; 'As bee-oo-tiful as a *Butterfly*, and as *Proud* as a Queen, wa-as *Pretty* little Polly *Perkins* of *Paddington* Green! Pom-ti *pom*-ti, pompty, pompty, as *Proud* as a Queen—' and the girls gyrated and twisted, their fixed grins never faltering, and the pianist nodded his head in time to his own thumping as the violinist scraped away busily and the man with the small drum and cymbals added his own clashing noise.

Gideon smiled, feeling suddenly very much at home; how

like Jonah to find a song that combined a lively tune with words that could offend no one; he must tell Abby of this one for she had been used to live in Paddington Green, long ago—

'Gideon!' Jonah came hurrying across the room towards him, weaving past the tables, now looking rather bleak with their chairs piled up on them. 'You are very good to come! Will you take some wine? Some victuals? Mary—' and he waved to a girl in a print dress who had been cleaning glasses at the long mahogany bar that covered the whole of the far wall. She nodded, and reached for a bottle and tray.

'I like your new song, Jonah!' Gideon said cheerfully, shaking hands. 'Where did you find it?'

'Eh? Oh, a new man – Harry Clifton. A clever young chap and one with promise, I think. Writes his own stuff. Glad you like it – we're trying the dance with the girls as a filler – we'll have to see how it goes tomorrow. We're having a complete new bill to start the week. New costumes, scenery – trying some fire-eaters and sword-swallowers too, found them at a circus in Bedford last winter season—

Gideon looked at him curiously. Jonah and he had never become close friends, tending to be polite to each other in a wary sort of fashion, each aware of the affection felt for both of them by Abby and both wishing to keep her happy by being reasonably cordial to each other; but there was no real *rapport* between them. Jonah was basically too withdrawn and lonely a man for Gideon not to feel slight embarrassment in his company, especially when he compared Jonah's domestic situation with his own. Yet despite this faint chill between them Gideon believed he knew his brother-in-law fairly well, and today he was behaving in a far from normal manner. This staccato chattering was most uncharacteristic, as was the way he seemed to be watching and waiting for – what?

Gideon did not know, and was most intrigued. He had assumed that Jonah wished to discuss with him a matter of business, for though they lacked closeness, Jonah respected Gideon's commercial acumen and regularly consulted him on matters to do with property or money in general. But perhaps this was something different?

54

Gideon accepted the glass of Madeira and piece of seed cake the girl brought him, and followed Jonah down the Rooms towards the stage with quite an eager step. He was as human as anyone else, and quite relished the idea of discovering some interesting information about his brother-in-law's life.

But Jonah seemed in no hurry to confide whatever it was to Gideon's ready ear. He dismissed the musicians and performers after one more run-through of their routine, and carefully lowered the gas-lights on the stage (and Gideon duly admired the new installation which offered as bright and yet as subtle an illumination as any stage ten times its size in London) and talked and talked and talked – but of not very important things.

He asked Gideon for his estimate of the numbers of people who might be expected to come to London when the Great Exhibition opened in May, and whether he would consider the spending of twenty pounds on playbills and flyposters to advertise the entertainment available at the Celia Rooms as a reasonable outlay for the return it might bring; and since they had discussed this selfsame subject many times before (for Jonah was quite fascinated by the power of advertising, and much enjoyed composing his own playbills and teaser posters for the printer), it was obvious to Gideon that this was not why he had been asked to attend at King Street.

Gideon became a little restive after half an hour of this and similar unimportances and tried some gentle prodding. Was Jonah to come to his daughter's entertainment this evening? Indeed he was, Jonah assured him. He would see the first show through here and be at Stanhope Terrace very shortly after ten. and looked forward greatly to seeing what Phoebe had devised for them all. And in responding so he showed no undue tension, so Gideon accepted that it was not concern for Phoebe that perturbed him, and started to talk of Oliver instead.

Had Jonah heard from his son? Indeed Jonah had and was much pleased that the boy was doing so well and was so happy. He was lodging with a most respectable family in the north of the city, he said, most respectable, and had developed an interest in evangelism, not the most fiery kind, but the practical sort that showed its piety in concern for its fellow men, and this must gladden the heart of any father whose son was so far from his watchful eye, at so young an age.

'For a boy of twenty is very vulnerable, Gideon, as I am sure you will agree. And I would rather know he was spending his leisure time perusing questions of belief and theology in the modern manner than rushing about with undesirable females.' And thinking of the rather solemn and even ponderous Oliver, so unlike his quicksilver sister, Gideon smiled and agreed.

After a good deal more of this inconsequential chat they lapsed into a silence. Gideon sipped his wine and ate his cake and looked at Jonah over the rim of his glass and decided to be patient. Whatever it was, no doubt Jonah would deliver himself of it in due course, he told himself, and with only a side-long glance at his watch, folded his arms and waited.

It burst out quite suddenly. 'What debt could a man be said to owe to the relations of his dead wife, Gideon?' Jonah asked abruptly. 'If there was no will, you understand? I am not at all anxious to start any wild goose chase, but I would wish to know.'

Gideon frowned sharply. 'What debt? Why, in what manner do you mean, Jonah? It depends on so many factors! Such as whether the dead person had accrued loans and so forth, and had signed documents to that effect and—'

'Oh, I am sure there was no such situation as that!' Jonah said swiftly. 'Celia would never have – at least, I do not think – I don't really know—' His voice dwindled away and he looked miserably at Gideon, his hands folded on the table before him, his chin tucked down a little so that he had a rather hang-dog look about him and Gideon felt a stab of irritation; he knew Jonah had suffered many losses and tragedies in his life, and had no doubt he was justified if he felt unhappy, but why did he have to look at a man so pathetically? Gideon's voice was a little waspish when he answered.

'Really, Jonah, you talk in riddles! What is all this? Your wife died some years ago now, and I would have thought all questions regarding the legal bestowal of any property had been long since settled.'

'It is not legal matters I am concerned about,' Jonah said, and now sat up a little straighter, as though aware of Gideon's irritation. 'The legal situation was, as you say, settled long ago.

'No, it is – it is *moral* concerns that worry me. Would you consider that it is possible for any of Celia's relations to make just demands upon me? Of any kind?'

Gideon looked at him for a long moment and then shook his head crisply. 'You will have to explain yourself much more clearly than this, Jonah. I cannot offer any guidance when I am not in full possession of all the facts.'

Jonah stood up and turned to walk away, and then came back to his chair to sit down again, every line of his body as he moved displaying his nervousness. 'Yes, I suppose that is reasonable enough – oh, damn it all! If only people would leave me in peace! I ask little enough of life, God knows. Just a little peace, and the chance to amass enough money to see Oliver and Phoebe fairly settled in life! All this disturbance – I don't like it.' He moved fretfully in his chair again, and Gideon leaned forwards and touched his hand and said calmly, 'Come on now, man! You've got yourself in a sorry tangle, whatever it is, and I daresay you'll feel much better if you get the chance to talk of it, so unbutton yourself, do!'

There was a short silence and then Jonah again stood up, but this time so that he could reach easily into the pocket of his coat. He withdrew a thick wad of folded sheets of paper, and handed it to Gideon who took it, unfolded it and then looked up questioningly.

'Aye,' Jonah said. 'It is a private letter, but I wish you would read it. It will explain my anxiety.'

Obediently, Gideon bent his head and began to read.

17, Princes Gardens,
Edinburgh
March 11th, 1851

My dear Brother-in-Law,

There! Is that not a salutation to surprise you? I am sure it is, as sure as I am that you have given no thought whatever to me these past many years – more than *I* wish to count, I do assure you! I feel some shame that I have not wrote to you before this, especially when I heard of my poor sister's death but I was so shocked in my mind when I heard the news at that time, and besides it did not reach the Edinburgh newspapers until some weeks after the melancholy happening, and it seemed to me at that time that to write to you of my own distress would be to open up slow-healing wounds.

So, enough of the past! You will wonder why after so many years of silence I should be writing to you now, but that is easy to explain. It is indeed a situation that might amuse you, remembering as I do that you will have as much cause as any to feel some animosity towards my mother. The matter lies thusly. It was less than three years after you and Celia left North Audley Street in such a to-do – and I can tell you now that mother was fit to die of rage over it all! – that I too felt it politic to leave her house. I was showing signs of growing into an actress of some ability and as I am sure you will understand *she* did not like that at all! So, to come to a point, I left her, came north, and eventually settled here in Edinburgh – a most beautiful city, if occupied by some very boring people! I yearned for many years for the interest of working in London, but my dear Mamma, in the goodness of her heart, made sure that this could not be! I made some success here, I will be straight with you, and would never come to London in aught but a big and important production. I am sure you will understand that! But my Mamma with all her influence – which is far from inconsiderable – made sure that no such offer ever came my way. Until now – and I am most cock-a-hoop about it all! I heard – as one hears theatre gossip, dear Jonah, and I have no doubt you will recall the way of the greenroom – that my mother no longer enjoyed the same influence she once had had at the Haymarket, and so the way was open. It takes but little to alert *me* my dear Jonah, and I at once made shifts which, I am happy to say, have resulted in a most respectable offer to me to lead a company at the Haymarket in 'Ivanhoe' – a play I much enjoy and have had some considerable success in, and there is no need for me to be unduly modest about my achievements here! So, I shall be coming to live in London for the Season, and most excited I am about it! I have taken a house at twenty-two Soho Square – it was all my agents could find for me, for because of the Exhibition, they tell me, London promises to be packed tight and no houses are to be had anywhere – and look forward indeed to receiving a call from you. You will come, will you not? There is so much to talk of, so much I would speak of with you! You can find me at any time after March 25th, and I am eager indeed for a sight of you. I must tell you that you will find me not as Lydia Lucas, for I married some years ago and was widowed but shortly after.

I remain, therefore, your affectionate sister,

Lydia Mohun

Gideon folded the letter slowly and gave it back to Jonah, who sat and twisted it between his fingers, and after a moment Gideon said, 'And did you find her as agreeable as her letter? She writes with great animation, does she not?'

'Oh, I have not visited her!' Jonah sounded quite shocked. 'I could not do that—'

'Why not?' Gideon was genuinely puzzled. 'Did she do you some injury when you saw her last? I understood it to be many years ago?'

'It *was* many years ago,' Jonah said miserably. 'She was just a child then. No, she did me no injury, I suppose, I mean, none directly. It is just that her mother – and Celia – oh, you do not understand! I should not have talked of it to you!'

There was a pause and then Gideon said gently, 'Of course you should – and I think I do understand. You were made very unhappy by so many of the things that happened. I can see it would be easier for you to deny that any of that family had existed, ever, and to keep well away from them.'

Jonah looked up and said with an almost pathetic eagerness, 'Yes – yes, that is precisely the case! And to tell you the honest truth, Gideon they do alarm me so, these women! Celia herself – I loved her dearly, indeed I did, but – well, she became

59

difficult in later years—' his voice dwindled and then strengthened again, '—and Lilith, her mother, you know – was altogether too much for one of my temperament! I cannot tell you, cannot express to you how – how *powerful* she was! She could set me into such a quake so easily—'

He stopped and stared at Gideon with a sort of blankness about his face that spoke much more clearly than did his words of the intensity of the memories that were sweeping him, and Gideon looked away in momentary embarrassment.

'And now this one – Lydia. I recall her as a child, and then she did not perturb me particularly, but she had some power in her even then, no question of it. Very full of vitality, you know! No one knows better than I how devastating the young can be! My own Phoebe – but Lydia, you see, has lost none of what she had, and has added more, I am convinced. She looks quite splendid, not in the least her age, nor at all cast down by the loss of her husband—'

'I thought you had not called upon her?'

Jonah flushed a brick red, and blinked and then said with some asperity, 'Oh, damn it! My own tongue will always be such a burden to me! No, I did not call. But I – I made it my business to observe her. Enough of that! All I am now asking you is whether you feel I owe her any part of this—' He swept his hand around, a comprehensive gesture which took in not just the Supper Rooms and its stage, but his private rooms above, his slowly building savings in the City banks, his whole life, and Gideon stared at him in genuine amazement.

'Why ever should you even think such a thing for a moment? How can this woman, sister-in-law though she be, have any title to any of your possessions? What maggot is this that is in your brain?' That any man could be as ignorant of the laws of property as this seemed to Gideon quite incredible.

'Oh, I know there can be no legal case – and I daresay she will not go to law – but the Supper Rooms are called by her sister's name, are they not? And it was Celia who started it all, worked so hard to establish it—'

'And you who have worked so hard this past ten years to build it,' Gideon said stoutly. 'No, Jonah, if this is all that is concerning you, I can tell you quite without fear of any argument that you are quite out of your attic to entertain any such notions! The property you have here, its goodwill, its value – it all belongs to you, solely, and eventually to your children. This sister of your dead wife has no claim upon any of it.'

He stood up and smiled down at Jonah, still sitting glumly at the table. 'Come, my dear man, you cannot really be so foolish as to fear any difficulty. If this Mrs. Mohun should attempt to make any claim upon you, call upon me and I shall put the matter at once into the hands of our man of law – you know him, I believe, Peter Norman – but I will be amazed if that ever becomes necessary. Even if she were destitute – which from her letter I would say she is not, and she is to play a big part in this play, I imagine, and that will net her some considerable money – even then, there would be no claim upon you.'

'I suppose in part I hoped it *was* just money,' Jonah said suddenly, still sitting at the table with his chin hunched into his collar.

'Eh?' Gideon bent a little to stare at him. 'What are you talking of now, Jonah?'

He looked up and for the first time smiled. 'I am sorry, Gideon! I talk nonsense, no doubt. It is very foolish of me. Perhaps my trouble is that I have too long to spend alone in my chambers above stairs after the Rooms here close, and none to talk to of the notions that afflict me in the small hours when I do not sleep well. I am sorry to have worried you so unnecessarily. I will accept your assurances that all is well, and that Mrs. Mohun cannot take any money from me because of Celia, and rest happy that it is still my Phoebe and Oliver for whom the Supper Rooms work! And I will see you tonight at your house.'

He stood up, and held out his hand. 'For now, then, Gideon, I will say—'

There was a flurry at the far end of the Rooms. The crimson curtain billowed and swayed, and they both turned to look, and Jonah started forwards suddenly, saying, 'Damn it all, will they never learn? We are not open for at least an hour yet—' And then stopped.

Again the curtain had billowed, but this time wide enough to allow two people to pass it and Gideon stood and watched as they both came up the long room, walking as easily and comfortably as though they lived there. A woman of medium height, dressed in a handsome fur pelisse and what was, even to Gideon's eye, a bonnet of the very latest fashion, one kid-gloved hand resting lightly on the arm of a tall and exceedingly handsome man, also dressed in the very latest of fashion. His hat shone with a positively insolent sheen over his crisply curling dark hair, his eyes were a very dark blue and quite outrageously bright, and he smiled with a lazy elegance which displayed the most even of white teeth. Altogether, thought Gideon with some distaste, a complete mountebank.

And then the two of them were standing in front of them and the woman was holding out both hands to Jonah.

'My dear Jonah! I would have known you anywhere! But what a neglectful wretch you are! Even after so long a time, it is not kind in you not to call upon me! But I bear no malice, and am here to call upon you instead. May I present my friend and colleague, Mr. Richard O'Hare—' and the glossy hat came off with a great flourish. '—Dickon, this is Jonah Lackland. I am sure we shall all be *great* friends. And will you not present me to *your* friend, Jonah? As a new arrival in Town I cannot wait to meet everyone – quite everyone!'

'Mrs. Lydia Mohun, Gideon,' Jonah said woodenly after a moment. 'My brother-in-law, Gideon Henriques, ma'am.'

At once she clapped her hands together, and laughed, a most pretty laugh full of soft gurgling and clearly a much practised one. 'Brother-in-law! Oh, this is too delightful! To arrive in London after so many years of exile, and at once to be surrounded by so many charming connections! I am indeed a most fortunate woman!'

And she put one hand lightly into Gideon's outstretched one, and smiled up at him with such warmth that Gideon felt his own lips curve into a matching smile as he looked at her, for she really was one of the prettiest and most beguiling women he had ever met.

# CHAPTER FIVE

SITTING beside his mother in her closed phaeton as it went sedately round and round the park, Jody felt more alert than he had for a long time. His major problem, always, was ennui; the days stretched so long and so often empty before him each morning that even his sharp wits were hard put to it to find some employment that would make him feel completely alive. His was a difficult situation to be in, heaven knew; the income of a gentleman of leisure was his, and freed him totally from the need of lesser men to follow some profession, or worse still, a trade; but the source of his income and his family history made him totally unacceptable to the company of other young gentlemen of leisure and the resulting loneliness and pointlessness of his life was often hard to bear.

He had been at one time interested in the possibility of a stage career. He had the looks, he had told his Mamma (and she had agreed that without question), so why not? But she had been most earnest in her entreaties that he should not even consider it; the people of the theatre would treat him so unkindly, would steal away his youth and health. Who should know better than she? And he had allowed himself to be deterred (how could it be otherwise when he knew quite well that any attempt to set his face against hers in such a matter would result in the drying-up of his means of sustenance?), but had sometimes wondered if her protection was not so much aimed at shielding him from the rigours and cruelties of a theatrical career, as herself from the loss of his company. A man acting on stage each day could hardly be expected to spend much time with his mother – and that was something Jody did do, day in day out, until sometimes he almost hated her.

And yet he knew that was unjust. He did in fact love her

very dearly, in his own way. He knew himself to be warmly wrapped in her adoration, and it was good to be so. He enjoyed it, and was glad to respond. But there were too many times when he felt she smothered him with her company and he ached to be away from her.

But not today. Today, as he sat with his head resting on the crimson velvet squabs of the very comfortable carriage, looking at her as she sat back in her shadowy corner with her eyes just visible behind her creamy lace veil, he was full of interest in her and her affairs. Ever since he had told her of what was toward at the Haymarket she had been behaving strangely. She had been withdrawn and irritable, even with him, and he ached to know why. He had tried some probing questions about Lydia Mohun, and why her name had had so powerful an effect on his mother, but she had shut up like an oyster, and that was strange indeed from her, she who was usually so pathetically eager to talk to him, to engage his interest. And, absurdly, the effect of this was to make him infinitely more interested in her and her affairs than he could remember being for a long time.

He stretched his legs a little, and turned his head to look out at the passing scene and reached out to open the window, and at once Lilith put up her hand to her veil.

'Oh, Mamma,' he said a little irritably. 'You really do make too much of it altogether. Your veil cannot blow that much if I open the window, and even if it does, who is here to see but me? And I do not care in the least.'

'I cannot bear that you should see it,' she said. 'You know I cannot.'

'I sometimes wonder if it is as bad a disfigurement as you would have me believe,' he said a little more gently. 'It is many years now since I saw you without that eternal veil, and, you know, it is possible that you make too much of it altogether! I have seen many women about with shocking pockmarks and they do not wear veils! Whatever sort of scar it is cannot be as ugly as Mrs. Chester's, I am sure—'

'Would you compare my situation with a *housekeeper's*? What does it matter that a woman who spends her time chasing kitchenmaids should look as she does? We speak of me.'

There was a short silence as the phaeton curved round into Park Lane on its way to Upper Brook Street and so home to Grosvenor Square, and Jody stirred himself again and said with a somewhat spurious brightness, 'Mamma! Let us pretend that you have no scar at all, and let me take a box at the theatre for you! No, do not behave so frightened!—' for she had shrunk back into her corner, '—but think about it! You have not seen a play these many years, and it was your whole life, after all! It is silly to cut yourself off so. Let me take a box, and we can arrive early, and I shall sit in such a way that no one in the theatre will be able to see you, or more than a shadow of you anyway, and they will say, "Who is she?" and "What is the secret of the lady in the box?" and so forth! It will be capital sport quite apart from the pleasure of the play. And—'

For a moment it had seemed she was actually considering the idea seriously, but then she shook her head so firmly that the veil swung wide and gave a glimpse of her chin. 'No! I am sure you mean kind, Jody, but no. You cannot understand, no doubt, but I who was considered the most beautiful woman in London for so many years to risk being seen and pitied – no, I am not made of such stuff. Besides there is nothing I wish to see at any theatre. I may not attend performances, but I read all the reports of every production, and I know what is happening. And there is nothing at all of my interest—'

'Not even *Ivanhoe*?' he said slyly.

'That does not open for at least another month, as well you know!' she said sharply. 'And do stop tormenting me about it all! I wish I had said nothing about the wretched business in the first place.'

'Well, wish or not, you did. And now I am afire with interest! Whatever did this Mohun woman do that you are so set about? Truly, Mamma, I am quite mad with curiosity! If you will not tell me, I swear I shall have to set out to find out by myself!'

'You will not!' she leaned forward and gripped his wrist so hard that he winced.

'Here, take care! What are you doing?' He pulled his hand away and rubbed it, frowning at her. 'What in the world are you making such a fuss about? I never saw you so—'

'Jody, please, listen to me. I have no doubt you *are* most curious about it all, but I do not wish to burden you with a lot – of ancient history or myself with having to talk of it. Sufficient, surely, that I believe I have cause to feel as I do. Leave it be. That is all I ask. Just leave it be and we will be comfortable again and forget the wretched business was ever mentioned.'

He looked at her curiously, and then after momentary silence, as the phaeton made its turn into the Square, he said, 'No, I cannot let it be. Not until you answer some questions. For example, do you hate this woman?'

She had leaned back again, and turned her head away from him, but there was no pause at all in her reply. 'Yes, yes, I do. I have cause—'

'I shall not tease you about the cause,' he said at once. 'I promise. But it seems to me that what perturbs you most is that she should be playing in your theatre – well, it was almost yours, was it not, in the days when you played there? I can remember how it was, when I was small—'

'Yes, it was mine. The audience were mine, the stage was mine, and almost the bricks and mortar were mine—'

'Yes, well! That is what I mean. Is it not the thought that this Mohun, whoever she is, should be on *your* stage playing to *your* audience that so upsets you?'

'Yes! Why must you plague me so? I told you I don't wish to speak of it! But yes, that is part of it—'

He grinned at her, and leaned forward and took her hands in both of his. 'Foolish Mamma! Why did you not admit this to me earlier? I could perhaps have done something to – shall we say *arrange* things in a manner you would prefer! It is a little late now, of course, and will cost a little more to put in hand. But nothing is impossible! If you ask it of me, I will arrange matters so that the Mohun will return to her savage Scottish wilderness as fast as ever she came to London and the Hay-market! I know well enough that you lost your own control over the productions there by selling out on my behalf – but bless you, Mamma, it is more than ownership of shares of an enterprise that makes it possible to be involved in that enterprise. Especially when it is of the theatrical performances we speak! Why, think what you can do for the mere price of a seat in the pit! You have the free run of the building – well, almost free, for you cannot go into the backstage parts I grant you, without due reason – but you can enter the greenroom if it pleases you to do so. And you can sit and watch the play, and applaud, and cheer, can you not?'

The phaeton had slowed, and was coming to a stop, and the carriage shook as the footman sprang down from the back and came round to set the steps and open the door to hand Lilith out, and Jody spoke more rapidly. '—And of course, if the play displeases you, you can boo and jeer and shout and generally show all those around that you feel as you do!'

He jerked his head at the footman to make him move aside and himself sprang out and held out his hand to assist his mother to alight. 'Think of it, Mamma!' He spoke into her ear now as he walked beside her up the sweep of steps that led to the front door. 'Just think of what it would be like if on a first night a lot of people in the house took a dislike to a performer! Why, would not the noise be indescribable? Indeed, if they were firm enough in their dislike it would be near impossible for the actor – or actress come to that – to lift voice enough to be heard!'

She stopped very still, one foot on the doorstep, and turned her head slowly to peer at him through her veil.

'Would it not indeed!' she said after a moment. 'I remember one night, when I first appeared, the cheers were so loud and rapturous it was fully five minutes before I could say a word, and I had to come to the front of the stage to take my bow and kiss hands to them before they would be silent.'

'I am sure it was like that more than once!' he said, and patted the hand held in the crook of his elbow. 'And I am sure you never heard the other sort of noise – that greets the unbe-loved—'

She moved again as the door opened and Rashett, the most

recent of the many butlers who had worked in the house, stepped back with a bow as his employer and her son walked in.

'No.' Standing there in her black and white tiled hall, slowly pulling the gloves from her fingers, she looked to Jody a very slight figure and he was filled with a sudden surge of affection tinged with guilt; he really should not be so devious with her, not when she was so lonely and so helpless, locked in her veil and her empty days. But then she lifted her head and looked round at the hallway and the tilt of her chin and that proprietorial way she had of looking at her possessions – almost as though she were making a swift inventory – had its usual effect, and irritation and sense of real frustration sent his gentler feelings back where they belonged, into limbo.

'So, Mamma, I leave it with you!' He spoke in as light a tone as he could muster, tossing his hat and gloves at Rashett, and turning towards the stairs. 'You must let me know if there are any small commissions you would have me undertake on your behalf. The sort of commission I have in mind will be costly, of course, but there, that is of small moment to you, I daresay, if matters should fall out as you wish in consequence. You have but to ask me, remember!'

He ran up the stairs with the springing lightness that he was at some pains to cultivate, and she stood there and watched him go, and when he looked back from the top of the stairs to raise his hand to her before going along the wide passageway to his own room for his afternoon brandy and cigar, he wished heartily, and not for the first time, that she would get rid of that wretched veil. Not so much because he wished to see the scar which she so assiduously kept hidden but because the sight of her face would help him to know what she was thinking. And he would dearly like to know, that moment, the effectiveness of the bait he had so carefully dropped.

'You do not intend to go, surely?' Richard said, and reached over her shoulder to pick up a length of Chantilly lace from the heap of fabrics spread before them on the shopkeeper's counter. 'That is a splendid piece now! I think I should like

68

that for my second act, when I am about to set out for the castle, you know, and—'

'No, you shan't!' she said and pulled it from his hand with a neat twist of her wrist. 'It will look dreadful on you – make you quite muddy in the complexion! And I want it for my act one entrance. Yes, I think I *shall* go! Why not? It might be quite amusing—'

She was arranging the Chantilly lace around her shoulders, and peacocking in front of the mirror held carefully for her by the shopkeeper's lanky apprentice. 'Indeed, I am sure I am right about this! The amber colour suits me admirably, don't you agree?' She cocked her head inquiringly at the apprentice who reddened and swallowed and blinked and bobbed his head, all at once, and she laughed her bubbly laugh so that he fell instantly and helplessly in love with her, a passion that was to consume him for years to come, while Lydia, content with the effect she had made, turned back to Richard at the counter and immediately forgot the adoring apprentice for ever. 'Dickon, try that piece of blue silk – yes, that one. Now *that* will suit you magnificently, because of your eyes.'

'Mmm,' he said consideringly, replacing her at the mirror, to the misery of the apprentice. 'Hold the thing still, boy! That's better. Yes, I quite like this – amusing, did you say? How could it be? An evening spent with a tedious moneygrubbing cit and his tedious moneygrubbing wife and tedious moneygrubbing children and—'

'—and my far from tedious moneygrubbing brother-in-law! Come, Dickon, you cannot find him disagreeable. Shy, a little, and a shade brusque in consequence, but he is still very handsome! I remember him as a boy, when he was drooping after my mother and sister – oh, I thought him the very acme of male perfection! And though I can now see that he is not precisely Apollo Belvedere, he remains a man of much charm.'

Richard threw the blue silk at the shopkeeper who caught it expertly and went away to parcel it up together with the other pieces of satin and lace and muslin and velvets they had chosen, and looked at Lydia with a scowl.

'If you wish to waste your time with some dismal piece of your past, then it is no matter to me – *I* have no wish to cramp your style in any way, I do promise you! If you want to sit and sigh with him, never let it be said I stood in your way! Go if you wish and—'

'Oh, Pooh! Such a pet to fly into!'

She giggled then, and with a ghost of a wink at the apprentice, who bade fair to swoon on the spot in consequence, tucked her hand into the crook of Richard's elbow and began to walk him up and down the shop as they waited for their parcels to be ready for them. 'Now, do stop being so silly, my dear Dickon, for you know as well as you know your own name that I adore you, that I have no wish to look at any other man at all, in any serious way, and that I am but amusing myself when I talk to others! You know how much it amuses you to see them gawp and stammer and watch you take me home, half-eaten by jealousy! It is but a game, I do promise you – and I wish to go to this party at Stanhope Terrace tonight in part for the game and in part, you know, for the family ties. I have been alone so long, Dickon! A woman enjoys the cosy prosing that happens in families, but I have none! I was born one of three you know – no, four! – but here I am with no mother, no sister, no brother left to me. All quite cut off, I am! My sister dead, my mother hating me, my brother God knows where – for he set out to go to America you know, five years ago, and never have I heard a word from him since – and now I find my long-lost brother-in-law, and hear that I have a niece and a nephew – come, you cannot grudge me this! Not you with all the vast family you enjoy!'

'Enjoy!' He snorted at that. 'That parcel of grabbers and bloodsuckers? If you had to finance the hungry mouths of as many damned relations as I do, you wouldn't be so delighted to have nieces and nephews! Mine cost me a fortune, I can tell you, and—'

'Aye, and think how dearly they all love you, and admire you!' she said wheedlingly. 'And how much you enjoy their adulation! You would not surely wish me to have less? It cannot detract from the pleasure we find together, darling

Dickon! Please – come with me tonight! That pleasant man asked so agreeably and—'

'Pleasant!' Richard, who had been almost mollified, became very sharp again. 'A cool customer that one is! Sleek as a cat, and as arrogant as – as – pah! How you can call him pleasant I cannot imagine!'

And indeed Gideon had looked very coolly indeed at O'Hara when first introduced to him, and that had rankled. It had been Lydia who had made that long white face lose its chill, Lydia who had made it soften and crack into a smile – and it could not be denied that it was a most attractive smile – Lydia who had been so cordially invited to join the Henriques family at their party that evening. The invitation to himself had been included very much as an afterthought, though delivered with punctilious good manners, simply because Lydia had reached out and tucked her hand into his elbow in that confiding, even proprietorial fashion of hers. Richard O'Hare was not the man to enjoy being regarded as any person's accessory, even a person as elegant and charming – and ultimately useful – as Mrs. Mohun.

So it took Lydia quite five minutes of her best efforts finally to convince him that there was pleasure to be found in spending an evening watching amateur tableaux *vivants*, that he would not be at all set in the shade by any other person, as far as she was concerned, and above all that it would be good business sense to entrench themselves in the society of such respectable London citizens as the Henriques and Lacklands.

'For depend upon it, Dickon,' she said earnestly, 'we must make good from the start of this engagement! I have fought hard and long to get here to London to show what I can do, and there will be many wishing me ill! Mrs. Stanton, for a start, and other ladies I prefer not to waste my breath naming. I want us to do good business from the very start. I want this to be the greatest success the Haymarket has had since my mother left 'em. Indeed, I am determined it shall be so! And the more acquaintances we make this next month while we are in rehearsal, the better, for London will be full of tradespeople and men of business as we get nearer to the Exhibition's opening,

71

and it may be hard to establish ourselves properly as a result! You must see the sense of it! Here I am fresh from the provinces, yet I have already the entrée to a useful section of London society. You really must not spoil it all, my love!'

'Well, I suppose so,' he said, as the shopkeeper handed them their elegantly tied parcels and with much bowing and scraping followed them from the shop (leaving the apprentice still holding the mirror and gawping adoringly after Lydia) to hand them into their waiting carriage. 'If that is how it is, then there is *some* value in it, I dare say. Not that it won't be a dead bore from start to finish! Tea and ratafia biscuits and men talking interminably of money! Can't you just imagine it! And the women – can't you just see 'em! Row upon row of hideous ugly females, that's what there'll be. O Lor'!'

She settled comfortably into the phaeton, gathering up the reins and nodding at the little tiger who left the horses' heads at once to leap behind. 'Ugly women! Well, that may be so! But I am sure you can bear that, Dickon darling, as long as I am there!' and her whip flickered and the horses stamped and Richard sat and stared glumly over his folded arms at the prospect of a most dismal evening ahead.

# CHAPTER SIX

THIS was the most perfect time of day for Abby. Her babies were settled in their cribs, snugly asleep after their bread-and-milk and story-telling, with Ellie sitting watchfully beside the nursery fire, her skirts crumpled inelegantly above her wide-spread knees and her lap full of sewing; her business had been neatly locked up for the night, with the huge machines lying dustily silent in the vast room that smelled so strongly of wintergreen and ginger, bismuth and squills and paregoric, and the books with the long columns of figures that spoke so eloquently of continuing success secure in the big iron safe; and her household had slipped smoothly into evening gear with the cook sweating in the kitchen and the butler setting the dinner table and maids running busily everywhere with their starched cap ribbons flying. Now was the time when Abby could stretch out on her chaise-longue for half an hour, to be warmed by the flames in her wide fireplace and listen contentedly to Gideon giving news of his day.

But tonight it was not the usual source of satisfaction, this half-hour of peace before it was necessary to dress for dinner and their evening party. For a start, Gideon had come to her room late, and so had quite destroyed the sensuous feelings she had entertained for quite a large part of the afternoon. They were, heaven knew, a most respectable pair, the Henriques, however stormy their early days together had been – and sometimes she would remember the painful times when she had been so convinced that there could be no future for her with the man she so dearly loved, with a pang of fear for what she had almost lost combined with gratitude that all had ended so happily – but that did not mean that they were not deeply passionate. And many were the times when, during the dwindling winter afternoons, their rest time before dinner was occupied in a far from restful way, when the chaise-longue that stood so elegantly before the fire shared their far from elegant embraces.

But not tonight. Tonight she had removed her stays and put on her prettiest peignoir to no purpose, for he came rather breathlessly into her room a bare ten minutes before her maid would come to help her dress, thus leaving time for nothing but conversation. So her tone was a little sharp when she greeted him.

'Well, Gideon! At what stage of your day was your time so stolen from you? Did you find your mother well?'

Abby tried never to show any resentment of her parents-in-law, truly tried very hard, bitterly hurtful though their complete rejection of her, and her children, was, but there were times when it would have taken a superhuman woman to bite her tongue. And Abby, though a practical woman, though a most intelligent and affectionate and indeed wise woman, was not superhuman.

'Oh, my mother—' Gideon said. 'I had almost forgot I saw her this morning! No, she is well, as is all at Lombard Street—' They never mentioned his father's name in any discussion between them. There was so little point in doing so. But they always exchanged news of him, in their own way. 'In fact, I spent rather less time with her than usual, for there was nothing to be dealt with regarding business, and she was expecting visitors. There are some of her more remote cousins here from Madrid, I understand. I am sorry I am late, my love, but I was somewhat delayed at King Street, by Jonah – he really does get some absurd notions into his head – and then of course, Freddy! You will recall he wished to talk to me tonight.'

Her awareness of her own injustice in being annoyed with him, since it was her brother and her son who had delayed him rather than his parents, sharpened her tongue rather than the reverse. 'Freddy! Indeed! And what masculine matters are they between you two that I must be excluded? Am I even permitted to ask?'

He had by now removed his coat and was in his shirt-sleeves in front of the mirror over the fireplace trying to undo his high collar, but at the sound of her voice he at once stopped, peered at her reflection for a moment and then smiled, that narrow-lipped, slightly lopsided smile that she knew so well and which could still tie a small knot in her belly when she saw it. And he turned and came to the chaise-longue and sat down beside her, putting his hands on her shoulders and looking down at her with his eyes narrowed with humour.

'Ah, Abby, my love, have I spoiled some delectable little plan you had made by being late? Was the loss of this quarter hour more than a mere loss of time?' And he bent and kissed her, slipping his hands down her shoulders and across her breasts under her peignoir until he was holding her waist. 'I know the feeling! The times when Isabel demands just one more story, and Sarah must perforce have a drink of water before she will let you go – you cannot imagine how thirsty her extra drinks make me!'

She giggled softly, quite mollified, and linked her hands behind his neck. 'Indeed I can! You wretch! It is not gentle-manly in you to remind me what a brazen hussy I am!'

He kissed her again, her cheeks, her eyelids, her chin. 'And why should I concern myself with matters of gentlemanliness when you would so hate it if I did? Whenever did mere gentility come between us? You are a delightful hussy, indeed, thoroughly brazen, and I would not have you otherwise! Forgive me? And we shall retire early to bed like Darby and Joan and—'

'Early! Not tonight. Had you forgot Phoebe's party?'

He lifted his face from her neck and grimaced. 'Damn it, I had! And there is a matter I must tell you of regarding it, too! You see what an effect you can have on me?'

He stood up and went back to the mirror to wrestle again with his collar. 'And after eight years too! The Femme Fatale of Stanhope Terrace! The Terror of Tyburnia!'

She clasped her hands behind her head, and watched him. 'Not for much longer – if ever I was! Wait until you see Phoebe tonight! I have seen some of her costumes, and truly, she is quite, quite delectable! What was it you had to tell me regarding her party?'

'Ah, yes – well, I have bidden two more guests, my love. I hope this will not incommode you at all?'

'Two more? But who? There will be no problems I daresay – I cannot imagine two more will add much to the crush which I suspect will be frightful anyway; and I told Cook this morning she had over-estimated the amounts needed for supper. But do tell me!'

'I was at Jonah's this afternoon, as I told you, and he had most interesting news! His wife's sister has come to London!'

She frowned sharply at that, and sat up straighter. 'Celia's *sister*? But who – wait, now, I can barely remember – I believe there was a brother as well as a sister was there not? And the sister was younger than Celia and—'

'Her name is Lydia. Lydia Mohun. She is a widow, just come down from Edinburgh to be in a new production at the Haymarket, and Jonah, I can assure you, was quite *bouleversé* by it all! He had some notion she would come down on him for money, but it is clear she has no intention of such a thing. She is dressed very expensive and wears extremely good diamonds. There is no reason to think for a moment she is any sort a pauper! But Jonah thought—'

She got to her feet, and came to help him untie the recalci- trant shoe-lace with which he was struggling. 'You've seen her?'

'Well, that was what was so amusing! There we are talking of the lady, and in she comes for all the world like an actress answering a cue! The whole episode was like a bad play, I do assure you! There is Jonah just telling me he is happy with what I have assured him is his freedom from cause to worry and in comes this most exquisite creature, dressed to the nines and I must say a pleasure to look at, on the arm of a rather disagreeable character—'

She was still crouched at his feet and looked up at him with a sharp tilt of her chin. 'Disagreeable?'

'Oh, shockingly overdressed, I thought, and too handsome to be anything but a rake of the worst sort—'

'More overdressed than she?'

He looked down at her for a moment and then laughed. 'Well, I suppose you have the right of it! They were very much a pair! But on her, you know, it looked – well there was no hint of vulgar show about it! I would not be ashamed ever to present her to you, and indeed I thought – she is Phoebe's aunt, after all! She showed a very pretty concern for news of her family, I must say, and with Jonah standing there with his mouth clamped shut as though he were struck dumb, what could I do but give it? And she seemed so genuinely interested in meeting her niece that I thought the least I could do was to bid her here tonight. You know yourself how you dislike the matter of formal calls, my love! You always say you are a woman of business as well as mistress of your household, and hate interminably wasting time in the way other women do, those who lack your involvement in affairs! And of course, as an actress she is in the same situation. So, I told her of our party here tonight – it was inevitable in fact, for I was telling her of Phoebe's taste for home theatricals since it seemed to be a matter of family links, you know, and – well, I asked her! I trust you do not object, my love? And I am sure Phoebe will be enchanted! The lady is an aunt any young lady could find pleasure in!'

'And what about her companion? I imagine he is your other extra guest?'

Her maid had come softly into the room, carrying the brass can of hot water ready for Abby's toilet, and was moving soft-footedly about setting out her gown and preparing her hair brushes, and Gideon moved to his dressing-room door, carrying his shoes in one hand and his collar and cravat in the other.

'Oh, yes, I had to, I'm afraid. They were clearly very much together. But he will bear watching, I think. Too smooth altogether, much too smooth. He was wearing a blue cravat, Abby! Such vulgarity! Annie! Is Mansfield ready for me?'

The maid bobbed and said breathily, 'Yes, sir, and Cook says as dinner'll 'ave to be sharp on the hour, if she's to be all ready proper like for the party, please, sir, and I was to tell you both, sir, ma'am, meanin' no disrespect, sir—'

'Then I had best put myself into fast speed! I bade them for ten o'clock, Abby! I shall be most interested to hear your views on Phoebe's aunt, I must say. A charming woman, charming—'

And he was gone, leaving Abby to wash and gown herself and allow her hair to be dressed, in a most thoughtful mood. She could not recall ever hearing Gideon speak so admiringly of any other woman. Not even before they were wed, not even during those long years when they had been but business colleagues, and had never whispered a word of their shared affection for each other, had he displayed so much enthusiasm for anybody. And although Abby knew better than any woman ever could that she had no shred of cause to feel the least pang of anxiety about her husband's abiding affection for her, she did not like it. She did not like it one bit.

Freddy stood as close as he could to the curtains that shrouded the drawing-room archway, leaning against the wall so that he was quite shaded; a difficult feat for the room was blazing with gaslight, and candles had been brought in in tall brass candelabra to add to the glitter of the occasion. He did not wish to be observed observing Phoebe, feeling that in some way his emotions would show too clearly on his face. And he wanted to keep all of that well battened down until such time as he had the opportunity to communicate it all to Phoebe herself. In a curious way he felt it would in some sort be an insult to Phoebe if anyone else were to know what was toward before Phoebe did.

For Gideon had assured him that there was no financial reason why he should not marry.

'Your income is assured, dear boy, certainly for the next ten years, as far as I am concerned. And even if the business should then collapse and no longer bring you the sizeable income it now does – an eventuality which is so unlikely as to be absurd to consider – why, by then you will be a surgeon of repute, I have no doubt, and fully capable of earning enough to support a wife and family!'

Freddy had reddened suddenly at that; to find his much admired stepfather treating his request for information – and by implication, for advice and guidance – in so serious a manner had been very gratifying. Gideon had always treated him with courtesy and indeed affection all his life. Even before his mother had married him, Freddy had known the tall thin dark man to be his friend. But there had always been the gap of age between them; Gideon so much the man, Freddy so much the boy – until now. And Freddy was so touched and warmed by this sense of masculine fellowship that he blurted it out without really thinking about it.

'Oh, Gideon, *am* I doing the right thing, do you believe? I know we are both very young to consider matrimony, but I have loved her so long and so much that I sometimes feel we are positively middle-aged, and that if I do not wed her soon, we will both be too old! Absurd, I know, but so do I feel—'

'Not absurd, dear boy,' Gideon had said, and touched his shoulder reassuringly. 'You are far from absurd. I look back on the lonely years I had before I dared to speak to your Mamma of my affection for her, and I do regret them, even though now we are so happy. Life is too short, I am convinced, to waste any of it. You are a sensible, caring sort of young man, Freddy, and one I much admire. Your father would have been deeply proud of you had he lived to know you, of that I am certain. Phoebe is a fortunate young lady indeed to have attached you to her so firmly. How does *she* feel about so young a marriage?'

'Oh, I do not know!' Freddy sounded quite shocked. 'I have not spoken to her yet, you understand! I could not, to be sure, until I was certain that the financial aspects were possible, and that you agreed I was in a position to declare myself!'

There was a short silence and then Gideon said carefully, 'Freddy, my dear boy, I had not realized – I mean – have you thought of the possibility that she will not share your enthusiasm for an early wedding?'

'Oh, as to that, she will listen to me! She always has, bless her! Even when we were small, you know, she agreed that I knew best and that she would do as I said she must!' Freddy's lips curved reminiscently. 'Such games and villainies as we got up to, you can't imagine—'

'Indeed, I can! I knew of many of them, as did your

79

Mamma, but we thought it politic to say nothing! None of them were all that villainous, really. The occasional broken window, perhaps, or stolen fruit tarts from the kitchen! Oh, we knew!'

Freddy laughed. 'Well, there you are, Gideon! There will be no problem there, I am sure. Phoebe may seem a giddy girl, and there are times when indeed she is very tiresome with her peacockings and performings, but she is so good a girl and so very tender and affectionate at bottom! No, I have no fears on that score. My only doubt was whether you would agree that my ideas were practicable!'

'And what of her father?'

'Uncle Jonah? Well, what of him? I have been a little concerned, I do not deny, but I cannot imagine he will take the idea in dislike!'

'One never knows.' Gideon stood up and began to prowl around the room a little restlessly, not looking at his stepson. 'One never knows how parents will be, Freddy. One expects them always to want what is best for their children, and indeed they usually do. But their views of what is best and their offspring's views – that is where there may be parting of the ways.'

He stood still then and looked rather sombrely at Freddy. 'Remember that it is possible, my boy, will you? I would not wish you to call all your ships home in full confidence only to find some have foundered.'

Freddy shook his head firmly. 'Oh, I am not being so foolish, Gideon, I do assure you! I have thought of it all so carefully, and I have come to the conclusion that I fear no objection from Uncle Jonah because there cannot be any! Phoebe has lived here with me half my life. I have loved her and cared for and taught her and protected her in every way I could, and Uncle Jonah knows me to be a person he can trust. We are on excellent terms, I do assure you! And with you to tell him, as I trust you will when the times comes, that I am a secure man of money, why there can be no stop in our way!'

He stood up, and shot his cuffs. 'I will go and dress for dinner and then, after the party, I shall tell Phoebe of it all!

And then we shall speak to Mamma and then to Uncle Jonah.'

He produced a grin that threatened to split his face, so wide and happy was it. 'Oh, Gideon, isn't it *splendid* to feel like this? I am indeed so lucky a man!' And he leaned forward and seized one of Gideon's hands in both his and shook it with great vigour, and reddened so much that even his hair seemed to deepen in colour, and then hurried out of the room to rush upstairs and dress.

Now he stood in the shadows of the curtains in the big drawing-room, watching her as she went about among her guests, and felt he would burst with love of her. She looked so entirely perfect, so soft, so shining, so exactly what a girl should be that if he had sat down with a pen and paper to make a detailed list of all the attributes a girl should have, he could not have improved in any way upon the one he now looked at.

She was moving as light as a piece of fluff from group to group of her guests, her huge crinoline dipping and lifting as she twirled and twisted past them so that sometimes her small feet in their kid slippers showed tantalizingly, and sometimes, very daringly, even a glimpse of her white silk ankles; and no one could have said for a moment that she was deliberately so displaying herself, although Freddy and the rest of her family knew perfectly well that she was, because she did it so charmingly and with such style. And Freddy did not blame her in the least, and felt none of the pangs of jealousy lovers are supposed to feel when others are given the privilege of admiring the usually secret aspects of their ladies; indeed, all Freddy felt when he saw the way other men's eyes widened and darkened at the sight of her, the way they turned away from their own female companions to gain a better view of their hostess, was simple pride. These others might admire her, might desire her, might look at her with hungry eyes, that did not matter a whit to Freddy, for she belonged to him, and only to him, and always had ever since she was a tiny girl to be bullied and taught and adored.

The chatter in the room built up in direct proportion to the heat as more and more people arrived to fill the long drawing-room with crinolines and sober black trousers and – among the younger and more fashionable men – gleaming oiled hair and even the very modern mutton-chop whiskers. The young swells of Tyburnia were as alive to the trends of the moment as any of the aristocrats of Mayfair and Belgravia, and the Stanhope Terrace drawing-room showed their elegance to perfection. The trio of musicians in the far corner scraping away on fiddles to give an air of sprightliness to the occasion sweated under the attack of warmth from candles and gas mantles and the women's fans fluttered and trembled as they waved them busily before their hot and shining faces. The room smelled of flowers and candle wax and chypre and, very faintly, of human bodies glowing a little more than was really comfortable. A most successful crush indeed.

It was just a little before ten when the room was swept by a new movement, as Phoebe and several of her friends went hurrying about whispering to some, bidding others to move to the far end of the room, and gradually the event of the evening took shape. Most of the guests took themselves to the front of the room, to cluster below the pair of big windows on stools and low sofas, the young gentlemen very elegantly sitting themselves al fresco upon the red Turkey carpet, while two servants brought in red silk screens which they drew across the end of the room to hide the door into the library and the smaller windows that looked down into the garden. Candles were rearranged and gaslights turned down in such a way that the part of the room where the audience sat was in shadow, while the far end behind the screens was brilliantly lit. The musicians who had been enjoying a moment's respite to catch their breath launched themselves into a stately pavane, after a breathy and too audible 'one-two-three' from their heavily sweating leader, and the servants drew back the screens with a rattle to display the entertainment.

And very lovely it was to see, Freddy told himself after his first slightly shocked reaction. Very lovely. And classical, of course—

Several young ladies in Roman style drapes were arranged in tasteful poses about a long couch which was flanked by two young gentlemen – who looked quite agonizingly uncomfortable in their complicated swirls of white linen, obviously sheets arranged to look like senatorial togas – and leaning towards it in such a way that the eyes of all beholders were drawn quite irresistibly to the occupant of the couch. The lights were so arranged that the strongest pool of illumination fell upon it. And there in all her loveliness lay Phoebe.

She was wearing a gown that was very tight – quite immodestly tight, it could not be denied – and which displayed a good deal more of her than even Freddy felt was quite proper. For the first time he could remember he felt a twinge of disquiet as he heard the faint hiss of indrawn breath from the men in the audience. For Phoebe did look inviting. It could not be denied that the total effect of her costume – which was rather more Egyptian, Freddy decided, than Roman, a fact which puzzled him – was far from innocent in its sensuousness.

'Cleopatra at Caesar's Palace!' announced a breathy little voice from the side of the makeshift stage, and after a second the audience applauded and voices were raised in approval.

'Very pretty!' someone said. 'Too delightful!' others agreed, though it was noticeable that most of the comments came from the men; but Freddy, whose hearing was acute, caught the sound of his mother's voice saying in some asperity, 'The wretched child! I told her that one was quite unsuitable and she told me it would not be used!' And then the applause increased and he heard no more.

The screens rattled to a close and after a rush of feet and more frenzied playing from the musicians to cover the sound of furniture being moved while the audience giggled and flirted cheerfully, they parted again, this time to display Phoebe quite gorgeously arrayed in golden silk and imperiously striking a kneeling man in rather skimpy hose with a fencing foil.

'Queen Elizabeth knights Raleigh at Tilbury!' announced the little voice beside the screens, now seen to belong to a rather plain little friend of Phoebe who adored her much prettier companion and was always willing therefore to do the tasks no one else wanted. Again the applause, again the comments, but this time a little less enthusiastically; for there was little doubt that splendid though the Queen Elizabeth costume was, it did lack the interest of the far less ornate Cleopatra one.

Nothing could quite surpass the effect that had had, Freddy thought, and watched with some gloom as the screens closed again, the same interval for furniture-shifting and costume-changing elapsed, and they parted again, this time on a most pathetic sight – Phoebe in sombre black and white alone and kneeling before a footstool which was covered with a piece of elderly brown carpet to make it appear to be a wooden block, and her hands clasped most fervently as she stared at the draw-ing-room ceiling, her face a perfect vision of patient accept-ance and forgiveness.

'Mary, Queen of Scots!' announced the plain friend, her voice quite choked with emotion, and this time the audience applauded much more rapturously, for indeed the total effect was very compelling. Especially as this time Phoebe had no companions at all on her stage.

Freddy became aware of people behind him, late arrivals who had been standing there some time, indeed since before the first tableau, but now he registered their presence because of the tone of the male voice that said, 'Clever! Very, very clever! Last thing you'd expect to find at a party like *this*!' And the scorn the voice managed to inject into the last word was so intense that Freddy turned his head to peer into the shadows to see who had spoken.

But he could not see more than a shape and only heard a woman's soft gurgling voice murmur, 'Hush, Dickon, do! You really must remember that you have a powerful voice! I wouldn't have the child hear you for the world!'

'I'm paying her a compliment, dammit,' the voice said, lower this time, but still strong and very deep. 'And it is clever! Wasted on this—' and his voice slid down into a rumble from which Freddy could extract no words at all, but the gurgling voice laughed and said something, and the man responded with a deep laugh of his own and Freddy felt a surge of irritation. Damn these people; who were they to laugh at what happened in *his* house and at *his* party? And then turned back to the screens which were parting yet again, reminding himself with some sharpness that it was really Phoebe's party and not his.

This time she stood swathed to the neck in gauzy, many-coloured draperies with her arms spread wide and a golden fillet about her forehead over her dark curls which had been unbound and lay tumbled over her shoulders. There was silver lace drifting from her arms and at her feet crouched various of her friends dressed somewhat surprisingly – and obviously very uncomfortably – as cats, rabbits, birds and even, most ambitiously, a long green serpent.

'The Gift of the Rainbow!' cried the announcer and everyone laughed and applauded mightily, and after holding her pose for just one more long minute, Phoebe dropped her arms and stepped forward to bow and then curtsy, and the applause increased and people called, 'Bravo!' and she curtsied again, staring out at all of them with her face glowing with pride and satisfaction and total delight. She had never looked more delicious, Freddy thought, and never been so totally unaware of him. And for a moment he felt very cold indeed in that hot room.

The next fifteen minutes went by in a flurry of rearrangement as the room was cleared of the impedimenta of the tableaux, and people milled about talking. Abby disappeared to help Phoebe dress again and, no doubt, Freddy thought, to tell her roundly of her opinion of the first tableau and its costume, and all the time Freddy stood in the shadows by the curtain. He had looked round to see who it was who had spoken in the darkness in so insulting a fashion – as he now felt it was – but a group of giggling girls had come surging into the hallway and filled his field of vision entirely. No one could see anything beyond the vast hoops of their crinolines; and since he did not wish to be embroiled in conversation with them (and he knew quite well that many of his Phoebe's friends would be more than willing to flirt and chatter with him) he turned back into the room to stare at the library door and wait for Phoebe to emerge. Probably the strangers had come into the room in the flurry at the end of the performance, he told himself; and he did not care anyway who they were or what they had to say. He had other matters to consider. But then, he saw Jonah at the far side of the room talking to Gideon, and beside them a couple of people he had never seen before, people dressed, as far as he could tell (for they stood with their backs to him) in the first stare of fashion. The man's coat was cut with almost insulting perfection and the woman's crinoline was in a deep scarlet silk that was very striking. Were *they* the ill-mannered gossipers?

At last Phoebe emerged, Abby beside her, and he started forward, but was delayed by the crush of people moving towards him, for the butler had just sonorously announced that supper was served below in the dining-room, and these thirsty, hungry guests were not the sort to wait for others to lead the way. So he had to stand back and wait, and found himself, at last, face to face with Phoebe.

'Phoebe!' He started forward again. 'For heaven's sake, girl, what took you so long? Now do come and have some supper! I have to talk to you, and it really is—'

'Oh, Freddy!' she looked up at him with eyes so sparkling and so wide that it was almost as though she would drown in her own gaiety. 'Dear Freddy, was I not *perfect*? Admit it! And was not my Cleopatra costume very, very outrageous? Aunt Abby is quite furious with me! So funny!' And she giggled and turned her head to look up at the man whose arm she was holding. 'Mr. O'Hare says it is the best tableau he has ever seen, and he should know, for he is a great actor, Freddy! Is it not capital? Here is my new aunt as well – such an excitement this evening, I am sure I shall quite swoon away!'

'Supper,' Freddy said gruffly and held out one crooked arm. 'Shall we go down?' He would not look at the man to whose arm she was clinging; he was the man in the insulting coat, and was standing there beside Phoebe in silence, one hand covering hers with apparent negligence as it lay on his arm, and one leg held in a pose of studied nonchalance that quite made Freddy's gorge rise.

'Oh, darling Freddy, I cannot, for Mr. O'Hare is taking me down, are you not? He wishes to talk to me of my tableaux. Imagine!' and she was gone, drifting past in a fluff of yellow gauze; and still not a word had O'Hare said.

Freddy lifted his eyes at last and looked up at the man as he

86

passed him, staring into a pair of very dark blue eyes that looked at him as though they knew every atom of his business.

'Your servant, sir,' he said and his deep voice was inevitably the one that had come from the shadows behind Freddy during the Mary, Queen of Scots pose. 'Forgive us if we do not delay. Miss Phoebe tells me she is quite *parched* with thirst—' and they were away down the stairs, leaving Freddy staring after them, his arm still absurdly crooked ready to receive Phoebe's hand.

# CHAPTER SEVEN

FREDDY worked next day as though it were the last he would ever work. He went through the rounds of dressings with a face so grim that even the nurses hesitated to speak to him, and the patients did no more than take one scared look at him and then shut their eyes and grit their teeth until he had finished. Not that he caused them any unnecessary pain, for determined though he was to push his way through his work in so concentrated a fashion that he would not have time to think of Phoebe, he did not forget the agony a mistimed movement of his could cause, or the way the patients suffered from the pain of their suppurating wounds. He had suffered enough pain himself at the sight of their tears and the sound of their entreaties.

And when the ward rounds were finished, and his fellow students took themselves off to the tavern across the street next to the church for ale to wash the stink of pus out of their nostrils and the taste of bloody surgery from their throats, he stayed behind and set himself the task of copying his notes on the techniques of amputation from his commonplace book into his permanent leather-covered record of his studies, knowing full well that the talking among the other students would inevitably turn to last night's entertainment and the girls they knew or didn't know – and he would not be able to remain aloof. And to talk of or think of last night's events he would not and could not.

But even as he listed the arteries and nerves that fed the buttocks and thigh, and drew the shapes of the muscles that clustered about the hip joint, her face came drifting up, coming between him and the white page so that he swore and had to erase half a drawing and start again. How could she have looked so beautiful, how could she have been so totally desirable, so perfect a girl to ask to become a man's wife and then behave so cruelly: That she did not know he had intended to speak to her so seriously he knew; that his feeling that some blame should attach to her for spoiling his plans when she was unaware of them was unjust, he also knew; but still it rankled.

And what rankled most was that she had gone down to supper with the loathsome O'Hare and furthermore had returned from supper with him too, and danced with him, and then sat and chattered to her new-found aunt, and altogether behaved as though the most important person in her life now or ever, Freddy himself, was just not there. Freddy could not remember ever feeling so bereft and so angry.

It was late into the afternoon – a grey and dull afternoon that demanded the gaslights be lit in the long wards even before five o'clock – when his grandfather came into the dispensary where with half a dozen other students Freddy was listening to a Fellow of the Society of Apothecaries lecturing on the properties of the volatile oils.

He stood there in the doorway for a moment and the lecturer looked up and faltered and then stopped, for even the senior staff of Nellie's showed a healthy respect for the old man, and Abel frowned sharply and said, 'Do go on, man – I wish only to speak to Caspar. Come here, will you?' and Freddy followed him from the room, feeling the eyes of the other students on his back and finding himself not a little irritated by it. His grandfather was beginning to show a good deal more partiality than would endear him to his fellows, and he was not sure he liked it.

'I have a rare opportunity for one of my students this evening, and I would prefer it be you rather than any other. Not because it is you, y'understand, but because the reports I have of your progress make it clear you're the one that would benefit most by it. Don't go getting any notion I'm making some sort of pet of you, since it ain't my style, or ever will be.'

Freddy reddened. The old man seemed sometimes to read his mind, he thought uncomfortably, and then reddened even more when Abel laughed and said, 'And never fear it'll get about among the others that you're being privileged. Quite the reverse in fact, for they can leave the hospital and be about their private business by six o'clock and you'll be working till well gone the dinner hour. I've sent a message to your mother's house so they won't fret themselves over your absence.'

'I am to remain here tonight, sir?' Freddy said carefully, and suddenly felt his heart lift. Not to go home and face Phoebe over the dinner table – that would show her! She would sit there looking at his empty chair and be alarmed and anxious at his absence, and miss him sorely. The prospect of Phoebe's suffering in this way warmed him, and he turned a positively eager face to his grandather. 'To work at some special matter, perhaps?'

'Not here,' Abel said, and jerked his head to make Freddy follow him to his private room. 'The case is such that we cannot get it here, though that would be better. No, you are to go out, and a very unpleasant outing it will be, never doubt it!' He looked shrewdly at the young face. 'If you can handle yourself with dignity and good sense in the conditions you'll find yourself in tonight, then you'll have the makings of a real surgeon in you. If you can't – well then, we'll both know whether we're wasting our time teaching you.'

A sudden vision of the big, hot scented room in Panton Street rose before Freddy's eyes, the room full of half-dressed women sitting about languorously and invitingly on red velvet sofas, and he said hesitantly, 'Are we – er – are we to make the same visit we did the other day, sir?'

'Eh? Oh, to Lucy's? No – not to Lucy's!' He laughed suddenly then. 'By God, you'll wish it were Lucy's the moment you set foot in Purty Bill's, that I can tell you! Lucy's!' He shook his head and laughed again, and then stopped and said gruffly, 'She died. The night after you saw her.'

'Oh,' Freddy did not know quite what was expected of him. 'I am sorry, sir.'

'Are you indeed? And why the devil should you be sorry, tell me that? You knew nothing of Lucy, did you?'

'No, sir, I did not know her. But she seemed a most pleasant person, in the short conversation I had with her. And clearly you held her in some esteem. So I offer such condolence to you as I can.'

There was a short silence and then Abel said, 'Well, yes, you are right. I should not have been so short with you. I did care for her, a great deal, for she had been my good friend since I was a child. She gave me more of affection than any I ever knew before her. And I miss her, even more than I would have thought possible.'

There was an uncomfortable silence, and then Freddy said tentatively, 'Purty Bill's, sir?'

'Eh? Oh, yes. Purty Bill's.' Again Abel gave one of those short barks of laughter to which he was prone. 'Wait until you see him, Frederick! He is beyond any shadow of doubt the most hideous specimen of humanity you're ever likely to clap eyes upon! What a face! You could frighten babies into taking Gregory Powder as though it was cream cake with that face! That's why they call him Purty Bill – but you'll see. Now, get your coat and be quick about it! Snow has been there some time and I would not have him kept waiting more than is needful.'

They walked, Freddy with his coat collar turned up against the sharp cold, for though April was beckoning on the horizon March had by no means released its chill grip on the metropolis, and Abel with his hands thrust deep into his pockets.

'No hansom,' he said shortly when he saw Freddy look hopefully up and down the street as they stood on the top step of the hospital. 'Not for where we're going. No driver will go there. Carry this – you've younger muscles than I have and they need the effort to make 'em grow—' And he thrust a heavy bag into Freddy's cold hand and then went down the steps with a gait as sure and as swift as a boy's, leaving Freddy to come panting a little behind him.

They walked through the curving filthy alleys which pushed so hard against the hospital, thrusting ever more deeply into the slums away from the brightly lit thoroughfares of the Strand and Bow Street and Covent Garden. It was not yet quite dark, the last of the daylight lingering over the western rooftops behind them, but the sky ahead as they moved eastwards was filled with a deep grey heaviness that seemed to press down on Freddy's head. There were people about, a lot of them, but they did not walk, as did Freddy and Abel, in the middle of the filthy streets, but went slinking along close beside the filthy walls of the ramshackle houses that leaned over the gutters, and again Freddy shivered and lengthened his step, wanting to hurry his grandfather and himself out of this threatening gloom.

'Find it disagreeable, Freddy?' Abel said suddenly. 'Mislike the smells, do you?'

'Any man would, sir,' Freddy said. 'I cannot believe you do not find it unpleasant yourself.'

'Oh, for my part, I do not regard these streets as so dreadful! I grew up in 'em after all!'

Freddy turned his head to peer at him in the darkness. 'Yes, sir?' he said uncertainly.

'Aye, yes sir,' Abel said mockingly. 'You see that child there? Use your eyes, boy, 'tis not so dark you cannot see if you try – aye, that's the one. The boy sitting on the doorstep. Well, I was such a one.'

Freddy could see the child now, a scrap of humanity with a very white face peering up at them from the shadows of the doorstep he sat on, thin bony legs sticking out beneath a few scraps of grey rags, his whole body drooping and still.

'How old do you suppose he is, Freddy, eh?' Abel said. 'Come here, boy – aye, you there – come here if you can use a brown or two!'

The boy sat still a moment longer, crouching lower in the corner and staring up at them with a face blank of all expression, but clearly filled with doubt, and then suddenly seemed to make up his mind and came slithering forwards to stand in front of Abel, his body held stiffly to one side and his shoulder hunched as though he expected a blow to land on him. Abel reached forward with one hand and took the boy by the shoulder, holding him with apparent ease but, Freddy could see by the whiteness of his knuckles, very firmly indeed, and the boy cowered and whimpered; but Abel reached into his pocket with his other hand and took out some money, and held it out to the child

'Here you are, boy – take three browns and buy yourself a supper – Freddy, how old do you suppose he is?'

'How old?' Freddy looked down on the child who stood, still bent a little but less fearful now as he clutched the three pennies he had taken from Abel's hand, and peered up at the two tall men from beneath the fringe of dirty hair, the eyes dull and heavy but very watchful. 'I cannot say sir, perhaps eight or nine years? He looks not much larger than my sister Isabel, and she is seven, but he has an air of being perhaps a little older than that. Say eight, sir—'

'Well, boy? Do you know how old you are?'

The boy tried to pull away, but Abel tugged him back and spoke again, more gently. 'No need to be afraid, child. None at all. Tell me the answer to my question, and not only shall you have your three browns, but if you come tomorrow to Nellie's we'll see if we can't find some employment for you that will earn you your dinner for tomorrow as well.'

'Nellie's?' the boy said hoarsely, and now came closer to peer up at Abel's face in the gloom. 'Oh, it's you, is it? Di'n't know, did I? Should'er said, yer should. What yer wants to know fer, Mr. Lackland? What's it matter?'

He was sounding quite perky now, and his face was for the first time showing some animation. Abel let go of his shoulder, but the boy did not run, clearly feeling he was in safe company. 'What's it worth?'

'I told you – tomorrow's dinner. I want to know to teach this young man here some of the facts he needs to make him a better surgeon. So come on. We have little time to waste on you—'

The boy wriggled and slid away into the shadows. 'Firteen. That's what I am, firteen. Old enough to deal wiv you, and a couple more like yer – don' ferget – promised me m'dinner termorrer – I'll be there—'

'Thirteen, Freddy,' Abel said, and started to walk again, faster than ever so that Freddy had almost to run to keep up. 'Nearer a man than a child. And so undersized and wizened you thought him a baby of no more than your sister's age.'

'But why? Is it a matter of their drinking? We were told by Dr. Burchell in his lectures on physic that it is drink – largely gin – that is the cause of their poor physique and that it is their natural savagery that keeps them from understanding of morality of the sort that would keep them away from the evil that it does to them—'

'That is the fashionable view, and Burchell and I have had many an argument about it. He is one that believes with the Malthusians that we should not treat the poor, that we should not interfere with the pressure of their numbers, but leave them to die, thus avoiding the starvation of the future generations our care allows them to spawn. But for me – I was one such! Had I not found a way out of these gutters, then where would you be? Where would Nellie's be? And where would Burchell be? It is on Nellie's patients that he learns enough of his skills to make him the fashionable physician he is, and one that can demand large fees from the richer sort. Who drink as well, of course, but their claret no doubt is less vicious in his eyes than these people's gin—'

'It is not a natural state of their physiques, then, sir? That makes them so different in kind to the rest of us?' Freddy spoke a little awkwardly. He had never shared the disgust for the patients that many of his fellow students showed, but he had also never been able to regard them as people at all like himself or his family. His grandfather's cool admission that he had himself been a gutter child had shaken Freddy rather more than he would have expected such information to. He would have to ask his mother about it, he thought uneasily. There was clearly much more he would need to know about his antecedents. Especially if he and Phoebe—

He pulled his mind back to Abel, who was still walking with great speed.

'A natural state? No it is not. Feed you and house you and treat you as these are from the moment of their birth, and you will become as dull and lifeless as they. It is necessary you learn this fact, Frederick. You will make no sort of surgeon until you do. Come – this way. We cut across High Holborn and into Gray's Inn Lane. We are going to Saffron Hill—'

'Saffron Hill? But that is—'

'Aye!' Abel said almost cheerfully, as they left the alleys

94

behind them and crossed the brightly lit and populous High Holborn, with its gleaming shop windows and cursing drivers and plunging horses, its busy citizens thronging the narrow pavements as they made their way from the City counting-houses and banking-rooms towards their homes in the western and northern suburbs that sprawled far into the curving hills that surrounded London. 'Aye, you are probably going to say that is the place where the thieves lie thickest on the ground. And so they do, so they do! The Peelers have had half their force watching Saffron Hill from the day Sir Robert started 'em. But there are other people there as well, their women, you know, and their children—'

'Why are we going there, sir?' Freddy said a little breathlessly, as his grandfather pushed his way through the crowds on the pavement to cross Gray's Inn Lane and then turned into Cross Street.

'Why? Because John Snow has a case there he wishes to treat and when John Snow calls on me, I go. He is a good man, a splendid physician and one who is using more of the new methods of pain-killing than any in London. Even Simpson in Edinburgh has not had his experience, for all the noise he makes about it. That man – all Scotch bombast and talk and fighting with his fellows and what is the use of it? A waste of good time—'

Freddy grinned a little in the darkness. From all he had heard of the redoubtable Simpson in faraway Edinburgh with his irascible temper, his sharp tongue and his total and indeed downright scornful disregard for any opinion or feelings other than his own, the two men had much in common. But he did not dare say so.

'Snow sent a message that he had a case in need of me. That I was to be prepared for surgery, that the woman could not be brought to me, and that he would provide an anaesthetic treatment to aid me, but that I would need an assistant. You're the assistant – and you will need your wits about you here—'

They had arrived in a broad open space, with greasy cobbles underfoot and tall heavy buildings pressing forward over it so that the sky above seemed to be squeezed out of existence.

There were a few smoky oil flares burning against the blackened walls and at the far side Freddy could see a splash of light across the muddy ground that opened out into a smoky fan of warmth. It was thrown up from a half-open trapdoor set low in the wall, and towards this Abel led him with a steady gait, as though he walked this way every day of his life and could not put a foot wrong. Behind him Freddy slithered and tripped, for the ground was very rough as well as slippery with years of collected ordure and garbage, and stacked with barrels and old boxes and heaps of assorted timber and metal.

Abel ducked his head and went in under the trapdoor, and perforce Freddy followed him, his throat constricting at the smell, a mixture of half-burned dirty oil, sewage, unwashed human bodies and stewed vegetables. There were hollowed wooden steps on the other side and down these the two of them picked their way.

As they reached the bottom there was a sudden hoarse shout, and at once all the lights went out, as abruptly as if there had been one concerted breath to blow them, and a sudden heavy silence, and then Abel called irritably, 'God damn your eyes, you idiots! It is Lackland – give me a glim there!'

Freddy almost felt the wave of relief that seemed to come surging from the hidden people and then tinders scraped and matches flared, and the lights came back and he stood blinking round at what was laid out for his view.

They were in a vast cellar, perhaps fifty feet square, with walls of heavy stone and a ceiling made of great beams of unplaned timber. The weight of the building above seemed to make the walls bulge, and they gleamed with wetness, dripping here and there into greasy black pools on the packed earth floor.

In the middle of the huge expanse was a fireplace built of a few bricks and slabs of broken stone, upon which a heap of coals glowed dully, for when the lights had been put out someone had thrown a sheet of metal over it to hide its light and only now was it beginning to burn up again. Around this sat people, huddled into small groups or sitting alone hunched over their knees, staring dully at the interlopers.

Freddy blinked and tried to count them and gave up – there must have been as many as thirty surrounding that pitiful heap of coals, and beyond them, disappearing into the distant shadows, were others. He could feel them, hear them, smell them, was aware of watchful eyes on him, and instinctively he hunched his shoulders and held the bag he had been carrying closer to his chest.

There was a movement in the distant shadows and then a light moved and came towards them, bobbing high, and Freddy tried to see beyond it to the person who was carrying it. Almost as though he had been asked, the man brought the lamp nearer to his face so that he could be seen, and Freddy took an involuntary step backward.

He had seen pockmarked faces; who hadn't? The regular epidemics of smallpox that swept the city left their trademark on hundreds, but he could not recall ever seeing one quite so hideously deformed as this. The man had a totally hairless face, the place where his eyebrows would have been seeming to be ridges of greyish twisted flesh. His lips were pulled sideways into a permanent grin by the way the skin had healed across the right cheek, and the eyelids, quite lashless, were puffy and wrinkled as a frog's. From behind their thick folds a pair of greenish-blue eyes peered out with suspicion above a pair of shoulders as vast as those of an ox, muscled like a drayman's and bulging through the cloth of the once elegant coat that was tightly buttoned across the straining chest.

This must be Purty Bill, Freddy thought. No one so ugly could be called anything else, and involuntarily he smiled at the thought. And at once the man's face changed, shifting and twisting awkwardly, and after a moment Freddy realized that he was smiling back.

'Is it yerselves, yer 'onners? Oh, I'm that glad to see yer! Dr. Snow's been a-sendin' out of lookers this past hour and gone, and the poor woman's fit to die – she's bleedin' like a stuck pig, that she is – will yer come on, now, and yer young assistant man with yer – this way, if yer please, an' if I don't say it later, let me say it now, we're as grateful as 'tis possible to be that yer came, as good as 'alf the angels in all 'eaven, that you are—'

He was leading them across the great cellar as he spoke, his voice a soft monotone, and the people squatting as near to the warmth of the poor fire as they could get peered at them with incurious faces as they passed and then returned their attention to the big stewpot one of them was stirring over the heat, releasing a smell of burned bacon and stale vegetables that made Freddy feel momentarily queasy, and all too aware of the beef and bread he had so hastily swallowed before leaving Nellie's.

At the far side of the cellar Purty Bill threw open a door, so low a door that they both had to bend almost double to get through it. And on the other side was another cellar, much smaller but just as wet and dank, just as cold and dark, just as badly lit by penny dips and smoky lamps.

And in the middle of it, on a heap of old blankets and rags, lay a woman. A young woman. Freddy could tell that by the richness and thickness of her hair, a deep red in colour and which, surprisingly, had been recently washed. Its cleanliness shone almost insolently in this dismal place, as though it were a light by itself. But the face beneath it was white, quite dreadfully white, so that Freddy thought for a moment that it was a dead face.

But then the eyes opened, and the head moved slightly as the figure that had been crouched beside her stood up to reveal itself as that of John Snow.

'Is that you Lackland?' The voice was sharp and a little tired. 'I'm glad to see you, man. If we don't get this done in the next half hour, I'm not answerable for the consequences. We're ready when you are.'

Abel was shrugging out of his coat, and Freddy took his lead and did the same. 'What is the case? I cannot operate till I know what the devil it is I'm supposed to be operating upon!'

Snow came forward and taking Abel's elbow in one hand led him a little aside while Purty Bill stood with his lamp held aloft and looking down on the pale young woman in the rag bed with his eyes wide and considering. Freddy turned his own gaze away, for suddenly he felt embarrassed, as though he were

98

intruding on some very private moment, and moved a little closer to his grandfather and Snow.

'—the man's making vast sums from these poor devils, and I for one am sick of it! If we can save this girl, I swear she'll shop him – but I cannot see how we can bring him to book until such time as I do have a willing witness! If you can pull her out of this one, we can get the villain dealt with – and perhaps stop a few more like him! But she's bled fit to die for a long time and I'm not too sanguine myself.'

The two men turned and looked back at the girl on the bed, and now Freddy could see his grandfather's face and it was grim and tight with anger.

'A perforated uterus, I suppose?'

'It cannot be otherwise. She was five months gone, and the muscle must have been very soft. There's guarding of the belly and though I've tipped her as you can see and packed her tight as I could, she's oozing. I can give her chloroform now, for I have all ready, but can you get the vessels tied in time? That is the question that concerns me most.'

'We can't know until we try,' Abel said, and his voice sounded very loud in the dingy cellar. 'Frederick! Unpack the bag! And set the instruments ready to my hand. Bill, get out of here, and shut the door behind you. We're to perform an operation here that needs time and quiet – so see to it we're not disturbed. Frederick, what the devil is taking you so long?'

His sleeves were already up, and his jacket coat had been thrown on the floor behind him as he came and crouched beside the woman. 'Goddamn it, Snow, must I operate on my knees? Is there nothing we can use as a table? No – God almighty! – Oh, all right! Manage I must if I must – you'd best get started. Watch him, Frederick. There's matter here for you to learn about.'

And he pushed the woman's ragged skirts away, thrust the tattered – but clean – petticoats beneath them above the waist, and began gently to move his hands across the pale belly that was exposed to their view, and Freddy turned his head to look at Snow. He would never be used to the casual nudity of the surgical patient. It offended him deeply, not because of any erotic effect – of which there was none – but because of the helplessness of the patients. Poor, ill, in pain they might be; did they have to be humiliated as well? This question he often asked himself and in this he felt that in averting at least his own gaze he restored to the woman on her rag bed a shred of her damaged dignity. Snow would be better to look at, so look he did.

And at once remembered that lecture that had so affected him, for Snow had covered the helpless face with a piece of fabric and was dripping on to it the colourless liquid from the selfsame green bottle, as the now almost familiar sickly, sweetish smell began to fill the cold air, swirling hazily through the shadows beyond the light of the guttering candles and the sooty lamps.

The woman took a few shuddering breaths, and began to snore, softly, with a thick and almost casual buzz, and her eyes were partly open so that they stared with blue surprise into the darkness above. And Freddy watched and listened and held his grandfather's instruments according to his barked instructions, and felt he had moved into some sort of strange dream of someone else's devising, and someone else's sleep.

# CHAPTER EIGHT

It had taken only a little effort on Jody's part to find the whereabouts of the Mohun woman.

He had not been able to make inquiries at the Haymarket theatre, which would have been the obvious place to start, for the whole town knew rehearsals for *Ivanhoe* were in full swing there, because since his mother's loss of involvement with the Haymarket's finances the management had taken an almost fiendish delight in barring the young Lucas from the special visiting privileges he had once enjoyed.

So, instead, he turned his attention to the shops near the theatre, sure as he could be that sooner or later he would be able to discover to which address her necessary purchases were sent.

And so it fell out; he was buying cigars in Fribourg and Treyer's, leaning on the counter and taking his time over deciding between the richness of Havanas and the milder Dutch variety, when a man in the green baize apron of a servant came in and asked for a '—box of Mr. O'Hare's seven shillin' specials, to be sent rahnd to the theyater right away, Mrs. Mohun says, and step about it—'

An apprentice packed up a box of large cabanas and handed it over, as Jody still leaned negligently there on the counter, and asked for payment, and the man grinned and took the box and said airily, 'What d'you fink, mate? Cash on the nail? Not from this feller! Send the bill rahnd to So'o Square like always. Madam Mohun'll cough up!'

The apprentice grinned. 'She's 'ot stuff, from all accounts—'

'None o' yer lip! I'm not tellin' the likes o' *you* the details of their private lives just so's you can dribble over 'em! Not that I couldn't if I wanted!' and he laughed and the apprentice grinned and the man went off whistling, leaving Jody lazily watching the apprentice write the bill ready to be sent out. He had been able to read upside down for many years, and had often found it to be a most valuable accomplishment.

And now, standing on the bottom step of Lydia Mohun's house, he felt decidedly perky. The stratagem upon which he had embarked had really gone too ridiculously well so far. His mother, on the very evening of the day he had mentioned the matter, had given him fifty pounds, saying only, 'To use as you think fit, my love, to further my interests! I know you have your poor mamma's concern close to your heart, so I shall not quiz you in the details of your expenditure! But I shall look forward to hearing news of the effect of it.' And she had laughed and he had smiled and they had settled to an evening of card-playing which both enjoyed more than usual.

And then the ease with which he had found Mrs. Mohun, followed by the fortunate discovery that she was holding a crush at her house that night – all had fallen out in the best of ways for him. He had never been one to go uninvited to a party, regarding it as a low provincial habit, but he did not doubt his ability to do so with aplomb. And once he had scraped acquaintance, there was no knowing what might be possible!

A party of rather noisy young men came tumbling from a carriage that drew up at the kerb behind him, and four of them went rattling up the steps past him in such a cheerful way that it was the most natural thing in the world that Jody should join them. He handed his hat to the butler together with the rest of them, and passed easily into the hallway without any person querying either his name or his right to be there.

His lips pursed in admiring approval as he made his way up the richly carpeted staircase through the crowds of chattering people; this was indeed a very smart house done up in the first crack of fashion, deliciously warm (such a pleasant change from the icy draughts that blew about most London houses he visited!), brilliantly illuminated with the most elegant of gaso-liers and wall brackets, and clearly very expensive indeed.

The people were equally expensive in their dress, but, as he soon realized, not quite as cracklingly fashionable as their surroundings. There was a certain raffishness about them, an air of knowingness, an alert and calculating observation from sharp eyes that showed they were not, by and large, the aristocrats of the town. The people who belonged to the very top stratum of society drawled and drooped and certainly never showed the animation and deep curiosity these people did. They belonged to the race-course and the rich City counting-houses and Fleet Street as well as to the theatre (there were faces he recognized from the other side of the footlights) and quite a few were of the sort who seemed to belong to nowhere and everywhere; people with a style of living that clearly cost a great deal, but with no gentlemanly occupation or respectable source of private income that could be demonstrated. These Jody recognized at once, for was he not just such a one himself? He felt very much at home in this company.

Even if he had not had business of his own to pursue in this house, he would have enjoyed the evening. There was music in the ballroom at the back of the house, very sprightly and as modern as the décor, and plenty of agreeable people to talk to. There was delightful food at supper time, and Jody, who had always had a great affection for his stomach, ate quantities of York ham and truffled chicken galantine, cold game pies and iced puddings; but with a rare abstemiousness drank only three glasses of the excellent claret cup. He felt he needed his wits about him for the most important part of the evening which was still to come.

It was well past midnight when the crowd began to thin out, leaving their hostess with much affection and cries of admiration for her delicious party, and he leaned against the drawing-room door watching her, now really able to see her for the first time.

Quite what he had expected to see he did not know. It was not until the moment when he could actually observe the lady at close quarters that he was able to think about such expectations at all and he realized with a little shock of surprise that she was quite young. His assumption had been that Mrs. Mohun was a contemporary of his mother's; why else should

Mamma have such a hate against her? But this lady was clearly not much above thirty, and it was quite obvious that she could easily pass as one ten younger if she so chose.

Jody found it interesting that she did not choose to do as most pretty women did, and try to ape junior ways. Far from it, in fact, for she was dressed in clothes that betrayed at once her maturity and sophistication without for a moment detracting from her charm and beauty. The contrast between her elegant amber silk gown with its modish crinoline and outrageous décolletage and the insipid pink fluffiness of the gown of the girl – who looked to be a bare seventeen or so – who was standing beside her as guests made their adieux, was very clever. The girl, Jody saw, was really enchantingly pretty, with dark curly hair and long-lashed grey eyes, dimpled and curved to a nicety. But she faded into a mere ordinariness next to Mrs. Mohun who was so much more handsome, though there was a curious likeness between them. She too was dark and curly of hair, she too had a luscious shapeliness, but she had an added dimension that made her so much more worth looking at.

Whatever it was she had done to so offend his mother, Jody thought, he would be surprised if her good looks did not have something to do with it.

Looking yet again at the curve of the cheek above the long neck, at the way her strong white teeth shone as she laughed at something one of the men had whispered into her ear, he was stirred by a vague sense of recognition. She looked, somehow, like a person he had once met. But surely that was not possible? This woman came from Edinburgh, after all. And then he recalled, with a surge of irritated puzzlement, his mother's reaction. Clearly Mrs. Mohun *had* been in London at some time, for how else could his mother know her and have been injured by her? Lilith had certainly never been to Scotland! Really, he could hardly wait another minute for a chance to talk to her; there was so much he wished to know.

His chance came very shortly. She turned towards the door as yet another group of guests made their farewells, and caught his eyes and looked at him consideringly for a moment, seeming to take some sort of inventory, and then nodded very slightly; her lips curved, and as clearly as if she had said the words he could hear her thoughts; 'An interloper! Now who, and why, and when is he going?'

At once he moved forward and came to stand in front of her, very aware as he did so of the girl standing behind her and looking curiously at him. It was as though two pairs of matching faces were studying him, and he wondered briefly if the girl were Mrs Mohun's daughter, and then dismissed it. The age difference between them was too small to allow for that.

'Madam,' he said and took her hand and kissed it with a somewhat flowery gesture of the sort he knew most women found quite irresistible. 'I ask your pardon. I am here without invitation. You do not know me, and have every right to turn me out of your door at the end of your butler's foot. I take my dignity in my hands in approaching you, and also my hopes and fears. Hopes that you will admit me to your acquaintance, fears that you will be so incensed by my impudence in coming unbidden to your house that you will not.' And he looked up at her under his lashes in a way that he again knew to be usually most effective with women.

But this one was different. She looked at him very coolly for a long moment and then turned her head towards the girl behind her. 'I hope you took close note of that speech, Phoebe! Beguiling, charming, well-mannered and totally false. You have been given the opportunity – I cannot call it privilege – of observing a complete rogue in action!'

He stood very erect and looked at her with his head on one side, and then, very slowly, smiled, and she stared back at him with so straight a face that for one dreadful moment he thought he had miscalculated and she was indeed going to turn him away.

But then she relaxed and smiled back and then, to his intense relief she giggled, and he joined in until they were both laughing delightedly at each other, while Phoebe stood and stared at them in puzzlement.

A tall man in a very elegant dark red coat – one very *outré* in style which had attracted Jody's attention earlier in the evening – detached himself from a group of people by the window and joined them.

'And what is it that is so very funny, Lydia, my love?' he

said, in a soft faintly accented drawl, and he came and stood between the two women, slipping an arm round both their waists in a manner that displayed his proprietorial rights very clearly indeed.

'Why, this young villain here! Comes marching into my party as cool as you please, and then comes and tells me of it! I have known of uninvited guests before, but they always had the manners to do without the politeness of bidding farewell, just as they did without a bidding to attend. But not this one! He deserves whipping for his insolence.' She smiled then. 'But welcoming for his wit.'

'And may I know your name, sir? If you are to be regarded so favourably by a hostess you have used so ill, the least you can do is allow her to receive an introduction.'

The girl in pink had moved a little aside so that the tall man had perforce to let go of her and Jody was amused to notice the heightened flush of embarrassment on her cheeks. Whoever she was, she did not belong as completely in this *milieu* as she might; she had reacted to the familiarity of the arm about her waist like every other missish schoolgirl of good upbringing he had ever met; boringly, in other words. He dismissed her from his calculations. Close as she appeared to be to Mrs. Mohun, she was not as close, not as important, as this man, and it was these two he must put himself out to beguile into some sort of friendship. If his plan was to work.

So he sketched an old-fashioned bow and said, 'Jonathan Lucas, at your service, ma'am. I know you to be the enchanting Mrs. Mohun and take this opportunity to welcome you to London. We have great need of such a talent as I have heard yours to be.'

She was standing very still and staring at him with a faint frown on her face.

'Lucas, did you say?'

He was now enjoying himself hugely. 'Why, yes, ma'am. Is it a name that is known to you? That is too much for me to hope! Not that it is an entirely undistinguished name, I believe. Not, I haste to say, for any exploits of my own. I am indeed a villainous wretch as you, with what is a rare perspicacity in a beautiful woman, realized. I am also a lazy wretch and a poor wretch, who must pick up what crumbs of comfort he can, where he can—'

'You are a great talker,' she said absently, still looking at him with that very close and intense look. 'Have you always been so? You are not very old, I believe – would it be impertinent of me to ask you how old?'

'You put me to the blush, ma'am. I am not proud of being as young as I am. But I cannot lie to you, because I am sure you are far too clever not to discover me. And I have been quite mendacious enough already, have I not, in coming to your party as I did. I was born in 1834, ma'am. I am seventeen, but not, I trust, a callow seventeen. There are some of us who reach maturity earlier than others—' and his eyes slid sideways to look at Phoebe, still standing a little apart.

Lydia nodded, but still with that oddly remote air, and her eyes never left his face. 'Seventeen. Yes, I can see that would be – tell me – did you have a special motive in seeking to make my acquaintance in this manner? No doubt you could have arranged for yourself a more usual form of introduction? You are clearly a person who moves in society, and I cannot pretend that my parties are so select that you would find any great difficulty in obtaining an invitation.'

He smiled, and slipped his hands into his trouser pockets. He was feeling more and more relaxed by the moment.

'Well, yes, ma'am, you are right. I chose to make myself known to you in this rather uncouth way, since I have matters to discuss with you which might distress you. And I would not add to your distress by being introduced by a friend of yours. You see, you may be so angered by what I have to tell you that your rage would spread, as it were, to encompass any who were connected with me. As I rather think it will, anyway.'

'He talks in silly riddles,' the tall man said with a sudden petulance and lowered his arm. 'I think he is just another stage-struck hobbledehoy who thinks to engage your attentions by mock-mysteries. I am not beguiled by it, if you are. Turn him out, Lyddy, for pity's sake! I am getting bored.'

Better and better, thought Jody. He is jealous—

'Oh, please, ma'am, you will not do so?' he said aloud, smiling widely at Lydia. 'I think you realize my mysteries, such as they are, are far from mock?'

'I know your name,' she said. 'Although it is far from being uncommon, of course—'

'My surname is not uncommon, perhaps. But there are more to names than surnames, are there not?'

Suddenly, and to his discomfiture, she laughed aloud. He felt release of tension in her, and it alarmed him, for it was all at once as though the control he had had of the conversation – and he had undoubtedly been in such a position of mastery – had slipped from his grasp.

'I *am* right!' she said and it came out almost like a crow of delight. 'Lilith Lucas! You are a connection of hers! Come, tell me. Immediately!'

'Well, yes, I am indeed,' he said, almost sulkily, and thrust his hands deeper into his pockets, scowling a little.

'And I will tell you what sort of connection!' she said gaily. 'Yes, I shall – do not you tell me and spoil my reputation for – what did you call it? Perspicacity? Let me see now—' and she set her forefinger to her forehead in an exaggerated gesture of thoughtfulness. 'I have it! You are her son! Her lamb of a child, her special precious child from whom she cannot bear to be parted in any way and who, despite his years and his much vaunted maturity, lives close tied to his Mamma's apron strings! Not that she ever wore an apron, of course, but you understand the metaphor, I am convinced.'

His face was scarlet with mortification. 'I suspect you make mockery of me, ma'am,' he said very stiffly.

'And did you not mock me, young wretch, and did you not insinuate yourself into my house in the coolest manner imaginable? Come, you must learn to take as good as you give! Well, well. Jonathan Lucas. To think that we meet in this manner! I am quite enchanted, I do assure you! I had expected one much more disagreeable, from all I had heard!'

Jody was nonplussed. In a matter of moments the whole situation had slid completely from him. This pretty woman who had seemed so pliable, so much putty between his fingers, and whose conversation he had been so much enjoying, had suddenly become almost sinister, seeming older and harder and sharper and he blinked and tightened his jaw, determined she should not see the effect she had had on him. This had to be salvaged, somehow, and it could not be if she knew how discomfited he was by her reactions.

But she knew. It showed in the broad smile across her face, in the way she tapped his arm with her fan, not precisely dismissively, not precisely mockingly, but with an air that made him feel very young.

'I am surprised you have wasted your time in listening to any talk about a person of so little importance as I,' he said and he knew his voice sounded wooden and cursed himself for it.

'Come, do not be so disturbed! You tried a trick that did not work! Well, not entirely, that is! You attended my party, after all, so that much you achieved. Whatever the rest of your plan was, I cannot know. All I can say to you is that you can now go back to her and tell her that I am not one whit—'

'Go back to whom?' he said softly, and felt a new surge of confidence. There were misunderstandings here, and he could use them.

'Why, to your mother! To Lilith Lucas, the great and beautiful Lilith Lucas! Who did all she could for so many years to – well, let it be.'

For a moment her face had hardened and flared into lines of anger, but almost as fast as it had happened she controlled it again, and once more laughed and tapped his wrist with her fan, and then slipped her hand into the crook of the tall man's elbow, moving close beside him in a provocative way. 'I shall not allow myself to be one whit disturbed by her and her tricks! The time is long since gone when *she* could have that effect on me.'

She looked consideringly at Jody again. 'I'll say this for her. I had heard that you were quite ruined by her. That she had reared a most selfish namby pamby – no sense to blush so! That was the talk at the Haymarket when I got there, and you might as well know it. And hugely I enjoyed it I can tell you! After all I suffered at that woman's hands I am not above finding pleasure in hearing she has reared a rod for her back as bitter as the one she once used on mine!'

Jody was staring at her with his mouth half open, trying to sort out his thoughts. At one moment he felt he knew what was happening, at the next he was filled with confusion, but before he could say more another group of people came drifting towards them, and Lydia became at once the perfect hostess, accepting their farewells with much graciousness, smiling and nodding and agreeing to plans for future junketings, and Jody was glad of the moment of respite. He still did not know what lay behind his mother's antipathy towards this woman, any more than he knew why it was so obviously and so heartily reciprocated. Enough it was there; there was no reason why he should not still carry out his plan. And, he thought shrewdly, there is no point in fencing any longer. This woman, who is genuinely very remarkable in her acuity, in the speed with which her understanding takes hold of a situation, is not one to play silly games with – except for pleasure. No, he must be direct with her.

By now the room was virtually empty, with only the girl and the tall man left besides Lydia and himself, and as Lydia came back from the door through which the last of her guests had just disappeared he took a deep breath and said baldly, 'There is a matter of business I would discuss with you, ma'am.'

'Is there?' She looked at him over her shoulder, a brilliant smile moving across her face to be replaced almost at once by a sudden jaw-cracking yawn. 'Lord, but I'm tired! Quite dead in my bones. Dearest Phoebe, you should be in your bed, I am sure. When your aunt and uncle permitted you to come to stay with me for this party, I assure you they had no idea I would lead you into such naughty ways as this. Past two in the morning and still out of your bed—'

She yawned again, and threw herself on to a long sofa, kicking off her golden slippers with a fine disregard for the display of ankle, and even calf, that the movement entailed.

'Dickon, as you love me, a last glass of wine, and then to bed – I am past thinking, truly I am. Was it a good party, do you think? A successful one? I flatter myself it went very well – better than most—'

She cocked an eye at Jody above the glass that Dickon had obediently brought to her. 'And at the end of it this funny young man to provide the *coup de grâce*—'

'A business matter, ma'am, I would like to discuss a business matter with you,' Jody said, and was pleased with himself, for his voice came out clear and steady and not as choked and strained as he feared it would.

She raised an eyebrow. 'Oh?'

'It would be easier if—' He looked at the tall man and then at Phoebe. 'It is a private matter.'

'Phoebe is about to say goodnight, are you not, my love?'

The girl in pink came at once to the sofa and bent to kiss the upraised face. 'Indeed, yes. Goodnight, dear aunt. It was a most splendid party, the best imaginable! I have not had so much pleasure since – oh, I do not remember! Thank you so much!'

'Bless you, my love, it gave me more pleasure to see you enjoying yourself than you obtained, I do assure you. To-morrow we shall have even more delight – you shall come to a rehearsal! Yes you shall! And we shall not tell any of them at Stanhope Terrace so there can be no head-shakings. Our secret! Goodnight!'

Phobe kissed her aunt again, most fervently, and then after a moment bobbed, pink-faced, at the tall man, who bowed a little mockingly back at her over his own wine glass, and went away in a flurry of frilled skirts.

'Dickon remains, young Jonathan Lucas,' Lydia said lazily. 'As long as I do, that is. And I must tell you now that it will not be above a few moments at best, for I am quite exhausted, and amusing though I find you, I really must go to bed. You can come another day with your business matter, perhaps—'

'No,' Jody said, very baldly. 'No. It must be now.' He doubted he would ever be able to face her again if he did not get the matter in hand at once and he took a deep breath, still looking at Dickon.

'I told you, he stays,' she said a little impatiently. 'Now, do get on with it! I will soon be bored as well as fatigued and when that happens I am quite unapproachable, I do assure you!'

'My mother has asked me to arrange a – a disturbance,' he said after a moment.

Dickon, who had been standing by the fire kicking the last embers into a final burst of flame, turned his head sharply. 'A disturbance?'

'At the theatre. On your first performance.'

The room sank into a silence, broken only by the faint hiss of the flames in the subsiding fire. And was broken at last by the last sound Jody had thought she would produce – that same giggle which had greeted his first approach to her.

'It will not be funny, ma'am,' he said loudly. 'Do not think it will be funny! I can tell you that I have such connections in this town that I could indeed cause a riot in the theatre such as would make you unable ever to hold your head up there again! I came to tell you this for your own good! I did not expect to be laughed at!'

'Laughed at! He did not expect to be laughed at!' she cried mockingly. 'You hear him, Dickon?'

'I hear him!' Dickon said, and moved towards the boy with a menace in his movements that was not entirely play-acting. 'And I'll have his guts out of him, and tied around his neck in a manner he will find is—'

She shook her head. 'Don't be so silly, Dickon! It won't be necessary! You can see why he is here! He wants us to pay him as much as she has to do it, in order *not* to do it! The oldest and most boring trick in the world, and this whippersnapper thinks he can pull it on me!'

She laughed again. 'Better still, he thinks he can do it to her! Unless she has changed beyond all recognition and whatever Celia – God rest her poor wicked soul in what peace she may – did to her face, her nature will be the same, of that I am sure! And you misjudge your mother sorely if you think you can ever succeed with so heavy a piece of fraud!'

Jody's face was white with mortification, with disappointment, and not a little with fear. Dickon was a very big man, and looked very angry standing there in front of him.

But Jody too had his store of courage and he whipped up every shred of it. 'I do not think you need concern yourself about how my mother will behave, ma'am. She is, after all, *my* mother and I think you will admit I am more likely to know her ways and how she might think than you would!'

She sat up, swinging her stockinged feet to the floor, and stared at him, and her face softened and then widened into a smile, but a very different one from the rather hard triumphant grin that had invested it before.

'You don't know, then?' she said softly, after a moment. 'You have no idea why she was willing to agree to such a scheme when you put it to her? As I am sure you did – you strike me as very much a young man who would think in such a way. Tell me, you really do not know?'

'If you mean do I know why she hates you, then I admit I do not,' Jody said, thrusting his hands back into his pockets in an attempt to look more insouciant than he felt. 'But I don't think it matters! Whatever bad blood exists between you both is your affair. All I am trying to do is a good turn to someone – you – against whom I hold no grudge. I would not wish my Mamma to spoil your first London performance! That is why I am here, and—'

'Well, *I* don't wish my Mamma to spoil my first London performance either! And with your aid, dear boy, she shall not!'

Lydia had got to her feet now, and came across the room towards him with a swish of silk, her smile wide and full of warmth.

'Come, we shall be friends. It is right and proper that we should! You are, after all, my half-brother! There! Is that not a surprise that you did not expect to receive this evening? I am sure it is! And so funny – so very, very funny!'

And Jody stood there with his hands in his pockets, staring at her and feeling as though the solid floorboards beneath his feet were melting to jelly.

# CHAPTER NINE

FREDDY reached home at half an hour past midnight, paying off the hackney cab in so abstracted a way that he inadvertently gave the man sixpence too much, which sent him trotting away very cheerfully indeed. He apologized to the yawning housemaid who had been told to wait up for him, and turned out the one remaining gaslight burning in the hall before making his way heavily upstairs. It seemed a year had passed since he had left the house this morning; and he was exhausted.

His room was blessedly welcoming, with the fire burning redly and a jug of hot water set before it still hot enough to make washing agreeable, and he stripped and scrubbed himself and climbed into his nightshirt, grateful to be rid of the day's dirt, but feeling obscurely that some of the filth of Purty Bill's cellar had seeped into his very skin and bone, and would never leave him.

Standing there in his long nightshirt, his bare toes curling a little against the warm pile of the rug before his fire, he made himself remember it. He felt somehow that until he had rehearsed again the whole long horror of it he would never be able to contain it in his mind. It would crawl into every corner of it, filling every available thought. But if he organized it and discussed it with himself then he would be able to shut it away in a corner, under control. For it would never leave him, that much was sure. As long as he lived he would remember her.

'Freddy – dear boy, may I come in?'

He started and looked up at the door to see his mother standing there with her woollen robe pulled close to her with one hand, and a steaming cup in the other.

'Eh? Oh, Mamma! What are you doing out of your bed so late? I am sorry if I disturbed you – I did not mean to—'

She came into the room, quietly closing the door behind her. 'I heard you arrive home, and I felt – oh, I don't know! You have never before stayed at the hospital so long, and I was concerned for you. I thought you might be hungry, so I have made you some gruel. No, do not look so disgusted! It is well laced with brandy and brown sugar, and so will be agreeable as well as nutritious!'

He laughed and took the cup from her. 'Oh, Mamma, you make me feel as though I were as young as Isabel! But I will not pretend I do not like such mollycoddling. Thank you.'

She sat down on the armchair beside his fire, tucking her feet under her and staring up at him. With her hair down about her shoulders she looked absurdly young to be so large a young man's mother. 'Isabel likes nothing better than to tell me of all that happens to her each day, when I am not here to see for myself. I do not suppose that old as you are you will find this so strange.'

He grinned down at her. 'Are you asking me to confide in you, or telling me?'

She smiled equably back. 'Neither! I am inviting you! You look a little strained, dear boy. Was it a very wearying day?'

'Excessively.' He began to drink the gruel, enjoying the way the brandy bit at his throat and warmed his belly. 'It usually is, you know. And then Grandpapa adding *that* on – well!'

She settled herself more comfortably in the chair. 'It is no use, Freddy! I came merely to give you the opportunity to tell me of your day's activity, if you so chose, Now, however, I am eaten with curiosity on my own account. *What* did my father add on, as you put it?'

He grimaced and finished his gruel, and then sat on the rug at her feet, curling his arms around his knees, his bare legs thrust forward a little to get the warmth of the dying fire. 'It is all very nasty, Mamma. I do not think a lady should be concerned with such—'

'Oh, lady! Pooh to that! I am no milk and water miss, Freddy, to be protected from nastiness! If you can tolerate it, so can I.'

'There was a woman in Saffron Hill,' he said abruptly. 'She had need of surgery.'

'Oh?'

'Aye. My grandfather had to remove – shall we say – a large portion of the contents of her abdomen. She had been severely injured.'

There was a little silence, and then she said carefully, 'In what manner? An accident?'

He shook his head. 'She was increasing, was but four months short of her time, and determined not to bear the infant. There is a man in the area, an evil creature from all accounts, who for a large sum of money will deal with such matters. Not a true surgeon, you understand. A quack!' His lip curled at the word, with all the disgust and young arrogance of the student who feels no one can know as much of anything as he does, except, perhaps, his own teachers. 'But it took this woman so long to find the money that she was too far gone when he did his work. So Grandfather said. He ripped her very severely, and she bled—'

His voice dwindled away, and then strengthened.

'My God, how she bled! When Grandfather opened the abdomen, which was very tense, you understand, the release of muscle pressure sent such a fountain in the air I thought it would reach the room above. Grandfather was – oh, extraordinary! He moved so fast I could hardly see his hands, and he found the major vessels which had been damaged and tied them. But it was too late, as Grandfather himself had warned. It had been the tension exerted by the shed blood, within the belly you see, which had prevented greater loss. But when Grandpapa tied the big vessels and evacuated the remaining blood, then other smaller vessels were revealed as ruptured, and by the time he tied those—' He shook his head. 'She seemed to dissolve, somehow. I was standing there handing the instruments, and watching Mr. Snow give her the chloroform, and she was breathing so deep and so very noisy and it got thinner and then halted and started again, and she gasped so very fast, but then she seemed to shrink, and was not gasping at all. Nor bleeding. There was Grandfather seeking for the last blood vessel, and I had seen the pulsing of the blood. I had watched it as it came up to the surface of the wound and then it just moved less and less, and stopped, and Grandfather swore fearfully and just pushed it all back and sewed her up. It was dreadful—'

He looked up at her with his eyes seeming very dark, so dilated were the pupils.

'I think that was the worst part, Mamma. He had been so gentle, you see, before. So very fast, but so careful! His hands moved – oh, with such control you know? And then suddenly, he was just swearing and shoving away at that dead flesh and sewing away as though she were – like some piece of carcass meat at a street butchery stall. It was that which made me feel so dreadful, I think. I know she was dead – we could all see that – but he should not have been so *rough* with her, even so! Not when her hair was so very well washed and she looked so—'

He shook his head, and swallowed and blinked, and then his eyes, which had been glazed, moved, and his vision focused again, and he looked at her face, really seeing it now; and at once scrambled to his feet.

'Oh, Mamma! Forgive me! I did not mean to shock you! There – I knew I shouldn't tell you. I knew how much you might be upset—'

She shook her head, and licked her lips, for her mouth had gone very dry, and she knew her face had whitened. 'I am sorry, Freddy – please to take no notice. I told you I would not be disturbed, and here I am as queasy as any silly school-room chit. I am ashamed.'

'Do not be! For I do not hesitate to tell you that the same thing happened to me. At one moment I am standing there holding instruments and the next, there is Snow with one hand shoved hard on the back of my neck and the other holding me by the seat of my breeks so that I am bent double! It was very degrading! I, so senior a student, to get qualmish at the sight of a little blood—'

'But it was not the blood that made you feel so ill, Freddy, was it? Any more than it was the talk of blood that made me—'

she bit her lip. 'Well, let be! It is not perhaps a matter that we should talk of so late—'

He was standing looking down at her, and after a moment said awkwardly, 'I am glad you understand it was not the blood, Mamma. I am quite used to blood, even the smell of it, which is sweet and not really disagreeable. No, it was not the blood—'

She took his hand and squeezed it. 'I am glad it was not. It was your concern for the poor creature as a – as a fellow creature in misery that touched you, I think, and that is right and proper. If you were to become the sort of surgeon who cared nothing for the person who inhabited the flesh upon which you worked, I would be most dispirited about you. It was because I did not think you were the sort of man to become hard and cruel – as some of them do – that I was content to agree when the matter of your career came under review.'

'Mamma, if it was not the talk of blood which made you feel as I did, what was it?' he said abruptly, still standing and holding her hands, and she reddened a little, and pulled her hands away.

'It is not a matter of such great importance, Freddy, that we should talk of it now! Tomorrow, some other day perhaps, when Gideon is able to be with us, and we can—'

He shook his head. 'No, I would prefer to talk with you. Gideon I trust and love, of course, and I am fortunate indeed in so kind a stepfather. But I prefer to talk to you. Is it that the woman was with child?'

She reddened even more. 'Oh dear! I would never have thought myself so sensitive on such a natural matter! When I was increasing with Isabel and Sarah, I was not one whit perturbed that you should know of it, and though there were some that considered me indelicate not to hide my state from you, I could not regard the matter as anything but a natural one for a mother and son to discuss. But this—'

He nodded. 'Aye. This. She had but four months to her time. Grandfather was so angry, Mamma. You cannot imagine—'

She smiled briefly at that. 'I think I can! I have known his tempers before now! Freddy—'

She stopped and swallowed and started again.

'Freddy, since you desire we should speak of it, I must finish the matter, I think, that came into my mind. It would be more – seemly, perhaps, were Gideon to talk to you, but—'

He turned and came back to stand beside her, for he had gone to stir the fire a little, and looked down at her with his lips curved into a smile.

'Oh, Mamma, are you to talk to me of matters that careful parents tell their sons when they go away from home for the first time? I do not think it necessary, you know! I am a medical student, after all, and there is much that I learn about upon the wards. There is little hid in delicacy, there, I do assure you.'

'I know. But this is different.' She lifted her chin and looked up at him very directly. 'Freddy, the love between a man and a woman is a most beautiful thing. There are those that will tell you that the best sort of love is the kind that is not afflicted with – with carnal desires. There are those that strive always to maintain purity in all matters, regarding the bodily pleasures of love as being in some sort foul. But it is not so, Freddy. I would not ever wish you to – to become lax about matters of love, you understand, to become one of those young men – and I believe there are many such in these modern times – who regard it lightly, as a personal pleasure that is one only they can enjoy. Women too—'

Her face was very red now but still she sat there looking up at him, making no attempt to hide her embarrassment.

'I must tell you Freddy, that I loved your father very dearly, and found such joy with him – such joy as I would wish all women to know, and all men as well, for I know he too – and with Gideon. Oh, Freddy, I am so fortunate a woman, and know of the – the *gentleness* of love, of the true purity of it, however the evangelists may try to say otherwise! I am not seeking, you must understand, to encourage you in any sort of vice or luxury, but I would be so sad if you did not realize that love between a man and a woman is good and beautiful and –

and Godly, I do believe! If what you saw today should give you a – a disgust of women, or a sense of horror at the manner – the manner in which we create new souls, I would be so very sad, so very anxious for you! I could wish you no greater felicity than that enjoyed by your father and stepfather. And me. I do hope you can understand what it is I am trying to tell you, Freddy. It is difficult for me, even though I am in a sort unlike other women, having more knowledge of the harshness of this world than most who have been gently reared—'

He took her hands again, and held them very tightly. 'It has not given me a disgust of – of true love, mamma. A disgust of men who use women and their frailty as cruelly as this man who so butchered that woman today – yes, I have a disgust of him! Oh, indeed, I have! There was a moment today when, had the evil creature come into that cellar, I would myself have set upon him and wrung his neck. And you know me to be a most pacific sort of man, Mamma! No, do not fret yourself, I am not likely to be so perturbed by such an experience. It saddened me deeply, but it could not affect the way I feel about the love that should be between a man and his wife—'

He moved away suddenly, and she looked after him, her forehead a little creased.

'I am glad,' she said uncertainly after a moment. 'I am very glad. For one day you will wed yourself, and I ask for no more for you than happiness. Real happiness.'

'As to that, I cannot say.' His voice sounded very flat.

'No,' she said, still uncertain. 'No, of course you cannot. But one day, I hope – I hope your eye will fall upon someone who will seem to you to be the wife you want and—'

'Mamma! I—' He lifted his head and looked at her, his anxiety about Phoebe trembling on his lips, longing to pour out to her all the anguish that had suddenly come surging up inside him again. He had thought himself to be concerned only with the happenings of the evening, thought his distress was due entirely to that, but the mere mention of marriage and all the day's earlier anguish came back, all the sense of rejection that had filled him ever since he had watched Phoebe chattering away to that O'Hare creature. But the sight of her sitting there looking at him so attentively made him stop and think, and almost without realizing he had done it, he shook his head.

No, the time to tell his Mamma of the future he planned with Phoebe was when Phoebe knew of it. He had spoken to Gideon only because of his status as his trustee and financial adviser and he knew he could trust Gideon to say nothing, even to his own wife. It would be a sort of betrayal of Phoebe to speak to his mother of his desires before he spoke to the object of them, and he could not do it, deeply comforting though it would be to tell her of all the pain he had suffered that day. But that, he told himself fiercely was childish, and now he was a man. He must behave like one.

'Mamma, we must indeed bid each other goodnight. I am fit to drop asleep as I stand here, and you must be as fatigued as I am. Thank you for the gruel, and for listening so patiently to my account of a most disagreeable experience, and please allow me to apologize for causing you that moment of discomfort.'

'There is no need to apologize,' she said almost absently, and went to him and lifted her chin and kissed his cheek. 'You are right, dear boy, of course. Goodnight, and sleep peacefully. You will feel much restored in the morning, I think.'

But as she went back softly along the dark carpet towards her own bedroom, she felt a twinge of anxiety deep within her. His reaction to the mention of marriage had been so sharp; did that mean that his eye had already found an object of admiration?

She slid gently into bed beside her sleeping husband who snuffled a little and turned over to throw an arm across her and to intertwine one long leg with hers, and she slipped her own arm beneath his head and held him close, and again he made the snuffling sound and moved close to her. But she lay awake beside him thinking hard, sleep far away from her, although she had been deeply in slumber when the sound of Freddy's footsteps on the stairs had roused her.

Like every mother, she told herself, she wished only happiness for her son. Like every mother, she gloried in the sight of her boy grown to confident manhood, and the day he chose himself a wife and became a man in every sense would be one of great joy. But if that is so, she argued with herself, why should I have felt that shaft of – whatever it was – resentment, loss, even desolation – when he spoke as he did? Surely, I am not going to be the dreadful sort of woman who ties her son so tightly to her bonnet strings that the poor creature can never struggle free, like Mrs. Branston, the widow who lived three houses along the terrace? Her son Monty was despised by all the young people among Phoebe's friends; many were the times when Abby had found it necessary to remonstrate with them for the unkind comments they had made about him after he had been swept away by his mother, who always took him with her when she made her morning calls. Oh, it would be quite intolerable if she were to become even the shadow of such a one.

She sighed, and turned over so that Gideon lay even more securely within the circle of her arms, and with her customary good sense tried to settle herself to sleep. No point in lying here worrying about it now, she told herself firmly. If Freddy had chosen his future wife then that was that. It was his affair, and she, his mother, could hope only to find pleasure in his happiness. She still had her daughters to love, after all, even if the time had come for Freddy to go away and set up his own establishment. Her daughters, and her dear Gideon. No woman could ask for more.

But as she slid at last into sleep, the faint sense of regret still lingered there deep in her mind. They had been so close, she and Freddy, all through those long years of her widowhood. To part with him, however much it was for his happiness, would be a dreadful wrench.

She dreamed of James, that night, for the first time in many, many years. James, her dead husband, but somehow, he had Freddy's face. It was not a pleasant dream.

# CHAPTER TEN

PHOEBE was so happy, she thought she might burst with it. She had always been a person to find much satisfaction in her life; as long as she had lived she could not remember ever being really miserable for very long. Of course, there had been the time when the people about her had been solemn and worn black clothes, and told her how tragic it was to be a motherless child, and she had obediently looked downcast since that had clearly been what everyone expected of her, but inside she had been quite blithe. She had not been particularly close to her Mamma, after all, and now she could not even remember what she had looked like.

Apart from that she had never really had any cause to be sad. Broken dolls, the refusal of some much coveted gown or bonnet, rain on a day which had been promised for a picnic – these had caused her tears to flow; but even then she had enjoyed the sensation of her sadness. To cry could be very enjoyable, and many were the times when she and her female friends would abandon themselves to the luxury of tears over a dead bird or a sad novel or a handsome man with a pale face and curly hair, just for the pleasure of it.

And because she had never been really unhappy, she had never known the peaks of joy either – until now. She sat in the front row of the red plush-covered seats in the pit of the great Haymarket theatre, her fur-trimmed pelisse about her shoulders to protect her from the chill draught that blew from the wide open stage – for the huge tableau curtains were pulled well back and the scene dock doors were open – her hands tucked into her muff, and blissfully watched her aunt, her very own aunt, up there in an elegant close-fitting gown of buff merino ('my rehearsal rag!' she had called it when Phoebe had admired it, and pinched her cheek and laughed) actually *rehearsing*.

And not only that; her aunt had promised her, with that casual good humour which Phoebe was already realizing was a hallmark of her character, that Phoebe herself should have a chance to take part in the piece.

'I shall tell the stage director that I have need of an extra lady to attend me in the big scene in act three, Phoebe, and you shall be dressed in the most handsome of costumes we can devise for you, and shall walk on! No lines, of course – it takes a deal of time before any aspiring actress can be given lines! – but a reasonable walk on. It will give you the smell of the business of a theatre and I daresay you will enjoy it.'

'Enjoy it!' Phoebe had gasped. 'Enjoy it! Oh, Aunt Lydia, I shall enjoy it above all things. I did not know until now how much I wished to be an actress. I have always vastly enjoyed the tableaux we do, of course, but now I know that the stage is what I was born for. To be an *actress*! Oh, Aunt Lydia, thank you!' And she kissed her aunt with such fervour it had made even that accomplished lady reel a little.

'Well, you should be an actress, I am convinced of it,' Lydia said, when she had set herself to rights again. 'It would be a wicked waste to let such prettiness and such talent be seen only in insipid drawing-room games. Has no one in your family ever considered the possibility? After all, it is a tradition with us, is it not? Your Mamma and Papa established their supper rooms as a place of theatre, and your Papa is a most skilful director of stage entertainment. I have seen his shows and enjoyed them greatly, although they are of course more for the vulgar taste than for the discerning theatre patron. But that is no bad thing – I am the last to scorn any people who show willing to pay to see performances, whatever the performances may be.'

'Well, yes, of course Papa is involved in the theatre, I suppose, though I never thought about it in that way. He does not actually perform, you see, does he? I suppose if I had thought of it at all, I had regarded him as a man of business, like Uncle Gideon. And Aunt Abby is not a whit interested in the theatre, nor is Freddy. They concern themselves with only disagreeable medical matters. So you cannot precisely say it is a family tradition, can you? I mean, there is you, of course, but I did not know of you until – oh, was it but a week or two ago? I cannot believe it!' and she laughed with such real pleasure that Lydia was enchanted even more with her, and again pinched her cheek with that affectionate gesture to which she was so prone.

And said nothing about the other member of their shared family from whom Phoebe might have been expected to draw some of her talent and good looks. Lydia was too easy-going and essentially happy a person to wish any distress to anyone, especially to herself, and telling Phoebe about her grandmother – of whom she patently knew nothing – would undoubtedly distress Lydia. She had joked when talking to Dickon about her lack of family connections with whom she could be comfortable, but in all truth she did feel a sense of deprivation in being one of so fragmented a clan. Her pleasure in Phoebe's company was not due entirely to the girl's own charm, considerable though that was; had she been a dull little mouse, Lydia thought shrewdly, I would have warmed to her, for I have need of her. As it is, I am fortunate to have found her so delightful a niece.

And now that delightful niece sat, filled to the brim with her own sense of delight, and watched her from the stalls, and Lydia caught her eye as she crossed downstage to fall on her knees with an impassioned declaration of deep-felt emotion before Dickon, standing arrogant and tall in a position which brought him precisely under the prompt side floods, and sketched a shadow of a wink. Which quite convulsed Phoebe with giggles, and irritated Dickon not a little. Silly creature, he thought savagely. Lydia is positively mawkish about her! Too boring.

The rehearsal moved on, gathering speed and polish as the rest of the cast followed the lead of the undoubtedly gifted principals. They worked as a smooth team, building trick upon trick until it seemed to the watching Phoebe that she was seeing actual people re-creating their lives before her very eyes. She was so enthralled that when the rehearsal for the third act reached the point where Lydia was to sweep on stage with her

Attendant Ladies, Phoebe was almost surprised, and when her aunt called her was able to go running up to the stage with no semblance of nervousness, because there had been no time for it to develop.

And because she was a quick-minded girl with a genuine gift for acting, however small and undeveloped, she was able to understand very quickly what was wanted of her, and moved on stage in her appointed place and with a natural grace.

The stage manager breathed a sigh of relief, for he had been expecting the usual gawkishness displayed by untried people who were inserted into productions to gratify the whims of leading players (though he had to admit it was usually the men who asked for 'little parts' for young ladies, rather than the women) and smiled at her amiably enough when the scene was finished. The rest of the cast, taking their cue from him, were equally affable, and Phoebe's cup was brimming. To be having so much enjoyment, and everyone being so agreeable! What more could life offer?

Jody, watching her from the wings, scowled a little. The wretched girl was a nuisance, he told himself, and one to be removed from his way as soon as possible, but he had to be careful. Lydia had made it very clear to him, once he had recovered from the shock of discovering that she was his sister, that she wanted there to be no talk at all about their relationship.

'Because, Jody, I tell you flat, I am not interested in troubles and difficulties. Madam Lilith is much hated here at the Haymarket for the many ways in which she meddled with its affairs – while she could.' She smiled at Jody with ineffable sweetness, and he felt his face redden. Did she know how his mother had lost her opportunity to meddle? How could she? It was not possible. Still, he felt uncomfortable. He would not wish his new-found sister to know how expensive a relative he was likely – indeed, intended – to be.

'And enough people here know you to be her son,' Lydia went on. 'So if you wish to spend any time here with me, it must be in the guise of my young friend, not as my young relation. You understand me? Not a word to *anyone* – only Dickon and I and you know, and that is all who will.'

She stopped for a moment, and then said with an uncharacteristic sharpness, 'Besides, it is not my wish that the news that we are friends should reach Grosvenor Square and the only way to prevent *that* is to keep quiet. And in demanding you be silent, I mean also with Miss Phoebe, for, dear child as she is, there is no doubt she is also a chatterbox, and if she knows you are her uncle – and how droll a thought that is! – of course, she will tell her father and her aunt and her cousins and all – and her father, I can tell you, has as little love for your precious Mamma as I have!'

'She is your Mamma as well!' Jody said sulkily.

'I prefer to ignore the fact. She made me very unhappy as a child, she sees me as an object of dislike – though I can assure you that I never did her any injustice or unkindness, apart, that is, from growing up to be handsome and talented – and so it is better we leave sleeping dogs lie. If you wish us to be friends, then I will be delighted, for I like young company, and you will be very welcome in my house. But not if you parade your kinship, or make any problems. And I know you are thinking of threatening me again with your wretched noise-makers at my first night, but you can forget that. Forewarned is forearmed, remember, and two can play at your games.'

So, he had had to bite his tongue and show all the politeness he could to that pest, young Phoebe. Look at her now, he thought disgustedly, hanging round Lydia like that and making such an exhibition of herself. Bad enough there was that hateful O'Hare with his sneers and slights; to have two such standing between him and his sister's company was too much!

For although Jody would not have been willing – or even able – to say it in so many words, he was in fact quite bedazzled by his newfound sister. He had discovered her to be not only a woman of beauty and wit but also of power. She had control of her life in a way that Jody found wholly admirable, being successful and much admired and with many friends. She also had much of her mother's money acumen, he had soon realized, being able both to amass money and invest it shrewdly. When he thought how much he had to struggle to get money for his own needs from his mother, when he thought how very strong and healthy Lilith was, in spite of her secluded life, and how far from decently dying and handing on her fortune, it was clear that another source of income now would be very useful to him. Indeed, essential. To borrow against his hopes of inheritance from his mother he could not do, for she would soon find out such a fact and that would, he was sure, effectively sew up her pockets. So, a rich and clever sister who found him amusing as well as impudent could be a great asset.

But a sister hemmed in with an admirer and a lively niece was less attractive. He really would have to do something about it, he told himself again, watching the way Lydia was petting Phoebe for having done so well at her first rehearsal. And strolled on to the stage to see if he could discover what that something might be.

He found it, but not as a result of his own efforts. Had Jody been one ever to consider the feelings of any but himself, he would have realized that his resentment of Phoebe was shared by his other object of dislike – O'Hare. He too was watching Lydia fussing over the girl and finding it more than a little irritating. It was not simply that while she was playing the mother hen with Phoebe she was ignoring him (although none had the right, in O'Hare's own opinion, to ignore O'Hare), but that it was all having a poor effect on the rest of the assembled company. Lydia, almost as soon as she had arrived at the Haymarket, had established herself as very much the Queen Bee, the centre of attention and the former of attitudes. The fact that she had chosen to find Dickon O'Hare as attractive as he found himself had done him a lot of good, for hitherto he had not been regarded with much affection by his colleagues. And however good an actor was he knew that if the people he worked with disliked him, he would find it difficult to establish himself with the public – for other actors have a way of getting back at performers they dislike, knowing how to make him look foolish, or give a poor show. While he had been Lydia's Dearest Friend, and had always been with her, the company had given him the same sort of affection and respect they gave her, seeing him as part of her. But now they were transferring all that, he suspected, to the wretched Phoebe. It really was not to be borne!

He watched the group clustering around Lydia in the centre of the stage as they rested before the recommencement of the act four run-through, and saw the insolent figure of Jody come sauntering lazily across the boards, and scowled even more. Another wretched relation. It was all too much! If he had been just a young hanger-on of the sort that usually came to gawp at the lovely Lydia, he could have handled the matter; for he knew better than any how to put callow youths to rout. If he had not been a relation, it might have been possible to persuade him to pay some court to the boring girl who was such a pest, and be rid of her – indeed, both of them – in that way. But since she was in fact his niece as well as Lydia's—

O'Hare stopped short in his thoughts, which had been running round his head in a most disorganized manner, and began to think to some purpose. And, gradually, he relaxed and strolled across the stage towards the central group, smiling lazily. Lydia looked up and greeted him with a wide smile.

'Why, Dickon! I thought you were sulking there in your corner. Have you come to join in our felicitations to our clever Phoebe? You cannot deny she did very well for a first time.'

Dickon looked down on the two curly heads, aunt and niece, side by side, and said easily, 'Indeed, I have. I told you when I first saw her that she had a talent that bid fair to outshine even yours.' And he put out one hand and set long fingers beneath Phoebe's chin, and tipped it up so that Phoebe had to look at him.

She really was looking very charming, Dickon thought, considering her dispassionately while seeming to be looking at her with great admiration. She was flushed and very bright-eyed, and her hair had tumbled out of its careful arrangement in a most beguiling way. Indeed, it would be little hardship to carry out his newborn ploy. Very deliberately he bent and kissed the parted lips gently, but with a good deal of skill. He knew better than most just how far to go to make a young girl feel amorous without making her fearful.

Phoebe immediately flushed an almost peony red, and pulled her head back and Dickon laughed very softly. 'There, did I startle you, my child? You must forgive me, I meant no impropriety. It was but to congratulate you on being so very talented a young lady.'

'Well, we really must settle to act four, if we are to be complete today,' Lydia said, and stood up, and Dickon was most satisfied with the faint edge he recognized in her voice. How foolish he had been to be resentful of Lydia's attachment to her new-found family, when it was so obvious – and so easy! – a matter to deal with. Immediately, he turned to her, and moving close, slid one hand into the crook of her elbow.

'Dear Lyddy, there is a matter we must sort out before we move into the rehearsal. That love scene we have in this act – now, cannot we try—'

He bent his head so that he was speaking in her ear as they moved away from the central group, and Jody, watching how his sister's back curved and swayed a little so that she was walking very close to him, felt his spirits droop again. For one splendid moment there, watching his sister's face as Dickon behaved so prettily to Phoebe, he had thought the solution to his problem was before him. If Phoebe were to engage the attentions of Dickon, that would not only remove both of them from Lydia's side, but would also make Lydia more than a little angry with them. She was not a lady, Jody thought, who would take kindly to being anywhere but the centre of everybody's attention. And if Phoebe and Dickon displaced her from that position with them, why, she would be more than ready for the balm his own attentions could provide. After a lifetime of soothing his captious mother out of her moods and miseries, none knew better than Jody how to make a woman feel beautiful!

But seeing the two of them so close together made him feel less hopeful of that particular outcome – until he shifted his gaze and looked at Phoebe. She was still sitting there on the stool beside Lydia's vacated chair, not listening at all to the cheerful chatter that was going on around her from the rest of the actors. Instead she was staring after Lydia and Dickon, with her lips still slightly parted and her eyes very bright. Dear me, thought Jody, and stuck the knob of his cane in his mouth, tapping it gently against his teeth. Dear me, perhaps I was not so wrong after all.

The rehearsal finished at last, after one more complete run-through of the first act as well as the fourth and fifth, by which time most of the actors were tired and irritable. When the stage manager called the dismissal, they cheered up immediately, moving with more alacrity than they had shown most of the afternoon, and within a matter of minutes the stage was cleared with only the stage manager tidying away the few props that had been left lying about, and Phoebe in her plush seat in the front row of the stalls.

She was far from being irritable; tired undoubtedly, but in her it took the form of feeling dreamlike and detached. She had watched the rest of the rehearsals with the same absorption with which she had watched all day, but all the time, beneath that absorption, lay the memory of the way Dickon had looked down at her with those absurdly blue eyes of his, the way his lips had felt on hers – warm and firm and yet very soft and gentle. Every so often, when she allowed her concentration on what was going forward on the stage to slip, the memory would become so vivid that it was almost as though she felt it again, that touch on her mouth; and her hands tingled and felt cold. It was quite unlike any of the sensations she had had when recalling kisses offered by shy and adoring young men in palm-filled conservatories at Stanhope Terrace parties, and there had been enough of those, heaven knew. So many in fact that she had found them more irritating than enjoyable. So to feel as she did because Mr. O'Hare had congratulated her with a kiss was really very strange.

Particularly so when she recalled how embarrassed she had been last evening at Aunt Lydia's party when he had set his arm about her waist. She had found that not in the least agreeable, for it had seemed to be so casual an embrace as to be positively insulting. She had felt as though he would have set his arm so had she been but a marble statue, or a piece of furniture. So why should she feel so now about having been kissed by him?

Because it was a very particular kiss, a little voice inside her whispered. Because he knew very well it was you, and not a marble statue. Because he intended you to feel it, so you did—

The stage manager had gone, leaving the stage lit only by one half-power gas jet, and still she sat there, waiting dreamily for her aunt to come and collect her, as she had been told she must. The vast theatre was dark now, as the dwindling afternoon light which had been coming in through the open scene dock doors was shut away, and all the illumination the auditorium had was from the open double doors behind the stalls, which led to the foyer and the promenade. So, when she felt the hand on hers, she almost screamed with the surprise, and whirled to peer in the darkness, to see who had so crept up on her.

'Oh! It's you – you did startle me—' she said, and her breath was very uneven. The result, no doubt of the surprise, she told herself. Of course. The surprise.

'And who would you have been expecting?' Dickon said, in that soft Irish drawl that she had not really noticed before, but now felt was really one of the most agreeable sounds a voice could have. 'Were you expecting some young admirer to come seeking you?'

'Why, no – no, of course not. My aunt said – I was to wait here, you see, and she—'

'Now, how strange that so delightful and charming a young lady should not be expecting an admirer. You cannot tell me you do not have any!'

'No, of course not!' She was almost indignant. 'I mean, I have many friends, you understand, and—'

'Of course!'

She could hear the laughter in his voice and felt herself blush in the dimness. 'You really must not mock at me, Mr. O'Hare! I am sure you understand perfectly well what I meant.'

'Oh, please, I do not mock you!' He leaned a little closer, and his hand, very warm and big, closed over hers. 'I would never mock, not in any cruel way, I promise you. I find you delightful and a source of merriment, little Phoebe, but that is a measure

132

of my admiration! I do not for a moment wish you to think otherwise. I really am, I do assure you, one of your most fervent friends. If you will have me, that is. Please say you will. I could not be happy again if you were to take me in dislike.'

'Why ever should I?' she said, a little breathless still, but gradually gaining more control over herself. This sort of flirtatious conversation was something she understood, and could manage. Indeed, she was quite skilful at it, and often found it amusing, even if she did not particularly care for the young man with whom she shared it. But this time it was different. The silly phrases that tripped out so easily seemed full of real meaning although she knew quite well that by all the rules of flirting they could not be. The whole point of flirting was that it was a game, a nonsense to be enjoyed but never on any account to be taken seriously. But the puzzling thing was that she wanted the phrases to be full of real meaning even though she did not wish to become at all seriously involved with the alarming Mr. O'Hare. It was all very confusing.

They sat on there for another ten minutes, he still – apparently absentmindedly – holding her hand, and she equally absentmindedly not seeming to notice, but liking the contact very much, liking the way it made her feel so very alert as well as breathless. Almost as delightful a sensation as being in one of her tableaux, poised for the screens to be drawn aside so that the audience could see her.

They jumped almost guiltily when suddenly Lydia came sweeping on to the stage wrapped in furs and peered into the darkness of the auditorium.

'Phoebe! Are you there? My dear child, can you hear me? I had no idea it was so late, and we must take you immediately back to Stanhope Terrace, for your Aunt Abby will think we have quite stolen you, and will be in a state of great alarm. I do not know where Dickon can be, but when we find him I shall—'

'Here I am, Lyddy.' He squeezed Phoebe's hand briefly before letting it go and then stood up and moved forward, vaulting up on the stage with admirable ease. 'I did not know you were seeking both of us.'

'Oh!' She stood there for a moment, a little puzzled, a faint frown between her brows, and peered again into the dark rows of seats. 'Is Phoebe there as well?'

'Yes, aunt, here I am!' Phoebe called, and moved forward to be seen, and again Lydia said, 'Oh!' but this time with a different note in her voice, and she turned and looked sharply at Dickon.

'You wanted me, Lyddy?' he said and stood looking down at her, but making no attempt to touch her.

'I was going to ask you to accompany us to Stanhope Terrace,' she said after a moment. 'But really, it is of no consequence.'

'Of no consequence?' he said at once, and turned to smile down at Phoebe, holding out his hand to help her step on to the stage. 'How can you say such a thing? The safe delivery of Miss Phoebe is of the first consequence! I shall take her myself, at once, in a hack, my dear Lyddy. You go back to Soho Square, and do not disturb yourself playing the driver for so long a journey. It will be my pleasure!'

And he bent his head, and kissed her cheek in an almost casual manner, and then took Phoebe's hand in his and led her away towards the back of the stage and the stage door.

'Good-bye, aunt!' Phoebe called back over her shoulder. 'It has been such a splendid day! May I come again to you soon? In a day or two, perhaps?'

'Of course,' Lydia said, almost mechanically, still staring at them both with her forehead creased. 'Of course, dear child. A day or two. I shall look forward to it.'

And then they were both gone, leaving her to pull her furs closer about her and make her solitary way to her phaeton, waiting for her outside in the busy Haymarket. It was an unusual thing for Lydia to have to go unaccompanied to her home after a rehearsal. A very unusual thing, and not one that she particularly liked. She drove home at a much greater speed than she usually did and whipped up her horses so much more vigorously than usual that her little tiger pursed his lips in disapproval. Somethin' 'ad upset missus, he told himself. Somethin's upset 'er more than somewhat!

# CHAPTER ELEVEN

THE long journey back to Stanhope Terrace was just as delightful as the ten minutes spent in the darkness of the pit at the Haymarket had been. And just as confusing. Phoebe had prided herself for some time on being a lady of some sophistication; among her young female friends she was regarded as a most worldly person and much to be admired in consequence, and had always shared their view of her. Not for Phoebe the sudden attachments and yearnings to which other girls were subject. Not for Phoebe the immediate tremblings and flutterings that other girls fell into when a young man showed any partiality. Her style had always been to be most cool and even casual when the feelings of a male heart were poured at her feet. She had always been one to turn away any declaration of undying worship with a flick of her fan, an easy laugh, a pitying smile. It had not been a difficult pose to master; so far none of the worshipping young men had been in the least interesting to her. It had pleased her far more to bask in her girl-friends' admiration; it had been more entertaining to talk of clothes than affairs of the heart; it had been most amusing to mock her suitors.

Until now. Now she sat in a hackney carriage beside a man with her heart fluttering as much as the silliest of her friends', having to hold her hands close together inside her muff so that he should not observe their trembling, and her head averted ostensibly to look out at the passing streets but in reality to hide her blushing face behind the brim of her bonnet.

Not that he was still playing the flirting game with her. Far from it. He sat well over to his side of the carriage, his head thrown back against the dusty squabs, his gloved hands crossed on the silver knob of his stick, and talked of the merest generalities. This street was very fine, was it not, with ample space for the heavy traffic that used it; and had not London traffic become quite insupportable of late? Such a crush of cabs and carriages, carts and vans and chaises and phaetons – there were times when he thought the whole of the town would become solid with swearing drivers and plunging horses and that no power on earth would ever clear the streets.

She agreed a little breathlessly, peeping at him for a moment from behind her bonnet brim, and was a little put out to find that far from looking at her, he was in all truth looking out of the window at the traffic. So, she tried a little conversation of her own, and was pleased with herself to discover her voice was well within her control, although she was a little trembly still.

Was he interested in the Exhibition? She for her part was looking forward to it most eagerly, for from all accounts it was to be a most marvellous display. She had walked quite often in the park to see Mr. Paxton and his men build the huge glass palace that was to house it all, and the mind could hardly encompass the size of it, did he not agree?

Indeed he did; it quite filled one with wonder at the industry of the people, especially of this country, to realize that so vast a space could be filled with their artefacts. Of course, they would have to wait for the opening in a few weeks' time to see if Prince Albert's great scheme was going to succeed, but he, O'Hare, believed it would. Unfashionable though it might be to admire the Prince Consort – and many people made much mock of him, did they not, at fashionable parties? – (and Phoebe bridled pleasurably at the way he assumed she went often to fashionable parties where guests spoke disparagingly of the Prince Consort), but for his part, he found the Prince a most interesting person. He was indeed industrious, and perhaps a little dull in conversation, as his critics were fond of saying, but when one considered how hard the dear man worked for his adopted country, it quite made one's eyes moisten . . .

They reached Stanhope Terrace as the evening light finally faded, and lights flared at doorways to fill the streets with smoky illumination. He handed her down from the carriage with the most punctilious of care, but he did not pay the driver at once, simply jerking his head at him, and the man couched his whip and the horse whinnied softly and drooped its head, tipping up one hoof to rest it delicately on the rim of the shoe.

Phoebe felt her spirits sink a little. She had not known quite what she expected him to do, but had in a general way assumed he would escort her to the drawing-room and engage a little in conversation with her aunt, in the usual manner of young men who had accompanied her on an afternoon drive or a shopping expedition. But he was not a usual young man, of course, and she should have realized that, for he handed her up the steps to the front door, and when Kent the butler opened it, and stood back to allow them entry, merely took her gloved hand in his, bowed over it and said in his deep soft voice, 'Your servant, ma'am,' and then turned and went swiftly back to the cab, leaving her saying, 'Good-bye. And thank you for—' to the empty air. And feeling remarkably empty herself.

She stood inside the front door slowly untying her bonnet strings, and staring unseeingly across the brightly lit hallway. How very strange a day it had been! How very exciting and wonderful and altogether splendid. And how very low she now felt. Her eyes suddenly prickled a little and she blinked hard. Too absurd!

Kent took away her bonnet and pelisse and muff, and she stood at the foot of the stairs for a moment, considering. Should she seek out her aunt immediately and tell her she had returned, or go to her room and bath and change and wait until dinner-time to greet them all? She had been away for two whole days, after all, and that was unusual. Perhaps they would be distressed if she did not go to them at once with her news. Then, thinking of her news, she decided that she needed time to collect herself, and that a bath and the opportunity to titi-vate a little would help her recover her usual good humour – because for someone who was always happy and who had this very day discovered herself to be so happy she could burst with it, she felt remarkably mournful.

'Phoebe!'

She looked up, startled, and peering a little, for the stairs were not as well lit as the lower hall, where the gaslight reflected brightly from the polished black and white tiles, and said uncertainly, 'Who is it?'

He came downstairs with a clatter. 'Who is it? Have you been so busy about your affairs that you cannot even recall who I might be?' he said waspishly. 'Who should it be?'

'Oh, Freddy,' she said flatly.

'Aye, Freddy!' He had not meant to be so sharp with her, wanted nothing more now than to take hold of her and set his arms about her and hug her close as he usually did, but he had been in such a state of alarm about her that he could not now fully control his emotions. 'What do you mean by returning home at this hour? Where have you been?' he snapped, and stared at her with his forehead creased like a map with his displeasure.

He had woken late after his busy night of surgery, and had not had time to take family breakfast and share family conversation as he usually did, contenting himself with a cup of coffee brought to him by Kent (who acted as his valet as well as butler to the household) before rushing away to the hospital. There he had had a dispiriting day, for his grandfather had been in the most foul of moods (and knowing that it was in part due to his angry distress at the loss of the patient in Purty Bill's cellar did not alter the fact that his sharp words and sour comments made Freddy smart) and the other students had been decidedly mocking about his status as the Guv'nor's Pet.

Then, another of his own surgical patients had died, a boy of seven who had had an infection of the tibia demanding a below-the-knee amputation. He had seemed to be getting on very well, with only a minimum of laudable pus showing itself on the stump wound, but while Freddy had been dressing it the boy, who had been feverish all night and very restless, moved sharply, pulling away from Freddy's hands.

Whether it was that which caused it, or whether it had been inevitable, it was impossible to say, but the wound opened as one of the rotting ligatures burst, and the artery slipped its tie as well and sent the boy's life blood spurting horribly. By the time Freddy and the nurse had managed to seize the child and put heavy pressure on the wound, he had become so exsanguinated that there was little that could be done. The wound was repaired, but the child had died at four in the afternoon leaving Freddy feeling sick and exhausted and overwhelmingly angry with the world he lived in. The boy had been so lively and so hopeful and so very brave about his treatment. It was cruel that he should have had to suffer so much and to no avail.

So, by the time he left the hospital he was in very low spirits, wanting only the comfort of home and above all of Phoebe's company. All the way back (and he walked, feeling the need of the extra time walking took to shake off the evils of the day before he reached the peace of Stanhope Terrace) he rehearsed what he would say to her. How he would make no comment at all about her captious behaviour at her party, for he could see now that it was not her fault. That wretched man had been not only an ill-mannered guest, but also a pushy and unpleasant person who had forced his attentions on the young lady of the house. It was not fair to blame her because she was well mannered and had behaved prettily to a bidden guest.

No, he would not speak of that, but only of their future, of the plans he had made for them to be happy together for always as they had been in the past. Only now in their own home, with their own possessions about them. As a married pair.

So sure had he been of his welcome that when Kent had told him blandly that 'Miss Phoebe is away from home' when he demanded which room she might be found in, he stared at the man with his mouth open, and then said, 'Eh?' in a positively street arab fashion.

'She is away from home, sir,' Kent said patiently. ('Poor feller – looked fit to drop 'e did. Nasty time 'e 'as of it at that there 'orspital,' he had said to Cook later, recounting, as he always did, every detail of the day above stairs) and then, taking pity on his evident bewilderment, elaborated.

'She went yesterday, sir, to stay, as I understood it, with her aunt. Her *new* aunt, sir!' The entire servants' hall was agog for news of this fresh arrival in the family's midst, and Kent hoped for a moment that Mr. Freddy's obvious annoyance at the fact he had imported would encourage him to be indiscreet and blurt out some titbit of useful information. But Freddy merely scowled, so Kent took away his hat and coat and left him in the hallway to stand undecided trying to sort out his feelings.

Gone to stay with a new aunt? Not been here for two days? How could such a thing be, when he knew nothing of it? And then he remembered. Remembered that he himself had been away from home all day yesterday until the very latest time of night, and that he had himself found some sharp-edged satisfaction in believing that Phoebe would be distressed at his absence. The memory of the way he had regarded with equanimity – indeed with pleasure – the prospect of Phoebe's being distressed at his absence from the family dinner-table now made him feel most disagreeable. The biter bit – a most hateful sensation.

His ire rose in him as he thought of it all, and he flung away upstairs to seek his mother. He had not intended to talk to her about his plans for Phoebe and himself, and still did not intend to, but there would be balm in conversation with her.

But she too was away from home. It was not long since quarter day, and some business matters had fallen in arrears. He recalled now that she had told him of this a few days ago, making the point that she and Gideon would have to spend much time closeted with Henry Sydenham, their general manager, to put the books to rights. So not only was she absent from home; so was Gideon. No one was about to give him company but the babies in the nursery, and even they would be busy about their bread and milk and bedtime baths, for it was now past five o'clock. So he sat miserably in the drawing-room, staring out at the darkening streets, and felt as hard done by a young man as any in London.

But as the clock crept round and only the hiss of the flames in the grate and the distant clatter of dishes from the dining-room below where Kent and his minions were setting the table gave him company, his irritation sharpened into alarm. He sent for Kent and asked at what time Miss Phoebe had left the house yesterday, and was told that she had gone to visit her aunt in Soho Square at eleven in the morning, to share a luncheon, and that a message had been returned begging that her maid be sent with her necessaries, for, as he understood it, Madam had consented that Miss Phoebe should remain with her aunt for a party at her house that night.

'Katy, her maid, she comes back this afternoon, sir, sayin' as 'ow Miss Phoebe 'ad gone abroad with 'er h'aunt, and would be back later. That was at – well, must 'a' bin about two o'clock, sir.'

So Freddy had to sit on chafing at the window and staring out, unable to admit to himself that he was watching for her. He told himself that he was there simply to kill time. He was too tired to work at his books, as he usually did when he had an hour to spare, and no one to talk to.

But he watched every carriage that arrived at the end of the terrace, straining his eyes against the diminishing light, and feeling anxiety build up in him. It was so late! It must mean she had been hurt; there had been some sort of accident in the busy streets, her carriage had overturned, she had been set on by a pickpocket and been injured. And when at last a cab stopped outside the house and he saw her being handed out the sense of joy because she was alive and well came bursting up in him so that he leaped to his feet, and reached up to the sash of the window, preparing to open it and lean out and call to her. And then stopped, as he realized who it was who was so punctiliously leading her to the steps. Only that damned actor would wear so flamboyant a garment as that coat, which was probably of as outrageous a colour as its cut was perfect. Even in this bad light his linen gleamed with insolent perfection above his cravat and his silk hat shone with richness.

By the time Freddy reached the top of the stairs his relief had been almost overcome by his anger. To be so late, and to return with that man! It was the outside of enough. And then he saw her standing there in the middle of the hallway with her head down in a most uncharacteristically dejected stance, her hands dangling loosely at her sides, every line of her bespeaking some underlying emotion that was disagreeable, and felt a chill rise in him. Why should she look like that? Had that man said something, done something to annoy her? If he had, he would have Frederick James Caspar to deal with, that was for sure!

But even as he thought it, even as he spoke her name and started downstairs towards her, the other thought rose unbidden in his mind. Was she dejected not because of O'Hare's behaviour, but because of her own feelings regarding him? That was something not to be thought of! So when he spoke, he was much sharper and harsher than he had ever been in his dealings with her.

She looked at him blankly for a moment, and then said, 'At this hour? What do you mean, at this hour? It is not so late, surely! Are my aunt and uncle here and ready for their dinner?'

'No, of course not!' he said impatiently. 'But you know quite well that it is dark, has been for – well, some time now. It is not right that a young lady should be away from her home so late in the day when—'

'Oh, Freddy, do stop prosing at me!' she said wearily, and started to climb the stairs. 'You make too much fuss altogether! I am not a child any more, although you delight in treating me so, and I really cannot see why I should have to put up with your scolding when I am tired. I am going to bath and dress for dinner – and—'

As she passed him he seized her arm by the elbow and said urgently, 'No! No. That must wait. I have been waiting to talk to you these – oh, for two days! This is the first chance I have had, and I do not intend to let it go! I did not mean to be so churlish about your late arrival, but I was anxious for you – and then to see that man. . . .'

She stopped, and turned her head to look at him. 'What man?' Her voice was suddenly very silky.

'Oh, that dreadful actor feller,' Freddy said impatiently. 'He is the outside of enough, and I am surprised your Aunt Lydia should allow such a man to hang about her, let alone hang about you. I dare say your aunt is a very good sort of woman, at heart, but I suppose she cannot always control the sort of people she will meet in her life – but it is too bad you should have to tolerate such—'

'I tolerate nothing I do not choose to, Freddy!' she said, and he stopped and looked at her a little more closely, at the slightly raised colour in her cheeks, the glitter in her eyes, and again his spirits sank within him.

'We must talk, Phoebe,' he said after a moment, deliberately keeping his voice expressionless. 'Please? My mother and Gideon will return shortly, and then it will be dinner-time, and it will be difficult. There will be time for you to dress, I do promise you. Please.'

She stood there a moment longer, her chin still held up and still with that slightly challenging air about her, and then her shoulders drooped a little, and she softened. After all, this was her Freddy, her own dearest Freddy who was so comfortable to be with, and who never meant any harm with his scoldings. She knew it was simply that he felt the need to take care of her, and it was very nice to be so protected. Like now, when she was fatigued and a little confused. To sit and be scolded by Freddy and pretend to take notice in the way they always played that little game would be quite soothing really.

So she nodded and tucked her hand into the crook of his elbow, and together they walked upstairs to the drawing-room. Freddy closed his own hand warmly over hers, and prepared to declare himself, to offer to the girl he loved above all others in the whole world his hand and his heart, for always.

# CHAPTER TWELVE

'It is no use prowling up and down the room in that fashion, Freddy!' she said a little petulantly. 'It makes it very difficult to talk properly, and my neck is getting tired, always having to turn to watch you so. Do sit down! You are behaving very odd!'

'I am not behaving odd!' he said, but came obediently to the sofa on the other side of the fireplace. He wanted to sit beside her, very close beside her, so that he could feel the warmth of her and smell the familiar scent of her, but he knew that not only would that make it difficult for him to talk sensibly, but that he did not have the right any more.

In the past when they had been so brother and sister-like it meant nothing more than cosiness and comfort and friendship. But now that he knew what he was to say to her to behave so before she was aware of his intentions would be in some sort an insult to her. He was very conscious of the significance of the situation in which he had placed himself, even if she was not.

'Please, Freddy!' she said and now she sounded more than a little impatient. 'I wish you would get on with whatever it is you have to say. You made a great point of not keeping me long from my bath and fresh gown, but if you do not put your tongue to it soon whatever it is I will not even get any dinner – and nor will you!'

'Phoebe,' he said urgently. 'Phoebe, I have wanted to speak to you for – for a long time. I have held my tongue until I knew for certain that I had a right to speak so. I have not addressed myself to Uncle Jonah, although this would of course be proper, because – well, our situation is not the normal one, is it? It is not as though I have been calling upon you at your father's establishment. We have lived in the same house now for a long time – close on a dozen years is it not? – so it seemed to me right that I should speak first to you of my intentions . . .'

She was sitting up very straight and staring at him with her mouth half open. He sat there in front of her, looking as he always had, with his red hair and his sandy freckled face, his earnest green eyes and his trick of holding his head a little to one side, and yet he sounded like a stranger. His voice had none of that easy jocularity she was used to in him, nor any of the mock seriousness he employed for his scoldings. He sounded like – what?

She shook her head a little, trying to deny to herself what she knew to be the case and could not. It was dreadful – because he sounded like all those foolish young men at parties who sat beside her under tropical plants in conservatories and tried to hold her hand with hot damp palms which not even their white gloves could keep agreeable to touch, who breathed hotly over her neck and made her want to giggle at the intensity of their words, the extravagance of their emotion.

But this was not one of those stupid boring young men, but *Freddy,* her dear Freddy, who had always been so reliable and funny and comfortable and agreeable to be with. Freddy, who had always been able to make her laugh in a comfortable, rather than a spiteful way, Freddy, who she had always shared best jokes with. It was more than she could bear and she put out one hand and said, urgently, 'Freddy, please, don't—'

But it was too late. He was already launched upon his speech and it bore every sign of having been carefully thought out and planned, even rehearsed a little.

'I am sure you know, dear Phoebe, that I have long nurtured the most tender of feelings for you. The fact of our shared childhood does not alter the fact that I have learned to love you in a manner that is a far from childish one. It has matured and grown into a very real passion, and one I take leave to hope can be reciprocated. I know you as few young men have ever been privileged to know the ladies they wish to make their wives, and it is indeed an index of your character and charm that even on so close an acquaintance, my love for you has grown!'

He grinned at her then, a hint of his old familiar easy-going self coming through his solemnity, and she opened her mouth to speak, wanting to stop him before he went on any further, hoping it was still not too late, but he leaned forwards and set one finger against her lips and shook his head.

'No, please to let me finish! I have planned it all so carefully, and if you interrupt me now, I shall forget some, and it is all so important. Dearest Phoebe, I must tell you, even though I know you do not care about such matters, that I am a man of some substance. The only person to whom I have spoken of my desires regarding you is Gideon, since he is my adviser on money matters, and as I have always suspected, I am what is regarded as a person of some wealth. I know you do not worry your head about such matters and it is right that you should not, but if we are to be wed – and – and to care for a family in the proper manner, of course the question of money must be gone into. And you can be assured a most satisfactory portion as my wife, one that will ensure you total comfort and security always. No, please not to speak yet, dear Phoebe! I know talk of money is disagreeable, so I will say no more on that score, hoping you will feel sufficiently assured that I have thought of all aspects of our future. All I ask of you, my dear, dear girl, is that you tell me you can be as happy to contemplate a future with me in a home of our own as I do with you. . . .'

He smiled again, a broad and most cheerful grin and slid forwards so that he was on his knees before her, looking up at her with his hands closed over both of hers on her lap.

'You see?' he said softly. 'I am on my knees to you. I know what a dear, romantic-minded girl you are, and I would not have my proposal to you to be lacking in the smallest particular! Dear, dear Miss Lackland, will you do me the honour to be my wife?' And he lifted his hands and took her face between them and very gently kissed her lips.

There was a long silence between them as he knelt there staring up at her with a faint smile curling his mouth, and she stared solemnly back, and then very slowly tears rose in her eyes and slid down her nose, and she sniffed and swallowed and he grinned even more widely if that were possible and pulled a handkerchief from his pocket and very tenderly wiped them away.

'As I said, my love, such a romantical, sentimental girl you are! I should have guessed you would weep. . . .'

She shook her head, and pulled away from him and said in a tight voice, 'Please, do go and sit down again, Freddy. I cannot talk to you while you kneel there in that silly fashion.'

He remained very still, holding the handkerchief in one hand and staring at her with the smile very slowly fading from his face. And then, as though suddenly aware of the ludicrousness of his posture, he got to his feet, and brushed his knees and went to stand with his back to the fire, his hands thrust deep in his trouser pockets.

'I did not mean it to be a silly fashion,' he said after a moment, and his voice too was tight. 'I thought I knew you well enough to believe you would wish me to behave in the traditional manner in what is, I cannot deny, a most traditional situation. I am not the first young man to make a proposal of marriage, of course, but it is the first time for *me*. I wished it all to be done in the proper manner.'

She heard the appeal in his voice, knew he was asking her to treat him gently, with respect and concern as well as love, but she could not answer it. It was as though some other creature had crept inside her skin with her, a sharp and cruel creature who did not care at all about appeals for gentleness, who found such things rather tedious, in fact. A creature who much preferred the company of men like O'Hare, sophisticated and amusing and witty men, to that of familiar boys she had grown up with.

'Oh, Freddy, do stop being so pompous!' she said and looked up at him with a very bright smile. 'Come, you did not really mean to be so silly, did you? This was some foolish maggot you got into your brain this evening, a notion you had because I was late, and it was dark, and you thought it would be a way to make me do as you told me! Let us please forget all about it and—'

'Forget all about it?' The words seemed to explode from him and she shrank back a little, almost for the first time seeing the size of him and feeling the weight of his presence, for he was towering above her in a way of which she had never before been aware.

'I offer you every part of myself. I offer you my entire future, every atom of love I have in me, and you tell me to *forget* it? Come, Phoebe, even you cannot be so flibbertigibbet as to ask that! I have no doubt it is fashionable among your friends to be so captious with a man, to treat a proposal in this shall-I-shan't-I manner, but I had thought there was enough between us for it to be possible for me to expect an honest reply from you! Do not play games with me, Phoebe! I have declared myself as truly and sincerely as I know how. Pay me the decency of treating me as I treated you!'

'Oh, Freddy, you make me feel so wretched!' At last the cruel other creature who had shared her skin with her was gone, and she could be as she always had been with him, her own affectionate self. 'If only you had not spoken so! You have spoiled everything – everything! We have always been such dear friends, and I have loved you so dearly – I mean, as people who live as close as we have inevitably must – and I had no wish ever to spoil any of it. And now you have! You have changed it all, and I do not like it – I do not like it one bit!' and the tears which had been temporarily stemmed now began to flow in real earnest and she wept bitterly.

But he made no move to come to comfort her this time, standing there and staring down at her with his face quite blank. After a while she stopped sobbing, and gulped and sniffed and rubbed her face with her wet hands and said piteously, 'You see? That is the first time in all the years we have been so happy together that you have let me weep alone. You have spoiled it *all*. The easy happy intercourse between us – it can never be the same again.'

'I did not wish it to be as it always had been,' he said after a moment. 'People grow up, Phoebe, they become men and women. We cannot stay children for ever, no matter how delightful it was to be a child. The days when we robbed the larder and played childish tricks upon our elders – they had to go! We are elders ourselves, now. It is Sarah and Isabel who

148

are the children. I thought that you could grow up as I have, could see the love that we always shared growing into a better love—'

'It can never be better!' she said swiftly. 'All those years of sharing and laughing and – none of that could be made better!'

'Oh, but it can, Phoebe, it car ' He came across to stand beside her again, looking down on her as she sat there, her hands still holding her tear-stained face. 'To love as children love is a delight of course, but to love as adults – oh, Phoebe, that is so much better! Do not shut your eyes to the living future in contemplating the dead past, my little love! It can and will be better, I promise you! I rushed you perhaps, I should have given you more time, for you are still so very young, after all, and—'

She stiffened then. 'I am not a child, Freddy, even if I recall our childhood days with so much pleasure! You must not think I feel as I do about – about your proposal because of some infantile attitude of mind! It is far from being so.'

He felt the chill again, and the moment of hope that had filled him subsided.

'Oh?' he said carefully. 'I am sorry if I misunderstood. I thought perhaps that—'

She lifted her head and looked at him very directly, and for all the tear-marks on her cheeks, she looked very much the young woman now and far from the pathetic little girl she had seemed to be in his eyes a few moments before.

'Then you thought wrong, Freddy. You thought I was still the child you had always known, who would do as you told her because she always had. But I have a mind of my own and tastes and interests of my own now and they do not necessarily fit entirely with yours.'

'You misjudge me,' he said stiffly, and moved away from her, returning to the safety of the hearthrug. 'I was not trying to treat you as a child, I promise you. I proposed marriage to you, Phoebe, and I would have thought that such a suggestion indicates very clearly indeed the light in which I see you. And it is not as a childish playmate.'

'And I must tell you I cannot accept your proposal, Freddy,

and deeply regret that you made it, for it spoils so much that was easy between us. And in refusing you, I thank you, and assure you I speak not as a child, but as a woman grown. I have other plans for my future, you see. My *own* plans.'

All the suspicion and hostility that he had felt against O'Hare came surging up in him again and he said savagely, 'That damnable man! Has he been making approaches to you? Is that what you are trying to tell me?'

She stared at him for a moment, genuinely puzzled, and then reddened and said sharply, 'If you mean Mr. O'Hare, you insult me as well as him! Were I to permit such familiarity from a gentleman I met barely a few days ago, I must indeed be a person whose virtue and honour must be called into question! You will apologize immediately for so—'

'Indeed, I beg your pardon,' he said at once. 'That was outrageous of me, and I trust you can forgive me. I meant no insult to you, you must realize that. But he with his theatrical falsity and greater knowledge of the world could – I thought perhaps he had played on you and dazzled you and—'

'And again you thought wrong,' she said coldly. 'I may give the impression of being a very inexperienced and foolish girl, perhaps, but I am not entirely a piece of wax to be melted by any man's attentions! Not even yours.' And she pushed firmly away the sudden memory of the way she had felt when Richard O'Hare had so tenderly kissed her on the stage of the Haymarket that afternoon. 'You thought wrong,' she said again, more strongly.

'Then perhaps you will explain to me how I should think to be right,' he said, and now his voice seemed filled with a sort of weariness. 'For I must tell you that I am so confused and bewildered by your – your response to me this afternoon that I am hard put to it to think anything, right or wrong.'

There was a silence and then she stood up and moved away from the pool of light in which she had been sitting towards the darker part of the room where the gaslight did not quite reach and the evening candles had not yet been lit.

'I have decided – that it, I have been advised—' she began and then stopped.

'Which?' he said and turned his head to look at her there in the shadows and ached a little at the sight of her. She was so lovely, standing there with her shoulders sloping a little, the curves of her breasts showing beneath the tight bodice of her afternoon gown and the narrowness of her waist above the half crinoline of her skirt.

'*I* have decided, and been advised it is a good decision,' she said, her voice strengthening a little. 'Do not make me angry again, Freddy, by suggesting I am incapable of thinking for myself.'

'I ask your pardon. And may I also ask what the decision is that you have made? If I am permitted to know, that is, the affairs of so strong-minded a woman!'

She lifted her chin, refusing to acknowledge that she was aware of the acid note in his voice. 'I am going to be an actress,' she said. 'My aunt says it is a talent I possess and that it would be wrong to waste it. She has promised to help me realize my ambition, and I am determined upon it.'

'You are – what did you say?' He laughed then, albeit uncertainly, and at once she flared up.

'Oh, I might have known you would think it amusing! You would think any matter which I interested myself with was ridiculous, the games of a child! Just because I am a female, the affairs of my mind are of course of small interest! You are such a one as I despise, do you know that? I thought you a cut above the stupid young men who live hereabouts and who come to pester me with their silly mawkish posturings of love, who think I am interested in little more than parties and playing, but you are just the same as all of them! You talk of love and romance as though it is the only matter to which I can bend my mind. But you do not think it enough of an interest to consume *you* wholly, do you? No, you have your studies to be a surgeon! You are a man, and therefore important, whereas I am but a woman, and therefore just a silly joke!'

She was well launched now, and began to march about the room flinging her words over her shoulder at him, and now it was his turn to feel the strain as his head moved this way and that to keep pace with her.

'You have laughed at my tableaux, have you not? Thought them just babies' games to keep me occupied in the long, dull afternoons! Well, it might have been so for the others, but not for me! I planned them, and I thought about them and organized them, and worked very hard to make them right. And though guests at parties saw them but as moments of entertainment, for me they were important, and real and – and – they were *important*!'

She turned and glared at him. 'Do you understand me? Important! And now I have met some people who understand this, who see I have some – some ability and who wish to help me develop it into something greater. I *am* going to be an actress and I am going to be a very successful one, and my aunt says it is possible, and so I shall do it! Already I have a part in her play – not a big part, no lines to speak, merely walking on, but I do not care! It is a beginning, and I shall do it, and you shall laugh in a very different way when you see me in the years to come when I am a great success and famous and – and—'

She stopped as suddenly as she had begun, looking at him with wide eyes, then shook her head, and burst into tears, standing there and sobbing in a most piteous manner. At once he moved across the room to comfort her, but she turned and ran to the door, pulling it open furiously and almost tumbling through it, and he followed her out to the hallway.

Beyond her he could see Gideon and Abby standing almost on the top steps, Kent behind them with a lamp in his hand, and all three with their faces reflecting amazement as Phoebe went whisking past them and fled along the hallway to the stairs to run to the floor above, to her room.

'My dear boy!' Abby said mildly. 'Are you well? I did not see you this morning.'

'I am very well, thank you, Mamma,' he said mechanically, staring after Phoebe, and then he moved forward uncertainly as though he were about to follow her.

'I would not, dear boy,' Gideon said softly, and came past Abby to take Freddy's elbow in a firm grip. 'It would not be of much use if you did, and besides, the height of impropriety! Come. We shall share a pre-prandial glass of sherry wine, I think. And if your Mamma will forgive us both, we will not change our dress for dinner tonight. You agree, my dear? We have no guests, and to dine comfortably in our day clothes would not be such a dreadful thing, I believe.'

'No, of course not. An excellent idea,' Abby said, and picking up her skirts completed her ascent of the stairs. 'Kent, please to tell Cook we should like dinner sent up on trays to my boudoir. We shall be cosy there tonight, the three of us.'

She caught Gideon's raised eyebrows and went on gently, 'I think Phoebe has had a most tiring stay with her Aunt Lydia, my dear, and needs to rest a little. I shall go up to her, and arrange, I think, for her meal in bed and to go early to sleep. I shall ring with instructions, Kent.'

The butler nodded and went away downstairs, agog with all he had observed, and Gideon, looking after him, sighed a little, and then tightened his grip on Freddy's arm and led him away to his study.

'That sherry, my boy. No, not a word, until we have taken it, and dined as well. Some matters deal better after being cogitated upon. *Silently.*'

# CHAPTER THIRTEEN

THE remains of their dinner had been removed and now they sat in a companionable silence, each staring at the flames of Abby's fire and all deep in their own thoughts.

Abby was now a little angry, not only because she now realized that her fears had been justified and she had indeed lost her son to another woman, but because that other woman – and how absurd to see Phoebe in that light – had behaved so unkindly to him. In the few moments she had had alone with Gideon before Freddy had joined them for their al fresco dinner she had told him that Phoebe had blurted out that Freddy had proposed and she had rejected him.

'There is more to it, I believe, than she told me, Gideon,' she had said. 'But the child was in such a taking I thought it better not to talk more myself or to let her do so. Ellie gave her some gruel and I sent her a small dose with some laudanum in it and I have no doubt she is fast asleep now. I am concerned indeed. I had suspected that Freddy had a *tendre* for someone, but I did not ever think it might be Phoebe. It was foolish of me, I suppose. It was the obvious place for his eye to alight. And I must confess to you that I wish it had not. She is a pretty and charming girl of course, and I love her dearly. How could I not after having had so much of the rearing of her? But there are aspects to her character that I do not entirely like. I – it worries me. For Freddy.'

'I knew,' Gideon said. 'No, do not look at me so, my love! I was not being in any way disloyal to you, believe me, in keeping my tongue between my teeth. He asked my guidance on the matter of his finances – he was so punctilious, Abby, you cannot imagine! It was very touching. I kept remembering the little boy he had been, and how he had behaved so wisely when you were so ill of the cholera and nearly died. Do you remember?'

'Yes,' she said softly. 'I remember,' and she held his hand tightly for a moment.

'Well, he came to me and said he wished no one, not even you, to know until he had spoken to Phoebe. And I promised him I would respect his confidence. You must forgive him, and me, for our silence. A man must be a man in his own way, Abby.'

She had kissed him then with a sudden passion. 'You are the best of stepfathers, dear Gideon. James would have been so grateful.'

'I am glad,' was all he had said, but he had held her tightly. And now he too was staring into the fire and thinking his own thoughts. Thoughts of the time when he also had ached for a woman who rejected his proposal, the time when he had wanted her and needed her and not been able to reach out to touch her. But I was fortunate, he thought. I at least knew she cared for me, even though there was no way at the time for it to be shown. I at least knew of her desires and that they matched mine. Poor Freddy.

And he turned his head and looked at the boy sitting there, wrapped in a comfortable old smoking-jacket with his hair tousled above his blank eyes. What was he thinking? Gideon wondered. Would he be able to confide his unhappiness to them both? And if he did, could they help? Thinking of the way Phoebe had looked when she had fled along the hallway, and the sort of girl she was – and he had observed her close enough, heaven knew, in her growing years – he was afraid for his stepson.

As though he were aware of his thoughts, Freddy looked up and smiled at him, a little abashed, and said gruffly, 'I feel I owe you both an apology.'

'Oh, I do not think so, Freddy,' Gideon said easily. 'You cannot be blamed. Some matters cannot ever be hidden.'

Freddy grimaced. 'I suppose not. I wish Kent had not been there, though. It is so disagreeable to know one is the object of gossip among the servants.'

155

'Oh, as to that!' Abby said, stirring in her chair. 'Do not think about it. One is always the object of servants' gossip. There is little else for them to be interested in, after all.'

The silence slid back for a while and then Freddy said awkwardly, 'I must explain, I think.'

'You do not have to,' Abby said. 'We put no pressure on you, Freddy.'

'That is why I must explain,' he said with a flash of acerbity. 'If you were the sort of Mamma who put any pressure on me to tell you of my affairs it would be the easiest thing in the world to escape your prying. It is because you are not that I find myself compelled to tell you all!'

Gideon laughed at that. 'A lesson I must remember when it comes to dealing with my daughters and their secrets, Freddy. You are a wise teacher!'

'I wish someone had been able to teach Phoebe more!' Freddy said. 'I know you had the care of her, Mamma, from the earliest days, but there are aspects to her that – oh, forgive me. I do not mean to sound carping. I – we – it was painful this afternoon.'

'It seemed to be so, from what I saw of you both,' Abby said equably, and leaned forward to stir the fire.

'Well, you are right. Oh, Mamma, she has such a maggot in her now! This wretched Aunt Lydia of hers – the notion she has put into Phoebe's head is the outside of enough!'

'Well?'

'She says she is going to be an actress! That she already has been given a part in her aunt's play at the Haymarket, and she is to continue in this road and become famous! Did you ever hear such a nonsense in all your life? Phoebe! I know she finds pleasure in her tableaux, and has some pleasant ability in that direction, but a girl does not have to make her drawing-room accomplishments into a public display, does she? Yet this is what she wants to do, and it is a dreadful notion, quite dreadful! I wish this wretched Mohun woman had never set foot here! She has made no attempt to come near Phoebe in all these years, and now of a sudden here she is filling her head with rubbishy notions like this!'

He looked up at his mother, his face a little twisted. 'I do not think I am deluding myself, Mamma, when I tell you I believe that had I spoken to her last week, before all this silly theatrical nonsense started, she would have accepted me! It is all the fault of that Mohun and her O'Hare friend!'

There was a short silence and then Gideon said carefully, 'I would not be too sure about that Freddy. I mean, that you must blame the sudden appearance on the scene of her aunt for this contretemps. Her aunt did not put anything into Phoebe that was not already there. . . .'

Abby was sitting up very straight and staring at Freddy, and she said sharply, as though she had not heard Gideon speak, 'Actress, did you say? She is going to be an *actress*?'

'Yes!' Freddy said disgustedly. 'Did you ever hear such a nonsense! But so she says.'

'Oh, poor Jonah!' Abby said softly. 'Poor, poor Jonah.'

Freddy looked at her in surprise. 'What did you say? Why poor Uncle Jonah?' He brightened suddenly. 'Do you mean that Uncle Jonah will be distressed by this suggestion?'

'Distressed?' Abby's eyes focused again and she stared at her son. 'Oh, indeed, he will be distressed. It is the very thing he would most dislike for his Phoebe, I think. That is why she lives with us, you will remember, Freddy.'

'I remember little of the time before Phoebe came to us! It is sometimes as though she has been here all my life.' Freddy said, and his voice drifted away and he turned his head to stare again at the fire.

'He was anxious she should not be – tainted by the work he and Celia did. Phoebe's mother. He thought the Supper Rooms a bad place for children to be and indeed so they were, in those days. He has made it all much more genteel now of course. Much more.'

Freddy had roused himself again, and was looking at his mother with his face creased a little. 'Will he forbid this, do you think?'

'If he can,' Gideon said heavily, and stood up. 'May I smoke a cigar in here, Abby? You will not mind? Thank you. He will if he can, Freddy. But sometimes what is there in a person has to be allowed to come out. Push it back down and it can make such troubles in the future that—'

Freddy shook his head impatiently. 'Gideon, that will solve all! If my uncle says she may not appear in this theatre play, why then, she may not! He is her father and of course she must do as he bids her! Oh, Gideon, please, will you apprise him of all that has happened? I know the Mohun woman is his sister-in-law but she is not one he has ever known well, you told me, and anyway, Mamma is his own sister, and much closer to him. If you two tell him Phoebe should not be permitted this folly, why then, perhaps she will be able to rid herself of all the nonsense they have stuffed her head with, and give her the time to – to make her life again. . . .'

'Even if he does forbid her, Freddy, do not assume that she will be as she was before her aunt came,' Gideon said gently. 'People once changed do not change back completely. They never can. All experience alters us, for good or ill. You must never forget that, Freddy.'

But Freddy thrust that aside. There would be other times to talk in a philosophical vein with Gideon, many of them. Now he was more interested in seeking an answer to his own need, and he pursued the matter with great vigour.

'It would not be proper for *me* to speak to Uncle Jonah, since I have not yet spoken to him of my intentions regarding Phoebe,' he said earnestly. 'But could not you? It is not simply on my behalf, after all. It will be very bad for Phoebe to spend time with these people – you must agree as to that! Even after the first day with them she is not herself! You saw how she was when you returned home.'

Again Gideon shook his head. 'You are mistaken, Freddy, if you think that all this has come entirely from other people. However, I will of course speak to Jonah, and I would have done so had you not asked me. I would be failing sadly in my duty as her guardian – as I am while she lives in my household – were I not to do so.'

Abby moved in her chair again and said slowly, 'He will be very distressed, Gigi.'

'Yes, I know he will. But what can we do? I do not feel I am able to set my face against Phoebe's desire to accept her aunt's interest in her. After all, I am but her uncle by virtue of my marriage to you. Lydia is of her blood.'

'And so am I.' Abby stood up then and turned her head to look at Freddy. 'So am I! And I share Freddy's concern about this plan. I cannot see that Lydia behaved at all properly in making such arrangements with Phoebe without first talking to her father or to me about it. Her mother's sister she may be, but she has stepped beyond the bounds of propriety, and I shall tell her so. You may sleep better tonight, Freddy. You have my promise that I shall intercede with Lydia on this matter—'

'And I with Jonah,' Gideon said, also turning to look at Freddy.

Freddy raised his head and looked up at them both standing there side by side, and both gazing at him with the same expression of concern upon their faces, and to his amazement and horror felt tears prickle behind his lids.

'Dear Mamma, Gideon – you are too kind,' he said, and his voice was very gruff. 'I do not deserve such – such. . . .'

'Indeed, you don't!' Gideon said and smiled. 'Do not think we concern ourselves only with you, dear boy! I wish for nothing more than peace in my home, and if I do not settle this little war between Madame Phoebe and you, why, peace would be the first casualty! I am being thoroughly selfish! Do you not agree, Abby?'

And she too smiled, and said cheerfully, 'Indeed, I do!' and the moment of emotion passed. But even though they spent the remainder of the evening in conversation on other matters, and all appeared to be calm and content enough, none of them slept well that night. The even tenor of their life had been much more disturbed than any of them would have been happy to admit.

'You are a damned fool, Lyddy, and I don't scruple to tell you so to your face!' Dickon said irritably. 'Fifteen pounds! And what for? Fifteen pounds for a whipper-snapper of a toad-eating little prig who would steal the ring from your finger if you do not keep your hands in your pockets and—'

'You are speaking of my brother, Dickon,' Lydia said and though her voice sounded as easy as it always did there was a glitter in her eyes as she stared at him above the rim of her chocolate cup. She was sitting up in bed wrapped in a green silk peignoir, her dark hair tumbled about her shoulders, and looking very delectable indeed. Dickon, who had been banished to his own room the night before as soon as he had returned to Soho Square from Stanhope Terrace by a maid who had told him blandly, 'Madam bids you goodnight, sir, for she has gone to bed early with the headache,' was very aware of the need for her that was in him, and it sharpened his irritation. So much so that he became incautious.

'So he says! And anyway, what if he is! Have you ever given a tuppenny damn about him in all the years since his birth: This sudden passion you have for surrounding yourself with dingy little relations, boring creatures who—'

She put her cup down with a clatter. 'You did not seem to find one of my boring relations quite as boring as all that yesterday! You had plenty of interest to show then! But now, because I have given a little money – which, may I remind you, is entirely mine to give – to a young man, you choose to become offended. I hesitate to suggest that your resentment of my gift to my *brother* stems from any fear that your own pocket will suffer in consequence, but the thought does occur to me. Just as it occurs to me that your interest in my *niece* is—'

She stopped and glared at him, for he had suddenly started to laugh, leaning back in the corner of the chaise-longue and showing his teeth in a wide grin. His arms were thrown casually wide to rest on the quilted back in such a way that his chest was clearly displayed under his loosely tied robe, and his bare legs were thrust forwards under its skirts in a very insolent manner – and a very attractive one. Even in her temper she was aware of that.

Dickon was suddenly feeling much better. She had been very cool indeed when he had come to her room this morning, as he always did, to share their morning chocolate, and had turned her cheek to his attempt to kiss her mouth and had then told him with a relish that he found very galling that she had spent a long and most agreeable evening with her young brother, and had allowed him to win heavily at cards. She had airily dismissed his complaint about the message delivered to him by her maid with an, 'oh, I was not in the humour for company! Until Jody came, and coaxed so prettily that I could not gainsay him!' and stared at him challengingly when he opened his mouth to expostulate.

And now he was laughing at her, genuinely finding amusement in the situation. His attentions to Phoebe had indeed hit her precisely as he had intended them to, and had furthermore made her so irritated that she had allowed that creeping Jody to take advantage of her. It was a most delightful twist and he thoroughly enjoyed it.

'Be quiet!' she said, staring at him with her eyes narrowed a little. 'Be quiet, do you hear me?'

He shook his head. 'My dear one, how can I help but laugh? You choose to be jealous of that silly little girl, so much that you let that even stupider boy mulct you of fifteen pounds by cheating at cards, and you expect me to keep my face straight? It is too much, it really is too much!' and again he threw back his head and laughed loudly.

She moved with a calm determination that made it seem as though her actions were slow and considered when in fact they were very swift indeed, picking up the chocolate pot that still sat half-filled on the tray beside her and throwing it, hardly seeming to take aim, but with a most true eye, for it hit him glancingly on the side of the head, sending a warm brown flood down his cheek and neck and on to his chest, and making his head whip to one side.

There was a short silence while she sat there with her arms folded and stared at him with her eyebrows raised. He glared back, his jaw hard beneath the chocolate stain and the rest of his face white with fury. And then, slowly, she began to giggle, letting it grow until it became a peal of laughter, and threw herself back on her pillows with her arms above her head in a perfect paroxysm of joy.

'Oh, if you could but see yourself!' she crowed, and tears ran down her cheeks as she laughed even harder. 'Just *see* yourself!'

He was across the room in a flash of bare legs, both hands held out in front of him, his fingers clawed. 'You hell bitch! You stinking, lousy cow, you. . . .'

His hands slithered a little on her silk clad shoulders, and he clawed them even more, strongly twisting the fabric round his fingers and tugging until the delicate stuff tore and he was pulling it away in great strips. She writhed and shrieked, reaching up for his face with her own hands twisted in a perfect imitation of his, but her nails were clogged with the chocolate that still adhered to him and anyway he twisted his head away from her reach, so she tugged at his robe instead. But it was made of firmer stuff and would not tear, so she seized the sleeve and held on until he pulled his arm from it in his struggle to get free – all of which brought him even nearer to her head, so that she could turn and set her teeth into his shoulder, which she did, very hard indeed.

Her maid, when she came running, for the crash of the pot and then of the tray as well as the roar of their voices had reached clear down to the kitchens, stood irresolutely in the doorway for a moment and then, her face flaming red, firmly pulled it closed again. She'd been with Mrs. Mohun many years, she told the housemaids and cook, waiting agog at the foot of the stairs to see who had been murdered, but never in all her born days had she ever seen such a scene as that exposed to her eyes this morning. And a sizeable increase in her money there would have to be if she was to stay in a household where such happenings were likely to occur, she added self-righteously.

Then giggled and, dropping her voice to a whisper, for the younger housemaids must certainly not be allowed to hear, told Cook with great relish and some embellishment every detail she had registered in that one horrified glance at the entwined couple on the tumbled bed.

The entwined couple themselves had stopped shouting, and after a while Cook and the maid exchanged glances, sent the housemaids sulking back below stairs, and themselves crept back to listen outside the door, their mouths half open and their eyes glazed as they tried to interpret the sounds they heard. But there was a silence from the other side of the white door, and they were disappointed; until they were rewarded by the sound of Dickon saying something indistinguishable, and she responding with one of those husky laughs that had made her so popular with so many theatregoers, even in straitlaced Edinburgh, and promised to do the same in London.

Lydia heard the faint rustle from the other side of the door, pushed her head more comfortably into the curve of Dickon's neck and grimaced. 'That'll cost me hard cash,' she said. 'I think she came in, you know?'

'More than it cost you last night to be so sisterly?' he said languorously and turned his head so that he could nuzzle her cheek.

'If you start that again, I shall hurt you in good earnest,' she said and giggled. 'Did I hurt you?'

'Yes. Abominably. But for you I suffer anything.'

'Except brothers.'

'And nieces. If you promise me to stop letting both of them occupy you so much, I promise never again to make you jealous. . . .'

She lifted her head at that, but he pushed it down again with one hand. 'I was not jealous! I to be jealous of a child like that? And my own kin, to boot? Not at all, and if you dare say such a thing again I shall send the chocolate away to be boiled hot as hell before I throw it. I was concerned for her, for she is but an inexperienced child and could be most hurt by you. She would fall head over ears in love with you and—'

'As you have?' he said softly.

'Not a bit! I scorn falling in love! It is mawkish and tiresome and very exhausting and furthermore shocking for the complexion. It keeps one awake at night. No, I do not fall in love, Dickon O'Hare. I do not deny I enjoy a little of the pleasures of love—'

'Enjoy! A little! Wretched woman, you near ate me alive, you know that?'

'You did not complain before! Shall I be less – vigorous in future? More melting and—'

'Heaven forbid,' he said fervently, and kissed her. 'Well, hellcat? Will we make a bargain? You stop making such pets of these two and *I* will treat your niece like a piece of Dresden china.'

'I wonder why you care so much?' she said lazily and stretched a little. 'Are you afraid the company will start to treat you less respectful and them more?'

'Not at all!' he said sharply, and rolled over, reaching for his robe which had fallen to the floor beside the bed. 'I certainly have no fears in that direction. But I do not wish ever to seem like one of a train of courtiers. If you and I are to be a team with this production – and any other thereafter – then I play lead. It has been many years since I had to fight for centre stage and I am not about to start again now, off stage or on it. Me, I am a performer of the first importance, and I will not allow anyone to steal my thunder!'

'Indeed you are a considerable performer,' she said softly and reached up to twist her arms about his neck and kiss him, wriggling her nakedness even closer to him, and they clung tightly together for a moment. 'Very well, wretch. You will not flirt with Phoebe, and I will turn Master Jody away. He is threatening to be a bore anyway – a young man of such greed, you cannot imagine! But Phoebe is different. You must allow me to keep her beside me, for I am most taken with the child. No thunder-stealing, I promise you, Dickon my dearest, but allow me to be kind to the child. I—' she lay very still for a moment, staring up at him with her brow faintly creased. 'It will sound foolish perhaps, but her mother – my sister, you know – we were not precisely close as children, but she was a good soul and treated me as well as a sister could in such a house. Better than my bitch of a mother ever did, and so I tell you. She died young, and I would like to enjoy the company of her daughter. And. . . .'

She grinned then, a jaunty sort of grin, but there was real emotion behind it.

'Besides, were I to have had a child, she might well be of

almost such an age as Phoebe. You must allow me to enjoy the game of mothering the girl, if it pleases me.'

She would never let him or anyone know how much she had grieved for the one child she had borne to the dull Simon Mohun, the year she had married him. But grieve she had, and still did, in her own way, always remembering the dead infant's birthdate, often comparing girls she met with her image of what her own daughter might have been like. And Phoebe, although three years older than her cousin would have been had she lived, fitted that dream image more than Lydia would ever have thought possible.

'Well, as long as the brother is turned away I do not mind the niece,' he said and got out of bed, his robe in his hand, stretching in such a way that she could admire his body, knowing himself to look lissom and muscular and very masculine indeed. Dickon had always prided himself on every aspect of his physique.

She smiled up at him, duly admiring, and then they both laughed; their understanding of each other, the lack of any need for any pretence of noble sentiments was as strong a bond as the physical satisfactions they shared.

'So be it,' she said. 'And now leave me to take my bath and bribe that wretched maid to keep her mouth shut, for I want no boring gossip to leave this house. We shall go to the Exhibition this afternoon, I think. There are opportunities available for visits to be made before it is officially opened, I believe. And we have no rehearsal today. I would like to see it before the mobs get there, you know.'

He stood there for another moment looking down at her, and then, very deliberately, shook his head. He had re-established their relationship and his own domination in the way he best understood; now he would reinforce it. She would know he was master out of bed as well as in it; she gained too much satisfaction from him, he told himself with considerable self-confidence, to risk losing him.

'No, I do not think so,' he said lazily, and shrugged on the robe and turned to go. 'I do not care for Exhibitions particularly. We shall consider what to do later. When I have dressed,' and he blew her a kiss, and went, leaving her sitting up in bed staring after him with her forehead creased and her jaw set in a firm line that Dickon should have seen and recognized for the warning it was.

But he did not, going away whistling cheerfully to his own room on the floor above. He had won this round, and would win any future ones, he told himself. And furthermore if he chose to might *still* enjoy a little dalliance with young Phoebe, who was, he had discovered, quite an amusing little creature, after all.

# CHAPTER FOURTEEN

SHE decided what to do as she stepped out of her bath into the hot towel her maid stood holding for her. She had lain there in the scented water considering hard, and vacillating between memories of the sensuous pleasures of the morning and thoughts of how much she would dislike to be deprived of such experiences in the future, and irritation at the arrogant manner in which he had blown that kiss at her and gone swinging away.

How dare he try to bully her in such a fashion, she who provided him with a home here in her very elegant and comfortable house, who paid so many of his bills and generally allowed him to make such use of her? She did not have to tolerate such treatment from any man; she had long ago discovered – indeed even before her marriage to the tedious Simon Mohun – that she was a woman of considerable attraction who could gain the attention of any man she desired. She of all women did not have to bow before such cavalier treatment from a Richard O'Hare!

And then she remembered again the way that very Richard O'Hare could make her feel, how his legs had twined themselves about hers, how his hands had moved across her body, and she shivered a little and sat up in her bath and soaped herself vigorously. Damn it all, but life was getting a deal more complicated than she liked! She had plenty of energy for her work, which she took very seriously, but disliked above all things to waste herself on the silly petty intrigues involved with the affections in which so many other – and lesser – women engaged. She really must find some way to entertain herself without this man, and show him how little she cared one way or the other.

Which was when the idea came to her, and she dressed herself swiftly, choosing clothes that were elegant and charming without being too blatantly so. For her plans, she needed to look the sort of woman any man would be proud to be seen with, but who could not ever be likely to attract the faintest hint of approbrium.

But before leaving her bedroom, she sat down at her little French gilt escritoire and scribbled a note in her careless sweeping hand-writing, folding it and sealing it with a faint smile curling her lips before giving it to her maid with instructions to hand it to Mr. O'Hare '—half an hour after I have gone. No sooner, no later, you understand!' And then went, running downstairs as lithe as a girl of half her age.

She chose to travel in a hack, leaving her phaeton safe in its mews, much to the tiger's disgust, and sent her maid to call one from the surrounding streets while she stood there on the top step of her house drawing on her gloves and looking about her.

The Square looked particularly delightful this spring morning, she told herself, and tilted her chin to squint up at the blue sky and the swooping birds that always seemed to be more thick in this corner of London than any other, perhaps because of the many eating-houses and food-shops that clustered thereabouts. A lovely day indeed, and her heart lifted. She was in the best of health, her new theatre project promised to be highly successful when it opened at the end of the month, and she had her man at her fingers' ends. So much so, she told herself as she went tripping down the steps when the cab arrived, that I am going to cock a snook at him and leave him feeling very sorry indeed for himself!

When she arrived at the Supper Rooms she was somewhat put out to discover that they were open for business. She had assumed, from the name of the establishment, that it was only available to customers at night-time, and she stood for a moment in the doorway blinking at the sight that greeted her. Every table was occupied, each with three or four customers, and every one of them was a man. Various heads turned as she hesitated there at the side of the looped-back velvet curtain, and the hubbub of voices that had filled the big room faltered, and was then resumed louder than ever.

She bit her lip and for the first time in many years found herself unsure of what to do. She had come here expecting to find it quiet, with only the proprietor and his staff about; now she felt herself filled with discomfiture, and after a moment she turned to go. Even she, with all her aplomb, could hardly take herself through this crowd of staring men in what was obviously regarded as a totally masculine luncheon place.

But even as she put out her hand towards the street door it opened again and a tall man came in to stand in the little entrance, silhouetted against the bright light of the street. At the sight of her standing there he took off his tall hat and bowed slightly, and a trifle redfaced she stepped aside, intending to leave as soon as he made room for her in the doorway.

'Mrs. Mohun!' the man said with a note of surprise in his well-bred voice. 'I did not expect to see you here today. Not, of course, that I expected to see you at all, you understand, but here – at luncheon—' There was a faintly scandalized sound in his voice now and she peered up at him as he moved farther forward into the room. Then her face cleared.

'Oh, Mr. Henriques! How very glad I am to see you! I have never been so mortified in my life! I had no idea that this was so popular a place with gentlemen at this time of day.'

She looked back over her shoulder and reddened a little more for several of the customers were still staring at her, some with an appraising look in their eyes which she found most disagreeable.

'Indeed, mortified is the only word! There are some there staring at me as though I were – well, breeding forbids me to say! I came but to see my brother-in-law, you see. I did not for one moment wish to behave with any impropriety.'

'My dear lady, how very unfortunate. I must tell Jonah that he should change the name of his rooms. You are quite right, of course, but habitués know, you see, and to be honest Jonah has few but his habitués using his establishment at this time of day. Please, allow me to escort you, if that will relieve you of embarrassment.'

'It would indeed,' she said gratefully, and slipped her hand into his elbow and turned to face the room with her head high and a very direct gaze and had the satisfaction of seeing several of the most arrant starers drop their own gaze and turn their heads away.

'Jonah has a table that is his own, and at which various of his friends take their luncheon. I came myself today since there is a matter I must discuss with him—' He stopped and she looked up at him curiously, for he seemed a little discomfited himself suddenly. 'But it is no matter,' he went on after a moment. 'I can talk to him some other time. . . .'

'You must not allow yourself to be one whit put out by my presence, Mr. Henriques,' she said quickly, as he stepped aside to allow her to make her way in front of him past the crowded tables towards the one he had indicated in the far corner under the lee of the little stage, now shrouded in its curtains. 'You have saved me considerable embarrassment, and I am grateful to you. But if there are matters for you to discuss without my presence, why then, I shall go away immediately.'

He shook his head, and moving with considerable grace, stepped in front of her and drew a chair forward so that she could sit at the table. 'You have matters of your own to discuss with Jonah, no doubt. Why else should you be here? It is, I think, I who must step aside to allow you the opportunity. . . .'

He sat down opposite her, setting his top hat on the floor beneath his chair, and she smiled at him with real pleasure, for he looked very neat and dapper sitting there and she was genuinely grateful to him.

'Well, let us call a truce, and agree that neither of us will speak of matters of business!' she said gaily. 'Although that is hardly fair of me, since my business matter is nothing of the sort. However. . . .'

There was a movement behind her and she turned her head to see Jonah pushing towards them through crowds of customers, and at once she smiled brilliantly and held out her hand.

'My dear brother-in-law!' she said, using all the skills of the theatre to project her voice as far as possible, and was gratified to see heads nod and people turn to each other as the news of the interloping female's identity sped from table to table. *Now* they would know she was a respectable lady, and no Covent Garden tail.

'My dear brother-in-law,' she repeated. '—I had no idea you were so completely the restaurateur that you provided midday repasts as well. Mr. Henriques here saved my blushes, not to say my reputation, I do assure you, when he arrived to find me thrown in the midst of all these important-looking gentlemen!'

'Oh— Lydia!' Jonah said and stared at her, a little nonplussed. 'Yes. Well, how very agreeable – I am delighted – you will take a little wine, perhaps. Why did you come? I mean – forgive me....'

'Oh dear, I have embarrassed you, now!' she said with a wide disarming smile. 'Please to forgive me! And indeed, I would like to take a little wine with you, and I am sure, Mr. Henriques, but you must sit here with us, for otherwise I will know I have caused you more distress than I could bear to consider!'

'Yes. By all means,' he said, still in that rather disjointed and awkward fashion, and turned his head to look for one of his waiters who nodded and went hurrying away. 'Yes, well, agreeable to see you, indeed. Most agreeable. I – er – trust you enjoyed the performance that Phoebe offered at her party when last we met....'

He looked at her with a mixture of eagerness and shyness on his face that she suddenly found quite touching. She put out her hand and patted his and said quietly, 'I was quite, quite enchanted! She is a delicious child, Jonah, and must give you such pride and pleasure. To have reared so lovely a daughter – that is a felicitation denied to many. I do congratulate you.'

It was almost pathetic to see the way his shoulders straightened and his composure returned at her words, and he leaned back in his chair and said, 'Why, as to that, I must say I too find my Phoebe the most delightful company. It is all too rare that I am able to indulge myself, however, for the pressures of work, you know – this is not precisely in the first stare of fashion, this establishment, but I do my best to run it well and to make it a place Phoebe and Oliver – you have not met him, but he is a good boy too, such a good boy, and so hard-working – a place they will find agreeable, you know. It – I could not be comfortable if they were to find it a source of – of shame and – well, to run it so, I must be here a great deal. If there is any virtue in Phoebe it is to my sister and good brother-in-law here that you must look, for they have had the care and rearing of her these many years now. . . .'

'Not at all,' Gideon said swiftly. 'She is very much her father's daughter, Mrs. Mohun, and it is our privilege that she be permitted to live with us.'

He stopped and looked at her very directly then and after a moment went on with a certain emphasis in his voice, 'She is a much loved young lady, you know, Mrs. Mohun. There are so many of us who are concerned with her welfare, and her future good fortune.'

'And you must add me to the number,' she said heartily. 'For I am quite entirely delighted to discover, so unexpectedly, that I am blessed with so charming a young connection. Ah, your wine, Jonah—' and she leaned back in her chair so that the waiter could set glasses before them, and fill them with champagne. 'How delightful to find you so modern in your tastes, Jonah! Too often one is given Madeira and sack to the exclusion of all else and very heavy I find them both in the middle of the day. This, on the other hand, is so refreshing! *Santé.*' And she drank delicately but with relish, then leaned back again in her chair to smile at the two men.

They both sat and looked back at her in silence, Jonah somewhat reassured by her declaration of affection for Phoebe but still at a very deep level suspicious and fearful, for was not this Lilith's daughter, and did not Lilith spread trouble wherever she was? It still seemed inconceivable to him that as beautiful and clever a woman as this should want nothing of him or his; however hard he tried he could not completely still his anxieties.

And Gideon too was prey to anxiety, but of a different sort. The more he saw of Mrs. Mohun the more sure he was that she meant no harm to anyone. A woman of such wit and beauty and gifts, he told himself shrewdly, had no call to be anything but good-natured; it was only the ill-favoured who needed to use unpleasant tactics to make their way in the world. But having decided that she was not a bad woman in any way, how could he put to Jonah, as he had promised Freddy he would, the possibility that her influence on her niece was to be deplored? It had been a long time since he had found himself in so delicate a situation, and he sighed softly and drank some of his wine.

She laughed, a low gurgling laugh that was very characteristic of her, Gideon was beginning to realize, and very charming.

'My, but you both look very solemn! On so lovely a spring day, too. Really, I cannot bear to see it! You must, positively *must* put your worries to rout and seek some pleasure! In fact, dear Jonah, that is why I am here today. I looked at the sky and the sun, bethought myself of the opportunity being offered to visit the Exhibition in the park before it officially commences and said to myself, "to the Exhibition I shall go!" But no lady could enjoy such a jaunt unaccompanied, and lacking a companion, I told myself there would be nothing wrong in seeking the protection and guidance of one of my family! Will you, in short, Jonah, undertake to guide me to the park this afternoon on a voyage of discovery?'

'I? Oh, dear me, no! What a notion!' Jonah said, looking aghast, and at once looked acutely embarrassed. 'Oh dear! I did not mean to sound so ill-mannered, but you took me so by surprise! No, of course Lydia, I would be happy – if it were possible – not that I am at all concerned with the Exhibition, you understand – I mean if it is your wish – however, the Rooms, you see – we are still very busy—' He threw out one hand to indicate how busy, and she pouted and peeped up at him from under her bonnet brim.

'Oh, Jonah, surely you have some assistant who can take charge for you in your absence? In my experience assistants are always delighted to have the opportunity to undertake a little responsibility, and it is good for them to discover how much they need the guidance of their master, for they miss him sorely in his absence! Come, do let me coax you—'

'Oh, indeed, if it were possible – no, really, no assistant –

none that is, who would be able – not at all–' Jonah was floundering miserably and Gideon, after a moment's hesitation, took pity on him.

'I will gladly escort you, Mrs. Mohun, if you wish,' he said and sketched another of those slightly old-fashioned bows he affected. 'I believe it is a spectacle well worth inspecting and one that will give me much pleasure to display to you. Jonah's loss will be my gain – if he will permit me?'

'Oh, yes, indeed, Gideon, most grateful, I mean. I am sure Lydia – you will enjoy – yes, a most interesting spectacle. . . .'

'Why, Jonah, you are so glad to be rid of me that it shows in every word you say!' Lydia said and leaned forward to take his hand in hers, much to his embarrassment. 'But I quite understand the necessity to stay here with your work, and acquit you of any ill manners! But one day, I hope, I shall be able to prevail upon you to show me some aspect of the London scene that I am not acquainted with because of my long absence in remote parts.'

'By all means, by all means,' Jonah said and stood up. 'Please will you forgive me, Gideon, Lydia? I – there are matters to deal with – I shall send you some food, if you will allow – there is a fricassée of chicken today that is excellent – you will enjoy it, I am sure – excuse me–' and he was gone, moving quickly through the crowded room; it was not until he reached the kitchens and was instructing the waiter on the order for his official table that he felt safe again.

Clearly his alarm about Lydia was fully justified after all, he told himself, fanning the embers of anxiety that always lay deep within him. She *was* trying to obtain something from him! She must be! Why else should such a woman seek him out in this blatant manner (and his disapproval of her slightly raffish ways added its own fuel to his private furnace) if not for gain? But what gain? He could not imagine she wanted only his company, for he was not a man ladies normally sought out in such a manner. And anyway, he told himself fretfully, such a liaison would be most improper. Most improper! She is my dead wife's sister, and any contact between us two must remain always on the level of mere family ties. However bohemian a lady she may be, she cannot, surely she cannot be so careless of the proprieties?

But he failed to convince himself that Lydia was anything but the trouble he had feared she would be, and he returned to the counting of bottles and the listing of dishes as they left the kitchens in a wretchedly unhappy state of mind.

The lady who was causing him his distress was, however, extremely happy sitting opposite Gideon and eating fricassée of chicken with a healthy appetite. She was now beginning to bask in the covert stares of the other people about them; even though her face was not yet as well known as it had been in Edinburgh, and eventually would be here in London once her play opened, she knew these people had recognized her for a person of some importance and far from being a woman to be despised as they had first thought her. So she performed a little for their benefit, laughing with that much more of a gurgle, talking with that much more vivacity, turning her head to show her handsome profile that much more deliberately.

Gideon, watching and listening while eating very little, was fascinated. He had never been a man to engage in any sort of dalliance, even the most innocent drawing-room sort, finding small talk boring and the company of his Abby more than enough for him. Many were the ladies who, over the years, had ogled him from behind their fans, or tried to engage his interest with their scintillating talk. But not until now had any succeeded; and in a little separate part of his mind he was amused by himself, for he knew perfectly well that the display of feminine charm to which he was being treated by his companion was far from meant for him alone. He too was aware of the starers and murmurers. How absurd, his separate little self whispered to him, how absurd to be captivated by a woman who is so busy captivating a roomful of total strangers!

'Is it not the most amusing of coincidences?' she was saying, sitting leaning well back in her chair and twirling the stem of her wine-glass between her fingers. 'We met here for the first time, and now we have met again in the self-same spot! You must never breathe a hint of the suggestion to Jonah, who would have a fit, I am sure, at so improper a thought, for he is so *very* proper, is he not? – but I suspect that really his Rooms are a house of assignation. We were both drawn here today, against our wills, almost, for it was meant by the fates that this *coincidence* should occur!'

This was too much even for the amused looking-on part of Gideon and he said repressively, 'Not at all! I am sure you mean only to make a joke, but I must ask you never to say such a thing to anyone. It would take very little to earn any London establishment the wrong sort of label, for this town is, as I suppose are most towns, a perfect hotbed of gossip. And I would be very distressed to see Jonah's enterprise here threatened in any way. As would his children—'

'Oh, forgive me!' she said at once, all contrite. 'You are quite right of course! I was only joking, as sophisticated people do joke with each other. I would never dream of making any comment about Jonah or his Rooms to stupid people who might misconstrue my meaning. You must acquit me of any malice, you know! Jonah is my brother, is he not, and his children my own relations? I am as jealous of their wellbeing as any person could be.'

He was silent for a moment, feeling himself pulled in two directions. This would be the perfect moment to speak to her of Phoebe and the suggestion that she appear in her aunt's play. The opportunity had presented itself so pat that it would, surely, be a positive dereliction of his duty not to speak of the matter.

But, he had arranged with Abby and Freddy that the matter would be dealt with by a concerted attack; he would speak to Jonah, his wife to Lydia. If he stepped into Abby's place, as it were, could it not have the wrong effect? It clearly might; two women speaking to each other on so delicate a matter must surely be able to deal more directly and effectively, just as two men would understand each other best.

No, he could not speak to his companion of the matter he most wished to discuss with her; but he could, he thought, brightening a little, he undoubtedly could arrange matters so that *Abby* might do so. A little plan formed in his mind, and he leaned forwards, and said, 'May I send for some more food for you, Mrs. Mohun? If not, I think perhaps we should make our way now to Hyde Park, for I believe the demand for unofficial entry to the Exhibition is great, and increases in the afternoons – and perhaps you will honour us by returning with me to Stanhope Terrace afterwards to take a little refreshment? My wife will be at home, for our infant daughter woke this morning with the earache, and demanded her Mamma's company most vociferously! But I know she will be happy to receive you.'

'How kind!' she said at once and stood up. 'I have eaten more than I require, indeed, and need no further refreshment than a little air and agreeable company. You are indeed most charming to offer it. Of course I will enjoy greatly a little feminine gossip with your wife afterwards – and with my niece. I am quite enchanted by her, you know! Such spirit, such understanding, and *so* pretty. . . .'

She chattered her way gaily through the Rooms, loftily ignoring every other person there but totally aware of every glance in her direction; chattered all the time Gideon stood on the kerb seeking for a hack, chattered as he handed her into it and then all the way to the park. And Gideon, for all the wry amusement his secret mind felt at her display, found her more and more delightful company with every word she spoke.

By the time O'Hare arrived at the Rooms he was in a towering rage. How *dare* she, after all that had happened between them that morning, how dare the wretched woman behave so to him? To send him so airy a note, with the scribbled injunction to 'amuse himself as best he might, for she was going to visit the Exhibition with her dear brother-in-law' had been offensive enough; to add as a post scriptum that he could 'usefully occupy his time getting his lines more carefully learned, since he had been far from word perfect at yesterday's rehearsals', had been a downright insult. So he swung himself in through the glass doors and past the velvet portière with great energy, so much so that Jonah, who was standing halfway down the Rooms talking to a table full of regular customers, almost

.cringed at the sight of him. But he behaved as a careful proprietor must, and moved swiftly to the door to speak to him.

'Mr. O'Hare? I am happy that we meet again,' he said,
trying to look as though he meant it. 'Will you take some
luncheon? Or a little wine, perhaps?'

'No thank you,' O'Hare said, and his voice was loud and
harsh. 'I seek only to speak to my – to your sister-in-law,' and
he glared at Jonah with great ferocity, and Jonah felt the tide
of anxiety which had quietened once Lydia had gone begin to
rise again.

'My – yes, my sister-in-law,' he said and looked round a little
vaguely, as though he genuinely expected to see her behind
him. 'Yes, of course – I quite see that – not here, of course. No,
not here. This is a gentlemen's luncheon place, you understand,
and the ladies do not normally – and of course, as soon as she
realized – she had a little chicken, but no more, and then of
course, she went away.'

He looked back at O'Hare who was staring at him with an
expression of such scorn on his face that Jonah felt himself
redden and a twinge of anger sent the anxiety back into the
deeper pool of his mind.

'You will, I trust, forgive me, Mr. O'Hare, but as a busy
man, with work to do, I am unable to entertain my – my *family*
and their friends with the degree of – of freedom I should like.
My sister-in-law, as I say, has gone away. She realized her
mistake at once in coming at this time of the day. If you wish to
partake of luncheon, my Rooms are yours—' and he stood back
a little as though he were about to lead the way to a table, –
'but if not, well then please to acquit me of any casualness of
manner, but must beg you to excuse me so that I can go about
my business.'

And he stared at O'Hare with his chin up and his colour a
little heightened. Dammit all, he told himself, this man is no
more than a wretched actor, one of those self-important,
puffed-up creatures I hire every day of my life, and turn off to
boot, and I will not have such a one trying to intimidate me!
Not in my own establishment!

But O'Hare seemed unimpressed by this stance of superiority, and was staring about the room with his brows twisted into a frown, trying to see who was there. It was obvious to the most cursory glance that there were no women present at all, not even among the servants, for the afternoon had progressed to the stage where customers were drifting away, the remainder requiring the services of just a couple of waiters to deal with the residue of the work.

'Gone away?' he said after a moment, turning back to stare at Jonah. 'Gone where, man, for God's sake?'

Jonah's lips hardened. 'Your tone, Mr. O'Hare, is not one I find agreeable,' he said sharply. 'If I can be of assistance to any *gentleman* that seeks my aid, as a gentleman, I am happy to offer it, but—'

'Oh, I am sorry!' O'Hare said in a moment. Damned turkey-cock! he thought savagely. Coming the heavy with me, and he no more than a damned publican, when you get down to it. But still Lydia's brother-in-law, and angry as he was with her he had still enough good sense left alive under his rage to prevent him from making an irredeemable enemy of a man she valued.

'You must forgive me,' he went on, 'but I am anxious on her behalf, you see. She is, you must recall, not accustomed to London ways, for all she was born in the metropolis, and I seek always to protect her, for she is very impulsive, you know, and could in all innocence step into a situation she would find disagreeable, not to say – well, I am sure you understand; and when I heard she had come here to see you – and I of course knew this to be unsuitable for her at this time of the day—' He was improvising wildly now and clearly with some success, for Jonah was visibly relaxing as he stared at him. '—I feared for her, for innocent creature that she is, she could find herself so put about and with no one to take care of her. . . .' He shrugged, and raised his eyebrows at Jonah in an invitation to establish a masculine *rapport* between them. 'Well, I am sure you will understand my concern for a lady I hold very dearly!'

And if she could see *that* picture of herself as an innocent, not to say stupid, female abroad in the dangerous big city, she'd be highly mortified, he told himself gleefully, and stared mournfully at Jonah, waiting for his answer.

Jonah gave it at once, totally accepting O'Hare's description of his sister-in-law as a vulnerable wide-eyed provincial, finding it balm to his anxious soul. Innocent provincials could never be the threat his own observation had warned him the lady might be.

'You need not be anxious for a moment,' he said cordially. 'For she is quite, quite safe, I do promise you. It was the most absurd coincidence – absurd! You will recall when you came here last – my brother-in-law Henriques, he was here with me? Well, he chose to come to take his luncheon here today, and arrived with Mrs. Mohun, which was of course, very good fortune, for I was at the time in the kitchens, and did not see her – well, as I say, he was here, and after they ate a little luncheon, he took her to the park for the Exhibition, for she was quite set upon making such an expedition, and I could not take her, as she had hoped, being so occupied here—'

'Henriques?' O'Hare said quickly. 'The man whose house we—'

'Yes, indeed. Gideon, my brother-in-law. He and my sister, you know, live at Stanhope Terrace where my daughter resides with them. You may remember she performed some tableaux—' Jonah was very comfortable now, even enjoying the conversation. 'As an actor yourself, I am sure you were interested! For my part, as a man who spends much time devising and directing small theatrical entertainments for my own stage here, I found them very well thought out, very well thought out indeed—'

'Oh, excellent, quite excellent,' O'Hare said, almost absently. He had forgotten, or rather, not really thought about the fact that this man was Phoebe's father. He had regarded her always as Lydia's niece, just as he had regarded this man as Lydia's brother-in-law. It was as though people only existed in relation to her. Damn the woman, he thought savagely then. Damn her, damn her! To be so altogether *necessary* to so many people – including him. He who had always escaped the snares women threw down for him, who had always prided himself on his ability to take what he wanted and give little or nothing in return, to be so *bouleversé* as to care about these boring people. . . .

But he hid his underlying emotions with all his actor's skill, and smiled at Jonah affably, replacing his hat upon his head and turning back towards the door. 'Then, if I wish to find the lady, clearly it is in the western parts of town I must seek her. I will make my way to the park and relieve your good brother-in-law of the burden of his charge. I have no doubt that he, like you, has work that must be done on this busy day. Good day to you, Mr. Lackland! Glad to have seen you again!'

And he was gone, leaving Jonah breathing easily again and able to go contentedly to his own late repast. He had handled the matter well, he told himself optimistically. First persuading Gideon to take Lydia and her demands from me, and secondly sending someone to take her from Gideon! For a moment he really felt he had achieved the whole plan from his own head and felt very pleased indeed with himself.

Outside on the pavement of King Street, where the detritus of the morning's market still littered the gutters and the sellers and buyers and porters of fruit and vegetables stood about enjoying the afternoon sunshine before setting out on the long journeys back to their fields and shops and backstreet homes, O'Hare stood thinking, his hat on the back of his head and his face grim. And then slowly he began to smile to himself, and turned and went swinging along to the Strand to hail a cab.

'Stanhope Terrace,' he told the driver, and settled back into the dusty leathery interior with a sigh of satisfaction. Lydia might be prancing about in the park staring at dismal Exhibitions, he told himself, but for his part, he was going to go visiting other charming ladies.

# CHAPTER FIFTEEN

ABBY was sitting beside the nursery fire with Sarah asleep on her lap while Ellie took Isabel for a walk. The fire had burned low, but was still throwing out ample heat, and the sun was slanting agreeably across the dark blue carpet, illuminating the handsome mahogany furniture and the big rocking-horse and Isabel's pride and joy, the tall dolls' house.

Abby felt relaxed, and warm and comfortable and, even though the cause was Sarah's illness, happy to have time to sit here in the nursery of which she was really quite proud. Not for her children the shabby outworn furnishings banished from the rest of the house but thought 'good enough for the children'; not for her the uncomfortably bumpy horsehair sofas and broken chairs and torn carpets that had been very much a feature of her own nursery days. Her Mamma, she remembered sleepily now, had been a careful housewife – too careful to permit her children any hint of luxury. But I like *my* children to be comfortable.

Sitting there with her head resting against the back of the tall rocker, and with Sarah's heavy downy head buried in her neck, she sighed softly and gave herself over to the sheer joy of being herself. Her good fortune was so very apparent to her at times like this, when she felt the warmth and security and comfort of her house about her. It was not only the house that felt safe – it was all the people who belonged to it. Her dear Gideon, so totally reliable and loving, her daughters, so soft and warm and utterly beautiful, her son, so sensible and hard-working, her niece. . . .

She stopped in her thoughts then, contemplating Phoebe, and felt that twinge of anxiety that was so often the effect of such thinking. It was not simply because she had rejected

Freddy's proposal, she told herself, that I am anxious about her. And, admit it, a little angry. There is more to it than that. She is so very captious, swinging from the heights of joy at one moment to the gloomiest of depths at the next, when she declares the world to be a hateful, horrid place, and one she would gladly quit. That habit of mind had been understandable, if a little worrying, when she was a small child; but now she is almost a woman grown, and should have more control over her emotions and her thinking.

Abby closed her eyes for a moment, trying to shut away the real source of her anxiety, but it would not go, and so she let the picture arise in her mind: the picture of Phoebe's mother Celia, with her white face, and the heavy grey eyes looking out at her world with so suspicious and yet withdrawn an expression in them; the vision of her lying there, floating in the Long Water. . . .

Abby snapped her eyes open, and began, very gently, to rock in her chair. The baby snuffled and moved her damp head against her mother's neck and slid deeper into sleep. I never saw her, Abby told herself. I never *saw* her afterwards. I was simply told how it happened. Why is it that now, whenever I think of Celia, I see her lying dead in the water? And why is it when I think of Phoebe, I am always so frightened? Is it reasonable to be so alarmed? After all, she is as much her father's daughter as her mother's, as much the result of our careful upbringing as of her infant experience. Her poor mother never had the benefits and the security and love her daughter had – so why assume the daughter's behaviour must in any way reflect the mother's? It is not entirely true that all ills, be they of the mind or of the heart or of the body, are inherited. So why be fearful now? Is it really that you do not wish to consider the possibility of marriage with Freddy? Is it in truth your hunger to hold your son by your side that makes you so dubious about Phoebe?

She sighed again and moved the heavy baby a little, easing her cramped arm. Well, there was no sense in thinking about it now. She had promised Freddy she would do what she could to persuade Lydia to agree that his Phoebe should not be an actress, and she would keep her promise, even if a little bit of her mind, a very secret little bit would almost like to see her enter her family's profession, if it meant she would have to go away and leave Freddy behind in London, working at his books. . . .

Behind her the door opened, and the little between-maid stood there red-faced and awkward, twisting her apron between her swollen water-roughened fingers. 'Please, 'm, Kent and the others is aht for the afternoon an' Ellie ain't 'ere, 'm, and this gennelman 'as come an' says as 'e wants to talk to yer, 'm, but 'e says as 'ow—'

'He says as how he won't go away.' The little maid looked over her shoulder, quite terrified but also very captivated by the handsomeness of the man who had spoken, and now gently but firmly pushed her to one side to come into the room. 'Please, Mrs. Henriques, don't move! You look so very charming sitting there, that it must give any man pleasure to be privileged to see you, and besides I would not have you disturb yourself for the world, when I have been so ill-mannered as to overcome the scruples of your servant.' And he looked at the little between-maid and then cocked an amused eyebrow at Abby.

For a moment Abby was torn between irritation at being so unceremoniously disturbed when she had told her staff quite clearly that she was not at home to callers and gratification at the way this very handsome man looked at her with such approval. The irritation almost won, and she opened her mouth to express some of it, but caught the gawping stare of the little maid, almost hidden behind her visitor, and said instead, 'That is all right, Jane. You may go and tell Cook to prepare tea for the drawing-room as soon as Ellie returns.'

The little maid blinked, closed her mouth and nodded, all at once, and went regretfully away, leaving the man standing there just inside the door and looking down at Abby with a faint smile on his face, a smile which wrinkled the skin round his startlingly blue eyes in a very attractive manner. So attractive, that Abby felt her irritation melt away altogether, and she smiled at him over Sarah's sleeping head – for she had not stirred throughout the disturbance – and said softly, 'Well, Mr.

O'Hare, I am sure you had your reason for so determined an assault upon my afternoon's peace! Please to take a chair and settle yourself. You will forgive me if I do not make any shift to play the complete hostess, but as you see, my baby has greater need of my ministrations than even the most welcome of guests. She has the earache, you know, and although she is much better, she needs to sleep a little longer yet. So, your pardon.'

'Please, it is my privilege to see you looking so madonna-like and lovely,' O'Hare said smoothly, and shrugged off his coat and sat down in a chair which he hooked towards the fire with one easy movement. 'And I cannot pretend that my affairs are so urgent that they warrant this intrusion. But to tell the truth, I was so amused by your little maid, who just gulped and muttered at me, that I could not forbear to follow her and try my luck. I could not know, of course that you would be settled so domestically by your nursery fire.'

'You must not mock Jane, Mr. O'Hare,' Abby said a little reprovingly. 'She lacks the advantages that make a better address possible for other servants.'

'I am all contrition. You are right, of course. It is not kind in me to be sharp with so pathetic a creature. Am I forgiven?'

'Of course. I trust you are well, and enjoying your stay in London?'

He stretched his legs towards the fire and settled himself more comfortably in the chair. 'Oh, indeed, you must not mistake the case! I am not entirely new to London, you know. I have been appearing in some of our best theatres for the past three years or so. But this is, I cannot deny, my first exceeding big part.'

'Oh dear! I trust I have not offended you by being so ignorant of your reputation. I am sure it is an excellent one, and well known to people who profess to a greater awareness of the doings of the London stage than I am able to do. I have been much occupied in recent years with my family, as well as with my family business, of course.'

He looked at her curiously. 'Business? Come, you cannot tell me you are one of this new breed of women who, like the

Queen herself, follow the complicated dealings of large enterprises?'

'Why not? I am indeed. I was widowed for many years, Mr. O'Hare, and needed to provide for my son and myself. So, it was necessary that I occupy myself gainfully. I have long dealt a great deal with the running of the apothecary business of Caspar's. My husband now of course has the major involvement, but I am not entirely in the background. Although as I say, I have not had much time for such entertainment as theatre-going since—'

He shrugged. 'Please you must not concern yourself with that. It is of no importance. So, you are a business woman! A remarkable situation!'

She reddened slightly, aware of a faintly mocking note in his voice. 'Well, it is not so strange, after all, in your experience, Mr. O'Hare! The ladies with whom you work in the theatre are after all business women as well, are they not? I may deal in herbs and drugs and plasters, while they deal in – well, themselves, I suppose! Their talents certainly, and their lovely appearance.'

He smiled. 'Well, you could say that. I had not quite thought of it so. It is perhaps, because you are a lady of such – tolerant views, that you are able to recognize the value of an actress. I can assure you that there are some people we meet who regard them as very low indeed!'

There was a short silence in which Abby contemplated him thoughtfully over Sarah's head, while he stared into the embers of the fire. It seemed almost to be meant in some providential way that she should discuss the matter of Phoebe's new ambition with this man; who could know better than he whether or not this would be a reasonable occupation for the girl? She herself had little judgement on the matter; she had seen Phoebe's performances often enough – indeed from her earliest baby days when she had acted the Mother Goose stories for them all – but she could not decide if she was more than merely accomplished. And yet the words hesitated on her lips. To quiz him about her niece would surely be in some measure disloyal? And suppose he assured her that Phoebe *was* talented, and had a real career in front of her? What then? Could she in all honour keep her word to Freddy, and plead with Lydia to put an end to the acting idea, knowing that?

He turned his head and caught her glance, and smiled at once, the practised and very beautiful smile of the actor. It chilled her in a curious way, and she closed her lips on her unasked questions and smiled back, albeit in a rather wintry fashion.

'I feel some guilt now in disturbing you,' he said easily. 'I had expected to find Lydia with you, you see, and came to relieve your kind husband of responsibility for her. But I must suppose I am ahead of them, and they will be here in due course. . . .'

Her brows drew in a little and she looked at him in some surprise. 'Lydia? My husband? I do not understand you. I believe my husband to be at the counting-house at Caspar's. He usually is at this time of day.'

He hardly moved, and his face too seemed to remain still, and yet he managed to sketch a picture of a man embarrassed to have spoken thoughtlessly, a man who has all unknowingly revealed a secret fact to one who should not know it, and he did it without for one moment removing that very direct blue gaze from her face.

'Oh?' he said silkily and smiled with ineffable sweetness. 'Perhaps I misunderstood. You brother, Mr. Lackland, you know, happened to let fall to me that they had taken lunch together at his establishment, and then gone to the Exhibition, to avail themselves of the opportunities being offered to those visitors who wish to see the display before the official opening. He did not say that this was not a matter to be bruited abroad, or I would not have said – although of course, I did not tell him I had decided to come here to collect her! We have no re-hearsal today, of course, but there are some costume designs to be discussed and I thought – ah, well! No doubt Lydia will remember. Eventually!'

He lifted his chin a little, still smiling that gentle, even lazy, smile, and she looked back at him very directly and said in a tight little voice, 'I think, Mr. O'Hare, that you mean some malice!'

He was taken aback at that, opening his eyes very widely at

her. 'Malice? Oh, come now, Mrs. Henriques! How can you say so! When I have come merely to—'

'To tell me, in your own actorish fashion, that my husband is involved in some form of dalliance with Mrs. Mohun. Come, Mr. O'Hare, you are not dealing here with one of your slippery backstage friends, who no doubt are accustomed to this sort of unpleasant tittle-tattling and the sort of immoral behaviour you are imputing to my husband, but to a practical woman of business. Yes, indeed, of *business*! And I cannot be doing with such – such gossiping ways as—'

He was tight with anger now, and spoke without attempting to hide the sneer in his voice. 'I am sorry if my *actorish* ways offend you! The same ways clearly do not offend your husband, since he is spending his afternoon squiring about the park one with a much more polished *actorish* manner than mine. And as for saying I impute immorality to your husband – dear me, Mrs. Henriques, you embarrass me, you really do! I said nothing to cause you such a reaction, and I can only suppose, since you leapt to this conclusion, that you have in the past had some cause to do so.'

She did not move, sitting there in her rocker with her arms about her sleeping baby, and she kept her voice very low and controlled; but still it cut across the quiet room like a knife. 'Mr. O'Hare, you will leave this room and this house immediately. I wish to have no further discussion with you on this or any other matter. Good afternoon!'

He sat there undecided for a moment, feeling his anger seep away. He had indeed, been feeling very malicious when he had come to Stanhope Terrace, but he had not for one moment intended to cause such a furore that he would end up being thrown out of the house. ·

Too late he remembered how necessary it was to him not to offend the relations Lydia had just found and now seemed to set such store by, and he opened his mouth to remonstrate with the white-faced angry woman who sat staring at him with an expression of quite implacable dislike on her face. Damn it all, he thought, aggrieved, how was I to know the wretched woman would be so deficient in all the arts of conversation as to go as straight as a dart to the point? Who in his right mind would ever expect any woman with any pretensions to sophistication or intelligence to behave in so mutton-headed a fashion?

He opened his mouth to speak again but she sat there staring at him still, with that same expression of disgust on her face, and although he was almost half as big again as she was, although he was a man full grown and a most successful one to boot, he felt himself quail like any child who has suffered a reprimand, and moving almost sulkily he rose and picked up his hat and coat.

'Well, you seem quite to have misunderstood me,' he said after a moment, hoping yet to retrieve the situation. 'I meant no harm at all, of course, for I would hardly have come here if I had done! I merely sought to find Mrs. Mohun and to thank your husband for his care of her. However, I clearly have distressed you, no doubt by disturbing you when you are anxious about your baby's illness, and can only ask your forgiveness. I shall wait upon your husband at some other time, and seek his pardon also.'

And he bowed a little stiffly and went away, closing the door behind him on that white face still staring at him with a look of sheer loathing on it. And in spite of his apparent insouciance, he felt far from comfortable. Very far from comfortable indeed.

Phoebe heard the footsteps on the stairs and debated with herself whether to come out and see who it was. She had heard the front door knocker, had heard that stupid Jane answer it, and the deep voice of some caller or other, but she had not been in the mood for a drawing-room conversation and had hidden herself at once behind the big window curtains, only to emerge feeling very foolish when, after a long and uncomfortable five minutes, she had realized that the caller, whoever it was, was not seeking her, unusual a case though that was, but someone else, for he had gone past the drawing-room door, and on up to the floor above. The doctor for Sarah, she thought, and flung herself back on to the sofa beside the fire to stare again into the embers, seeking an answer to her miseries.

Yesterday at this time she had been so happy! There had been Aunt Lydia, and the theatre, and the rehearsal and the promise of excitement to come with the play, and of course there had been Dickon O'Hare, though she would not think about him; and then Freddy had spoiled it all.

She had brooded long on that, going over and over it in her mind all morning, from the time she rose late, long after everyone else had gone about their day's affairs, and feeling still rather fuddled with the dose Aunt Abby had made her swallow, all through the lunch of bread and milk Ellie had forced on her (for Ellie still treated her as a child, in need of childhood remedies for all her ills) until now. And still she was confused.

At first she was angry with Freddy with spoiling everything. All those lovely happy playing years seemed to have melted away when he had looked at her with that same silly adoring look that the other men used when they spoke to her. All the funny times they had enjoyed, the way he had laughed at her and mocked at her for her stupid ignorance, the way he had been able to answer all her questions, solve all her problems, intercede for her with Ellie and his mother when necessary, all quite ruined.

But then she had thought again, and decided it was not ruined after all. He must, he surely must, have more sense than the stupid boys who could not take their *congés*. They would sulk and follow her about in the street when she went abroad, had even stood beneath her window staring up at it (for she had seen them and laughed at them from behind her curtains), but surely Freddy could not be so absurd? He would philosophically accept the fact that she did not wish to marry him, and life would go on as it had before, with him always there to talk to and lean on when she needed to talk and lean, and to share jokes with when she was in the mood to do so.

And then she thought about marrying him, after all. Would it be so bad a thing? He loved her dearly, and she loved him, if not precisely in the breathless romantic way her friends expected a girl to love the man she would marry, but very comfortably. To have her own home and Freddy to take care of her could be very agreeable. Not that she had any lack of comfort and pleasure here in Aunt Abby's and Uncle Gideon's house; they loved her well, and she knew it. But there was silly Ellie, who controlled – or attempted to control – her life in a way that was very tiresome. Having her own establishment and her own servants could be great fun, and with no one to say her nay in anything, life could be. . . .

No one to say her nay. That was where the dream shattered, for Freddy was very good indeed at saying nay, would say it vigorously and often as he had been doing for most of her life. If she were married to him, he would, she shrewdly suspected, be even more likely to balk her. He would be her husband then, and in charge of her life, whereas now he was at least a suitor, and more likely to try to appease her.

Which brought the next idea, which was to play the game of pretend for a little while, and keep him hopefully dangling, waiting for the answer he wanted to his proposal. She gave that very serious consideration indeed, seeing it as an excellent source of comfort. Why, if she were known in the family as Freddy's almost-betrothed, and if, whenever she was about her own affairs, she told her aunt and uncle she was abroad with Freddy, they would not be at all anxious, and if Freddy found out she had used his name thus, he would not tell his mother and stepfather, for fear of upsetting his Phoebe and making her refuse him. . . .

But that idea had to be abandoned too. And not simply because she had no wish to be cruel, for to tell the truth she could not regard such behaviour as cruel, since it was a natural way for any girl to behave. When young females were so hemmed about with controls and chaperones, they had to use every shift they might to make their lives supportable. No, she dismissed it because it would not serve. However hard she bent her imagination she could not visualize a Freddy who was all complaisance and appeasement, for it was not his style at all. If she were to misbehave, he would complain about it loud and long, whether it would incur her wrath or not. He always had, and it was very apparent to her that he always would.

There had not even been the pleasure of a rehearsal and a meeting with her Aunt Lydia to salvage her day from the depths of misery in which she found herself. An early message had come by hand to tell her that her aunt had quite forgotten to tell her that there was to be no rehearsal today, but that she would gladly see her at Soho Square the next day, when they could be cosy together and talk of the future and the play.

Phoebe had torn up the note and stamped about and shouted at Ellie (who took it as the normal behaviour of a young lady recently in receipt of a proposal, about which all the servants knew all there was to know, for the news had spread rapidly through the green baize door that led to the kitchen quarters) and wept.

And now she sat in the drawing-room alone, for everyone apart from her Aunt Abby was out, and she was boringly wrapped up in the baby, and wondered whether to go and see who it might be who had gone up the stairs to see her aunt, and who was now coming down again.

'It's only the doctor,' she told herself but still went across the room to the drawing-room to peep out, for anything was better than this heavy load of ennui.

And found herself peeping up at Richard O'Hare.

He was just passing the drawing-room as she opened it a trifle, and looked round the jamb, and he stopped at once and looked down at her standing there, and after a long moment, smiled. And not only because it was polite to do so, and not only because he was seeking a way to recoup his situation with the Henriques family and had suddenly realized that Phoebe might provide the answer, but because she really did look so delightful.

Her nose was a little red, her hair was disordered, and she was wearing a simple gown in an apple green that was rather insipid and which had the skimpiest of ribbons on it. Yet she looked charming, if woebegone, and he smiled even more widely at the amazement on her face. Setting his hand on the drawing-room door to open it a little wider, he said gently, 'Good afternoon, Miss Phoebe! Have you time for a little conversation with a caller?'

# CHAPTER SIXTEEN

As miserable as she had been so far today, so was she now happy. She walked along the gravelled path beside him, her hand tucked into his elbow, and felt herself positively bathed in the envious glances of the other women they passed. That he was attractive and charming she knew, of course, but she had so far valued his company entirely because of the effect he had on her. Now she was realizing the added balm there was in finding herself squired by a man other women would gladly steal from her, and she preened and glowed with satisfaction.

And he, knowing precisely how she felt and meaning her to feel so, looked down at her and smiled and gently, with great skill, pressed her hand so that a shiver ran up her spine.

'You look entirely beautiful, Miss Phoebe!' he said. 'You are not a young lady who needs, as so many do, the artifice of splendid gown and bonnet to put a brave face forwards, for I believe you could look entrancing in a sack, but there is no doubt that the gown you are wearing is a perfect foil for you!'

She bridled and blushed and smiled and dropped her lashes on to her cheeks, all in one smooth movement. 'This is a very old gown, and not at all modish, and well you know it, Mr. O'Hare, fashionable man as you are! I could not have dared to go and change it, though, for I am sure I would have been apprehended and stopped.' She giggled. 'Oh, it was so funny, was it not? And they would be so angry if they knew.'

She tossed her head then in a manner she felt to be suitable for the sentiment she was expressing. 'And I do not care a fig how angry they are! I was so miserable that you seemed to me when you arrived to be a positive Sir Galahad!'

'Tell me, why were you so miserable?'

They walked on a little in silence, while she debated whether to tell him the truth or not, and then decided she would, for it did not put her in any unattractive light.

'I – I had to – I received a – a proposal of marriage last night,' she said in a low voice. 'It – it caused me much pain.'

'Pain? Now, why? To be the recipient of a young man's offer of heart and hand is surely not a painful experience but one that young ladies regularly desire to enjoy!'

She shook her head. 'This was painful to me.'

'But you have not said why – unless it was not from a young man, but from some hateful old roué your family had selected for you.'

At the note of faint mockery in his voice she looked up at him, but his face was perfectly serious, and for a moment she played with the idea of going along with the fantasy he had offered her, for it was a very beguiling one; how charming to be seen as the Victim of a Cruel Guardian, being Sold into a Loveless Match! But her common sense overcame her taste for the dramatic and she said, 'No! Of course not!'

At once he smiled. 'Had you said yes, then I would have known you to be romancing, for I have met your father and cannot imagine he would ever put any pressure upon you to do anything you did not wish to. He seems to be a positively adoring parent!'

'Oh, he is! Dear Papa will do anything I ask! He is the kindest man imaginable.'

'So, why was this proposal you received so painful? Was it from a young man you disliked?'

'Indeed, no! If it had been, it would have been merely tiresome. I have had many of those and to tell the truth they are more likely to make me laugh than weep.'

He looked down at her with a new interest in his face. 'Then this was serious?'

'Oh dear, yes, it was! That is why it was all so miserable. He is so dear a friend, you see, and one I have known all my life – I would not have him sad for the world and if I could have stopped him, I would truly, but – well, I could not. And now it is all so miserable, for it will never be the same again between us—'

Her voice trailed away, and for a little while she just walked on beside him, lost in her thoughts, and looking at her he realized that she was not posturing at all now, but being perfectly honest, and his curiosity was piqued.

'And who might this paragon be, who distressed you so by loving you too well? I sympathize with him – you seem to be a lady it would be all too easy to love too well.'

She blushed prettily. 'Oh, it is no one you know, of course—'

'But tell me! I am agog! Any matter that is of interest to you interests me—'

'Oh, well, why not? My cousin, Mr. O'Hare, he is my cousin. My Aunt Abby's son, Freddy, from when she was a widow, you know?'

He laughed at that. 'Such an elegant way to explain it. But I know what you mean. Your Aunt Abby's son, eh? Well, it is understandable, if you have lived cheek by jowl so long, that he should be quite under your spell—'

Beneath the almost automatic flirtatiousness of his tone, his mind was working fast. Mrs. Henriques' son? Now that was interesting! Here he was, enjoying an illicit stroll with the object of her son's affections. That would show these wretched people they could not meddle in his affairs! He could not quite see how benefit could accrue to him from this situation, but he felt instinctively that it could. Time would tell. And he closed his own warm hand over hers tucked there so neatly into his elbow, and again applied that faint pressure that he knew from experience to have so devastating an effect on young and susceptible ladies.

He led her, talking lightly and still with that glittering vein of almost but not quite naughty flirtatiousness, towards the great soaring glass mountain that shone at them through the sunlit trees. The paths were well populated with other walkers, all making their way towards the same goal, and his eyes darted about as he sought the faces he knew. There would be no point at all in his expedition if Lydia did not see him with her niece on his arm, and in this crowd he would have to make some effort to ensure they did not miss each other. But after a while he realized that since the other pair had set out on their expedition so much earlier, they must already be inside the Exhibition, and more likely to be encountered strolling about among the crowds within.

So he speeded his pace somewhat, and they threaded their way past the other walkers, she laughing a little breathlessly at his raillery, and by dint of some extra persuasion offered in the form of a half-sovereign to a man standing beside one of the myriad side doors that led into the great sparkle that was Paxton's Exhibition building, obtained entry. And she stood there just inside, her neck craning as she stared upwards, and gaped and clapped her hands with genuine delight, and he smiled at her, finding her pleasure a pleasure to watch.

That she should be so entranced with the building, he had to admit, was in no way to be laid at the door of her naïveté. The place was indeed breathtaking, the great glass walls soaring away into the air like some vast translucent bubble, the struts of metal that held the panes seeming as delicate as the filaments in a spider's web. Beneath their feet were layers of plaited straw matting, giving off a faintly earthy smell, and this, added to the presence of great trees in early leaf thrusting their branches up towards the sun that shone with what seemed redoubled brightness above the glass canopy, added to the sense of being trapped in some sort of fairyland. The higgledy-piggledy collection of objects that lay about in unbelievable confusion made it seem, furthermore, like a goblin treasure cave. There were whole engines and fragments of engines made of heavy grey silken iron that glowed sulkily in the all-pervading light. There was brass that gleamed with an unbelievable golden sheen. There was wood, carved into ludicrous and painful shapes, there were immense marble statues (from one of which Phoebe averted her eyes in modesty, before taking another quick peep; a massive marble lion lay looking up in some surprise at the totally naked lady who sat on his back insouciantly paring the claws of one vast paw with an almost equally vast pair of clippers); there was bamboo furniture and lacquered screens and colour, colour, colour, everywhere.

'It is very remarkable,' Phoebe said in a small awed voice after a moment. 'I knew it was big – Freddy told me it covers

nineteen acres and is three times bigger than St. Paul's – and of
course I have looked at it often from outside. But inside – oh
my, it is very—'

'Remarkable,' he said, and moved forwards through heaped-
up exhibits until they were standing in the middle of the great
central aisle that led away almost to infinity on each side. 'It is
indeed. I am glad they did not remove the trees. They add a
great deal of – I wonder, would it ever be possible to use real
trees, in tubs, perhaps, on a stage? Now, there is an idea that—'

'It'd make yer life a misery, squire, a' so I tells yer!'

They both turned to see a small and very wrinkled old man
in a moleskin waistcoat, frieze trousers tied at the knee with
rough string, and a flat billycock hat on the back of his head,
staring up at them from his perch on the pedestal of a statue
that depicted a handsome young female wearing only a chain
about her wrists and looking most soulful. 'A misery, mate, an'
that's all about it!'

'Oh?' O'Hare was amused and pressed Phoebe's hand in a
conspiratorial manner. She looked down at the little man and
tried to show she was not at all discommoded by being held
there face to face with so very realistic a depiction of the naked
female form. She knew somewhere deep inside her that Mr.
O'Hare was not behaving as a gentleman should. Had Freddy
been with her, he would never have permitted her to be embarrassed at the sight of the statue, would have hurried her immediately away. But she was not with Freddy, she reminded
herself, dear but boring old Freddy. This was Richard O'Hare
and a much more agreeable and exciting companion; and
anyway if she was to be an actress she must learn to be a little
more devil-may-care in her attitudes.

'You must tell us why!' Richard was saying in the special
voice he always used when speaking to his social inferiors –
friendly but making it clear they were to remain at arm's
length. 'If His Royal Highness and the designers saw fit to
leave the trees within this splendid building, I imagine they
were aware of the manner in which the trees could be kept in
health!'

'T'ain't the trees as is the trouble,' the little man said, and sniffed, and picking up a large enamelled jug from the ground at his side took a deep swig. 'Care for a wet?' he added, holding out the jug invitingly.

O'Hare shook his head, grimacing slightly. 'Then what is?'

'Sparrers,' the little man said succinctly.

'Sparrows?'

'Yers! Sparrers! Take a look an' see for yerself!' He waved his hand comprehensively and they both turned their heads to look about them and saw very clearly the evidence of the presence of small birds plentifully scattered about on many of the exhibits, especially those that lay near the great trunks of the trees.

'Still, can't moan, can I? Seein' as 'ow they gives me a job—' He stood up and picked up a bucket and a long-handled brush that lay beside him. 'For a while yet, anyways.' He grinned then and wiped his nose on the back of his hand. 'S'all right, now, yer see. Or will be. They asked the Dook o' Wellin'ton as what 'e'd do to get rid of 'em, and d'yer know what Ol' 'Ooky Nose says? "Why, ma'am," 'e says – for 'e was talkin' to the Queen at the time, bein' as 'ow 'e's a great friend of 'ers, and very proper 'e should be, seein' as 'ow 'e saved 'er an' all of us – with the 'elp o' the likes o' me an' me mates as fought the battle o' Waterloo for 'im – "Why, ma'am," 'e says, "Sparrer 'awks, ma'am." And so it's goin' ter be. They'm bringin' sparrer 'awks tomorrer or the next day, and then they'll be rid o' the sparrers, an' 'ave to find a new job fer me! So unless yer wants sparrers an' sparrer 'awks in theaytres, squire, I wouldn't reckon nothin' to puttin' trees on stages. But if yer do, come an' find me, an' I'll do the necessary!' And he grinned and went stumping away to start his ministrations with brush and bucket on a large and very cumbersome black iron bedstead embellished with brass cherubs at head and foot.

Richard laughed heartily, smiling down at Phoebe, and a little doubtfully she smiled back. Perhaps she was being too punctilious, she told herself, but she could not imagine Freddy finding such a story humorous, involving as it did such very disagreeable animal functions. Well, perhaps he would, really, but he would never expect her, as a young lady of any delicacy, to laugh. Although, she told herself optimistically, as O'Hare led her away down the long central aisle, perhaps the Queen had laughed? Yes, I am sure she did, for I am told she is a very lively lady, and has been known to quite shock the court, being as fond of dancing and parties as she is. Yes, the Queen would have laughed, and anyway, Freddy was far too protective altogether. That was why she was here with Mr. O'Hare – she smiled in a sudden access of good spirits and gripped his arm tightly and looked up at him and said impulsively, 'Oh, Mr. O'Hare, I am enjoying myself! Thank you so much for bringing me.'

'The pleasure is indeed all mine,' he said easily. 'I rather fear that before too long you will be exhausted, for there is much walking to do if we are to see what is here. I believe it is six hundred yards long – that is near a third of a mile! And there are all the side galleries as well – in one advertisement I saw in the *Morning Gazette* it promised fully eight miles of table space for the exhibitors.'

'Oh, I am sure we will not see all on one day! And I must come back of course, when it is properly opened, and not in quite so sorry a state of disorder. But let us see what we can today – I promise you I will not become tired, for I am very strong, you know, and not much given to sitting about in weary postures!'

And so they walked for a long time, up one side and down the other, weaving their way past half-arranged exhibits of pictures and chemical manufactures, musical instruments and agricultural machinery, porcelain baths and tubs and basins and wooden furniture and mysterious engines and contraptions of all sorts.

She stared and exclaimed and asked for explanations, which he offered to the best of his ability – and many of them were completely erroneous, but since she was as ignorant of the subject of engineering as he it did not matter a whit and both were content enough with what he said – but all the time his glances were darting everywhere looking for Lydia and Gideon; and as the afternoon moved inexorably forwards he became a little more edgy and irritable, and she became aware of the change in him and looked up and said a little timorously, 'Are you fatigued, Mr. O'Hare? I have been very selfish, I am sure, for I was so interested I did not stop to think you might be weary.'

He was all attention at once. 'No, of course I am not fatigued – though perhaps a little refreshment would be agreeable! And it is time you stopped being quite so formal, my dear Miss Phoébe, and addressed me as Richard! Or even Dickon, which is used by all my dearest friends. And I should like to include you in their number. Please say you will!'

She blushed at that, and stammered a little. 'Oh, indeed I could not, on so brief an acquaintance – in time, perhaps, but at present—'

'Come, try! And then we shall go and seek some refreshment before looking at whatever else there is here to look upon.'

She stood there in front of him, smiling and dimpling, and he looked over her head to throw another of his sweeping glances about the crowds. This time he thought he saw the familiar shape of that curved and elegant back, walking away along one of the side galleries beside a tall thin man in a high hat, who looked very like Gideon Henriques, as he remembered him. And at once he seized Phoebe's wrist and began to hurry after them.

'We shall clearly have to give you the chance to practise saying my name,' he said with a huge gaiety. 'And it will be easier over some food and drink! Come, there is a place I believe, at this side of the Park, through here . . .'

She was breathless by the time they reached the end of the gallery and the door which gave egress to the Park, but still he hurried her on, and not until they were out in the open air, where the long shadows showed the time to be approaching six o'clock at least, did his speed abate, and he stood there looking about at the strolling crowds with a faint scowl on his face, and again she looked up at him in some concern.

After a moment he seemed aware of her gaze, and looked at her, and managed a smile.

'Forgive me,' he said, 'but I thought I saw a – somebody I knew. But apparently not, because they have gone – or at least, cannot be seen there.'

'Perhaps they too were in need of some refreshment?' she said a little slyly, for she was, now she thought about it, very thirsty. At once he brightened.

'Of course! You are tired now, and I promised you – come, at once! We shall go – let me see. . . .' He looked about him, and then with an air of great assurance tucked her hand back into his elbow and led her to a path where their shadows drew out behind them as they walked westwards. 'To Kensington Gore – there is an excellent establishment there where we can obtain a most refreshing half-hour, I know!'

She was a little startled when she discovered that the establishment to which he was taking her was an hotel. She had assumed that it was to a tea shop they were going, for in recent years these agreeable places had appeared in many parts of London, and much did she enjoy visiting them with her friends to drink tea and eat little macaroon biscuits and slices of rich pound cake and even, on hot afternoons, the rich cream ices that were her favourite food.

She hesitated in the doorway, looking round at the heavy red carpets and curtains and gilded wood of the desk at one side, at the people sitting about on the heavily upholstered chairs and sofas, and then relaxed. They all looked very respectable, very respectable indeed, for there were small family groups, even including small children, in the lobby as well as groups of ladies. She had nothing to fear here and she followed him happily to a table in the corner and sat down gratefully.

'Oh, Richard, I am so tired after all!' she said and bent down to rub her ankles delicately through the apple green stuff of her gown. 'I did not know how tired until now!'

'I know the answer to that!' he said cheerfully, and waved to a waiter, and murmured in his ear. The waiter nodded and went away, and Richard leaned forwards over the small gilt table, and took her hand and said in that special low note he sometimes used and which made her feel so agreeable, 'Did you notice what you said then?'

'That I was tired?' she said, peeping up at him, and feeling the sensation of faint shiveriness that was beginning to be so familiar to her creep into her whole body, moving onwards from the grasp of his hand on hers.

'No. You said my name.' And he smiled, and lifted her hand and very deliberately turned it palm upwards, and kissed it, closing her fingers over the moist spot where his lips had touched, and she bit her lip and blushed an even rosier red, if that were possible.

'You – you really must not take advantage of me, Richard!' she said. 'For I – I am not quite as – as accustomed to the company of men as – as well, men of the town like you, even though I have pretended just a little, perhaps, that I am.'

'I would not dream of taking any advantage of your youth and innocence, dear Miss Phoebe,' he said, more touched than he would have thought possible by her sudden burst of honesty. 'But you really are very delightful and to kiss your hand is no very great sin, after all, and gave me so much pleasure. And I hope, you too—'

She did not answer, sitting there looking down at the table very modestly, but she made no attempt to take her hand from his, for it felt very comfortable there. Until the waiter came and he squeezed her closed fist before letting it go and the waiter set glasses in front of them and poured them brimful of a sparkling greenish wine.

She looked at it doubtfully and said, 'I had thought – not tea, Richard? Is it not a little – well, raffish, to take wine at this time of the day?'

'Raffish? Oh, a little, I suppose, for so young a lady – but so refreshing, and it is refreshment you need, is it not? And this is very harmless, I do assure you – just a light German wine, very fresh and cool and so delicious. If you do not like it, I shall order tea for you.'

Doubtfully, she sipped the wine, and indeed it was very good. There was the scent of flowers about it and it tasted just a little like the raisins they snatched from the bowl at Christmas time, when they played snapdragon, and the sparkle bit her tongue in a pleasant fashion. So she drank some more and then said, 'It is much nicer than the wine Uncle Gideon has for our parties. I know champagne is supposed to be very good, but I find it rather – well, dull, you know! But this tastes—'

'Like lemonade,' he said and emptied his own glass, and refilled it, and she laughed and said, 'Not quite!' and finished her own just as recklessly and let him refill it too.

She knew perfectly well that ladies should never drink enough wine to make themselves the least bit altered by it. She had been carefully reared to know that moderation in all things was the mark of the truly genteel, and was as shocked as anyone by tales that sometimes seeped into Stanhope Terrace drawing-rooms of people who regularly took too much wine and had to be put to bed by their servants as a result. She knew that drunkenness was the curse of the poor people of London, and the root cause of so much of their misery. She knew all that and more, perfectly well.

But what she did not know was what it felt like to be drunk. She had always assumed that it must feel very disagreeable indeed, for she had seen the grey-faced beggars who swept the crossings when she went shopping with Aunt Abby, had seen the ragged children who came seeking scraps at their kitchen door, had seen the hopelessness and misery on their faces. How could any habit that made a person look so dreadful possibly be pleasant?

So when she felt her head swim a little and felt the tiredness melt out of her, when the laughter came bubbling up and made her giggle so helplessly, when Richard's touch on her hand – which was more and more frequent – became even more exciting and shivery, she put it all down to being so young and happy and being with Richard. She did not for one moment realize that the second and then the third bottle of the delicious wine he sent for was too much. She did not realize that the way her tongue slid over perfectly familiar words was meant to be a warning to her. She just found it all very very enjoyable, and very very amusing, and was altogether the happiest she had ever been.

By the time they left the hotel, she clinging to his arm rather more carefully than she had been doing hitherto, the safe and respectable people she had seen when they entered and who had given the place a cachet of gentility had long since gone, and the lobby was occupied by people drinking wine, much as they had, and who looked decidedly other than the sort of people she was used to. The women were that little bit more lavishly dressed, with bodices that little bit more tight and low-cut, and faces that little bit redder about the cheeks and whiter about the nose and chin than ladies usually were.

Had she been more in command of herself she would have recognized the fact that these ladies were painted, and this could have been enough to shake her into an awareness of her situation. But somehow the sparkle that had been in the wine was now in her vision; everything she looked at seemed to be rimed with a glittering dust, so that nothing looked quite as it usually did. And she liked what she saw and giggled and held on to his arm even more tightly.

He stood beside her on the kerb in the dark blue dusk, looking down at her and trying to decide what to do. He was himself more than a trifle the worse for wear, and was a little annoyed with himself. He had set out today to show Madam Lydia just how independent of her he was, and now, because he had not been able to find her as he had intended to do, had allowed himself to act so recklessly as to get himself half drunk so early in the evening, and furthermore, to saddle himself with a giggling miss. He shook his head in an attempt to clear it and the lights of the hotel swung and swooped, leaving him feeling decidedly uncomfortable.

'I must go home, must I not, Dickon?' she said, peering up at him and smiling her wide and pretty smile, and he looked down on her and some of his pique melted away. Such a captivating child it was! Not a patch on its aunt, of course, the exciting and experienced and beautiful Lydia, but like enough to her to be very attractive.

He pinched her cheek and laughed and said, 'If I take you home in this state, your family will half kill me! You, my child, have taken rather more wine than is good for you, and we must be sure to rid you of it before your severe Aunt Abby and your sobersides uncle see you. Not to speak of the good Freddy!'

She pondered that for a while. 'I have had too much wine?' she said carefully at length and he smiled and said with equal ponderousness, 'You have had too much wine.'

There was a silence and then, almost against her will, she

giggled. 'That is very wicked, is it not, Dickon? I have always known that to take too much wine is very, very wicked.'

'Very wicked indeed. Especially if you do not have someone to take care of you when you are getting over it.'

'Have you not had too much wine?' she said peering up at him owlishly.

'Yes, just a little! But with me it is not important because I am able to understand what to do. So you need not worry.'

She stood there swaying slightly, and then nodded. 'I think I should worry but I – it is difficult to worry. I do not feel *able* to worry. I think perhaps I am very wicked indeed. . . .'

'And I think we must take you home. But not in a hack. I shall walk you home across the park, because by the time you get there you will be quite together again. And no one will know how naughty you have been. Come along.'

To do him justice, he meant no harm to her. He had never meant harm to her, finding her both charming and tedious, rather as a puppy is charming and tedious, simply seeing her as an object to be used as part of his dealings with Lydia, with whom he was far more tangled in his feelings than he wished to admit. But she was a very pretty child and he was a healthy and very vigorous man and the park was full of softness and sensuous whispering sounds as the night breezes began to go sliding through the young leaves on the trees, and the flowers smelled very rich and good, wafting on the night air; gillyflowers and early stocks and lily-of-the-valley.

So when she slipped on the dew-damp grass and he seized her to save her, and they found that her ankle had twisted and was painful, it was the most natural thing in the world that he should lift her up and carry her for part of the way, for she was light. And it was the most natural thing in the world, that, light as she was, he should become tired and need to rest, and when he gasped out, 'My – dear – Miss Phoebe – I must stop – just for a moment,' it seemed to her the most natural thing in the world that he should sink to the ground with her still held in his arms, and sit there on the grass holding her and breathing deeply so that her head rose and fell gently against the cloth of his coat.

She sat there with the warmth of his arms about her, and her head still spinning, so pleasantly that the first of the stars that now were tangled in the trees above her head seemed to swoop and dance and laugh at her, and she sighed a sigh of sheer pleasure, and turned her head towards him in the darkness to peer up at him and see if he were happy too.

He, his breath now under control again as he recovered from his efforts, looked down, and found that once more he needed to breathe very unevenly, for she was so very close to him that her own breath was warm against his cheek, and her lips, slightly parted, were gleaming softly in the fading blue light. And she smelled warm and feminine and altogether inviting, and the wine that still flowed in his veins gave one more sparkle, and she seemed to feel it too, and her lips widened in a very faint smile, Kissing her was altogether completely inevitable.

Neither of them was ever able in later years to remember the episode fully. They had kissed and clung close and kissed again, and the soft spring night had darkened around them.

For Phoebe, even carefully reared and genteel Phoebe, who so valued her reputation and herself that the smallest hint of forwardness on the part of any young man could call down a blistering wrath on his head, it was as though the world had changed completely. In this new world the right thing, the proper thing, the only natural thing to do was what they were doing, even though it meant his hands were moving across her body in a way she had never imagined possible, even though it meant she was caressing him in the same urgent and extraordinary manner, even though they were clinging to each other as though they would never be parted, ever.

And then for Phoebe it was suddenly as though this strange new world turned topsy-turvy in a rush of sensation that seized her in a violent grasp and made her back arch and her head pull back on her straining neck and her mouth pull wide in a hideous grimace. And then, sickeningly, the world righted itself, and she lay there gasping and shaking, feeling his weight upon her, aware of his own violent activity, as he pinned her down to the damp grass, and she tried to pull back from him, suddenly knowing what was happening. But it was too late, for now it was his turn to be grimacing and gasping, his back that was arched, his body that shook in spasms of urgent movement.

She lay there in the darkness and stared up at the shadow of a face above her and knew that the world had returned to its original form, but that she, Phoebe, had been utterly and completely changed, for always. As he took one last deep breath and finally subsided she felt the tears come sliding out of her eyes to go coursing down her cheeks, and she stared up at the star above her, still tangled in the branches, but now not dancing at all.

# CHAPTER SEVENTEEN

'I CANNOT comprehend you, Abby!' His face was tight with hurt anger, and for a moment she wanted to go to him, her arms wide and welcoming, wanted to tell him it was all a nonsense, that she was out of sorts, tired, she hadn't meant it. But her rage built up in her again, her fear and her doubts bubbling, and instead she almost spat her words at him.

'You cannot comprehend me! You cannot comprehend that I should be perturbed when some mountebank of an actor comes to me in my own nursery to tell me as cool as you please that my husband is cavorting about the town with – with – you dare to come in here, so late, and then tell me that *your* pride is hurt, *you* are hard done by because I complain! *You* are the one who has suffered – it is I who cannot comprehend, my friend, I who need a good deal more and a good deal better explanation than I have had so far!'

'Abby, we have been wed for eight years. Before that I spent all my young years, from boyhood onwards, devoted to you and your interests. Not once in all those years, not once have you had cause to complain of my behaviour as a husband. I have loved you dearly, I have protected you, cared for you, been completely at your service. And yet when a man who by your own estimation is little more than a mountebank comes and tells you some cock-and-bull story of my ill doings, so-called, you believe him implicitly against anything I may say! You are prepared to throw into the scales half a lifetime of love and – and concern against one fool's unsubstantial word, and let the balance come down against me. It – how can I possibly understand such a – how can I—'

He turned away to stand in front of the fireplace with his head bent, staring down at the embers glowing dully in the grate, but not so fast that she did not see the sudden gleam of tears on his lashes; and all her own distress and fear and guilt – for she knew she was wrong, cruelly wrong, to have attacked him as she had – overflowed and she was weeping in good earnest herself, sitting there very upright on her chair with her hands tightly clasped on her lap and the tears sliding silently down her face, her nose running, her throat almost solid with it all.

He turned to speak to her again and saw, and at once was beside her and on his knees, his hands tight over hers, and staring up into her face. 'Oh, Abby, Abby, don't weep, please don't weep. I cannot bear to see you thus! What can I do? Oh, my dear one, what can I do to make it better – I would not have you weep for the world. . . .'

He put his arms about her and held her close and after one rigid moment when she tried to resist him she gave in to the luxury of her tears and sobbed and coughed and sobbed again, while he gently patted her back and murmured incomprehensible sounds at her until the storm was past.

It seemed to Abby suddenly as though the clock had run backwards, and she was sitting in her counting-house, the old counting-house at the Irongate Wharf Road factory with Henry Sydenham just outside the door, stunned with mystification, and she clinging helplessly to the young Gideon, trying to control the weeping that had overtaken her, trying not to let go of herself as totally as she knew she had.

And as though he shared her memory he behaved now just as he had all those years ago, taking his handkerchief from his pocket and wiping away her tears and setting its soft cambric bay-rum-scented folds against her nose and saying softly, 'Blow!' so that she did, for all the world like a child, while he sat back on his haunches and looked up at her. Then he said very simply, 'Dear Abby. Dear, dear Abby. I do love you so very much. And I thought you knew.' And she shook her head, not in denial, but in an attempt to bring herself back to the present.

'Oh, of course I know! I am sorry, Gigi, I should not have – I did not mean – I was so *frightened*! You who are never late to be more than an hour past your usual time, and after that dreadful man had come here with his hateful – and then to bring *her* with you so that I could not speak to you, but had to sit there and do the polite and bottle it all – Oh, cannot you see how it was?'

'Of course I can. And I beg your pardon for causing you such distress. It was all so *silly*. She arrived at Jonah's when I had gone there to speak to him of the matter of Phoebe, as I had promised I would, and he, poor wretch, behaved like some rabbit caught by a stoat's stare, and gulped and gibbered for all the world like – well, you know how Jonah is! I took Lydia from his back in sheer brotherly concern – and she marched me about the damned Exhibition like some – some automaton! The dear Lord knows where she gets her energies, Abby, for I tell you she quite flattened me! I so needed the balm of your peace and care when I reached home, and well—' He smiled at her a trifle ruefully, and she smiled back, her lips still trembling, and held out her hands to him and he took them and held them very tightly.

But the damage had been done and she knew it; for the first time in all the years of their love she had doubted him, had feared for his constancy, and the hurt had gone deep. There had of course been many arguments between them over the years, for they were both people of much passion and strong views; it would be impossible for two such, loving each other as dearly as they did, to live together in total amity. But never had there been any disagreement between them as divisive as this. Whatever else had happened they had always known themselves as united as a pair of convolvulus plants, totally entwined in each other. And she, today, had tugged at the roots of that vigorous growth and much time would be needed before it would be as safe and strong again.

Suddenly she hated Phoebe, hated her with so powerful a surge of feeling that it quite made her shake, and she bit her lip, amazed at her own absurdity, for surely to blame Phoebe for it all was quite irrational. She had been the most unwitting member of this whole sorry tangle.

Wanting to make amends to Phoebe she said carefully to

Gideon, 'We shall not talk of it again. Tell me instead – did you speak to Jonah? About Phoebe?'

He shook his head. 'No, that was what was so galling! The lady gave neither of us a chance to do anything but deal with *her*. I cannot deny to you, Abby, and there is, believe me, no reason why I should, that hitherto I have thought her a likeable enough person, and indeed very fascinating in a curious sort of – well, foreign way. It is like seeing an Indian in a turban suddenly walking down the Oxford Road! One wishes to stare, and walk alongside for a while, but, by God, it soon palls! Such chatter, such artifice! Never think such a one is of interest to any but the most superficial of minds, Abby. There is as much depth to that lady – as to a gutter-puddle!'

She smiled at that. 'Well you need not overstate the case, my love, or you will have me feeling even more doubtful. I have met her, remember, and anyone less like a gutter-puddle—'

'Well, I am sure you know what I mean. Anyway, the matter of Phoebe remains unsettled. I considered mentioning it to Lydia, you know, but – well, I thought better of it. As a female you will, I have no doubt, have a better effect on her . . .'

Her lips tightened. 'I do not care if I never see the woman again!'

'Oh, Abby, please! Let us not—'

'But of course I shall. I promised Freddy—' She stopped then, and went on a little painfully after a while, 'Gideon, I am a little – I wonder if perhaps I am not a – not as good about Freddy as I should be. I wish him so much to be happy, want only what is best for him, and yet I find myself secretly wishing that – well, that he and Phoebe – oh, it is so unjust! I have had the rearing of her, she is my brother's child, and yet I look at her, and wish that perhaps she would go on the stage and be done with it, so that Freddy will take his *congé* and forget her – I fear that I am being—' she shook her head then and bit her lip and looked up at him appealingly.

'Oh, no, my love, not you!' He took her hands and lifted them to his lips and kissed them. 'Not you! You are not one to try to shackle your boy to your side. It is the most natural thing in the world that you should be fearful for him, for he is very young, and the most natural thing in the world that you should have doubts about his desire to wed his cousin. But such doubts cannot be considered in any way to be wicked. They are simply maternal and therefore very right and proper. Do acquit yourself of being any sort of female ogre! I would never permit it, even if you were so misguided as to try it – which you never would.'

'Well, you comfort me a little. But still, I doubt – but I will speak to Phoebe's aunt as I promised – and you, Gideon? When will you speak to Jonah?'

'As soon as I can tomorrow, I think. I shall visit him before lunchtime, for it is clearly difficult when he is at his busiest time of the day. I could go back tonight, of course, and perhaps – Freddy will be worrying, no doubt. . . .'

He looked at her anxiously, and she smiled up at his long face, whiter than usual and a shade drawn, and shook her head firmly.

·'No. You are tired and dispirited tonight, and need the peace of home. Freddy can wait until tomorrow, I am sure. And I tomorrow will wait on Lydia and together we shall tell Freddy in the evening what has happened. We cannot do more. . . .'

He got to his feet, and pulled his watch from his pocket, peering at it in the fading light of the evening.

'Well, we must at least tell Freddy what we plan – where is he? Good God, Abby, it is nearly half past seven! It will soon be dinnertime, and here I am still in my street dirt. I am positively ashamed. I must dress – where are Freddy and Phoebe? Have they left us alone deliberately? I would be most distressed to think they knew that we were – that we had had an altercation.'

She shook her head. 'To tell the truth, I have not seen either of them. Freddy told me at breakfast he would be late at the hospital tonight, but would return in time for dinner, and as for Phoebe – she slept late, after her dose last night, you know, I have been with Sarah all day, so I have not, to tell the truth, given her much thought. She will be feeling most neglected, poor child.'

She got to her feet in a rustle of silk skirts, and smoothed her gown neatly over her hips.

'Please to dress, Gideon, and I shall go and seek Phoebe and talk to her and coax her out of her mopes and tell her to join us all at dinner, and we shall be cosy again. . . .'

He kissed her, holding her very close for a moment, and then went obediently away to his dressing-room, yawning, to leave her to go to Phoebe's room in search of her.

But she was not to be found anywhere. Abby went from room to room of her big house, even as far as the kitchens, and was mystified to discover that no one had seen her since Ellie had given her her bread and milk at twelve o'clock.

'Told 'er to eat 'er vittles and stop her silly fussin', ma'am. I did,' Ellie said self-importantly, 'and then to tell the truth never give 'er another thought for there was Miss Sarah, the blessed lamb, as poorly as she may be, with 'er ear, and Miss Isabel in need of a bit o' fussin' 'erself, seein' as she was being set aside for Sarah, and I thought, well Miss Phoebe's well able to take care of 'erself for a little while—'

She looked up sharply from the pan of gruel she was cooking for Sarah's supper. 'Is somethin' the matter, ma'am? I know as Miss Phoebe 'ad got 'erself into a state, but never thought too much to it, for she's an up an' down sort o' girl, and always 'as bin, an' 'oo should know bettern'n me? You don't reckon as she's gorn off and done somethin' stupid, do you, ma'am?' Her eyes glinted a little. Ellie dearly loved a drama.

'Of course not,' Abby said crisply. 'Really, Ellie, you talk such nonsense! Never let me hear you speak so again. I merely asked where she is. I have no doubt she has gone to visit one of her friends, and did not disturb me to tell me, knowing that I was concerned with Sarah. . . .'

But she was anxious, nevertheless, and chiding herself for being as absurd as Ellie, took herself to the front door to peer out into the Terrace and up and down the road, seeking a glimpse of the slight figure and pretty curly head.

The Oxford Road, wide and smooth, ran away on each side, the lights from the houses throwing a thin illumination across the smooth cobbles. She took a deep breath, enjoying the scent of the trees and damp grass that came towards her from the blackness of the park on the far side. She had not set foot outside the door all day, she realized now almost with surprise; no wonder she was feeling out of sorts and edgy. She really must be more understanding about Phoebe and Freddy, and less selfish, she told herself with some severity, and again craned her neck to look along the road.

And then she saw her, coming out of the Victoria Gate, a slender figure silhouetted against the lights that came obliquely across the road from the big houses that made up Hyde Park Gardens opposite. She frowned sharply, for even from this distance she could see she was dishevelled, wearing only a gown and shawl, and without a bonnet on her head.

She moved forwards to try to view her more clearly, to see if she was alone, but the traffic which had been fairly thin for the past few moments thickened, and a Shillibeer's omnibus came lumbering along down the roadway, its lights bobbing and the horses snorting softly, and as it passed Victoria Gate the slender girlish shape disappeared behind it and she had to stand there waiting.

And when the omnibus, and the hacks and carts that were behind it, had passed and she looked again there was no one there at all to be seen. Whoever it was must have gone hurrying along the road under the shade of the trees, and was therefore no longer in view.

She stood there uncertainly for a moment, wondering, and then, irritated at herself, went inside again. It was quite ridiculous to think that the girl she had seen had been Phoebe. It had been the most fleeting of likenesses, surely, and from a considerable distance to boot; she was imagining it, and it was most unjust in her to even think that her well-reared niece would ever behave in so hoydenish a manner as to go into the Park, after dark, and wearing no more than a day gown and a shawl. That was not her style at all, she told herself firmly, and closed the front door and went away to write a quick note to send with Kent to the mother of Phoebe's best friend, to see if she had gone visiting there and forgotten the time. That would be the answer, she was sure.

As the big front door closed on to the dark street, a hack came clattering up the Oxford Road, and wheeled across the oncoming traffic, now thin again, to pull up with a clash of iron-shod hooves on stone in front of the tall steps, and Freddy got out wearily and began to dig in his pocket for the shillings to pay. The man took his fare and touched his hat with his whip and clicked his tongue at his horse and went away, leaving Freddy on the pavement putting the change into his trousers pocket.

He was tired, and deeply abstracted in his own thoughts, and when she came running across the road and along the pavement he didn't see her at first, not until she nearly cannoned into him; he blinked and shot out one arm and seized her by the shoulder and said in a voice filled with amazement, 'Phoebe? It is you, is it not? What on earth are you doing out here in the dark? And in such a – what is the matter?'

For now he could see her, in the light thrown from the drawing-room windows above, and he peered at her more closely and his brows came together in a tight frown. 'Phoebe, are you well? You look – what is the *matter?*'

She stared up at him, her face quite blank as though she did not know who he was, as though she had never seen him in her life before. He looked back at her, feeling a sudden cold gripping in his guts. Was this Phoebe? It looked like her, and she was wearing a gown he knew well, but this girl was so different from his Phoebe, staring at him with her eyes wide and blank and uncomprehending. And then she shook her head, and her blank wild stare cleared and he saw it was undoubtedly Phoebe and in his anxiety he reached out and took her shoulders and shook her, and said roughly, 'What in God's name, girl—'

At once she pulled away from him, stepping back, and, pulling her shawl more closely about her shoulders, stared very directly at him from under her untidy hair.

'It is no concern of yours, Freddy, where I have been, at what hour I go there, and at what hour I return. Do you understand that? I will not tolerate your quizzing and your prying and your – and your *smothering*. I am not your possession, but myself, do you understand me? Myself! I do as I choose, when I choose, and I am not answerable to any – any but my Papa. Certainly not to you! Don't you dare to approach me so ever again. Don't you dare to take hold of me in such a manner and shake me about! I will not stand for it! Keep away from me – I hate you! You hear me? I hate you. I always shall, and I would not wed you ever, not if – ever! Don't you ever dare to try to interfere in my life in any way, for if you do, I shall walk out of this house and I shall never return!'

And she turned and went running up the steps, and pulled on the bell, and when Kent opened it pushed past him and went running up the stairs, leaving Freddy staring after her from his place on the pavement, his head whirling and his face quite blank of any expression.

After dinner, which was a silent affair with just the three of them picking at their food, for Phoebe had refused to come down, sending word with Ellie that she was fatigued and still disturbed by her bad night and would go to bed early, he got to his feet and said punctiliously, 'If you will excuse me, Mamma, Gideon, I will leave you. I must do some work with my books.'

Gideon looked up and smiled at him. 'Freddy, before you go, I just wish you to know that although I went to your Uncle Jonah's today, I was not able to speak to him, not privately, you understand. But it is my firm intention to go tomorrow to see him regarding your affairs, and your Mamma—'

Abby looked up too, and managed to smile, although it was an effort. She was still deeply worried about Phoebe's strange absence and even stranger return.

'I shall go to Soho Square tomorrow, Freddy, to see Mrs. Mohun and—'

'No!'

They both jerked a little, their heads snapping up and back. It was almost ludicrous, almost as though they were mechanical toys from Isabel's box of Christmas fancies, and he felt a sort of laughter come welling up in him, but he bit his tongue and the moment of hysteria passed.

'No, Gideon, Mamma. I would prefer you did not. I know yesterday – yesterday I said that it would be a good thing –

well, that was yesterday, and I am glad indeed you have made no shift on my behalf to intervene in – in Phoebe's plans. I have given the matter some thought. . . .'

He looked at them bleakly, and to Abby, plagued as she was with her fatigue and anxiety, he suddenly seemed strange, a different person to the boy she had loved so long and so well. She blinked and looked again, but now he seemed his familiar self again, if a little strained, his face a shade whiter than usual beneath his freckles, his eyes shadowy green depths beneath the lock of red hair that lay across his forehead.

'I have given the matter some thought,' he said again. 'And I would not wish to put any pressure upon Phoebe. Any pressure at all. Whatever she does must be her affair. It is no way proper that – that I or you on my behalf, should – should intervene. I thank you for your – for the kind concern you showed in my behalf, but I ask you most earnestly not to – simply to do nothing.'

There was a long silence, and then Gideon said very gently, 'Of course, Freddy. It is as you wish.'

'Thank you, Gideon.'

He came round the table and bent to kiss his mother's cheek and then nodded, unsmiling, at Gideon and went to the door.

'Goodnight,' he said quietly, and went away, leaving them sitting at the ends of their long dining-table staring at each other across the cluttered expanse of polished mahogany.

# CHAPTER EIGHTEEN

'WELL, I am sure there is no need to be so very intense about it, Phoebe, my pet!' Lydia leaned forwards and peered very carefully at her reflection and then sighed softly and reached for a pair of tweezers from the jumble of brushes and hares'-foot puffs that lay before her. 'Indeed, never be intense, child, for it wrinkles the face dreadfully! Now hush – I do so hate having to do this, but it is very necessary, and demands much care. . . .'

She began to pluck individual hairs from her eyebrows, which looked to Phoebe to be a perfect shape already, her mouth pursed into an O of concentration, her forehead wrinkled so that each brow described a fine arch, and then at last set her tweezers down, and turned in her chair to smile at her niece.

She was wearing a full-sleeved white wrapper made of moiré silk, and the watery patterns in it twisted and turned in the sunlight that came pouring across her dressing-room floor from the narrow, high-set window, and her hair was unbound and lying on her shoulders in a lazy profusion. She looked fresh and cheerful and hardly as old as Phoebe herself, especially as Phoebe was looking today, for her face was tight and drawn, and had lost some of the animation that usually filled it.

'Indeed, Phoebe,' Lydia said, looking at her more closely. 'You already show signs of it! Of thinking too intensely, I mean! You look positively haggard, child – come, what is distressing you? Is there anything that is worrying you? I am your very own aunt, you know, and already care for you a great deal! And you may talk to me of any of your anxieties at any time!' And she set her head to one side and smiled invitingly, her eyes crinkling in a most engaging manner.

Phoebe looked back at her for a long moment, as the thoughts went whirling through her head. Tell Aunt Lydia? Tell her of the horrors of last night when she had lain in her bed all through the long clock-chiming hours staring up at the muslin curtains of her bed, and letting it all go through her head over and over again? Tell Aunt Lydia of the world spinning on its axis, of the way it had lurched and twisted and then come so suddenly and sickeningly to rights?

Tell Aunt Lydia. It would be so comforting to tell someone. Anyone at all. To hold it all within her was becoming so painful; she could not tell Aunt Abby, nor Ellie, and certainly not her dear Freddy – no, hateful Freddy, the Freddy she had always told her woes to, the Freddy who had always been there to help but was no longer. Above all, she could not tell him.

She stared back at her aunt and then opened her mouth. She would speak to her, she would tell her what had happened and tell her of her dawn decision. That she would never marry anyone – how could she now? – but would be an actress like Lydia herself and work and travel about and never talk to men in hotels over glasses of cool German wine, ever again.

Behind her the door opened, and she stiffened, knowing even before she turned her head who it was who stood there. It was as though there was a special aura surrounding him, some colour or scent that moved ahead of him and loudly, ringingly, announced his presence.

'Lyddy, my love, have you any powdered white to spare? That damned dresser they've given me has spilled every grain of it on the floor and then expects me to use the sweepings – I'll strangle the bloody idiot before we open, so help me God. . . .'

He was already past her where she sat in the small armchair that Lydia kept for visitors, and he looked down at her and after an infinitesimal pause very punctiliously bowed, a mere sketch of a bow, and she looked up at him, sitting very still with her hands clasped on her lap and with equal punctiliousness bowed her own head. It was a most perfunctory courtesy, and she stared back at him challengingly as her head came up. He looked away, apparently bored, and said flatly, 'Oh! Good morning, Miss Lackland! I am sorry – I did not mean to intrude.'

'Good morning,' she said, and was proud of herself, for her voice was very steady. 'There is no intrusion so far as I am concerned, Mr. O'Hare.'

Lydia's lips quirked a little as she looked from one to the other, and then she smiled more widely and turned to rummage through the pots and boxes that littered her dressing-table.

'Powdered white, powdered white, where, oh where, is the powdered white?' she sang, and then, finding it, whirled in her seat again and held it out to him. 'There you are, my love! Now you need not kill your dresser, which is just as well for even if we found you another you would be no better off, for all are as stupid as each other! But do not let him spill this, or we are both in dire trouble.' And she gave him a ghost of a wink and grinned up at him with enormous satisfaction and after a moment he bent and kissed her mouth, hard and with real passion, and when he raised his head he looked at Phoebe over Lydia's tumbled curls, his eyes quite blank. And she looked back equally blankly, her hands still folded on her lap with meticulous neatness.

'Bless you, my precious! I am making a new tint – I have a fancy that I can produce a blue eye paint that will make more than usual of what Nature has endowed me with. The little I managed to make before that fool ruined it all suited me vastly! I will come and show you – when you are free. Later. . . .'

And he was gone, slamming the door cheerfully behind him, and both the women left behind breathed again more easily, for both had received the messages he had been so carefully sending.

*He will never play tricks with me again,* Lydia told herself complacently, looking again at her mirrored reflection and turning her head from side to side to admire the clean line of her jaw. *He knows I mean it and it matters to him! I might even, perhaps, marry him. One day – we must see how he shapes up with this production – there's more to a marriage than four legs in a bed, after all. I could not bear to be tied again to a failure. Last time was tedious enough. . . .*

*He is going to pretend it did not happen. He is going to pretend it did not happen.* Phoebe's little voice, the one that had spent last night chattering so hatefully in her ear all through the sleepless hours, started again. But this time she was grateful for what it was saying, deeply grateful. *He is going to pretend it never happened, and it is so much the best, it couldn't be better, for then it will mean it didn't happen at all, it really was all stupid imagination, it didn't happen at all, for I know it did not and he shows it did not, it's going to be all right . . .*

And she turned towards her aunt with a new eagerness and smiled brilliantly at her. And neither of them remembered that Phoebe had been trembling on the brink of a confidence and Lydia had been playing the Understanding Aunt about to offer her worldly wisdom and advice. Or, perhaps, both chose to forget.

'Please, aunt, *will* you help me?' Phoebe said, returning to her earlier theme. 'I am so glad and grateful to you for allowing me this small part in this production, and I am enjoying it all so much. The rehearsals are so much pleasure, I cannot conceive of the delight it will be when the play is actually being performed before an audience! And I am quite determined upon it, you know! I wish to do exactly with my life as you have done, and be an actress always. Please to help me, Aunt Lydia, for there is no one else who is so clever and so successful as you and—'

'Hush, child! There you go, being intense again! It is not necessary, and quite spoils your lovely face! Of course I shall help you all I can. You are my dear niece and very pretty and clever besides, so it will be no hardship. Of course you must see how matters progress with this play, for no one can make any promises of what will happen. However good rehearsals may be, the strangest things may occur once the piece is set before a paying audience. But rest assured, my love, that you are well regarded so far. I cannot offer you more than that, can I?'

Impulsively Phoebe jumped to her feet and hurried across the room to hug her aunt tightly and kiss her cheek ardently. Lydia lifted her hand and patted the soft round arm that was flung across her bosom and smiled at her and thought fleetingly of the child of her own who might have been as pretty and as charmingly grateful as this niece; and was happy.

Rehearsals moved into their last week and the pressure began to build up at the Haymarket, as the newly painted flats began to arrive – for this was to be a most costly play with special sets built to a most ambitious design – and costumes and properties were checked and found wanting, and wardrobe mistresses and stage carpenters and stage managers and the director shouted at each other and the actors who shouted back and then burst into tears and had to be coaxed back to work.

In the middle of it all Lydia gyrated, beautiful, unruffled, always sure of herself, always ready to work, always perfect, never angry or temperamental, never anything but amused and light-hearted. But beneath it all she was deadly serious, as Phoebe soon discovered, for she would go over her lines night after night, for hours on end, with Phoebe cueing her, until she thought her eyes would never hold open again, and her neck ached, and her head felt as heavy as lead. Lydia would laugh and say gaily, 'Just once more, pet, and then we shall send you home in my phaeton and you can sleep – just once more.'

At home in Stanhope Terrace there was some concern for the new pattern into which Phoebe's life had fallen. Gideon had been most put about when he realized that Phoebe would never reach home at night until after ten or more, as well as being all day at the theatre for rehearsals; and when he was told by a Phoebe who was strangely calm and direct in her ways, and not at all the coaxing sparkling minx he was accustomed to, that once the play opened she would be at the theatre every night until midnight or more, he tried very hard to put a stop to it all.

But she looked at him and at Abby, who was sitting on the other side of the fireplace in the drawing-room, and said quietly, 'It is a matter upon which I am quite determined, Uncle Gideon. I must tell you that I love you dearly and am much appreciative of all you have done for me, but I am quite set upon this. I shall have a career as an actress, and if you seek to say me nay, I shall have to go to my Papa. And if he says me nay, which I doubt, then I must go and live with Aunt Lydia, who will I know, allow me, for she tells me I have talent and should persist in my efforts. And she is, after all, my mother's sister. I cannot be said not to be among my own people, and therefore not in safe hands. . . .'

When she had gone Gideon looked at Abby almost helplessly and she had shaken her head at him.

'No, Gideon, there is nothing to be said, I am afraid. She has lived with us for so long that even you perhaps believe she is your child. But she is not. She knows herself that her situation is unusual. She knows that her father is the ultimate guardian of her welfare, but she knows even more certainly that he is, for all he is so good and careful a man, a most vacillating creature, and she can persuade him to do anything she wants.'

She leaned forwards and touched his hand gently. 'Furthermore, my love, I think she knows that we will not distress Jonah in any way that can be avoided. She may seem a flibberty miss, but there is some depth to her! She has lived among us long enough to know how we all protect Jonah from problems. We will not go to him about her, and she knows so perfectly well. She will be here every Sunday when he visits of course, for there are no rehearsals then, and so far as he will be concerned all will be going on as usual, and all will be well. And I would not let him think otherwise, for what good would it do? She will do as she says, you know, and go to her Aunt Lydia's house. And that would break Jonah's heart. She has changed in some way – she is much more determined, I believe, than we would have thought possible. Let be, Gideon. We must simply watch and wait. . . .'

And though she tried not to feel so, she was glad Phoebe was showing such stubborn determination, for it meant that Freddy must accept, somehow, that his hopes were totally blighted. Phoebe had set her mind on her career, as she called it, and it was as though he did not exist any more for her. When they met now – which was rarely enough – they were punctilious in their politeness to each other, but that was all. The old cheerful banter, the laughter and the teasing between them had dried up like a summer stream.

That Freddy was suffering misery was apparent to all; he

went about the house with an air of grim determination to go on being as normal, but even the babies knew he was different. Isabel would run to meet him when he came home from the hospital, and stand in the hall and stare at him, and then go back quietly to the nursery, and Sarah would gurgle and pout at him at breakfast time, but only for a little while, soon turning her attention to her mamma and her bread and milk.

And Freddy went on, working later and later in the evenings, often sending messages that he would dine at the hospital, and looking ever thinner and more tightly controlled when he did appear at home. And Abby, aching for him, bit her tongue and said nothing. That he had to suffer because of Phoebe, whatever happened, was obvious, and better for him to suffer now and get it over with, she told herself, than to persuade the girl into wedding him, for that could open the door to a lifetime of misery. So she said nothing, but she watched him and worried over him and grieved a little, while Gideon watched and worried over her. The house at Stanhope Terrace which had been so sunny a place in March seemed, in this hopeful month of April, to be lying in a shadow of its own making.

It was the last day of ordinary rehearsals – for the last two days before the play opened were to be devoted to dress rehearsals, since the piece was so lavishly provided with costumes and equipment and trick battle effects that much extra time was needed to perfect the technical aspects – that Jody came to the stage door.

Lydia had, in fact, hardly given him a thought since their last meeting. She had promised Dickon she would turn the boy away from her, to please him, and having said so promptly forgot him. It was as though in making the decision to reject him she had somehow sent him a spectral message to that effect, so that he no longer came to visit. So when her dresser came to find her on the crowded stage to tell her that 'that young man as was 'angin' around you all last week's 'ere and demandin' you should let 'im come and talk to you', she stared and frowned, and could not think for a moment who it might be.

Jody, who had followed the woman on the stage, having managed to dodge past the doorkeeper (a man of some ferocity who had been known to throw such a punch at a stage door hanger-on that the poor wretch had been senseless for half a day) saw the blank uncomprehending expression on her face as she listened to the dresser's message, and felt new rage boil up in him. All he needed was a chilly welcome here, he thought, and he would explode with it all. No one had any right to make him suffer as he did, he told himself furiously. *No* one.

He had had a perfectly dreadful week and his nerves were set on the finest of knife-edges in consequence. He had returned home after his last visit to his sister, from the delicious card-playing brandy-drinking intimacy at her house, his pocket plump with her guineas and his self-esteem even plumper with her admiration, looking forward to a most agreeable few weeks. With such a sister in town life promised to get better and better.

But he had found the house at Grosvenor Square in a turmoil. His mother had taken ill during the evening, he had been told, and she had asked for him most particularly. 'And if you please, sir,' Rashett had gone on unctuously, 'when we told her as you were nowhere to be found, and it was thought you had gone out for the evening, very distressed did she become. She had an attack of nerves, sir, and we took it upon ourselves, in your absence, sir, to send for the physician, who did all he could to soothe her and gave her a draught to make her rest, and sat with her a long time. He said you was to be told, sir, that she was a very frail lady, and not to be crossed unduly, for he couldn't answer for the consequences if she was. He'll call again tomorrow, sir, to wait upon Madam and tell you of the matter in his own person. . . .'

Jody had cursed and stamped but there was little more he could do; she had had these attacks before, when the frustration and loneliness and bitterness of her life would suddenly combine and work in her to make her nearly demented, so that she would thrash about her bed and wail and moan dreadfully and cling to him with hot wet hands and stare up at him, her eyes gleaming through her veil (and even at her worst, she was never without it) begging him to love her, take care of her, never leave her. If he moved away from her by as much as a yard the wails would rise into a shriek, and she would throw herself about even more, having what looked very like a fit, but could not be, for she was able to control the length of time they lasted, so that Jody could not risk setting a foot outside her chamber door. Her maid would set up a truckle bed for him beside the great French four-poster and there he would remain day and night until she had at last had her fill of her *crise des nerfs* and settled to the peace of emotional and physical exhaustion. Then and only then would she let him leave her for a little while to 'take the air in the park. But come back soon, my beloved, for I cannot tell you how ill I feel while you are away—' and gradually he would be able to stretch his 'airings' more and more until things were back to normal, and he was able to go about his own affairs again.

This time it had been more than usually irksome to have to remain tied to Grosvenor Square and the ailing, wailing Lilith. In the past there had been some sustenance in knowing that there would be at least recompense for his devotion to the sickroom; after such episodes his Mamma would be lavish of her money, would settle debts without a murmur and refill his purse most satisfyingly. But this time he had not needed her money, and that had made staying with her a matter of enormous irritation. There had been his sister on the other side of town, living a life of easy, lavish hospitality, laughing, gay, full of bonhomie and casual affection, and above all, clearly an excellent source of income for an impoverished young brother. And he could not get near her!

And when at last he could bear it no longer, and had slammed out of his mother's room leaving her screaming her distress behind him, and gone almost running out of the house with the sound of her misery ringing in his ears, he had come here to the theatre to find that the sister about whom he had been thinking and yearning constantly for the best part of the week was clearly uninterested in his arrival. It was almost more than he could bear: the anger in him thickened to a sour curd of hate, and he glowered at her from beneath half-closed eyelids, trying to look very sophisticated but succeeding only in looking sulky and truculent.

'There is no sense in frowning at me like that, young man!' Lydia said sharply.

She was feeling a little edgy herself this morning, for the costume fittings had taken even longer than had been expected, and mistakes in the original measuring had meant many alterations had needed to be made as she stood there with the seamstresses crawling about her. It was hot, the costumes were heavy and she was tired. The last thing she needed was an argument with a bad-tempered child.

'I am much too busy to be bothered now with anything but my work. You really must go away, there's a good boy! There is no time to talk now, do you understand? Please to go away!'

Had he been at all sensitive to atmosphere, to the needs and feelings of others, Jody would have understood, gone cheerfully away and sent her flowers and gifts to coax her into a better humour; and had he done so he might well have succeeded in persuading her to break her promise to Dickon. But Jody not only knew nothing of the precariousness of his position with her; he also lacked any awareness at all of any needs but his own.

'There's a warm welcome to a beloved little brother!' he said sneeringly. 'I had hoped for better manners than that from one who has aspirations to be the toast of the town when her play opens!'

Her head snapped up at that and she looked swiftly about her to see if any had heard him, but none had reacted, for the hubbub and noise as the preparations for the final dress rehearsals reached their peak made it difficult to hear anything, and then looked at him with her eyes narrowed and her mouth set very tight.

'Do you dare to make your threats at me, young man?' Her voice was low, but very clear. 'Do you dare to try to tell *me* how to behave? A slimy, useless little hanger-on like you, to dare to take exception to *my* manners? By God, you little turd, I've skinned three like you before breakfast, and not known

I've done it! Who the bloody hell do you think you're talking to, you heap of crap?'

Jody whitened. Although he was no paragon of the gentlemanly virtues, and kept very low company indeed when he was in the humour, he had never heard language as coarse as this from any woman, not even one of the whores that worked the taverns where he would go with his horse-racing cronies; to hear such words coming with smooth ease from the lips of a woman as beautiful, as charming and as desirable as Lydia was incredibly shocking; and then, as the shock subsided a little, he realized just how insulting it was too, and how much she had meant to insult him. To have spoken in such terms to him meant more than the actual words, foul as they were; it showed him, as nothing else could have done, how low he was in her estimation, how little she cared about his opinion of her; and his reaction was a surge of sick pain deep in his belly that made him actually take a step backwards.

'Aye!' she said, and her voice was withering in its scorn. 'You may well look like that! Get out of here, do you hear me? Never let me set eyes on your revolting face again, for if I do, I will set dogs on you! And make no more threats, you hear me? Make none, nor try to carry them out, for there is more to me than meets the eye and never you forget it! Bite your tongue and go away – *now*.' And she turned her back on him and went sweeping across the stage, her heavy medieval robe trailing behind her in a great curve of imitation ermine and red velvet, leaving him still standing there in the middle of the surging hubbub, staring after her.

# CHAPTER NINETEEN

THE theatre was humming gently with activity. It had hardly
seemed possible during the past two long days and even longer
nights of agonizing problem-ridden rehearsals that this moment
could ever arrive, but it had. All was ready and poised on
the edge of the moment when the immense purple curtain
would swing wide to reveal the vast stage with its great castle
setting, the moment when the musicians in the pit would strike
up the overture especially commissioned for this production,
and the most dramatic moment of all, when the first actors
would go swinging into the pooled lights centre stage with their
costumes a riot of colour and deeply satisfying if somewhat
anachronistic splendour.

In the various dressing-rooms around the periphery of the
stage which was the focus of everybody's attentions, hopes and
fears, reactions and feelings were mixed. In the big shared
dressing-room set aside for the male supers, sweating, cursing
actors climbed into heavy cloaks and mock armour, buckling
on the great flat-sided swords in exceedingly decorated scab-
bards which, though made of the cheapest of materials, were
still at least as weighty as they would have been had they been
made of real iron and precious stones and tooled leather.

In the women's dressing-room on the far side of the stage
the dressers sweated equally copiously as they coaxed their
charges into heavy skirts and tight bodices and great pointed
head-dresses, rushing from one to another with needle and
thread to repair sudden rents, pulling in corset laces to urge a
too well-endowed middle-aged actress into the costume in
which she would try to convince the audience she was no more
than three and twenty, and pouring out the mugs of ale that all
of them constantly and loudly demanded. The little pots set

over spirit lamps reeked as the actresses ready to put on their make-up settled down to melt ham fat and mix in the powdered colours they most favoured, and above that heavy smell, scent and sweat and ale fumes mixed themselves into an even thicker effluvium, all laced with the hint of coal gas, for the gaslight used at the Haymarket was a far from perfect installation, Phoebe, sitting in a corner trying to contain her nerves while she waited for a dresser to be ready to help her with her costume, felt her gorge rise and had to open her mouth wide and take a few deep breaths to control her nausea.

'Frightened, ducks?' One of the other women gave her a companionable shove with a sharp elbow and grinned at her through the mirror. 'No need to be! You could fall flat on yer fanny in this production, and no one'd notice. Chances are you wouldn't even 'it the deck, we'll be so close packed in those castle scenes. Never seen so many supers for one production! Still, mustn't complain – the more work there is the better I like it. Beats bein' on the game, don't it?'

And she winked leeringly at Phoebe and leaned forwards to apply paint to an already glowing red mouth.

And Phoebe, not really understanding the import of her words, but recognizing the kindness meant in them, smiled weakly back and nodded and tried, yet again, to calm her nerves.

At least the family were not coming tonight. She had not been able to hide from the people at Stanhope Terrace the fact that this was to be the first performance, for there had been considerable publicity about the opening of the new production of *Ivanhoe*. She had told them all firmly, however, that she would prefer none of them to be there.

'For,' as she said with all the wisdom of the complete tyro, 'the play must settle down, you know. First nights are never the best, everyone says that. I naturally wish you all to see the play, but not yet—' And she thought a trifle uneasily about the likelihood that even when they did come they would not see her, for she had but the one walk-on, and in a very crowded scene at that in which most of the time she was pushed so far back on the stage that only the people in the first gallery would be likely to see anything of her, and then just the very tip of her pointed head-dress, looking extremely foreshortened. 'And anyway, my part is extremely small,' she finished lamely.

Abby was glad indeed not to attend, for she had never found much pleasure in the theatre. In her childhood it had been a form of entertainment forbidden to her, and on the first occasion when she had seen a play it had been a miserable business, involved as it was with her mother's distress and later illness – but that was one thing she preferred not to think of now, after all these years; so she merely nodded at Phoebe's words and said cheerfully enough, 'Well, as you please, my dear. Tell us when and if you wish us to attend, and I am sure we shall contrive,' and she smiled at her husband across the breakfast table, who nodded soberly back, and said nothing.

And although no one discussed the matter, and his name was never mentioned, there was a tacit agreement between the three of them that the matter would not even be mentioned to Freddy.

Jonah was a different matter. Phoebe had thought carefully about him, and had decided to tell him in the easiest manner possible what was afoot, but in terms that would make him regard it with indulgent affection rather than genuine concern about what might become a career.

So, on the last Sunday before the play was due to open, after the usual Sunday luncheon shared by the whole family, and after Jonah's usual pleasant games with Sarah and Isabel – for he had a way with little children which was very delightful, and the small girls adored their uncle – during their usual shared walk about the long garden that lay behind the house, she had tucked her hand confidingly into his elbow and said, 'I want to tell you something, Papa.'

'Aha,' he said, and smiled down at her with great affection. 'Let me guess! You require a new gown, or better still two new gowns! And some shoes, and a bonnet or two and—'

'Oh, Papa, I am not always so greedy, am I, that I only ever want to talk to make requests for more bounty?' She pouted as she peeped up at him, using all the familiar wiles that she knew most enchanted him, and which he encouraged in her, for all he knew how contrived they were; it was a sort of game they played between them and always had.

'Not greedy, precisely – but you are a pretty child and so have a taste for pretty things which borders on the hungry!'

'Well, this is not about pretty things – although we may talk about that perhaps some other time—' he laughed at that, squeezing her arm tightly. '—but something quite other! Dear Papa, Aunt Lydia, you know, has been so charming to me!'

'Oh?' There was a sudden chill in his voice and he turned his head and looked down at her with a faint frown on his face.

'You do not like her, Papa?'

'Oh, I could not say that!' He sounded almost shocked. 'It would be most improper of me to show dislike for a lady who has done me no wrong – no wrong at all. . . .' His voice slid away into the note of unsureness that was so characteristic of him, and then, with an effort, he went on, 'I cannot dislike her – but in a curious way, she does make me anxious, my love. I cannot deny that to you! She – well, she reminds me of matters I would prefer not to – well I do not wish to *forget* your Mamma precisely, but – and of course Lydia is her sister and there is much of similarity – well, they are not alike, you understand. . . .'

She laughed now, and it was her turn to give his arm an affectionate squeeze.

'Dear Papa, how you do hate to have matters the least bit altered! If you could have your way, I believe every day would be exactly like the one before and the one after, and nothing would ever change and no one would ever grow a moment older, and all would be for ever perfect!'

'It sounds very delightful,' he said, almost wistfully, and then laughed. 'You are right of course! I am a shocking old stick-in-the-mud! So, your aunt has been charming to you?'

'Oh, yes, Papa! So much so that to amuse me she says I may walk on stage in her new play. She says I may have a costume and pretend to be an actress, and walk about the theatre like all the other real performers! Is it not a most droll idea? It will be capital fun! Of course I will not have to be like the real actors, and work and learn words and poses, will I? Just the pretending!'

She was walking along without looking at him, swinging her

bonnet by its ribbons at the flowers which lined the path, and feeling her heart beating a little more quickly than usual in her breast, and wondering if he could, by some mysterious insight, tell that while she was not precisely telling him a lie, she was not telling him the complete truth, either. But if he became aware of her determination, she knew, at some deep instinctive level, that he would oppose it, even loving her as dearly as he did, even while wishing to be as indulgent as a father could be.

But he did not see past her little deception, and smiled at her and said heartily, 'Oh, is that all? Well, if it amuses you, why not? I can remember the same offer being made to me, many years ago, to walk on that very same stage – well, actually I was offered a line to say! But I found it dreadful, and not at all fun! If it pleases you, sweetheart, then by all means – but do not neglect your friends, or your accomplishments while you are playing at the theatre game, will you? Or you will find yourself very down in the dumps when all this is over!'

'Of course not, Papa,' she had said and kissed his cheek, and turned the subject to Oliver and the news of his latest letter filled with his doings in remote York, and breathed again.

But now, sitting in the corner of the big noisy dressing-room, surrounded by women who were far from being as elegant of speech or as delicate of person as those to whose company she was accustomed, she found herself wishing, for one fleeting moment, that she had told her father the truth, and given him the chance to forbid her. Then she could have enjoyed hugging her sense of grievance and delicious dreams about the might-have-been world she had missed, whereas as things were she was faced with rather more reality than she had anticipated. And again she took a deep breath and tried to convince herself that she did not feel sick.

Nearer the stage, in the individual dressing-rooms reserved for principals, Dickon was swearing at his dresser and working himself up into a fever of temper. He had long ago discovered that he performed better, especially in stormy dramatic parts – which Ivanhoe certainly was – when fired with emotion. To drum up real feeling out of his own depths was something he had never been able to do; and when he had discovered quite accidentally how superb a performance he gave after giving his dresser a drubbing, he turned the knowledge to good use. Which was why so often he found himself without a dresser at all, or with only the stupidest, for the word went round the backstage fraternity very quickly, and few would work with O'Hare.

Lydia, on the other hand, was conserving her energies. She had talked agreeably to Mrs. Plunkett, who was playing Rowena, and was a rather tepid actress who never showed to much advantage in rehearsal and was so quiet that she made little impact on her fellow-players, but came up competently enough in her performance. She had sent her good wishes to the rest of the cast, via her dresser, and had herself checked that every one of her costumes was ready, that her quick-change items were set in her own cubbyhole in the wings, and that her paint was mixed and waiting. She was every inch a professional, and never neglected the smallest detail connected with her work. And now she was taking the nap that was to her *de rigueur*, recharging her emotions and her physical strength with shallow sleep. Everyone who had ever worked with her knew just how sacrosanct were these last few minutes of peace before the evening truly began.

Which was why she did not explode with anger when the doorkeeper came sidling into the room, his cap in his hand and his face troubled. It would have been the easiest thing in the world to scream at the man and throw things, like Dickon, and for a moment she wanted to, but instead took a deep breath, and said crisply, 'Well? I trust you have disturbed me to good purpose?'

'Indeed, ma'am, I can't say!' The man said apologetically. 'But I saw 'em, and the idea started to work in me, and work in me, an' I just thought well, suppose I'm right, an' say nuthin', and it turns out I was right an' there's trouble an' me knew all the time an' never warned nobody? I thought on it and eventual thought as I'd better come an' tell *you*, ma'am, as you're the one as 'as got most 'orse-sense about 'er, if you'll pardon me for sayin' so.'

'I'll pardon anything if you get to the point,' Lydia said,

attempting to cover her irritation with banter but realizing that the man's anxiety, whatever the cause, was real.

'Well, ma'am.' His voice became confidential. 'I nipped out front, see, for a quick wet wiv me mate as sits front of 'ouse and watches over the audience a'comin' in. Like, wantin' to wish the play every success, an' all.' He smirked a little, and then catching the impatience in her expression, hurried on. 'An' I'm sittin' there in 'is little cubby-'ole an' from there you can see clear aht to the street, see? Clear as yer like. Well, I sees these fellers, don' I? Four of 'em there is, all a'talkin' an' a'laughin' and I tells yer they looks a right smooth lot, an' I'm just about to say as much to my mate, when these fellers move rahnd a bit, and then I sees this other feller—'

'Well?'

'Well! I'm a rackin' o' my brains to see 'oo 'e might be, 'cos I seen 'im somewhere an' well I knows it, only I can't recolleck, no matter 'ow I try. And then my mate 'e looks up an' says, casual as yer please, "Well, if that ain't young Lucas, old Madam Lilith's boy, an' a right little bastard 'e is," beggin' your presence, ma'am, an' then I recollecks! 'E's the one's been 'angin' around you, ain't he? An' went slammin' aht of 'ere t'other day lookin' fit to kill someone? Well, my mate tells me a few tales about this 'ere geezer, and 'ow 'e's a right little article, and no error, and says as 'ow 'e wouldn't trust 'im wiv 'is own grandma. And the next thing the boy's been an' gone an' disappeared, ain't 'e? And the four fellers as 'e was talkin' to have come an' bought tickets, and I looks at 'em, an' me mate looks at 'em and – well. . . .'

He gazed at her for a long lugubrious moment and then burst out, 'An' if they ain't an 'ostile claque, then I ain't bin workin' in the theayter this past ten years an' more! They got that look, ma'am, and I just reckon someone ought to go an' give 'em the once-over lightly, like, and get 'em out, if it can be done. There's only the four, but I seen what damage the likes o' them can cause – mind you—' and now caution descended again, '—mind you, I could be wrong. . . .'

She was sitting upon her sofa now and staring at him, and after a long pause while she looked at him with her eyes a little narrowed she nodded briskly and swung her legs to the ground.

'I believe you. Thank you for your good sense in coming to me. Come, show me through the peep.'

She led the way swiftly from her dressing-room through the clutter of sets waiting to be used in later scenes, past the men busily setting the lights burning at just the right level, through the tangle of ropes and stage braces and cleats, to the great fabric wall that was the curtain; and reaching up at the O.P. side, swung across the little flap that disguised the small peephole that some long-ago actress had ordered made so that she could count the value of the house, when it was one of her own special benefit performances.

She jerked her head at the man who stepped forwards and peered through and then said huskily, 'Look to yer right, ma'am, t'other side o' that there column, an' you'll not miss 'em. Right bruisers, they are.'

He moved sideways and she replaced him at the curtain and began to seek the men he meant, and found them at once. The four of them were sitting spread out in their stalls, legs outstretched insolently so that other incoming members of the audience had to step over them, one chewing on a great cigar and the others laughing and talking to each other. They were bruisers, as the doorkeeper had said: the sleeves of their coats bulged disagreeably with muscle and the buttons strained across their heavy chests. Paid bully-boys if ever there were any.

She stood there for a long moment, thinking. Jody had pretended to threaten her with a disturbance at her first night, but surely that had been just a gesture, a trick designed to get her attention and amuse her?

It might have been at first, she told herself after pondering a while. It might have been. But then he came here and I gave him a tongue-lashing and – she closed her eyes for a moment, trying to conjure up a memory of how he looked, and at once her actress's gift for meticulous observation came into play, and she saw his face, white, tight and ugly with anger. Yes, indeed, he had been a very humiliated and furious young man that day.

'Damn,' she whispered softly, and opened her eyes to see the doorkeeper staring anxiously at her.

'What do we do, ma'am? There's 'alf the audience in now an' any attempt as we makes to throw 'em out will play right into their 'ands. Anyway, they're payin' customers, and we got no call to do nothin' to 'em if they don't make no trouble, 'ave we? I know I said as someone oughta do 'em over, but I reckon they've got us on a spit, trussed an' ready for roastin'.'

'Hush. Let me think. . . .' she said, and then after a moment nodded to herself.

'Well, there is a way out, but 't'will be costly. For my part, I reckon it worth while. You shall take them a letter from me.'

'Me, ma'am?' He looked very alarmed. 'Not me, lady, not for tuppence! I'd as lief grab a lion by its tail as—'

'No need to be fearful, man! They'll not touch you, not when they see what you bring 'em! And if you won't do it for tuppence you'll surely do it for a half crown, hey? Aye, I thought that would stiffen your courage a little!'

She made him wait outside her dressing-room door, under her dresser's eye, while she opened her cash box, the one she kept safely hidden in her travelling trunk. She counted out the money without a qualm; she liked cash, struck a hard bargain with any management that employed her, and salted away her earnings most carefully, her show of lavish living being based on very clever shopping and planning indeed. But she was no miser, and when the need arose to spend money, she did so with a will. And the need had, she felt, most certainly arisen now.

The letter she wrote was terse, and very much to the point.

*Gentlemen: We of the Haymarket much appreciate your presence here tonight. So much so, we wish to reward you. Here is a purse containing the sum of five gold sovereigns. By the same messenger, I have sent another ten sovereigns to Rules restaurant in Maiden Lane, hard by the Strand, to be collected by the four gentlemen who arrive there and present this letter by way of identity. The money will await you only for half an hour; once the curtain goes up, of course, the*

237

*money will be locked away ready to be returned to me. I am sure my message is clear to you.*

*Post Scriptum: No doubt he who sent you here to see the play tonight will be a shade perturbed at your early departure. But I have no doubt you will find a way to remove the perturbation from his mind.*

She signed it with a flourish as 'The Lady Rebecca' and called the man in from the passageway outside and gave him his precise instructions.

And then she set about putting on her make-up and climbing into her costume in her usual mood of easy readiness, singing softly under her breath as she did so; and when she was quite complete, having moved throughout with unruffled calm, took one last look in the mirror and then went sweeping out into the passageway and across the wings to the stage to look once more through the tiny peephole at the four seats at the back.

They were unoccupied, and looked remarkably strange in that huge auditorium where every other seat was filled with an audience fluttering with fashionable clothes and glittering with diamonds and rustling with feathers. She let her lips curve into a satisfied smile, and dropped the little cover to the peephole with a contented nod. *That* little problem had been solved.

Had she been outside, in the little alleyway that led round to Orange Street and the stage door, she might have positively grinned with satisfaction; for when the four men emerged from the theatre, clutching their letter and the neat purse that had come with it, they had been accosted by a very irate young man who had asked them shrilly, 'What the devil do you mean, coming out before the damned play has even begun?'

And they had with some insistence invited him to come with them to the alleyway so that they could explain why. And were doing so, driving their explanations home with a force that was making Jody's nose bleed and his lips split and his head hurt most abominably.

But Lydia could not see that, for she was on stage waiting for the curtain to rise on what was to be the performance of her career.

# CHAPTER TWENTY

PHOEBE was very grateful that the play was such a success. It was not because she herself gained any satisfaction from it – the notices in the newspapers had rung with comments about the beauty of Mrs. Mohun, the great strength of Mr. O'Hare, the tenderness of Mrs. Plunkett, and said not a word about the foreshortened tip of a tall head-dress that was only visible from the first gallery – but because it gave her peace of mind by keeping her so busy.

Day after day she arrived at the theatre in her little carriage for which Gideon had thoughtfully provided one of the factory servants to drive for her (for although he was distressed by and disapproving of her activities he still regarded it as his duty to protect her) and put on the heavy costume and submitted to having paint put on her face by the dresser, even beginning to learn how to do it herself. Night after night she returned home to Stanhope Terrace exhausted with the tension of it all, the noise and stuffiness and heat backstage, to fall into bed and sleep heavily until half-way through the next morning. She would fill the hours between rising and going to the theatre with visits to and from her friends, all of whom were quite thrilled by it all, seeing her as both shocking and deeply enviable, a most agreeable combination. And so had no time to think at all about past experiences and past distresses.

And there was another source of satisfaction in the success of the play – Dickon O'Hare's personal success in it, which had the effect of removing him even farther from Phoebe's orbit. The critical writers and commentators in the many newspapers had singled him out for a good deal of praise, which he fully deserved, for his stage presence was magnificent, his voice was deep and thrilling and his interpretation of the part heroic in the extreme. This had caused him to receive rather more respect from the theatre's management, who gave him every one of the extras he demanded, from a new carpet in his dressing-room to an increased rate of payment, and also from the rest of the cast.

Lydia in particular made more of him than she had, her attitude changing subtly from that of a mistress who commanded a willing slave to that of an equal who admired a professional. The two of them became positively wrapped up in each other, spending all their free time together. Lydia seemed to have forgotten her new-found satisfaction in family ties, so involved was she with O'Hare and the satisfactions he had to offer her. So, on the few occasions when Phoebe met either of them about the theatre – and they were very few, for a junior super could expect little contact with the principal players – they seemed hardly to notice her. Lydia would smile vaguely and sweetly and say, 'Why, Phoebe! Is all well with you? You look so delightful, child – I am glad you are content. . . .' and touch her shoulder casually as she went sweeping past, never stopping to discover whether in fact Phoebe was content; while Dickon ignored her altogether. And that was the way she preferred it.

She had almost managed to convince herself that the shameful, alarming and altogether extraordinary episode in Hyde Park had never happened. She felt in herself a new maturity and a new self-awareness which expressed itself in part in impatience with her old friends, who seemed to her now to be shallow and childish and often boring; but she told herself firmly that this was because she was now An Actress. It was Life in the Theatre that had changed her; and she would sit before the mirror in her bedroom after her maid had helped her undress and gone yawning away to her own bed, examining her face minutely in the mirror, seeking signs of this new Phoebe she felt existed in her. But she looked, to her own eyes, as smooth and as young and as agreeable as ever. Which helped her to pretend that she had in all truth dreamed that evening under the whispering trees.

The weeks of May moved onwards, with all London seeming

to rotate about Hyde Park and its Crystal Palace. The opening
on the first day of May had been a most glittering occasion, to
which Gideon took his family, although Phoebe had refused
his invitation, saying she was tired and needed to rest before
the evening performance. Not for the world would she go there,
she told herself. Not ever again.

But hundreds of thousands of people did, foreigners of all
persuasions pouring into the town from every direction so that
the streets and shops and the restaurant rang with exotic
speech-rhythms and fluttered with gesticulating eloquent hands,
and Londoners too came day after day over the bridges from
Lambeth and Rotherhithe, Plaistow and Camberwell and
Clapham and even as far south as Streatham; from Poplar and
Bow and Stepney and Hackney; voluble, happy, excited, and
proud as peacocks that their city had been selected for the most
important event of the century.

Freddy too was aware of the Exhibition. He could hardly be
otherwise, for the press of crowds in London meant inevitably
that there were more people demanding help from Nellie's for
broken heads and damaged bones and sickness of all sorts – but
like Phoebe had refused Gideon's offer of the opportunity to
attend the opening ceremonies. He had assumed, naturally
enough, that Phoebe would be of the party, and could not have
borne to walk so close beside her, on so light-hearted an occasion, for fear his control would snap.

For Freddy now was rigid with control. He had put all the
emotional effort of which he was capable into pushing his love
for Phoebe far down into the depths of his mind. She did not
want him and there was no sense in trying to evade that fact.
Not for Freddy the wallowing in painful yearning that he had
seen displayed by other young men, for many of his fellow-
students were susceptible creatures who fell in and out of love
with tedious regularity. His love was too real for any display of
pain to be possible.

The only way to deal with it was to contain it, and contain it
he did, spending extra time dealing with casualties in the out-
patient rooms at Nellie's, learning to put on splints, sew up

gashes, apply bandages and plasters, working long hours over his books, studying with a ferocity that his grandfather observed and admired greatly. The sight of Freddy going through his day brandishing his involvement with his work like a red-hot sword before him made the old man feel almost young again. So had he been, long years ago, when he had been struggling to obtain his professional competence, so had he been when he pored over his books at Gower Street when he was not occupied with his deeply satisfying days at Guy's hospital. So had he been when a green youth like this wholly admirable grandson.

He watched the boy, and talked to him, and taught him in a way he had taught no other student ever. And at the end of the weary days of surgery he would take him to sit in his private sanctum where they would discuss for hours the problems of aneurysms and tumours and operative techniques, and Freddy would ask questions, and Abel would ponder over them and answer them; and slowly a *rapport* grew up between the two that was the only source of true contentment Freddy had in those long spring weeks of 1851.

Even more unhappy than Freddy in his own way, was Jody, lying in bed in his mother's room in Grosvenor Square, sick with pain and blood loss but above all with rage. It simmered in him, a constant undertow of feeling that from time to time rose to fill every crevice of his mind with hate and plans for revenge and future satisfaction. And because his intellectual resources were few – he had not read a book since he had flung a lexicon at his last governess's head when he was twelve – he had much time to make those plans about what he would do to Lydia Mohun, one day, when the opportunity arose.

His mother, on the other hand, was supremely happy. The night he had been dragged home to her was one she would not soon forget; she had been lying weeping on her bed, tossing and turning in her misery, when she had heard the hubbub in the hall far below. When no one came to reply to her shrieks for information, she had dragged herself from her silk sheets and, wrapped in her peignoir, had tottered to the stairhead.

And had stood there staring down in sick horror at the

242

tableau below; her servants standing grouped about the two men in their blue, tightly-buttoned uniforms, their top hats set firmly on the back of their heads, their hooked belts with the lanterns and rattles attached round their portly waists, carrying between them the battered bleeding shape that was her Jody. She had stood there swaying for one brief moment, and then, moving with a speed she had not shown for many years, gone skimming down the stairs towards them.

'Sorry to cause you alarm, ma'am,' the older of the two policemen had said, staring with enormous curiosity at this apparition in a peignoir and all-enveloping veil. 'But we discovered this young man lying in an alleyway just off 'Aymarket, and 'e muttered at us as this was 'is address, and so we brung 'im 'ere. Not that we truly believed this to be right, on account 'e don't look like a young gentleman as would live in so important an 'ouse. If you takes my meaning—'

'Jody,' she had said, and put her hand out. 'Oh, God, Jody.'

And he had opened his eyes, or at least one of them, for the other was so contused and swollen that the lid could not move, and sworn horribly, and she had wept with relief, and had him carried up to her own bed, and undressed and bathed him with her own hands while waiting for the surgeon to come.

And since then, while he had lain chafing under the splints and bandages that were so cruelly clasped about his broken leg, she had nursed him, and loved him, and cared for him, cooking special little messes to tempt his capricious appetite, sitting with him for hours and coaxing and persuading him to be happy; and the more he swore and shouted, the more she tried to soothe him, finding deeper contentment in his dependence on her than she had known for many years – since his infancy in fact – until eventually he settled into a sulky acceptance of her ministrations, even beginning to quite enjoy them.

He had considered telling his mother about the source of his injuries, and then dismissed it, eventually telling her only that he had been set on by ruffians and did not know who they were; also he had said that they had robbed him, the opportunity for taking extra money from her being too good to be missed.

That she had her own causes to hate her daughter he did not doubt, but that was her own affair. Whatever lay between the two women from the past he wanted no part of it. He would not add his fuel to those flames. To form an alliance with his mother against his sister was not at all an idea that appealed to him. He wanted to pay his debts in his own way, and one day, he would. One day. When he was well again and out of this prison of a bed. . . .

But when he was at last allowed to get out of bed, he was appalled by his own weakness, and had stood there clutching his mother's arm and weeping with temper and self-pity. And she had clucked over him and kissed him and told him that he would soon be well, soon gain the benefit of air and sunshine and—

He had swallowed and rubbed his face with one hand and then shouted at her, 'Sunshine? You talk of sunshine? Have you no eyes in your stupid head? The rain never stops, and if I set foot outside the house I am so weak I shall fall no doubt and break the other leg! Is that what you want?'

'Then we shall go to where the sunshine is,' she had crooned at him. 'So we shall. We shall close the house, and go to Italy – you would like that, would you not? A little sea voyage and then the Italian lakes, and sunshine and good food and wine to build your strength. . . .'

He considered that carefully, and then agreed. He had long wished to travel, most earnestly wished to escape the shackles of the Grosvenor Square house, but she had always refused any suggestion of such a thing when he made it; but now, he realized, he could have almost anything he wanted, so frightened had she been by his injuries. Perhaps Lydia had not done him quite the disservice she thought she had.

There was time and enough to get his own back on her, he told himself. Plenty of time. Let her sit there in her damned theatre and quake, wondering what he would do and when he would do it. He would make her wait. One day, when she had been lulled into a false sense of security by his silence, one day he would return to the attack. So did he tell himself, warming his self-esteem with agreeable visions of Lydia suffering agonies of fear because of what she had done, and threw himself into his mother's plans for their extended journey to Italy. And never for a moment considered the possibility that Lydia might be quite oblivious of the threat he posed, might even believe she had put an end to his meddling for always.

They left London for Dover in a train in which Lilith had reserved an entire compartment for herself and her son, for expense did not matter, she told herself stoutly, where Jody's health was concerned. And also because she was herself more frightened than she would care to admit by this, not only her first journey in the roaring, snoring monster that was a train, so different from the dear familiar stage coaches of her youth, but also her first departure from the security of Grosvenor Square (apart from her daily carriage exercise) since the day long ago when she had been brought back there so dreadfully hurt, carried by anxious servants, tended by the long-dead Hawks. . . .

She shivered and pulled the blind down against the bewilderingly cluttered platform outside, leaving Rashett, who was travelling with them as Jody's valet, to supervise the loading of the luggage and the bestowal of himself and of her maid in the second-class carriage farther down the train. And turned to Jody, and tried to smile at him through the folds of her veil. But he did not look at her, lost, once more, in thinking about how it would be, later this year or maybe next when they came back, and Lydia would discover just how powerful a man her young brother was. . . .

June was sadly wet, for the summer did not carry out the promise of warmth made by the glitter of April, and this too fed the Exhibition turnstiles, for to be within the soaring glass mountain when rain was pattering down on the acres of panes was very thrilling, people told each other, and went there again and again. And it fed the theatres and with them, Jonah's Supper Rooms, which to his surprise and considerable satisfaction, became almost fashionable among many of London's visitors. The word had gone around, particularly among the Germans, that there was entertainment of the sort that they could enjoy, and for which language barriers did not exist, at the Celia Supper Rooms, and from mid-morning onwards the tables were full of people vociferously demanding refreshment.

Jonah, eager to make the most of the opportunity and spurred on by visions of the amount of money he would be able to put into the secret hoards he had for Phoebe and Oliver, set to work with an energy that almost surprised him. He produced a totally new show for his little stage, which he alternated with the one currently running, a system which meant there was music and dancing and comic singing to be enjoyed at the Rooms from eleven in the morning until almost three the following morning. He doubled the numbers of his waiters, and crammed several more tables into his establishment, as well as increasing his prices. He had not been so busy, or made so much money, for years. He was exhausted, exhilarated and quite oblivious of anything but work; even of his beloved Phoebe, for although he still made his regular visits to Stanhope Terrace every Sunday, he had fallen into the habit of dozing off in his chair almost before luncheon was over. Gideon and Abby would creep away and leave him there, a little amused and perhaps a little glad that he was so unaware of others.

Abby in particular was uneasy about what she had to regard as her own disloyalty, for she felt, as a parent herself, that Jonah should be more aware of Phoebe's determination to follow an actress's life. But if she and Gideon told him, and removed from him his comfortable notion that it was all just a *jeu d'esprit* on Phoebe's part, would not that be doing a disservice to Phoebe? And, ultimately, to Jonah himself? For that Phoebe was determined on her course was abundantly clear to Abby.

She felt herself on the horns of a most painful dilemma, and so did all she could to devote herself to her husband and children in order not to have time to think about the problem, and let the weeks pleat into each other contentedly enough.

By early July the Exhibition had settled down to become London's leading attraction, even though the first huge crowds of visitors from abroad and the provinces had gone home again, leaving the city still very full but more manageable. The Haymarket ticket office was content, for the play was clearly proving to be the success of the season, and Dickon and Lydia were doubly content, for they had persuaded the management that as they were both such obvious draws, and were having such a profound effect on the continuing success of the production, a share of the proceeds on a percentage basis was surely what they needed rather than a salary.

'As well as a salary,' Lydia had amended sweetly, and smiled brilliantly at the sweating Mr. Buckstone, who shook his head and tried to expostulate, but failed to move her. So, a percentage of the profits they both had (Lydia more than Dickon, for she took Mr. Buckstone to one side and told him privately that if she did not she would find herself sorely tempted to accept the invitation sent to her to join the company at Drury Lane) and were very pleased with themselves in consequence.

So pleased, in fact, that Lydia decided that they, as principals, should give a little crush for the rest of the players.

'For you know, Dickon, it is important to keep them all sweet! It is not unknown for the lesser people in a successful play, once the first excitement of the good reports has died down, to become somewhat jealous of the principals! And when that happens, it can be very disagreeable.'

Dickon who had in his time both used the many tricks a small-part actor can use to discomfit a more important one, and suffered as the target of them as he moved up in his career, agreed that it could be very disagreeable, but was less anxious to consider party-giving than was Lydia.

'For,' he said, 'they are a greedy lot, and it can be a costly business. Why not tell Buckstone to do it, if you are so anxious for it? For my part I—'

'Because, my love, it must come from *us*, and be seen to come from us! It is we who wish to gain the appreciation of the supers, not Buckstone! I shall arrange it all -- but you shall pay half the bills. No, don't scowl! You can afford it now, and it is me you have to thank for that, for I was very persuasive indeed with Buckstone, was I not?'

So it was that on the Saturday of the last week in July, when the stage had been cleared as soon as the curtain had fallen, and the usual dozen calls had been taken by Lydia and Dickon, and Lydia had gracefully accepted the flowers that had, as always, come over the footlights in great sheaves from adoring admirers (and there were several men who came to the same seats night after night to sit and worship her), that the company party was given. Lydia, who did nothing by halves, had provided handsomely, with huge York hams from Jackson's shop in Piccadilly and game pies specially baked and sent round from Rules in Maiden Lane, for no one baked better pies than they, and a couple of barrels of fine Whitstable oysters specially brought down by a fast train, and great quantities of beer and wine and gin.

And the company, including the dressers and the stage workers – for Lydia was shrewd about the importance of treating everyone as though they were of great personal value to her – set to with the minimum of prompting.

Dickon, standing a little to the side of the stage, watched her as she moved among the crowd – for altogether there were some seventy people there – and sighed a little. He had not intended ever to allow himself to become at all entangled with any woman. He, with his outrageously handsome face and those speaking eyes had, from his childhood, been the one to enslave others; he had enjoyed the attentions and gifts and adoration of more women than he could remember. And he had intended to go on being the footloose and fancy-free swain, the user of love but never the sufferer by it.

And yet here he was totally bewitched by a woman! It was galling. But he had to admire his own perceptiveness in selecting this woman to be enslaved by. Her beauty alone would commend her to the average ruck of men; but when there was added on her wit, her hard common sense, her money acumen, and above all her passionate nature (and his lips curved reminiscently as he thought of that aspect of her) she was a prize beyond price. So he told himself, for he was prone to think in such hackneyed phrases, and began to plan when he would speak to her of marriage.

For that, he had decided, was how it must be. There was no other way he could hope to hold her except by honest marriage, much as he – like many actors he knew – despised such tradesmen's morality, for there was an independent streak in her that could, he knew, flourish into a stubbornness that could make her go her own way completely. And that he could not bear; now was the time, while she too was full of the euphoria of their shared success, now was the time to settle the matter.

He had been standing there for a time, the stage before him brilliantly lit and looking like a great seething cauldron as people ate and drank greedily and milled about from group to group. Voices rose as the levels in the bottles fell, and someone started to play a fiddle on the far side, making some of the younger actresses shriek with delight and start to caper; and as skirts and petticoats began to whirl as more of the half-drunk crowd began to dance, he moved farther back towards the shadows. He wanted no part of this, he told himself a little scornfully, dancing with such scum as some of these people were.

He was watching Lydia, who had been whirled into the hubbub by one of the men who played the part of a castle guard, a tall and well-muscled young Scot who was holding her a great deal closer than Dickon regarded as altogether necessary. He considered briefly the possibility of moving into the whirling mass of legs and bodies and seizing her to dance with him, and then dismissed it. To show himself jealous would not be at all clever. And moved yet farther back.

So far back that he was able to hear the small sound above the noise, and he turned his head and peered curiously into the shadows. The sound came again, a small moan, and then the all too familiar retching noise of illness, and he grinned a little; he'd take a real pleasure in telling Lydia how her money had been wasted by greedy actors who knew no better than to make such pigs of themselves that they threw her good liquor and victuals back at her!

His eyes were more accustomed to the dimness now and he could see, tucked away beside one of the great flats that made up the castle wall in act three, a white shape, and realized that whoever was being so ill there in the corner, it was no actor. That was the shape of a gown, not of trousers and jacket.

Uninterested, he turned back to look at the stage and then

felt rather than heard the person move from her corner and come to stand behind him, and turned his head again to look.

And saw Phoebe standing there, her face so white it looked almost grey, and her eyes red-rimmed.

She was leaning against the stacked flats and breathing deeply, her nostrils flaring and then relaxing, and her eyes half closed. Instinctively he put out one hand to steady her, fearing she was about to fall as she swayed towards him, and he caught her and half carried, half dragged her to a stool that was set beside the wall. He pushed her down, and with the practised hand of long experience, thrust her head down so that it was almost on her knees, and stood there waiting.

She recovered after a very few moments and slowly sat up, to sit resting her head against the wall behind her, quite oblivious of the dampness of the whitewashed bricks and the way she was crushing her bonnet, loosely tied by its ribbons and hanging across her shoulders over her shawl.

'Well, are you feeling better?' he said after a moment, and she nodded slightly, but still breathing rather deeply, and still looking very white.

'You must learn not to drink so much!' he said, trying to be jocular. 'So many of you young actresses think you can—'

Her eyes had snapped open suddenly and she was staring at him with a glint he could not quite understand, and for a moment he was uneasy, trying to discover why this silly girl's stare should so discommode him.

'I have only once in my life taken too much wine,' she said at length in a low voice, but with an edge to it that grated on his ears, and he felt himself redden for all the world like a gawky schoolboy.

He had, in all truth, for a while quite forgotten what had occurred between them that April evening in Hyde Park. Just as she had been trying to tell herself that none of it had ever happened, that it was all a mad and ugly dream, that she and Dickon O'Hare were no more to each other than passing acquaintances, so had he; and had to a great extent succeeded, for she had, heaven knew, given him every cause to believe she had chosen to obliterate the whole incident.

'I have taken nothing here this evening,' she said after a moment, and now her voice had lost that painful edge and sounded merely tired. 'Neither wine nor food. I have eaten little for several days.' She opened her eyes and stared up at him dully, and he looked back at her, trying to swamp the thoughts that were rising in him.

'Well, it is summer, and despite the bad weather summer disorders of this nature are common – no doubt you have taken something that disagreed with you—' He tried to sound placatory, as though he were jollying a sick child, but she shook her head, still staring at him with those red-rimmed eyes.

'Do you not think I tried to convince myself of that? I have been saying it for the past – oh, so long I forget. But there are other symptoms – must I explain in every detail?'

'I do not understand you,' he said uneasily, and moved back a step, looking down at her with his face blank as he tried very hard to control the anxiety that was now threatening to overwhelm him. This was Lydia's niece, God damn it, he was thinking feverishly. She had not talked so much of her this past few weeks, but she cares for the girl, and if aught happens to her, it will be – oh God, Lydia's niece—

'Don't you?' Her voice was harsh, and seemed to have gathered strength, and she moved forwards, sitting up more straight and putting her bonnet and gown to rights. 'I must go home. Will you seek a carriage for me? My uncle's driver will not come for an hour or more yet, and I cannot wait so long.'

He wanted to nod and agree, wanted to run and find her a hackney cab and be rid of her but he could not. He stood and stared down at her and said flatly again, 'I don't understand.' It was as though in saying it he could make her deny his fears, but she looked up at him and shook her head and said with an enormous tiredness, 'I am increasing, of course. How can you find that so hard to understand? I have feared it for weeks, and now I cannot deny it. I am to have a child.'

# CHAPTER TWENTY-ONE

'I HAVE told you, and there's an end of it,' Phoebe said. 'And if you cannot take that for an answer, then there is nothing more to be said.'

She was standing beside the window with her back to it so that her face was in shadow and only her body was outlined. He peered at her, trying to see her expression, but he could not, for although it was getting dark now, Kent had not yet lit the drawing-room gaslight.

It had been an agreeable Sunday, perhaps the pleasantest since Phoebe had refused him. He had enjoyed luncheon with Uncle Jonah, who had kept all of them in a roar with his very skilful imitations of some of his German customers, producing ridiculous orders for unheard-of foods in a thick guttural accent so that the children whooped and Abby wiped tears of laughter from her eyes, and Gideon grinned so widely that his face seemed to be a totally different shape to its usual long seriousness. Even Phoebe had seemed agreeably relaxed, leaning back in her chair and admiring her father, and clapping him approvingly when he had finished.

And all afternoon, in the walled rose-filled garden where the sun was hot, and to be enjoyed as rare in this very wet summer they were having, while Isabel bowled her hoop or demanded her father play ball with her, he had lain there outstretched in a long chair and watching her, experimentally testing his feelings.

Did it hurt as much as it had to see the way her cheek curved so softly when she turned her head to speak to her father, lying on a rug on the grass beside her basket chair? Did the sound of her voice have the same knife-sharp effect as she said something jokingly to Isabel, clambering over her to reach the ball

252

she had thrown so badly? Did the way she held her cup, with both hands curving round it and her shoulders hunched forwards as she drank the tea the servants brought out and laid with such punctilious care under the sycamore trees, seem as touching and young as it had used to?

He had to admit that it was all as painful as it had been, yet somehow in a different way. It was sweeter, with a vein of almost agreeable melancholy beneath it. There had been no bitterness there in him this afternoon, as there had been for all those long weeks; no anger to be controlled, no sudden rushes of hate for all he had suffered. To be deeply in love with a girl who had rejected you was painful, God knew, he told himself, lying there and squinting greenly into the leaves above his head, but it need not be agonizing. He could learn to live with it.

And then she had put her hand on his arm when the family had gone trooping back into the house as the afternoon dwindled into evening and said breathlessly, 'I must speak to you, Freddy. Please, as soon as Papa has gone—' And at once, the fragile mood of acceptance was shattered. Hope came leaping up in him like some great wave attacking a hitherto quiet beach, making his ears almost roar with the suddenness of it, and leaving him breathless and tongue-tied.

'Of course – if you wish – naturally—' he had stammered, and then turned away to help Kent carry the heavy tea table back to the house, and she had gone away across the grass with her blue muslin gown glimmering in the half-light, and he had watched and taken a deep breath, and pushed his wild ridiculous hopes back down where they belonged. She could not be wishing to say what he wanted to hear. Could she?

And then when Jonah had gone and Abby and Gideon had taken their fractious weary children away upstairs to put them to bed (for it was Ellie's evening off, the night when Abby and Gideon revelled in their parenthood, bathing and feeding and loving their children and each other in scenes of domestic felicity) he followed her into the drawing-room, and fumbled in his pocket for matches.

'No,' she said breathlessly. 'No lights, Freddy. I – I could not speak to you if you could see me.'

'As you please, Phoebe,' he had said, carefully keeping his voice modulated, refusing to let any of the eagerness that was in him show for a moment.

'Freddy, what I have to say to you is very, very bad,' she said after a moment, and he had stood there and looked at her silhouette against the window, and felt himself filled with a huge weariness. He had known his hope was unjustified, known it was all his own imagination, but all the same it had been there. He had let his own desire dictate to him, had for those few minutes between her speaking to him in the garden and their arrival here been filled with a rosy glow. And now it was dead. Whatever she had to say, however bad it was – and what could be so bad? Did she need money? Probably. She had always been woefully extravagant – it could not be anything as jolting as the effect of his own ridiculousness.

Or so he had thought. Until he stood there and listened, almost unbelieving, trying to take in the sense of the words she was using, listening to her level voice speaking as calmly and collectedly as though she were discussing the cut of a gown or the style of a new bonnet.

He had stammered, trying to comprehend it, and patiently, as though talking to a backward child she had repeated it, slowly and clearly. 'I am to have a child, Freddy. I need your help.'

'But who – how – I do not understand – it is not possible—' he had said, his mouth suddenly very dry so that he had to swallow, and in trying to do so his throat, equally dry, constricted so that he almost retched. 'I cannot—'

'I will never tell you,' she had said at once, and for the first time there seemed to be some real emotion in her voice. 'That must be clearly understood. I shall not tell you, or anyone, now or ever. You may ask and you may ask and you may ask, but you will get nowhere. It is my affair and not yours or anyone else's. I ask your help, Freddy, not your – not a catechism—'

'But how can I – what is anyone to do unless – it is not that I – I desire to catechize you, but what sort of help can I – oh, God, Phoebe, who did this to you?'

And although his voice did not change pitch or tone, he

254

knew his own misery came out in every syllable, and he put out one hand towards her, standing there very still in the middle of the room while she stood so far away in the window embrasure. Only a few feet of carpet between them, but so far away.

'I have told you and there's an end of it. And if you cannot take that for an answer, there is nothing more to be said.'

They stood there in the rapidly darkening room and from somewhere above their heads came the sound of scales being played very unskilfully on a piano. Isabel in the schoolroom, Freddy thought inconsequentially, Isabel not wanting to go to bed and so pretending she had to practise her piano lesson. Doh ray me fah so lah te *doh,* he sang inside his head, staring at Phoebe's shape against the window. *Doh* te la so far me ray doh – Isabel, little Isabel, with her curls and her round cheeks and her bobbing head, her tongue caught between her teeth as she concentrated, doh ray me fah so lah te doh – just like Phoebe had been used to do, while he sat beside her in their shared schoolroom there in the little house at Paddington Green. Doh te lah so fah me ray *doh.*

He did not know when the tears had started. He just knew that his cheeks were wet as they ran down, that his nose and throat were filled with it, and his chest seemed as though it would burst with it, and he clenched his fists and closed his eyes and tried to stop, but he could not, for the sobs, great wrenching sobs, came up needle-sharp into his throat, and forced their way past his teeth, and he was weeping as hopelessly as Sarah or Isabel, a child bereft.

'Please, Freddy, what good is that?' Her voice was tired and so flat that it sounded like a stranger's. 'Do you not think I have wept until I am half blind? Do you not think I have lain awake night after night, so wet with tears it was as though I were dissolving into nothing? Do you not think that is what I would have *wanted* to happen? If tears would help, I have shed enough to make all well for every stupid female in London.'

He shook his head and swallowed, and reached into his pocket for a handkerchief, and blew his nose and scrubbed his face and then, moving very heavily, crossed the room to sit in the armchair beside the dead fireplace, staring down at the fan of pleated white paper which filled the space where in winter the coals glowed so warmly. Winter, he thought. Was it winter when we were here and I told her how dearly I loved her and wanted her? It was a lifetime ago. And he was filled suddenly with a huge rage that made him shake so much that he had to fold his arms across his chest and hug himself to still it. And he did not know whether he was enraged more for himself than for her, and the knowledge of that added to his fury.

'Will you help, Freddy?' She had not moved from the window, but she had turned her head and was staring at him, and he lifted his head and looked at her and saw the faint glint as the fading light caught her eyes.

'Help you? Oh God, what can I do? You tell me nothing, so how can I help you? I imagine you – that you have some regard for – that the man, oh, God, don't you *see*? How can I make sure he behaves honourably if I do not know him?'

'I do not wish to be wed, Freddy!' she said, her voice almost pitying, as though he were again that backward child who needed such careful explanation of every detail. 'Do not misunderstand me! I have no wish to bear this child. If I did, of course, the matter would be different. But I do not. I ask you to *help* me.'

Now he understood. Now it came clearly to him, everything she had said, her refusal to tell him anything of the cause of her dilemma, all of it. He looked at her but he did not see her at all; but saw instead a girl in a mock schoolgirl dress, but cut so low that her breasts were all displayed, her hair about her shoulders, and her hand set urgently on his grandfather's coat sleeve. 'I ain't 'avin' no baby, not no'ow. They said if I tol' you, you'd *'elp* me, but I ain't 'avin' no baby!'

The girl in Panton Street. The girl in the house where women displayed themselves for sale to whoever came in, where the walls were hung with pictures of such explicitness that he had blushed to see them, and yet of which that girl had been quite oblivious. That girl and Phoebe. That bare-breasted gutter creature and his delicate, protected, beloved Phoebe. And this time he really did retch, his throat tightening against the sickness in him as though a huge fist had closed around it.

'I daresay there are others I could go to.' Still her voice had that remote considering sound about it, as though she were talking of some minor matter, some easily settled debate about the colour of a new pelisse. 'I have been about the theatre long enough now to know there are some sources of assistance for such as need them. But I who have a family so deeply engaged in the affairs of apothecaries and surgeons do not, I hope, have to seek such aid. But I will if I must.'

'Phoebe—' he swallowed, and thrust his hands into his pockets, trying to be as calm and as sensible as she was, feeling for the first time in all the years they had been so close to each other that she was the wise one, the older one, the clever one, and he the simple little flibberty child who needed to ask questions, needed to have all explained to him. 'Phoebe, what has happened to you? I have known you and loved you as long as I can remember. I thought I knew every part of you, all your moods and ideas – and – and now I do not understand anything! That you should speak of such things, that you should have heard such talk and – and *understood* it – I cannot – you are not my Phoebe any more.'

'I never was,' she said after a tiny pause. 'I never was.'

And again the pain of his own loss came bubbling up in him, but this time he understood it more clearly. His anguish on her behalf, for her suffering and distress, was real enough, but stronger than that, deeper than that, ran the sense of his own rejection. He had offered her a lifetime of love and devotion and care, and asked nothing more than that she should hold his hand, perhaps kiss him in a gentle affectionate sort of way, and she had refused that and instead given to some stranger, some fly-by-night she had found in that theatre, all of her self that mattered; her abandonment, her passion, all the years of young growing and living that had added up to the desirable and adorable and wholly perfect creature she had been in his eyes.

And his pain became fury and he moved across the room swiftly, so swiftly he hardly realized he had moved at all, his hands upraised, and without stopping swung his arm back and with his open palm hit the side of her face so sharply that her head swung round and there was a faint click from the bones in her neck that came like a jeering echo of the sound of his slap.

They both stood there very still, he with his arm held awkwardly across his chest where it had been carried by the force of his movement, she with her head twisted to one side, and the silence between them grew until it seemed to be shrieking in his ears; and then she drew a long shuddering breath and slowly, almost creakingly, turned her head so that she could look up at him, and said wearily, 'Very well. *Now* will you help me?'

And suddenly, she was Phoebe again. Silly little Phoebe who had so simple a view of morality that she had always believed the small child's belief in the essential fairness of life. If you were hurt, someone had to kiss you better. If you were naughty, you had to be hurt afterwards. Then and only then was the slate clean. And because he had hurt her, she had the right to expect his help rather than merely ask it; and although he wanted to explain to her, to show her the enormity of what she had done to him, he could not. In letting his rage leak out of the ends of his fingers he had tacitly committed himself to her viewpoint. He had to help her, will he, nil he. She had a right.

'I will need information,' he said harshly, turning away and going back to stand before the empty fireplace. Odd how that fan of paper stood there, so prim and polite, hiding the emptiness of the grate. He would need a fan of paper to hold before the emptiness in his own life, now. 'You understand what I mean?'

'About my – personal details?' she said, and now her voice sounded familiar, a little tremulous, leaning on him, deferring to him. 'I have written it down. I was worried, so I wrote it down. Dates and – and things—' Her voice trailed away and then gathered strength. 'It is in my commonplace book. I will go and fetch it.'

'Commonplace?' he said and laughed suddenly. 'How very strange!'

She hesitated at the door. 'Yes, I suppose so. All of it is very strange. I – Freddy, I want you to know – it was not – I am not a bad person, really. Am I? I did not intend it to happen, nor I think did he, but the wine was very nice and tasted of Christmas. The raisins, you know? And it was not designed that I should fall and hurt my ankle – you must understand that. I am not like the other people at the theatre. Although some of them are very genteel ladies, really. Not so fortunate perhaps as some—'

'You were going for your commonplace book,' he said. 'If you cannot remember the information without it.'

'I – it is easier for you to read it than me to say it,' she said. 'Please to wait for me. . . .'

The door had almost closed behind her when his voice called her back.

'Phoebe. While you are bringing it – I want you to think about something. I am not demanding you tell me. Not any more. But think about whether you should not tell me who it was who did this to you. Not because I wish to seek him out and – and damage him in any way, but so that – in case you suffer again yourself. You are young and do not always understand things as I do. And I have seen enough of the people who come to us at the hospital to know that – that such an experience as you have had can profoundly change a woman. She may allow herself to be hurt again and again because she has some mistaken notion of – of affection for the man who treated her so cruelly. That is why I want to know – to help you.'

He was seeing them in his mind's eye; the women swollen with pregnancy, their faces thin and drawn and blurred with bruises, eyes puffed and purple from the contact of a human fist, arms hanging uselessly broken, saying flatly, 'It was me man wot did it. Nah – 'e din't mean it. 'E never does, reelly—' and refusing any offer of sanctuary in the hospital because 'Me man'd 'it me wuss if I din't get 'ome ternight.'

He had been amazed and sickened by them, and asked Abel how it was any woman, even gutter women like this, could choose to stay with men who treated them so ill. Abel had looked at him with those narrow green eyes under the heavy dark brows clouded with a considering expression, and then said, 'It is because the man awakened them to their own passions, Freddy. A man must take care, a thinking man, that is, how he treats women. What is to him little more than an agreeable adventure, a romp between a pair of sheets with a giddy girl, can be to her a key that opens a door she can never close again. It is as true for ladies of breeding as for these creatures. I have seen them in my private practice, women who suffer much to propagate, Freddy. More than we can ever know, however much we think we see. . . .'

' He had to protect her from that, he thought with a sudden urgency. The damage that had been done was incalculable enough. There must be a way to protect her from more.

And underneath his thoughts, he knew he lied. He wanted to know because he *did* want to seek him out and damage him. In many ways.

She stood and looked at him there in the almost dark room, at the square solidity of him, and wanted to tell him. All of it. The way the world had twisted and turned and been so joyous, and yet so dreadful afterwards. She ached to tell him. But behind that ache lay another; the memory of the way that Dickon had looked down on her sitting there on the little stool leaning against the damp brick wall and said flatly, 'You are a liar. If you say to anyone, anyone at all, that there has been any liaison between us, I will deny it. And why should you be believed above me? Did any see this episode? Did anyone know that you and I ever spent any time together? Why, on the very day you are *supposed* to have been so ill-used by me, I was with your aunt. That very morning, I was with your aunt—' and his mouth had curled in a curious way that had made her feel suddenly very ashamed, and she had dropped her gaze. '—and she above all will not believe your lies! No, my child. Whatever you do, do not tell anyone that I have any involvement with you! It will get you nowhere! But if you keep your mouth shut, I can help you – tell you where to go—'

'Where to go?' She had looked up at him there in the musty dusty shadowy wings beside the glittering stage and been puzzled. She had not yet been able to think at all about what she would do, how she would manage, had not thought of the future in any way. 'Where to go for what?'

'Why, to be rid of it, for God's sake,' he had said irritably.

'Are you a complete ninnyhammer? There are ways and means, woman, ways and means! There are people making a good living in the removal business – and I will make arrangements for you if you wish it. And pay for it, and that's not tuppence, I can tell you! But one word from you to imply I had aught to do with your dilemma, and I wash my hands of you. Understand? Not a word. Which none would believe anyway. . . .'

And she had watched him go sauntering back on to the stage, watched him move through the throng towards her aunt, put his arm about her waist and bend his head to kiss her, saw the eager, almost girlish way in which Lydia's head came up and she responded to him. And she had to believe him. Who would believe her? Who would ever believe her?

So she shook her head, and said, 'No, Freddy. I know you mean kindly, but no. I will never say. Not to anyone, ever. I will go and fetch my book. I won't be long. . . .'

# CHAPTER TWENTY-TWO

HE woke very suddenly thinking, 'O'Hare'. He had not even realized he had fallen asleep until that moment; he had lain there for hours staring at the ceiling, watching the faint moon-thrown shadows creep across the room and then die, hearing the occasional clop of a late cab and random cries of roisterers drifting home give way to the early morning traffic bringing poultry and eggs and milk and fruit and vegetables into London's markets from the remote farms of Middlesex and Oxfordshire, trying to live with the knowledge not only of what had happened to Phoebe, but what would have to happen yet.

And all through those long hours he had not allowed himself to think of who might be the architect of all his misery; until now, waking so suddenly that he sat bolt upright in bed and said the name aloud to the blackness of the before-dawn sky beyond his bedroom window.

O'Hare.

The smooth mountebank, the man in the insolent clothes. The man he had seen and disliked and then almost forgotten. Who else could it be? Who else did she know? He would not let himself consider the possibility that she had become so light, so careless and so venial that she allowed herself to become in-volved with any other man at the theatre, any of the many lesser versions of the hated O'Hare who probably infested the place; to think so would be to offer an even greater insult to her. Not, he thought bleakly, that she was, in polite people's eyes, insultable at all. If any of them knew of her situation she would be thrown out completely from any semblance of good society. A pariah woman so far beyond notice as to be as good as dead.

He turned again in his rumpled sheets, and pushed the bolster more firmly beneath his cheek. Well, suppose he was right? What then? He could do nothing about it without her corroboration, and that he could not obtain from her. He knew that. But once let this dreadful business be over and done with, and then, indeed *then* would he deal with the matter. If it were really necessary to do, for she would at least no longer be in any contact with the dreadful, hateful, sickening world that was the theatre. She must surely, at last, abandon this lunatic ambition of hers, seeing just how dangerous it was. She would again come home to live a normal life, and perhaps—

And now, at last, he looked honestly at the one thought which had been trying so hard to get through to his awareness and which he had most resolutely kept battened down. His own feelings about her. Suppose she did come back? Suppose she did come to him and say, 'Freddy, I was wrong. I do not wish to be an actress. I will marry you,' would he seize her in his arms and kiss her and be jubilant? Would he go to their elders, to Abby and Gideon and Jonah, and tell them of the news and set to making plans for weddings and wedding trips and a home with a nursery and—

He rolled over in bed again, punching at the bolster furiously. He could not think about it, he would not think about it, he would concern himself only with the practicalities of the situation. He had answered her plea for help. He had told her he would aid her. And now he had to do it.

How?

He could not take her hand and lead her up the steps of Nellie's to the ward where the women lay after having their operations. Quite apart from the horror of such a place – where no man could take a gentlewoman to lie, for it was full of whores and worn-out drudges, the dregs of Covent Garden and Seven Dials – there was the problem of Abel. He was in firm control of his hospital, in spite of the fact that now there were so many other surgeons and apothecaries and physicians working there. Each day he made his rounds of every ward, going from bed to bed, checking on names, on diseases, on treatments, whether they were his own patients or not. Phoebe, were he even to consider taking her to be a patient there, would be recognized by Abel before twenty-four hours had passed. Even though Abel saw little of this granddaughter of his, because of some long ago argument between her father Jonah and himself, he knew her. And would concern himself with her very much indeed.

There had to be some other way. And though he lay there as the dawn moved greyly through his window bringing with it another day of thin rain and summer chill, though he twisted and turned and thought of every avenue he could, he saw no way in which he could keep his promise to the girl who lay in a bed in a room just across the hallway from his own and who was probably sleeping soundly, feeling safe again now that she had come to him.

They breakfasted *en famille,* as usual, but Freddy's sleep-starved pallor and Phoebe's total lack of appetite went unnoticed, for both Abby and Gideon were very abstracted with their own business affairs. Today was to see the launching into operation of the new big multiple pill-making machine on to which so much of the future success of Caspar's was pinned, and Gideon was busily checking the lists which bore details of the quantities of drugs to be used and the number of pills to be made while Abby was going over the instruction sheets which had been prepared for the operatives. Since none of them could read, she had herself planned for them a series of pictures which showed which handle had to be pushed when, which ratchets fitted which cogs, and the precise order in which each action had to be performed. Any deviation from the rules laid down by the design of the equipment could result in the most costly damage, and Abby was well aware of the fact; so when Freddy and then Phoebe came into the breakfast parlour she hardly raised her head when she murmured, 'Good morning.' Only Gideon looked up for a moment to say a little vaguely, 'Phoebe? You do not usually honour us with your presence at breakfast!'

'Oh, you forget there was no performance last night, so I slept early, Uncle,' she said lightly, her back to him as she helped herself to food she would not eat from the sideboard.

But even before she had finished the sentence he had stopped listening, his head once more bent over his sheaf of paper.

Ellie came in to collect the children, both of whom were quieter than usual this morning, and said sourly, 'There's 'Enry Syden'am out in the 'all, and at this ungodly hour, too! Not eight o'clock yet, it ain't, an' there 'e is, askin' for you an' the master, cheeky as you please! I told 'im, that I did—'

'Then you took too much upon yourself,' Abby said crisply, and got to her feet in a whisper of dark green serge, settling the neat white lace collar and cuffs with hasty fingers, and urging Gideon to hurry up, for there was much to be done before the machinery could start its tests. And the two of them went rushing away, Abby dropping a swift kiss on Freddy's head as she passed him, and on Phoebe's dutifully upturned cheek, and Ellie followed them out with the children, muttering darkly, as she so often did, about people who told people nothing about what was going on and expected people to be mind-readers or suchlike magicians.

They sat there in the backwash of quietness, neither looking at the other, and then Phoebe lifted her head and said painfully, 'Have you forgiven me, Freddy?'

'Forgiven you?' He shrugged slightly, grimacing. 'How can you ask so absurd a question? You did not break my new hobbyhorse this time, or tell Ellie it was I who took the pigeon pie from the larder. Such childish episodes can be forgiven and if not precisely forgotten at least remembered with amusement. This is a rather different situation.'

'You think I am still a child, do you not, Freddy? That I do not comprehend what I have done, how wicked I have been – how enormous a burden I have put upon you in seeking your help? But I am not a child, Freddy. I told you that when you asked me to marry you and you did not understand. You still don't. Although I have grown up even more since then.'

He looked at her, sitting there on the other side of the table, and shook his head slightly. 'I do not see you as a child, Phoebe. I could never do that, ever again.'

And indeed she looked different now. She was thinner, her loss of appetite over the past days now showing in finer planes in her cheeks, in a faint hollowing of her temples; and almost as though she wished to show the world her new-found and painful maturity she had dressed in a manner that was unusual for her. Not the pale blue or lemon which she had loved because they set off her dark curls so intoxicatingly, but a sober brown merino, with the least possible braiding about the collar and sleeves, fitting tightly at the bodice but not as billowing of skirt as she usually wore. Her hair had been pulled back from her face into an imitation of Abby's neat knot, although several of the unruly curls had escaped to lie on her neck and forehead. He looked at her, and swallowed and tried to smile, but he could not. She looked so very lonely, sitting there.

'When I ask your forgiveness, Freddy, it is not because I seek absolution, you know. I meant only to ask if we were – oh, friends again! I suppose I am greedy because I would like to feel that you are – you are helping me because you wish to, as much as because I asked you to. That is what I meant. No – don't answer. I think perhaps it would be better for both of us if we did not explore our feelings any further. We will, if you please, keep it businesslike—'

She stood up. 'I do not know precisely what is to happen, Freddy. Shall I go to the theatre as usual? There is no matinée today, of course, so I may stay here until five o'clock. After that, of course, I must go—'

He looked up at her sharply. 'You intend to *remain* in this play?' And his voice was incredulous.

She lifted her brows at him. 'Of course! Quite apart from anything else, it would appear very odd if I were suddenly to be absent. It is most unprofessional to miss performances, unless one is very ill, or—' She stopped then and her mask of maturity slipped a little. 'Freddy, will I be – ill? Will I be hurt and be—' She shook her head suddenly and turned away, trying to hide the rush of tears, and he looked at her and could not bear it.

Swiftly he went round the table to put out his hands and she looked up at him with her grey eyes swimming and held out her own hands. He took them and then put his arms round her and she sighed very deeply and moved closely and settled her head on his chest; and he stood there swaying rhythmically, just as he did when Isabel or Sarah needed soothing, and murmured softly in a wordless monotone as she wept silently.

'I will do all I can, as soon as I can. Please, Phoebe, try not to think about it at all, will you? Difficult, I know, but you will gain no benefit from fretting. I will make what inquiries I may today, and as soon as possible, I will see what can be arranged. There is little time to be wasted anyway—'

She looked up at him. 'Should I have told you sooner, Freddy?'

He grinned a little wryly. 'If it could have been so much sooner that it was before any of it happened, yes. But—' He shrugged. 'I must go now, Phoebe. Will you be all right? I wish Mamma were here today. . . .'

She shook her head, rubbing her wet face with the back of her hand in a determined fashion. 'I shall be perfectly all right. Of course I shall! And I shall try not to think about it, as you said. But please, Freddy, do try to be *soon*. I can manage most things if there is something actually happening, you know.'


He spent the morning in the operating room with his grandfather, who was in an expansive and communicative mood. The first operation of the day, with Mr. Snow standing at the patient's head with the drip bottle and cloth that Freddy was beginning to regard as part of him, promised to be so interesting that even Freddy was able to be totally absorbed in it, standing there craning his neck with the rest of the students, trying to gain as good a view as possible before Abel started.

'I have told you before, gentlemen,' Abel boomed at them, 'That the advent of chloroform, especially in the hands of our good friend here, Dr. Snow, has made it possible for me, like other surgeons, to sacrifice mere speed to delicacy of action, and you will, I think, agree that in this morning's first case there is much need for delicacy, and not simply because the patient is a female.'

The students gave the little titter of laughter that was clearly expected of them and Abel looked up at them and nodded with a rare benignity.

'You observe the massive swelling of the belly. This is, I believe, due to a tumour growing upon the generative organ, the ovary. It has been established that such growths are common, and may be harmless, but all too often suffer torsion and strangulation or rupture, whereupon the patient suffers extremely severe griping pains, moves into a state of collapse, and may die very rapidly. I have performed a number of anatomy room dissections on such that have died of the disease, and been most struck by the health of the remaining organs. This condition is not like the cancerous ones in which the growth affects all its touches, and even areas of the body it does not, for we have seen great growths appearing in lungs and liver when obviously there was a much worse growth elsewhere that started the contagion. No, gentlemen, the situation is clear that in these ovarian tumours, which frequently afflict young females, the growth, were it to be safely removed, would not leave behind any legacy of disease to make our efforts a waste of time. Also, early removal of the mass, before strangulation or rupture occurs, clearly gives us a patient with a better chance of recovery. It is of little satisfaction to succeed with the operation but fail to keep the patient alive.'

He peered up again at the students. 'So, to this patient! Some twenty years of age, a better fed and cared for female than some, she was sent to me by my colleague Dr. Chadwick by whom she is employed as a nursemaid. He feared she was like the rest of her sort and, though she denied it, was with child without benefit of clergy.'

Again the students tittered, this time with a little more certainty, and Freddy felt a lurch of memory that was so sharp that he felt sick. He swayed and the red-headed student beside him grinned and nudged him with one shoulder, offering the friendly support that sometimes was much needed in the operating theatres (for Abel had been known to be exceedingly acerbic towards any student who had the temerity to faint), but Freddy shook his head and managed to smile reassuringly and returned his attention to the table.

'—without damaging adjacent organs,' his grandfather was saying. 'One handles carefully, and with delicacy not only of

268

touch, but of cleanliness. Aye, I know many of you have been vastly amused by my finicky ways. I have heard your ribaldry, never fear—' The red-headed student standing beside Freddy suddenly flushed and moved back behind his neighbour. 'But it is not merely old-maidish ways that makes me demand washed hands and scrubbed instruments and good white linen when I work.'

Snow looked up then, and smiled thinly. 'You're not alone in that, of course, Abel. I took a case last week for Tom Spencer Wells, at the Samaritan dispensary for women. He is beginning to show much interest in these ovariotomies, and insists always that the success he has – and his record is good – is due as much to his concern for clean working conditions as to any dexterity he may have.'

'Aye,' Abel grunted. 'And he is a wise young man. We are fortunate that he chose to settle here in London when he left the Navy two years ago. He came to me to study some aspects of female anatomy when he first arrived.'

He had turned to the bowl held ready by the nurse and was washing his hands with great concentration. 'Why it matters to be clean, we do not precisely know. I have some ideas of my own upon this – I have always been much exercised in my mind about the manner in which contagion spreads, and there is much in the sepsis that afflicts our surgical patients that seems to me to have a contagious source. That we must find the reason for the pus is undoubted. This patient on the table here, even since the advent of pain-dealing methods which have made so much work so much more possible to us, is in as great a danger as that any soldier on a battlefield must experience. Anything we can do to protect against that danger we must do, whether we understand the reasons or not. So I wash my hands and my instruments and also the patient, everything I can, like the most old-maidish of spinsters, since it seems to help. Now, gentlemen, to work!'

Freddy watched almost dreamily. He was once more swept away, not by the excitement of the dramatic tension of it all, real as that was, but by the beauty of the scenes that unfolded before his eyes. Just as once before he had found himself entrapped by the sight of a living, breathing body revealing itself to that prying darting scalpel, so he was again.

Abel's knife moved smoothly and yet with seeming casualness, slitting the belly from the navel to the crest of bone above the pubic hair as easily as if the knife were red-hot and the flesh beneath fashioned of ice. But there was more flexibility to the tissues than that, and Freddy watched, his mouth a little open, as the assistant standing close beside Abel reached out and touched each spurting little vessel that leaped out in the wake of the knife with a bead of hot pitch. The pitch bubbled and blackened on the yellow flesh, and the bleeding stopped and the faint sickly smell of burned flesh rose lazily in the air; and then Abel with a sharp movement pulled the incision gaping wide and slipped in the great blades of metal he had had fashioned for the purpose by a blacksmith whose quinsy he had once cured, and the assistant seized the looped handles and pulled, and there it lay in the shallow depression, the heaving gleaming pearliness of the peritoneum.

And Freddy marvelled yet again at the difference there was between living flesh and the dead butcher's meat upon which he had had to practise all through the hateful hours in the anatomy room. It was so tenderly reflective, throwing such soft gleams of light from its pellucid surface, and it was almost with regret that he saw the slit appear as his grandfather slid another knife beneath the tiny hole he had pinched out with his forceps, holding his finger beneath the membrane so that no inadvertent damage could be done to the underlying organs.

And then it was there, pulled out of the wound and looking like a great membraneous vegetable, smooth, round, growing on a thick stalk and with the Fallopian tube curving almost shyly away towards the uterus, still lying low in the belly. And Abel said almost involuntarily, 'Beautiful!' and the whole room seemed to shift as students craned to see and then grinned at each other. It had been hidden, inaccessible, totally remote, a secret threat to the life of the girl lying there on the narrow table so stertorously breathing and so totally unaware. And now it was in Abel's hand, as harmless as the knobbed potato it looked like. And they grinned with satisfaction as he tied ligatures firmly about the pedicle and with the assistant's hot pitch at the ready, began to slice it away; until at last the tumour lay in a dish, looking shrunken now, its opalescent surface gleam already fading as it died.

Abel nodded at Snow in satisfaction and said, 'I shall repair her now – you may limit your chloroform as soon as you please—' and began to tuck back the now shrunken-looking Fallopian tube. He sewed up the peritoneum with a needle of such fineness Freddy could hardly see it, using stitches made of silk, and as he watched those broad fingers moving as surely as ever he had seen his mother's move over her embroidery, he sighed with real pleasure. To watch such skill was as satisfying as eating or drinking, for it left behind it the same sensation of fullness and contentment.

The sewing of the muscle layer and then the skin seemed to be over almost before he had begun and then Abel was dissecting the growth to show them its contents, telling them all to make notes about the operation, to describe its progress and observe the results, and several of the students were set to help in bandaging the now snorting and restless patient before carrying her back to her bed in the ward to recover.

But Freddy hesitated, looking at his grandfather, and wondering suddenly if perhaps he could be approached in the matter of Phoebe after all. He need not tell him who the patient was, or even that there was one; he could simply ask him while he was in so cheerful a humour, as though it were in the normal line of a student's learning. . . .

The remainder of the morning's operations, involving as they did simple amputations, were of little interest, but he remained throughout and at the end, when the last student had gone to take the luncheon he had so abundantly earned, he moved back to stand beside the operating table where his grandfather was putting on his coat again, standing there in quiet colloquy with Snow.

'Sir,' he said, and then as both men turned and looked at him inquiringly felt his face redden; suddenly it was as though they could see beyond the blankness of his face, could read all the true facts simply by looking at him, just as that tumour had been taken from its secret hiding-place by the lazy insolent movement of a knife.

'Well, lad? Have you had an interesting morning?' Abel looked at him genially and then slapped his shoulder. 'You'll make a surgeon yet, my boy, if you go on being so eager. I saw the expression upon your face, and it pleased me, it pleased me well. It is a matter of heart, my boy, more than it is of wit or hand.'

'It needs those too,' Snow said in his lugubrious way, and Abel laughed.

'Aye, it needs those too. Well, young Frederick, what thought you of my ovariotomy? An elegant piece of butchery, was it not?'

'Indeed sir. Much better than the operation I saw you do in Purty Bill's cellar.'

Abel frowned at that, some of his *bonhomie* seeping away. 'Yes, that was a bad business, a bad business. She died in spite of all we did. It was inevitable she would.'

'Why?' Freddy looked at him very directly. 'I did not have the chance to ask you before, sir. Why did she die?'

'Why? Because she had been outrageously interfered with, Frederick! I thought you understood that! She had been with child and some damned villain had interfered!'

'Does it always happen so?' He had to know. Even at the risk of alerting his grandfather to a possible reason for his questions, he had to know. 'Do all such interferences kill patients?'

Snow snorted. 'By God, no, they don't! If some of 'em put their skills to doing decent surgery they'd be an asset to the profession! Especially those that work the whorehouse circuits. Delicate operators some of these women—'

'Women?' Freddy looked at him, aghast. 'Women *surgeons*, sir?'

There was a great crack of laughter from Abel. 'God forfend! No, boy, there can never be such a thing as a female surgeon! Snow refers to the cathouse keepers who know how to empty a uterus of its contents in so skilful a manner that they do the minimum of harm. But for everyone like that there are the sort of evil creatures who do the damage you saw that night in Saffron Hill. They maim and dig and cut so deep they leave their women dying in pools of their own blood.'

He was beside the door now, standing holding it open invitingly. 'Come, Snow. We are to meet Edwin Chadwick and give him news of his servant, you will remember. And you have work to do, Frederick, I have no doubt—'

'It is only – the lower sort of women who have these operations, sir? The whores and the thieves and that sort?' Freddy persisted, staring up at the older man and trying with all the willpower he had to keep his voice inconsequential.

But Abel looked at him sharply and said, 'Who has been asking you questions, Freddy? Have you been approached by some young devil you know to get him out of trouble? Is there a girl of good family looking for this sort of care? Because if that is so, I tell you as I have told you before, it is an evil trade and not to be countenanced! Read the Hippocratic oath! There is meat there for you! – come, Snow!'

And he was gone, clattering down the wooden stairs outside leaving Snow hovering at the door and looking back at Freddy standing very still and blank-faced in the middle of the big room.

He sighed softly. 'If it is as your grandfather suspects, Frederick, and you have been asked advice or even direct help on this matter by a – a *friend* – then take my advice and refuse it. There are such people working for the better class of women to send him – or her – to. They are all, of course, expensive – very expensive. Surgeons of poor technique in any other sort of work, they do nowt but this, and get rich on it. Tell your friend to inquire at an apothecary in the better parts of town, St. James's, perhaps. They will know. Or, of course, at a house of ease—'

Freddy looked at him with his head a little to one side, more curious than surprised. 'You do not seem to share my grandfather's disgust for the subject, sir? I did not ask, I assure you, for any – any *personal* reason, but because I have thought – I have been concerned about the woman whose operation I observed in Saffron Hill, you understand. But to hear you speak, why—'

Snow shrugged. 'I am a man of principle as much as any other, but I know also of the reality of life for women. But your grandfather – he is a great man, Frederick, a great surgeon, and it was the sight of a dead woman with her belly huge because she died in her travail which made him a surgeon. Ask him to tell you of it, one day when he is in a communicative humour! He told me once – and told me too how he promised himself because of that occasion that he would spend all the rest of his life working to make women's load an easier one. He's in love with gynaecology! That is what you must understand! He could never regard the deliberate destruction of a babe and the womb that bore it as owt but sinful.'

His northern accent which had been blunted by his years of living in London had sharpened suddenly. 'Never talk to Lackland of the bringing about of miscarriages, lad, unless you want your ears skinned! And if ever you need such help yourself or if any come to ask you to aid 'em, be wise. Send 'em to the people that know – to the apothecaries and whorehouses.'

# CHAPTER TWENTY-THREE

NANCY put the cup in front of him, slapping it down on the table with a barely contained ferocity that sent the hot gin and water slopping on to the scrubbed boards and said roughly, 'Well, drink it! It won't do yer no 'arm!'

He shook his head and then catching her eye, for she was staring at him most fiercely, put out his hand and picked up the cup and sipped; and it was more agreeable than he would have expected, for she had flavoured it with sugar and lemon and the heat of it was comforting.

They were sitting in a room at the back of the house to which she had led him after finding him scarlet-faced and almost speechless with embarrassment in the middle of the big hallway of the house in Panton Street. He had not stopped to think what might happen when he got there; he had simply called a cab and gone, running up the steps of the house to knock at the door peremptorily. And when it had opened, so swiftly it was almost as though someone had been standing behind it waiting for his summons, he had taken off his hat and said politely, 'Mrs. Bartlett, if you please?' And a soft, white and very bare feminine arm had come out of the shadows and pulled him in and shut the door behind him, and he had stood there blinking in the half light, so dim after the brightness of the streets outside, and said again a little uncertainly, 'Mrs. Bartlett?'

Someone had laughed, and he felt hands on his shoulders trying to pull his jacket from him, and he whirled, full of alarm, and then realized that he was surrounded by girls, these same exotic girls with their painted faces and dreadful, exciting, revolting, breathtaking clothes; one slid her arms about his neck from behind, while another slithered very close to him and put her hands up to hold his face between them and then kissed him very wetly on his mouth, pushing her pointed tongue against his clenched lips, and he had almost flailed his arms trying to pull away without actually hitting out at the girl herself, for whatever else she was, she was a female and as such to be protected. And there had been laughter, and a couple of jeers and more urgent pulling hands, and then Nancy's voice, harsh as a crow's, cutting across the soft babble; and they had melted away from him back into the rooms beyond.

'Well, I'll be a monkey's uncle!' she had said after a moment, coming closer to peer into his face. 'You, Mr. Frederick, is it? What're you doin' 'ere? Oh, Gawd, if yer gran-pa was to know 'e'd 'ave my 'ide! I'll send yer somewhere else, if yer must 'ave a girl, but don't come 'ere boy! 'E's a proud man, yer gran'pa, and 'e wouldn't like it above 'alf—'

'I did not come here for a girl,' he said with what dignity he could. 'I wished to speak to you on a matter of some urgency, and it was not a matter which could be dealt with at the hospital. Anyway, they told me you were not to be there until tomorrow, and it was of some urgency I should speak to you—'

Whether it was the stuffiness of the house, or the scent of the pastilles burning in the little brass dishes set about the place and sending their musky heavy perfume curling lazily through the air, or whether it was lack of sleep and excess of anxiety, he did not know, but suddenly he felt himself swaying, and his eyes were dazzled and he felt her rough hand on his sleeve and heard her say as if from a huge distance, 'Oh, Gawd, what now? Don't go measurin' yer length or castin' up yer accounts 'ere, for the love o' Pete – come on – come on. . . .'

She had taken his arm firmly and, making him lean on her, had led him to the kitchen, a room with a stone-flagged floor, a vast pine dresser adorned with blue and white plates and cups covering one wall, a great scrubbed table in the centre with rough wooden chairs about it, and a sea-coal fire burning redly in the open range, a room so blessedly ordinary and everyday that he felt better at once, and could stand without her support. But she pushed him down to sit in the old armchair she had dragged up to the table, and bustled about to make him her restorative drink. And now as he sipped it, staring at her over the edge of the cup, he felt himself relaxed and comfortable in a way he would not have thought possible when he had left home that morning.

'Well, better, are yer?' She looked down at him with a half grin on her face and he realized for the first time that she had been genuinely anxious on his behalf. He nodded and smiled back and said, 'Thank you,' with real gratitude in his voice, and she grinned even wider and then sat down opposite him, plonking her bare elbows on to the rough surface, and supporting her chin on her fists.

'Well, you said as it was urgent. You don't want a girl, but it's urgent. Which makes a change from the fellers as come 'ere as a rule. They always reckons it's urgent an' all, but it's always a girl with them.'

He looked at her curiously. 'You're quite different here, aren't you?'

'Eh? Oh, you mean from the 'ospital? Well, yes, s'pose I am! There I'm in charge, see? Got to see all's done right and tight, that those stinkin' nurses gets on with the work, and does it the way Mr. Abel likes it—' Her face softened. 'And what 'e wants is what matters, 'n it? But 'ere – well, it's different! I'm in charge 'ere as well, mind you. Own the place, don't I? Legacy, like—'

'I – yes, I heard of the lady's death. I am sorry,' he said formally, and she shot a very direct glance at him and said soberly, 'Ta. She was my good friend, and a lovely woman, an' I miss 'er sorely an' ain't ashamed to say so. She was that funny, an' all!' She laughed suddenly, a sharp little bark of laughter. 'She could make a cat laugh, could old Lucy! Looked after me all 'er life, and then leaves me a Madam! Me! That's the ripest joke of all—'

She sat with her eyes looking a little glazed, contemplating the ripeness of the joke, and then, almost seeming to shake herself, returned her attention to him. 'Well? So what is it as is so urgent you couldn't wait till I was back at Nellie's tomorrer? Better come aht wiv it!'

He put down the cup very deliberately, and his new-found

and fragile peace of mind disappeared as suddenly as it had arrived. He had not thought how he would put it precisely, and now he was facing her he felt a sudden panic. How could he tell her what he wanted? How could he say it in so many words without revealing more than he wanted to, or had any right to? It was Phoebe's secret, after all, not his.

'I have a friend,' he said carefully and she looked at him with her eyes seeming to become very tired suddenly. 'Everyone's got friends,' she said shortly.

'Yes, well, I mean – she has asked me – oh, it is so difficult! If I say more than I should and you cannot help my friend, can I be sure you will tell no one else of our conversation? For it is a matter of such delicacy, and—'

She sighed softly, still staring at him with that tired expression and said flatly, 'Someone spawnin'?'

He blinked at her. 'I beg your pardon?'

'Someone in a bit o' trouble? Some wench got 'erself a bun in the oven?'

He went very red again and stared at her miserably. To think of Phoebe in such terms was suddenly sickening in a truly physical sense, and he swallowed to push the wave of nausea down. She shook her head irritably and said, 'Oh, you stupid wet lump o' jelly! You 'alf-witted nothin', you! If you got to go sniffin' around skirts, and for the life o' me I don't see why you men can't keep yer minds above yer bellybuttons, why can't yer be *careful*? There's ways and means, ways an' means! But no, you got to find some poor bitch of a female as doesn't know which way's up and go and get 'er stuck wiv it! If you got to 'ave a woman, come to the likes o' me for Gawd's sake! Girls like mine know 'ow to look after theirselves, or got me to sort out their troubles for 'em. But no, you can't do nothin' so sensible, can you—'

'I seek help for a young *lady*, Mrs. Bartlett,' he said with all the dignity he could. 'She is a person of gentle rearing, and has been struck with her misfortune through no fault of her own—'

'Like I said,' and her voice was as jeering as ever. 'Some stupid little piece as doesn't know—'

'Please!' He was being as punctilious as he knew how to be,

struggling to get past the look of cold hostility on her face, wanting to shout at her, but needing her too much to risk being anything other than placatory. 'Please to hear me out! She came to me as her – as a friend and a connection, and sought my aid. I wish above all that she would wed me, if she will not—' He stopped and closed his eyes for a moment. He had been about to say, 'if she will not wed O'Hare', but how could he? She had not told him it was O'Hare; that was only his guess. And even if it were true did he really wish her to marry the man? That was something not to be thought of.

He opened his eyes and tried again. 'She is quite adamant. I do not know where she learned of such matters—' Again he stopped and then went on painfully. 'Well, I do know, I suppose. In the past few months she has come under the influence of people and a place that – well, never mind. I prefer not to speak of it. All I can tell you, Mrs. Bartlett, is that she is my – that I care deeply for her and if she is determined on this course then I must support and guide her through it, for if it is not I, she will go to some other who will – and I have seen the dreadful things that can happen – I could not—' and again he shook his head, unable to go on.

She stood up, moving heavily, and came round the table, pulling her sleeves down on to her wrists as she went for they had been rolled up above her elbows in her usual workmanlike way. ' 'Ow far gone is she?'

'I – I have the dates she gave me here.' He reached into his pocket and pulled out the scrap of paper and gave it to her. She smoothed it out and looked and checked with her fingers, counting, her lips moving, then she nodded and said, 'Aye. About three months or thereabouts. Bit later'n I like as a rule—'

'You?' He stared up at her, his face blank with disbelief. 'You? Do *you* deal with these matters? I thought you would know of some surgeon that—'

'Surgeons!' She almost spat the word. 'There's no surgeon other than yer gran'pa as I'd give tuppence for! All butchers, every bloody one of 'em. And I've stood there and watched enough of 'em operate, I can tell yer! Yer gran'pa does a lovely job though – lovely—' She smiled suddenly, her whole face lifting, and he wanted to look away in embarrassment, for the adoration that filled her showed as plainly as if it had been written on her forehead in scarlet letters. 'But 'e's too honourable a bloke to touch this sort o' thing. The girls as I've seen through to their time 'ere that 'e's brought me from Nellie's! They come to 'im to ask 'im to do the necessary and 'e goes mad at 'em and then brings 'em to me, and when they've been delivered, the babies get took to Mrs. Lackland – she's by way of bein' yer step-gran'ma, I suppose – and to yer aunt Martha and their charitable society – them London Ladies – and they gets 'em put out to good 'omes where they'll be reared proper. Even my girls 'e won't touch, not in that way. Not 'is style, see, not 'is style at all. An' seein' I takes good care o' my girls an' wouldn't let none touch 'em as I wouldn't let touch me, then what can I do? 'Ad to learn, years ago, din't I? Lucy taught me—' She grinned reminiscently. 'Lovely lady, Lucy was, and as nifty at the removal business as any you ever saw!'

'*Will* you help my friend, Mrs. Bartlett?' He said it very directly, standing up as he spoke and looking down at her from his greater height, but still feeling very much the suppliant. 'I believe I could trust you to treat her kindly and to – to treat her well. Please, will you? I will pay whatever is necessary – money is of no concern in the matter—'

She turned on him then, her face twisted with fury. 'Money? Do you think I do this for money? If you was a couple o' years younger I'd wash yer mouth aht wiv soap fer sayin' that! I may be a Madam, but I makes my money honest! I don't get it comin' an' goin! I'll do it because you're Abel's boy an' because I reckon you ain't so much wicked as bloody stupid. You got 'er into trouble but at least yer doin' all you can to get 'er out, so I'll 'elp yer – but not for money—'

He opened his mouth to remonstrate, to assure her that he was totally innocent, that he was indeed the most wronged participant in the whole sorry story, but even as she stared back at him he closed his mouth. How could he? How could he suggest to this woman, willing to help him though she was and earthy and practical as she was, how could he explain that

Phoebe, his beloved Phoebe, had gone and behaved in such a manner as to need such help? To say so would be to label her as clearly as if he had dressed her like the girls in the house beyond this commonplace kitchen, and he could not do that. Better that he should be blamed as a seducer than Phoebe branded, even in this woman's eyes, as a whore. And again he closed his eyes against the hatefulness of it all.

'She'll 'ave to stay 'ere a couple o' days,' Nancy's voice came cool and crisp and he opened his eyes again and looked at her. 'Will that be somethin' you can arrange easy? Or will 'er Ma and Pa be askin' awkward questions?'

He looked nonplussed for a moment. 'I daresay we can tell the family she has gone to visit friends,' he said after a moment. 'Phoebe – we will think of someone, no doubt.'

'All right. Bring 'er 'ere tomorrow afternoon then, with a couple o' clean shifts in 'er bag and 'er tongue betwixt 'er teeth. Because if ever a word gets aht that I'm agreeable to doin' this work, then there'd be all 'ell let loose. An' I'd say she and you was stinkin' liars anyway. . . .'

She stopped by the door, her hand on the latch, and looked back over her shoulder at him with her eyes bearing a considering expression and then seemed to make a decision, and came back into the room and stood close to him staring up into his face.

'You was there the day Mr. Snow give that special lecture, wasn't yer? The one about the use o' that there chloroform?'

He nodded, mystified.

'Well, there's a thought! Listen, young Mr. Frederick. This 'ere operation ain't exactly what you'd call a picnic, see? It's painful and it's nasty, and the girls don't enjoy it. If you recly care for this girl o' yours, why then, you'll not want 'er to suffer more'n is necessary, right?'

'Of course not – but—'

'But nothin'! You got 'er into this, an' you can take yer share o' gettin' 'er aht! You're bringin' 'er 'ere to me, an' that's one thing – but I don't see why you should get away wiv it – not 'avin' none o' the pain, nor even seein' it. So you can give 'er the chloroform. Why not? It'll 'elp 'er, poor cow, and it'll show you what you did in 'avin' yer bit o' fun. Trouble wiv you men is you just don't know what it is you does. Never sees the pain of it, or the ugliness of it – all the mess an' the blood and all. No, don't look at me like that! You got 'er in this state so you can do yer bit to gettin' 'er out! Bring 'er 'ere tomorrer, like I said, and bring a bottle o' yer chloroform wiv yer. I won't set a finger to 'er if you don't. . . .'

Phoebe had been totally silent from the moment they met at the end of the Terrace out of sight of the house. She had stood there on the pavement edge, a sober shawl about her shoulders and wearing a poke bonnet over an even quieter dress, and he had leaned out of the cab window and seen her and his belly had twisted with pity, for she had looked so small and vulnerable standing there alone. He had lifted her into the cab, and taken her bag, and she had sat curled away from him in the corner against the dusty squabs as the driver clicked his tongue and lashed out with his whip and the scrawny horse went clopping away down the Oxford Road towards Panton Street. And still she had said not a word.

He knew how she had planned it, knew that Abby had been told that Lydia was giving a special party and sought her niece's aid; knew that Phoebe had concocted a story about the Soho Square house being too full to accommodate her maid and being able to share the attentions of her Aunt Lydia's. And he could guess how her day had been, how the long hours had dragged away towards five o'clock when he had promised to meet her and take her to be 'looked after' which were the only words either of them could use to cover the situation.

He had asked her before leaving for his day's work at the hospital whether there was any risk of the people at the theatre making inquiries after her when it was noticed she was not at the performance, but she had shaken her head wearily at that.

'I sent a message to Aunt Lydia that I was required here at home for a few days since one of the children had the fever. She will make no inquiries, nor even send a message, because she has, I know, a great dislike of fever and much fears it. There will be no problems there.' She had lifted her gaze to

his. 'I am becoming a most accomplished liar, am I not?' Her
voice was bitter. 'I have never been one to regard the occasional mendacity as such a sin, but I had never thought I
could become as – as wicked as I am now.'

He had ached to put his arms about her, but had controlled
that, keeping his hands firmly in his pockets. 'Not wicked,
Phoebe. Foolish, perhaps. Misled, I think—'

She had shaken her head furiously at him. 'No! Do stop, for
heavens' sake, treating me as a child to whom things happen
entirely without my volition! That may sometimes be the case,
I cannot deny, for I do not know all there is to know, but I
cannot be entirely the innocent fool you would try to see me as!
What I do, I do! If you deny me any – any will in this matter
you deny me any sort of life at all! You must understand that!'

He stared at her for a long moment and then said wonderingly, 'You have changed, Phoebe.'

'And what else would you expect? I cannot be the silly
seventeen-year-old for ever! I am a woman grown, now.' She
had lifted her chin with a sort of perverse pride which he found
first touching and then infuriating. And he had thought all day,
whenever the work in the wards and operating theatre gave
him a moment to allow his own thoughts any rein, of her new
maturity and wondered at it.

But she was not seeming mature now. She was very much
the frightened child, and he slid across the cramped space between them in the swaying leather and horse-scented cab and
put his arm about her shoulders. She leaned against him in
gratitude, holding on to him with hands that had white
knuckles under her mittens. 'Don't be afraid, Phoebe,' he whispered into her ear. 'It will not be so bad! And – and it is all
arranged. I shall give you something to help you sleep. You will
know nothing of it, nothing at all.'

She looked up at him, her eyes questioning, and he murmured, 'Chloroform, my love. It is a new way to help people
feel no pain. You have heard of it, I am sure. . . .' and she
nodded, and then put her head back on his shoulder and the
rest of the journey passed in silence, both of them lost in their
own thoughts.

At Panton Street it all happened so quickly that Freddy felt almost breathless. His hand had barely touched the knocker on the big painted door when it was open and Nancy was chivvying them both inside, hurrying him away to sit in the kitchen to 'wait till yer wanted', and taking Phoebe away in a rush. And it was barely ten minutes later when Nancy put her head round the door again and said, gruffly, 'Come on. An' put a move on. Can't sit around 'ere all day.'

He followed her up the carpeted stairs, along the even more richly carpeted hallway, to a flight of plain wooden stairs which led up to the attics, clutching the ribbed green glass bottle in his hand inside his pocket, and feeling his pulses beat thickly in his throat. He would have been frightened at giving his first chloroform inhalation had he been at the hospital with Mr. Snow at his side to guide him, and dealing with a patient who was only a patient and had no other significance for him. Here he had to swallow not only that fear but the added terror for Phoebe that was rising in him like a great black tide and threatening to overwhelm his mind altogether.

As they turned from the stairhead to go along bare dusty boards of the attic passageway, Nancy walking ahead of him, he wanted to turn and run, to go clattering down those stairs and out into the dirt and noise and blessed normality of the street outside and the traffic he could hear making its muffled din through the high sloping windows that lit the bareness of the walls, and for a moment he actually tried to turn his body away. But she was at the door, pushing it open and staring challengingly at him.

'Well?' She said harshly. 'Are yer comin' in or not? Because if yer don't then it don't get done. An' you and yer young lady friend is left right where you are. Take yer choice!'

# CHAPTER TWENTY-FOUR

HE had placed himself as he had seen Snow do, behind the patient's head and looking down on her, and it helped to steady his nerve, for she looked quite different from this angle, remote and unfamiliar. He concentrated on looking at her face, at the way the frilled nightcap with its pretty lemon ribbons had been tied firmly about her curly hair and her night shift was fastened also with exactly matching ribbons, so that he did not have to look at anything else in the room.

But he could not help but be aware of it all. The curtains were closed so that the room was dim, lit only by a tall oil lamp which was standing on a table at the foot of the narrow couch on which Phoebe, covered by a rough linen sheet, was lying. In front of the oil lamp there were bowls and towels and heaps of grey charpie and also implements; a pair of long-handled sponge forceps, obviously borrowed from the big cupboard in the operating room at Nellie's, and edged curettes with sharp little teeth, and curved metal retractors, heavily weighted and gleaming dully. He pulled his eyes back once more to look at Phoebe, lying there below him with her eyes tightly closed and her hands clutching the edges of the sheet.

'Well, you can start whenever you like, Mr. Frederick,' Nancy said, and she moved nearer to the foot of the couch, tying a voluminous white apron about her thick waist and using one booted foot to hook a low stool from its place beneath the table. She sat herself down firmly and stared at him, her chin up, and he nodded, feeling his neck stiff and creaking, and took the ribbed green bottle from his pocket. His hands felt very cold.

'Phoebe,' he said softly and below him the eyes seemed to close even more tightly for a moment and then slowly opened, and it looked so odd, seeing the lids sweep downwards rather than upwards, and the way the lower lids of those grey eyes he knew so well seemed to have grown such long lower lashes and lost the richness of the upper ones; and a sort of wild giggle arose in him, and he bit his tongue to control it.

'Yes,' she said, and her voice came suddenly loud and clear in the quiet room and sounded so matter-of-fact that he was brought back from the edge of his moment of hysteria with a bump. 'Yes. You are going to start, I know. Please to get on with it, Freddy, for it is much worse waiting, you know—'

The eyes closed again, and the hands tightened even more on the edge of the sheet and the courage that was in her seemed to go flowing outwards and upwards and filled him too, and when he spoke again his voice was as clear and matter-of-fact as hers had been.

'I am going to put this cloth over your face, Phoebe. It will seem strange at first, but bear with it. I will drip the chloroform on it, and if you will breathe deeply you will soon be asleep, and when you awake all will be well.'

She made no move, only her lips seemed to tighten a little and her nostrils to dilate, and gently he put across her nose and mouth the folded lawn handkerchief he had prepared, and pulling the cork from the green bottle with a crooked little finger very gently he dripped two or three beads on to the cloth.

They made little spreading damp marks and he watched them with a sort of remote wonder, just as he had enjoyed watching the ripples spread in the Long Water on their childhood walks in the park, when the plopping fish had risen to a gnat or a bird had swooped to catch a dragonfly. The heavy sweet scent slowly drifted upwards and he took a shallow breath, remembering Snow's lecture, and again tipped the bottle, this time sending rather more of the chloroform into the neat folds.

She breathed deeply, clearly trying to obey his instructions, and once again he tipped the bottle, and now she started to roll her head, so that the cloth shifted, and moving swiftly he pushed it back and tilted out even more chloroform.

At once she began to moan and gasp, her hands coming up to pull at the cloth and he held on and said sharply, 'Mrs. Bartlett!'

She was there almost before he had finished saying her name, her hard red hands clamping themselves about Phoebe's bird-thin wrists, pulling the hands down and away, moving her heavy body so that she was lying across the heaving shoulders and he could use his own spare hand then to grasp Phoebe under her chin and hold on firmly. Gradually her struggles lessened, became as pathetic and fluttering as a bird's in a net, and once more he soaked the folded cloth with the sweet heaviness of the drug. Beneath his hand he felt how she slumped, slowly, but clearly no longer aware of anything at all. He lifted one eyelid with his fingertip and the blank pupil stared unseeingly back at him. When he let go the lid remained open, the eye still staring, and he shivered but could not reach out again to pull the eyelid down, for this was altogether too reminiscent of the times he had to perform that action for the staring senseless dead in the wards of Nellie's.

Nancy moved back to the foot of the couch, and as she went put out her hand and with one rough gesture tugged the sheet from Phoebe, leaving her lying there in her shift; and he was deeply and furiously affronted, and involuntarily put out his hand.

And she looked up at him and grinned, a hard and glittering grin, and said with a cheerfulness that made him want to hit out at her, 'You'll see worse insults nor that before we're done, Mr. Frederick!'

He didn't want to watch. He had promised himself he would not watch, would keep his gaze firmly on her face, would pretend that nothing else was going on but his use of chloroform, and to an extent he managed to do just that. Even when Nancy thrust a strip of old sheet behind Phoebe's bare knees and dragged up on it to make her legs fold up into her chest, tying the ends to the sides of the couch; even when she set her rough red hands on each soft knee and so casually and yet so brutally thrust them apart, he managed not to look, aware only that she had done it. All he saw was his own right hand holding the ribbed green bottle and the left with the thumb holding the linen mask in place and the first two fingers hooked under her chin, and he stared at them, willing his gaze to stay fixed.

But now and again, however hard he tried to prevent it, his eyes moved, came up and stared, and he could see Nancy's face there framed between Phoebe's bent knees, grim, frowning and with the lower lip caught between the strong yellowish teeth as she worked, moving smoothly and easily.

It seemed to go on for a long time, just the sound of Phoebe's deep sighing breathing and the distant muffled rattle of the traffic in the street far below impinging on his awareness, and then Nancy said loudly, 'Oh, Christ!' Startled, he looked up and saw there was a spurt of redness against her apron front that was spreading and opening out into a great crimson flower. 'Oh, Christ!' she said again, and then she was standing up and with one hand balled into a fist was leaning hard on Phoebe's belly, pressing down, her face resting against one bent leg and her other hand quite invisible.

He stared at her in horror, feeling the blood running away from his face, knowing he had gone grey, and Nancy's own face, twisted with concentration and beaded with sweat, grimaced, and then slowly she moved away, letting go; and he did not look at Phoebe at all, staring only at the other woman, at that blank expanse of sandy freckled skin. And when she took a deep breath and looked up at him and said laconically, 'That's all right then. Only a little 'un – it's when those big arteries goes as it's a real bugger—' he took a huge shuddering breath himself and had to bend his head to regain his equilibrium.

It was the sensation of movement under his left hand that restored him, and he saw Phoebe was rolling her eyes a little under those half-open lids, and realizing what was happening, he began to drip the chloroform again. It would be too dreadful to contemplate how she would feel if she woke now to find herself in this position, so exposed, so spattered with her own blood, so altogether vulnerable.

'It 'appens sometimes,' Nancy said with a sudden air of conversational normality. 'You gets the lot aht, and all's fine and then there's some little bleeder there as starts off its spurtin', and you don't know if it's one that's just a little 'un an'll stop, or you've managed to 'it a big one that never will. I saw one once lyin' 'ere and bleedin' to death, and though we took it in turns, me and Lucy, to do it right – you know, you shove one 'and in from under and t'other on the belly an' you squeeze the womb betwixt 'em on account that stops the bleeding – it made no never mind. She must 've 'ad a big one, see, growing right where we pulled the babe aht—'

'What did you do?' The question came from him as though this were the most natural thing in the world, as though they were both at Nellie's on an ordinary working day and she was a surgeon giving a lecture to an eager student. 'What did you do?'

She raised her eyes, her hands still busy and looked at him with a curiously limpid gaze. 'Do? Took 'er to Nellie's to the anatomy room, o' course! Nothin' else we could do, was there? But it was the only time we ever 'ad one like that, glory be. Put me off for a month, that did. Swore I'd never do another. Till some poor cow come to me swearin' as she'd cut 'er throat before she'd 'ave any baby, an' I'd be responsible for 'er goin' to 'er Maker either way – so I did it. An that one was all right—'

She sighed softly. 'Well, that's about it, Mr. Frederick. I got all of it. She's a bit soft there, and she may bleed a little to-night, but I'll take care of 'er, never fear. She's a fine strong girl and she'll do—'

She was busy with wet cloths now, washing the blood spatters away from those long pale legs, pulling down the shift, rearranging the rough sheet, and slowly, creakingly, and feeling very old, he put the almost empty chloroform bottle down on the floor beside him and peeled the cloth away from Phoebe's pale face, and they both stood staring down at her.

Her eyes, still half open, were filled with tears, the involuntary tears of unconsciousness, and her face was patchy with areas of redness, showing clearly where his fingers had held her chin, and where his thumb had rested against her cheek through the mask. Her mouth was half open and she was breathing heavily, and he reached forwards and with a soft

289

gesture wiped the traces of spittle away from the flaccid lips. Nancy beside him moved heavily and said in an inconsequential sort of way, 'Pretty little girl, ain't she? Can't blame yer, I s'pose. Young men is young men, an' always will be. But remember another time, Mr. Frederick, will you? Remember as it's fun when you starts, maybe, but sooner or later, one way or the other, it's bad for the females. They 'ave it rotten whatever turns out – 'oo is she, or shouldn't I ask?'

He took a deep breath. 'She is my cousin, Mrs. Bartlett,' he said, and his voice sounded cracked in his own ears. 'My cousin. Her father and my mother are brother and sister—'

She snapped her head up and stared at him. 'Oh, Gawd. Oh, my Gawd! Is she Mr. Abel's granddaughter then? Oh, Gawd—'

'Aye,' he said. 'Would it have made a difference if you had known?'

She looked down at the face beneath them, and Phoebe moaned softly and turned her head and retched, and at once Nancy put out her hand and held her chin to one side while she reached for a dish to set expertly beneath her mouth.

'I don't know,' she said. 'I don't know. There's nothin' I wouldn't do for Mr. Abel. Nothin' at all – but this – oh, Gawd, I don't know.' She lifted her head and looked at him and he tried to smile at her.

'I want you to know, Mrs. Bartlett. I – it is necessary to me that you should know. It was not—' He licked his dry lips. 'I had no part to play in this matter.'

She stared at him, her hands still holding Phoebe's head and the dish, and slowly her eyes filled with tears, and he looked back at her, almost embarrassed, for he could never have imagined that this harsh and battered woman with her sparse faded hair and her red creased face could experience the tender feelings that now so clearly filled her.

'Oh, you poor little sod,' she said softly after a moment. 'You poor pathetic little – did she use ter be yer girl, then? Is that why she come to you?'

He looked down at Phoebe and now the lids were fluttering and she opened her eyes and stared up at him wildly and he put out one hand and said softly, 'Don't fret you, Phoebe, don't fret. You're all right. It's Freddy here, don't cry—' for she was weeping now, tears running down the sides of her cheeks and her nose was running too, and he took a clean handkerchief from his pocket and gently wiped her face, and went on crooning, reassuringly, monotonously, as he had done for her so often when she was little.

And slowly the tears stopped and she turned awkwardly on the narrow couch and slept, and still Nancy stood there, the dish in her hand, and stared at him.

'My girl?' he said at last, raising his eyes and looking back at her. 'A strange way to say it perhaps, but I suppose you could – yes. She has lived with us, my mother and me, since she was a very small child, you see. So she had always been my girl. She always will be. You will take good care of her, Mrs. Bartlett? She is very precious.'

She nodded. 'Yes, I'll take good care of her,' she said roughly, and turned away with an air of sudden awkward embarrassment, and went to the cluttered table and began to tidy it, hiding the bloody bowl and its contents from his view with her body. He looked at her gratefully, at the broad back with the rolls of muscle showing beneath the print calico of her gown, and then he bent and very softly kissed Phoebe's sleeping heedless face.

And went away, back to the hospital to work late in the long lamplit wards, overheated and musty on this warm July night, to talk to other bedfast women, to soothe others' pains after operations, to touch others' outstretched hands seeking the comfort of a human contact, leaving the only patient he really cared about behind in Panton Street.

# CHAPTER TWENTY-FIVE

QUITE what he had expected he did not know. He had not been able to think beyond the situation itself, the need to arrange matters for her, the fear – unspoken even in the depths of his own mind – that she would die as a result.

But she had not died. She had remained with Nancy at Panton Street for three days, eating the plentiful and very nourishing food that the older women set implacably in front of her at regular intervals, sleeping and eating again, and had then returned quietly to Stanhope Terrace to tell Abby and Gideon that yes, thank you, the party had been most enjoyable, and Aunt Lydia had begged her to remain a day or two afterwards to help set all to rights, for she had used her best china and never permitted any of the servants to touch it (which the careful housewife in Abby found quite understandable, if surprising in the far from housewifely Lydia) and had gone about her usual daily activities as though nothing had happened.

It was that which Freddy found so extraordinary. He had come home from Nellie's to find her already returned, as had been arranged by Nancy. 'For,' she had told Freddy at the hospital the day after the operation, 'Miss reckons as it could cause troubles if you was to go to see 'er an' if you was to take 'er 'ome when the times comes, for it could set tongues to waggin'. I'll see to it she goes back with a respectable-looking female and that'll be that.' And he had been forced to agree, for it did make sense.

So when he had come into the dining-room for dinner on the fourth day after her operation, late from the hospital and so lacking time to be told anything by the servants, and had seen her sitting there calmly in her usual place, he had said involuntarily, 'Phoebe! My dear – you are back! Are you well? I have been so worried. . . .'

She had raised a limpid gaze to his and said calmly, 'Well? Of course I am! Why should I not be? You are becoming quite auntish, Freddy, even more so than Aunt Abby! She did not perturb herself because I was at Aunt Lydia's! So why should you?'

Abby looked up from the dish of lobsters she had been inspecting and nodded at Kent who bore it back to the sideboard. 'Dear me! Is behaving like an aunt something to be regarded as a cause for criticism? I must be careful in future!'

'Oh, Aunt Abby, you know quite well what I meant!' She dimpled at Abby with great charm. 'It is natural when *you* are so careful of me, but it is hardly to be expected in rackety young men, even if they are cousins! Do you not agree, Uncle Gideon?'

'Eh? Oh, my dear child, do not bring me into this argument, I do beg you! And let us please not have any arguments at all. It is a rare pleasure for us all to dine together like this, as we did in the days before you became so enamoured of the life theatrical, and I would wish us to enjoy it.'

'Well, I believe I should be able to return tomorrow, so we will not dine so after tonight. Aunt Lydia was very auntish indeed as well, for she would not let me go to the theatre these past four performances since there was one of the company was said to have a fever and she has such great fears of the fever! She would only perform herself on condition the stage was set almost alight with pastilles and her dressing-room forbidden to any visitors. But it appears it was all a hum and the man has been suffering from no more than the ague, and Aunt Lydia says I may return tomorrow. But she sent me home tonight since you had not seen me for so many days, and she thought you would prefer it so. . . .'

Listening to the lies tripping so prettily from her lips, watching her sparkle and chatter as she always had done, seeing the bloom of health on her cheeks – for Nancy's care and feeding had been very effective – he felt suddenly sick. And even more perturbed by the assumption that lay beneath her chatter, and when dinner at last was over and they were following Abby and Gideon from the room he tugged on her elbow and made her wait until the elders were out of earshot.

'What is this about going back to the theatre tomorrow?' he hissed at her. 'Are you quite mad? Surely, after all that has happened—'

'Freddy, I have not thanked you for your help,' she interrupted him. 'I would not wish you to think I am not full of gratitude. Indeed I am. But now, please, will you complete the good work you have done?'

'Complete it? I do not understand you—'

She put her hand on his sleeve and looked up into his face very earnestly. 'Please, Freddy, never speak of it ever again. Pretend none of it ever happened. I am the same as I was before – just the same. There has been no fear and no dreadfulness and no Panton Street – nothing. It was all a stupid dream, a bad one and a stupid one, and it did not happen—'

He shook his head slowly, 'But it did.'

'No, it did not.' She was very insistent suddenly, her knuckles whitening against his sleeve. 'Do try to understand, dear, dear Freddy! I do not wish to pretend you did not help me – never think I am ungrateful—'

'I do not want gratitude.'

'—but I could not live with myself ever again if I thought – if it was not all a bad dream, a nothing. It must be expunged, completely. For both of us! Do you understand? It must never have happened—'

'I – but you will not go back to the theatre? That is not to make things as they were before.'

'But of course it is! I was with Aunt Lydia at the theatre and making plans to be as great an actress as she is and so I still am! Nothing need ever change that. . . .'

'No!' He spoke more loudly than he had realized and she dropped her hand from his sleeve, and her lips tightened as she looked up at him. Then she turned and went running upstairs towards the drawing-room, and he followed her, too angry now to care about discretion. 'Phoebe! This is totally absurd, totally absurd! You are not one of these dreadful people, you do not have to spend your time among them, in search of some absurd daydream! There are some things you can pretend, some things you can say did not happen, but there must come a time when you grow up and realize that you cannot live a dream as though it were *real* life! And that is what you are doing—'

They had reached the upper hallway, and Gideon was standing at the drawing-room door looking at them questioningly as they reached the top of the stairs, Phoebe's face set and very determined. Freddy red with his barely controlled anger.

'Dear me!' he said mildly. 'This is very reminiscent of the days when you were both in the schoolroom! Has she broken one of your favourite model ships again, Freddy?'

Freddy coloured even more deeply at the rebuke, and said hotly, 'For heaven's sake, Gideon! She is talking of returning to the theatre. She is still talking about all this nonsense of being an actress like her aunt, and—'

Gideon raised his eyebrows. 'I know, Freddy. We all know. We have talked much of the matter. And we have told Phoebe of our views, have we not? There is little more we can do, as you have yourself agreed. Why should you start talking of the matter again now?'

Phoebe had turned her head and was staring at him with her face quite expressionless, just looking at him, and he stared back at her and opened his mouth. And closed it again.

'Dear Freddy,' Phoebe said after a moment, and turned to look at Gideon, and laughed a low bubbling laugh that sounded, suddenly, very like Lydia's. 'He seeks to keep me still a child as I was when he could tell me what to do and I always did it. He has not noticed I am a grown woman now, has he? But I know he means me well. Do not worry about our little argument, Uncle Gideon. It is all quite over. Is it not, Freddy?'

And he looked at her, standing there beside her uncle, her hand tucked in his elbow and staring challengingly at him, and nodded slowly and said, 'Yes. Quite over.'

But of course it was not. He tried to do as she asked and

295

pretend none of it had ever happened, but it was impossible. Every time he thought of her spending the long hours of the performances there among the same people who had led to her misery – and in a curious way he now felt that all the people at the Haymarket were her seducers, and not just the suspected O'Hare – he was filled with an urgent need to do something about it. It was not possible just to settle back and watch her and hope that she would be well and safe from any future mishap. And though he could not honestly admit the thought to himself there was little doubt that deep in his mind lay the knowledge that he could not really trust her. Not now.

He managed to contain his distress and anxiety for a week and then capitulated. Something would have to be done to get her away from the contagion of the theatre, but what? He could not ask his mother or stepfather's aid, not without revealing why it had now become so imperative a matter, and that was unthinkable. He equally could not go to her father, for what could Jonah do with such knowledge? She would either twist him about her little finger, or, if she could not, would do as she threatened and go to her Aunt Lydia and throw herself upon her care.

Lydia. It hit him almost as a blow. It was there that the key to the whole problem lay. If *she* told her niece that the theatre was not suitable for her, surely, surely Phoebe would have to accept it? He saw Lydia suddenly as the cork in the neck of a bottle. There trapped inside lay all Phoebe's other relations, all the people who really cared for her welfare, but as long as Lydia blocked them they were impotent. Well, he would be the one to pull that cork, he told himself, and felt suddenly, enormously, better.

He did not make any attempt to deal with the matter in a businesslike manner. He would write no letters seeking interviews, he told himself, but would simply call in a sociable sort of way, and broach the subject quite suddenly. That way there would be no risk of Lydia telling Phoebe of his approaches, and so no risk that Phoebe could beguile her aunt against his request even before he had made it. And knowing Phoebe as he did there was no doubt in his mind that she could gain her own way without difficulty, given the time to set to work. Well, she should not have such time.

He chose a Monday morning to call at Soho Square, remembering that this was the only day of the week that did not follow a late evening performance. That it was inconvenient for him was undoubted; there would be much trouble at the hospital for him when he was missed from his lectures and his work, but that was something that would have to be tolerated, he told himself, as his cab took him through the narrow streets, busy with fruitsellers' stalls and noisy children and the fat, pavement-gossiping Italian women who were so much a feature of the district. And anyway there would be a curious poignancy in being the object of Abel's wrath when it was because of Abel's granddaughter he was playing the truant.

The footman who let him into the house looked askance at his demand to see Mrs. Mohun and his insistence that he would wait for her return when he was given a bland, 'Not at home' response. But he led him to a small *salon* to wait, and went away leaving him to kick his heels in the white and gold room, trying to marshal his thoughts and plan precisely which words he would use.

He was disconcerted, to say the least, when at last a maid came and told him Madam would see him upstairs and he was led, not as he would have expected, to a morning-room or drawing-room, but to a large and very cluttered bedroom full of little tables and gold chairs and ornaments and plump stuffed footstools. He stood there hesitating at the door, looking at the bed heaped with satin cushions and an embroidered counterpane, in the middle of which lay Lydia with her hair tumbled very untidily on her shoulders.

'Oh, do come in!' she cried, and pushed a tray bearing a chocolate pot and cups to one side. 'I am so astounded that anyone should come visiting at so extraordinary an hour that I thought I really must see who it might be! My man gave me your card, but I seem to have mislaid it—' and she made a few ineffectual pulls at her bed coverings and then looked up at him with her head set on one side, smiling widely. 'Your face is familiar, I know! But it is so very early that I can, I trust, be forgiven for not being able to put a name to it—'

'It is past noon, ma'am,' he said a little stiffly, trying to behave as insouciantly as though he were entertained in ladies' bedchambers every day of his life. 'I am very sorry if I discommode you.'

'Past noon? My dear young man, I never rise before two! Not when there is a play in performance!'

'I chose today because there was no performance last night,' he said still feeling himself stiff and awkward. 'I had assumed that on Mondays you were like—'

'Like ordinary people?' she said, tilting her head at him again and his face flamed as she read his thoughts so accurately. 'Well, you were wrong. I am *never* like ordinary people, thank God! You still have not told me who you are.'

'Frederick Caspar, ma'am!' and he bowed, moving rather clumsily and knowing how absurd such drawing-room manners looked in this setting. 'We met first at Stanhope Terrace – my mother is—'

'Oh!' she said, and sat up a little straighter. 'You are Gideon's son? How interesting! You don't look at all like him—'

'He is my stepfather,' Freddy said flatly. 'My mother, I was about to say, is aunt to Phoebe on her father's side. As you are on her mother's. . . .'

'Ah! Light begins to dawn! It is not because you wished to see *me* that you came here at so ungodly an hour, but because of Phoebe! Well, we old women must face the fact that eventually the young beauties come along to supersede us!' And she wriggled a little against her pillows so that her bedgown slipped even further from her shoulders and smiled at him equably, obviously not one whit concerned about the thought of Phoebe as a rival.

'I am able to see Phoebe whenever I wish – well, almost,' he said. 'When she is not at the theatre with you, of course. I did indeed come here because of Phoebe, but to speak of her, not to see her.'

'Well, don't stand there so stiff and awkward, boy!' She

sounded suddenly a little impatient. 'Come in and sit down and tell me of what it is you wish to – *speak*. But I tell you this before you start. If you are trying to persuade me to act as cupid's go-between, you may save your breath to cool your broth! Aunt I may be but matchmaker, never. You must speak to her direct yourself for that. Or, of course, ask her other aunt to do the office for you. She is, after all, your Mamma! Or does she mislike the idea?' and she grinned at him wickedly.

He had come farther into the room at her command, and was now standing uncomfortably at the foot of the bed, and she made another impatient gesture. Obediently, if a little gingerly, he sat down on the edge of it, feeling the slipperiness of the silk beneath him, and it made his face redden again in that hateful – because it was so juvenile – manner. Irritation at himself sharpened his tone.

'I am perfectly capable, ma'am, of prosecuting my own affairs if I have them. It is not upon my own affairs I come, I repeat, but upon Phoebe's. I am interested in her well-being, as her cousin, a member of her family and one who as such must have her welfare at heart. There is no more to it than that, I assure you.'

'O ho! touched you on the raw, have I? Well, if that is how it is to be, it is. You have no romantic interest in my niece, you have never even noticed what a bewitching girl she is, and you need my aid in furthering her welfare, in spite of the vast number of other aunts and uncles and papas and such like that she has! I *quite* understand! So, explain your errand.'

It was getting worse and worse and he knew it. The interview had started on the wrong foot, promised to get more wrong yet, and though he wanted to please her he still could not govern his tongue. So much of the fear and anger and the sheer pain of the past weeks was there in him needing – indeed clamouring – to be released that it came tumbling out in a welter of words.

'I am very perturbed, ma'am, at the company she is keeping! Until this theatrical business started with her she was a happy and contented young lady who was busy with her friends, her interests, her natural occupations. But all this has changed since she has been keeping company with this collection of – of mountebanks and creatures who – well, in short, the people she now consorts with are not suitable for her, do not show her in any way a mirror in which a respectable girl of good family can observe herself with satisfaction, and we are all most concerned that she should be encouraged to return to the way of life to which she was reared and which is most suitable for her. However talented she may be in the matter of these drawing-room tableaux in which she was used to find satisfaction, it is clear to me at any rate that she does not have – the character or the hardness of spirit that would enable her to live a life as an actress that would be of satisfaction to her, or give any contentment to her friends and family. And I for one thank God for it. She is too delicate, too carefully reared, too—'

'Too much a lady?' Her voice was very soft, sitting there against her satin pillows, and gazing at him with eyes wide and apparently untroubled. 'Too sensitive, not made of the rough clay that theatre people are? Is that it?'

He should have been warned, should have heard the hardness underlying that honeyed voice, but he was too well launched upon his tirade for that.

'Precisely! They are vulgar and coarse and stupid and know nothing of what is due to a girl like Phoebe! She is not one of these tawdry painted trollops that hang about theatres, for heaven's sake! She is – she is *Phoebe* and you must know that you are wrong to allow her to consort with such creatures! She listens to you, and maintains that if we or her father seek to stop her in this mad plan she has devised with your aid, she will run away and come to live with you! You must know it is all lunacy, and must surely be as concerned as we are to put a stop to it!'

'Have you quite finished, Mr. Caspar? Quite, quite finished?' She leaned forwards, smiling sweetly. 'Have you any other comments to make upon the characters and behaviour of my friends, my colleagues, indeed myself? Have you quite done with your little lecture? You had better be – because if you don't get your bloody little jumped-up stupid self out of here, and go to the hell and damnation that is surely awaiting you, you will get a beating the like of which you have never had before, and which I, because of my evil character and painted trollopy ways, will be more than able to inflict upon you! You hear me? Get out, get out, get *out*!'

# CHAPTER TWENTY-SIX

'FREDDY, I cannot imagine what possessed you!' Abby said again, and looked at him almost helplessly. 'Why, for a start, did *you* go to her, anyway? We had agreed at first that I should go to her, and that Gideon would speak to Uncle Jonah, and then you bade us both to let be, and we did. And now you tell me you had a dreadful argument with Mrs. Mohun, and expect *me* to follow you? I cannot do it, Freddy! It is not reasonable of you to ask it. There is only one way to persuade Phoebe that this is not the career for her – if it is not – and that is for Uncle Jonah to—'

'*If* it is not? Mamma! For God's sake, how can you ever think it is anything but dreadful for her? How can you, knowing her as you do, having had the rearing of her, see her in such surroundings and not be fearful for her? I am almost frantic with worry—'

'Dear boy, I know you are! I can see clearly your distress, and I feel for you, darling, I truly do. But I fear also that you do not see Phoebe with clear eyes. She is, I agree, a well-brought-up girl – or at least I hope so, for I have treated her as my own child. But she is, you must recall, her mother's daughter. And her grandmother – well—' Abby shrugged. '*She* was an actress, you know. A very great one, from all accounts. I only ever saw her perform once, and I am no judge, but I recall her very vividly as one of such – well, she was so very much *there* on the stage, you know? Not one to be overlooked – and I have often seen in Phoebe some signs of her grandmother and her ways. She has her beauty, that is sure—'

'Oh, grandmothers!' Freddy said impatiently. 'There is more than one person involved in a family, Mamma! And you are her aunt, and a lady, and sensible and with good manners and –

why can you not see that it is as natural for Phoebe to be like you and aunt Martha and such of her relations as are worth being like, as like these raffish, dreadful—'

'Freddy, do stop!' Abby got up from her *chaise-longue*, and went to stand beside him where he was sitting hunched in the small armchair beside the empty fireplace in her boudoir. 'You are becoming quite absurd over this matter! I had hoped – had thought you had accepted your *congé*, that you realized that Phoebe was not for you, and could begin to make different plans for your future. I must of course admire constancy, dear heart, but there is a point at which constancy becomes a foolish stubbornness. And loyal person though you are, and so dear and caring and good, you have also always been sensible. I would not have expected you to go on and on in a lost cause as you are. . . .'

He looked up at her, aching to tell her why his anxiety about Phoebe had been so suddenly rekindled, wanting to describe to her the horrors of that darkened room at the top of the house in Panton Street, the way each night since then he had dreamed about it, of the way Nancy's voice had cried out and then her apron had been so richly crimson, and he had been so sick with fear. But he could not tell this gentle warm face above him looking down on his with so much anxious concern of such hideous sickening matters. How could he expect his own mother to cope with the knowledge of what the girl she had reared as her own daughter had done? And he suddenly re-membered the way she had looked the first time he had been taken to see her after Isabel was born, remembered the almost exalted expression on her face as she held out the shawled bundle to show him his new sister and knew that she would suffer even more from the knowledge than he had, if that were possible.

But still she had to be told of the urgency of the matter, and he tried, as best he could, to seek a way to express his fear without saying too much. It would be difficult for both of them, but it had to be done.

He got to his feet and began to prowl around her room, moving from table to sofa to window and back again, choosing his words with all the delicacy he could, and all the time she watched him and listened and said nothing, standing there in front of the mantelshelf with her head reflected in the mirror behind her.

'Mamma, there is something I must tell you – and I do not wish you to think I speak from – from jealousy, or some – some attempt to persuade myself that I can turn the clock back and make Phoebe listen to my proposal again and give a different answer. It is not that. It is that I am so frightened for her – she may not be marrying me, but that does not alter the years of – of love and concern and just – well, looking after her that I have done. I must still take care of her. You see?'

He looked up at her: still she was silent, but she nodded her head at him just once and he went on, a little more calmly now.

'Well, Mamma, I believe there is some risk to her from the men at the theatre. More precisely, one of them. I have heard what she has said and – I have tried to warn her – in a way – but it is difficult. And I believe my warnings were too late. The man O'Hare. The one who came here the night of the tableaux – you remember? – Yes. You remember. Well, I think – he may have—' He stopped. 'Must I spell it out, Mamma, in every detail? It is so difficult for me.'

There was a long silence, and then she said carefully, 'Freddy, are you trying to say he has seduced her?'

He sighed deeply and with enormous relief. 'Yes, Mamma. I believe he has. Her affections may or may not have been engaged – I do not know. And I do not know for sure that it *is* O'Hare. But someone in that theatre – and who if not him? – has used her most dreadfully – and will do so again, surely, if she remains there and – I cannot bear it, Mamma! She must be got away!'

'How do you know, Freddy?' She was looking at him very directly and again that urgent need to be honest with her, to tell her all he knew of all that had happened, rose in him and he actually opened his mouth. But closed it again and shook his head.

'Mamma, please, will you let me keep my own counsel on

this? I would wish to tell you all, but I cannot. Will you believe me that this is the case, that I know from Phoebe herself and not mere jealous suspicion? It is so, and I am so frightened for her! Please, Mamma, do something to help her!'

She looked at him for a long time, her eyes a little blank, and he watched her anxiously, feeling suddenly very young and helpless again, as though the clock had indeed turned ten years back and he was an anxious ten-year-old looking to the source of all his comfort for peace and reassurance. And felt the same bursting sense of relief when she nodded slowly and said, 'Very well! I shall go to see her. Since you wish me to. But Freddy – please do not expect too much. She is – you have offended her, and it will be far from easy. But I will try my best.'

'I would have been better impressed had your son come himself to tender his apologies, Mrs. Henriques!' Lydia said, challengingly. 'Do you not feel I have a right to feel sorely used?'

'Indeed, I do. Had I not felt so, Mrs. Mohun, I would hardly have started my conversation with you as I did. I was very humble, was I not?'

Lydia laughed at that, and leaned back with a luxurious little gesture of her shoulders. They were sitting in her small *salon,* she outstretched on a long gold sofa, her guest perched rather uneasily on a gilt chair, a table laden with the trappings of tea between them. Outside the rain drummed heavily on the windows, pouring down the panes with all the fury of a summer storm, but now she did not mind it. She had been sitting there bored and thoroughly dispirited by the weather, annoyed with Dickon for having to go for a new costume fitting, and even more annoyed with herself for feeling so, knowing as she did that it had been necessary for him to go. She had intended to drive herself out in the park, but the rain had started even before she had left her bed and she had fretted and fumed with boredom all afternoon. The announcement of Mrs. Henriques's call had come as a welcome respite, and although she had played for a moment with the idea of sending her away with some lofty message, to pay back her son for his insufferable impudence, her boredom had won. She had told the footman to bring the visitor in.

Now, looking at her consideringly across the table, she was glad she had. The woman was not quite the boring milk-and-water creature she had assumed her to be. There was more to her than there was to other wives and mothers of hopeful families she had met, although she could not for the life of her have explained why. It was not so much what she said, perhaps, as how she said it. Certainly she had made her apologies for her son's ill-mannered outburst crisply and with no hint of embarrassment in her even tones, looking at her with clear grey eyes and a calm expression on her face. Not a beautiful face, Lydia thought with all the complacency of a woman whose beauty was deep in her bones and so not likely to be tarnished by age, but with a certain handsomeness that was not to be sneered at.

'It will, perhaps, help you to be more tolerant of his young outburst if you understand the root of it,' Abby said, and bent her head to smooth her gloves on her lap, showing signs of discomfiture for the first time. 'He has long had a *tendre* for my niece, you must understand.'

'I do indeed. Looking at my niece I take it for granted that many young men have *tendres* for her,' Lydia said, and Abby looked up and smiled slightly.

'Yes. She is our mutual niece, is she not? One almost forgets—'

'I do not! It gives me much satisfaction that she should be so.' Lydia hesitated for a moment and then, reacting to the warmth she felt for this pleasant-faced woman, said impulsively, 'Indeed, she is a little more than – particularly important to me. You have three children, have you not? I remember your husband talked quite interminably of his daughters the day we walked in the park and saw the Exhibition! It must gratify you to have so devoted a husband and father, Mrs. Henriques. I, on the other hand have no children, nor a devoted husband.' Her lips curved a little. 'As yet. And Phoebe – well, I needed a niece! It is most agreeable that she should be so pretty and animated, so very like her mother's family and—'

She stopped and laughed, looking sideways at Abby. 'Oh

dear! I meant no offence. Your own family is of course very handsome also. I recall your brother Jonah, in his youth – before he married Celia – quite devastatingly handsome. I was a very worshipping child, I do assure you! But there is that other side of Phoebe, is there not? The animation, you know, the desire to achieve some sort of – ah, well. We need not go on about it! I am sure you understand.'

Abby looked up at her and nodded. 'Yes, I understand. I believe you do care for your niece as much as any of us. That is why I wished to talk to you today.'

'Oh? Then you did not come only to salvage your son's reputation with me?'

'Not entirely. Although it is linked with that of course. He would not have been so – intemperate in his speech had he not been so agitated about his cousin's welfare. As I said before, he is deeply attached to her.'

'Well, no doubt he is! I can well understand that he would be jealous of her attachment to the theatre. But there it is – the men who love people like Phoebe and me, they must suffer for it! They must share us with our art!' And she stretched her arms above her head and yawned, catlike, showing sharp little white teeth and a pointed pink tongue, and although there was a hint of self-mockery in her posture and an amused glint in her eyes, there was also in her voice the ring of sincerity. She meant precisely what she said.

'It is not of her attachment to the theatre that he is jealous,' Abby said, her voice very level. 'But to one of the people in it.'

'Oh?' Lydia cocked her head again in that inquiring way of hers. 'Has she found someone among the company to replace your Freddy in her affections?'

'Her affection for Freddy is nothing to do with the matter,' Abby said. 'I do not speak of Freddy, but of Phoebe. Mrs. Mohun—' she hesitated. 'There is a matter that I must tell you that I ask to keep a complete confidence between us. I take, I know a considerable risk in speaking of it, but I trust you. I believe you to be a woman who may be – different perhaps in her attitudes to the conventions, and one who cares little for the surface forms of life—' She smiled again at that. 'Much as I am, indeed. For despite the fact that Gideon and I and our children live so respectably we are a little unusual. He is a Jew, you know, and there was much opposition to our marriage on both sides. And I am a woman who is much occupied with masculine affairs. The family business is one upon which I am much engaged, and I work regularly in our own manu-factory—'

'I was right about you,' Lydia said, sitting up a little more straight, and looking at Abby with a new expression on her face. 'I felt you were different.'

'Well, I believe I am. A little. I have always followed my heart more than many would have believed.'

She lifted her head and looked very directly at the other woman. 'For example, I asked my present husband to be my lover rather than become his wife when he asked me. And I – anticipated my first marriage. Freddy was born barely six months after we were wed, James and I—'

'Did you, by God?' Lydia said softly, and then grinned widely. 'Did you! Well, you gratify me, Abby. May I call you so? We could be great friends, you and I. We are cut of similar cloth. And you must call me Lydia—'

'I told you this not because I wish to ingratiate myself with you, nor to make myself more interesting in your eyes,' Abby said. 'I speak so because of Phoebe.'

'Phoebe, yes – Phoebe. She is enamoured of an actor in the company, you say?'

There was a long pause. 'More than that, I suspect. Tell me, Mrs. Mohun – Lydia. Did my niece come to stay with you for a party a week or two ago? Was one of the company put down with a fever which so alarmed you that you bade her not to come to performances?'

Lydia stared at her, nonplussed. 'But you know quite well why she missed those performances! Your children had the fever—'

Gently Abby shook her head. 'No, Lydia. My children were quite well. It was the theatre that had the fever.'

'But Phoebe said—'

'Yes. Phoebe said.'

The silence drew out and then Lydia said uncertainly, 'But I do not understand. At least, I don't think I do—'

'You do, I believe. If you allow yourself. My son, you must recall, is a medical student, with my father, at Queen Eleanor's hospital.'

'So?'

'It was he who told me that the reason for his deep concern regarding his cousin is his belief that she has been seduced by some member of the company at the theatre.'

'Seduced?' Slowly a smile started on Lydia's face, and began to spread wider. 'Seduced? Our little Phoebe? Bless my soul! She is indeed her aunt's niece! I was a little younger than she, as I recall, not far past my sixteenth birthday, though I thought myself very late on the scene! Her aunt's niece — and from all you say, that is so for you as well—'

She began to laugh. 'Oh, this is too rich! Here is your poor son striking great postures of distress — tell me, is he one of these modern evangelists? No, hardly, with a Jew for a step-father — but still clearly one who has these stiff-necked modern ideas about the way men and women should comport themselves, and here am I, and you, with a past history of our own, being sought to rescue her! I suppose that is what he wishes? He demanded her banishment from the theatre from me, so I imagine he sent you to make the same request. Oh, indeed, too rich!'

'You do not seem to have understood the point I sought to make about Phoebe's absence from both of us, Mrs. Mohun. Where was she during those four days? And my son — the matter of his occupation does not seem significant to you?'

Lydia frowned, feeling a new chill in Abby's voice. 'No, I see nothing of great significance in that — but I do wonder, now I think of it, what Phoebe was doing if she wasn't at home with you as I thought, nor at the theatre with me—'

Abby sighed suddenly, and shook her head. 'You are not the perspicacious lady I thought you,' she said crisply. 'It was quite clear to me, knowing my son as I do and seeing how deeply distressed he was, and having, I must repeat, spent my life in a less protected way than some. I have employed women in my factory for many years, Lydia. I have seen them come and go, seen them grow anxious and fearful and then not come to work for a few days, only to return showing every sign of being much relieved of some distress. Come, you too are a woman of the world! It cannot be unusual for actresses also to need the services of one that has some understanding of the surgeon's trade?'

There was a long silence, and then Lydia sat upright, swinging her legs to the ground and staring at Abby with her mouth slightly open. And then she laughed.

'So that was what – well, well! Phoebe! How exceedingly sensible of her to have managed all so well! And how fortunate she was to have so helpful a cousin! He must be a gentleman of some aplomb, your Freddy, to have dealt so with a girl he cared for, in such straits because of some other man! Or – I would not wish to cast any ill-natured accusations at your boy, Abby, but are you sure the source of Phoebe's troubles *was* another man? But I am foolish! It must have been! Why else should he come here and treat me so rough in his attempt to wrest the girl away from the company, if he were himself the one who – no! It is clear that he is indeed a very good-hearted person. You must be very proud of him, my dear!'

'That is by-the-by. The matter under review now is surely Phoebe and her future. I share with Freddy the belief that she would be better served were we – her elders and also her true friends – all agreed that she should abandon her plan to join you in your life as an actress.'

Abby was sitting very upright now, her hands still crossed neatly on her lap, and with a surface appearance of calm, but the line of her jaw was tight, and her eyes wide as she stared at Lydia. However well she had carried off the conversation – and she knew she had – it had been very painful for her. Bad enough to know that the girl she had reared so carefully and learned to feel such affection for was little more than a trollop; worse still to have to reveal such facts to another person.

But Lydia seemed quite unaware of any distress in her, and simply stared back with her brows raised in genuine surprise.

'Abandon the plan? But why? What would be the point? If she were some tender virgin at risk of harm, perhaps I might agree with you! But you tell me she is past that and furthermore has managed her affairs with considerable dispatch, not to say efficiency. Clearly she is one who will go on managing. She will do well, our Phoebe!'

Now it was Abby's turn to look surprised. 'Come, Lydia, you cannot wish her to go on in this manner! She is only seventeen! What will she be by the time she is twenty if we leave her in this *milieu?*'

Lydia leaned forwards and poured another cup of tea for herself, and then sat back comfortably and began to sip it, looking at Abby over the rim of the delicate porcelain cup.

'What will she be? Why, who can say? She has a small talent, and if she has the opportunities put her way she may become a considerable performer. On stage, that is. For the rest – well, perhaps she will have a house of her own, and pretty things in it and jewels and elegant gowns—' Her eyes crinkled a little with real amusement. 'I did not achieve the agreeable state in which you now find me until I was well past twenty, because I was foolish enough to get married! She has been much cleverer than I! I am full of admiration for her, I do assure you! No, Abby, my dear, please not to fret yourself over our niece. She has had her baptism of fire and will do well enough, I have not the least doubt. Now, will you have some more tea? And let us, please talk of other matters! I am quite fascinated to hear more of your life, and to discover how it is one who seems so very much the lady should have so open and unshockable a mind. Quite fascinated!'

Abby stood up, shaking out her skirts, and began to pull on her gloves. 'That is your last word on the subject?'

'Oh, indeed it is! To tell the truth I am becoming bored by all this fuss about one little girl and her peccadilloes. First Freddy, and now you! No, I will talk no more of it. But as I say, I will be happy to talk with you of—'

Abby shook her head, and turned and went to the door. 'I think there is little point in my remaining longer with you, Lydia. Much as I regret the need, I think her father must be consulted on the matter. He is, after all, the person who should be most concerned. . . .'

She stopped sharply and then went on very smoothly, but with an edge to her tone, 'I am, I must confess, a little surprised that you showed no interest in who might be the author of Phoebe's difficulties.'

'Oh, as to that, the company is very large, you know! I cannot know all the people with whom she might become – shall we say – *friends*.'

'Oh, I am sure you cannot!' Abby said, and smiled a little tight smile. 'I, of course, don't know any of them. Except for one, of course. Mr. O'Hare, I think his name was. The gentleman who took her down to supper when you both came to our evening party, you will recall. Good afternoon, Lydia. I shall find my own way out.'

# CHAPTER TWENTY-SEVEN

JONAH stood on the corner of Carlisle Street, staring across the Square past King Charles's statue and the rich heaviness of the trees, particularly lush in this wet summer they were having, looking at Lydia's house. It seemed to have been so long since he had last stood here worrying about the occupant of that house, but it was hardly more than four months. Eighteen weeks, in fact. Eighteen weeks during which he had been first alarmed, and then reassured; eighteen weeks of sitting on the edge of a precipice and not knowing it, eighteen weeks of inaction, wasted because of his stupid ignorance, his own failure to recognize the risk.

For a moment he felt anger rise in him a great tide; if she had been standing there before him, he would have hit out at her, would have lashed her with his tongue, and all that had to be said. But that sank almost as soon as he was aware of it, changing back to the sick clotted fear that had filled him ever since Gideon had started, so painfully and unhappily, to explain the situation to him. And the fear swirled and melted and re-formed into tears and he let them course down his face, not caring who might see him.

Not that there was much chance for anyone to see him. It was dark, a city darkness edged with the lights from the houses about the Square and the occasional lanterns ranged along the railings in the centre and thinned to a yellow glow by the naphtha flares the street pie-sellers used to display their goods. Few of the passers-by, sauntering along arm in arm or rushing past on some urgent errand, had any interest in the heavily-coated man they could hardly see who stood there on the dark corner, silently staring into the leaf-whispering emptiness.

He was trying to plan what he would say, as well as how he

would say it. He knew he had a long time to wait. Gideon had left him at nine o'clock, begging him not to be too agitated, and assuring him he would return at half past eleven to accompany him on his visit to his sister-in-law when she came home from the theatre. And he had fully intended to stay there at the Supper Rooms to wait for him. He had fully intended to behave in as circumspect a manner as it was possible for a man in so painful a situation to behave. He would attend the house in Soho Square, accompanied by his friend and brother-in-law, and tell her firmly that she was to instruct his daughter to leave the Haymarket company immediately, was to understand that on no account was she to offer her any further hospitality, was on no account, indeed, ever to see her again.

But his resolve had failed. Gideon had not been gone more than fifteen minutes when Jonah had told his head waiter that he was going out, had rushed up to his room to seize the first coat that came to his hand and then gone, half walking and half running, all the way to the Square.

And now here he stood, trying to think and trying not to remember. Gideon's voice had been so hesitant, so careful, and yet so affectionate, and again his eyes pricked as he heard in his memory that soft tone. So much distress for so many people, and all because of this hateful, dangerous, wicked woman. So many hateful, dangerous wicked women there had been to destroy his life. First Lilith, and now Lydia. They had come between him and his wife Celia, and now they were coming between him and his Phoebe. And more than coming between. They were changing them, taking them and making them into new people as hateful as themselves. They had done it to Celia, taken her eager lovingness, her caring, wanting nature and made it suspicious and frightened and cruel. And now they were taking his own little girl, with her warm and loving heart and making her—

He shivered, and thrust his hands deep into his pockets. It was not cold, the air being heavy with a July sullenness that almost overcame the dampness left by the day's rain, but still he was cold, his hands feeling like dead lumps of meat, his legs and feet sluggish and awkward with the chill that filled him.

They were trying to change her, Lilith and Lydia, change her into one of the miserable and unhappy creatures who haunted the streets of Covent Garden, whose raddled faces and scrawny bodies he saw every day of his life. They were making her into one of the dead-eyed ones, the leering ones, the hungry ones. The ones he himself on half a dozen or so hateful disgusting occasions during the long lonely years since Celia's death, had been driven to use. He felt sick, hugely and horribly sick, and bent his head trying to control his stomach. His Phoebe, like that? Surely not! Surely never. Not if he could get her away now, protect her from this woman who had come spanking into this Square eighteen weeks ago, driving her own carriage so insolently and so unheedingly. He had saved his Phoebe before from such a one, long ago when she had been little more than a baby, had plucked her from the hurly-burly of her mother's Supper Rooms and taken her to safety in her aunt's house. Surely he could do that again?

She had been soiled a little then, he remembered, seeing in his mind's eye a vast half-drunken coster sitting with sprawling knees on a stool, nuzzling the neck of seven-year-old Phoebe, holding her with his huge hairy arms clamped about the delicacy of her frilled skirts, and the sick feeling came back. He had thought no damage had been done then, but had he been too late after all? Had she been so contaminated by that long-ago touch that she had never really recovered? It could not be so, and he would not believe it was so; he and Gideon, when Gideon came, would deal with this woman, and make sure it was not so.

He stood there for a long time, turning over and over in his mind the iniquities of Lydia, remembering everything he had ever known about her and her mother, making himself recall every detail of them. Anything not to think of Phoebe and what Gideon had told him; anything not to remember his Celia and how she had suffered. Anything, above all, not to have to remember his own misery.

Quite when he realized he did not have to wait until she returned home he did not know. He suddenly found himself whirling and running along Carlisle Street in search of a hack, heard himself shout, 'The Haymarket Theatre!' to the driver he at last found clopping dispiritedly along Broad Street, and not until he leaned back in the dusty odorous interior did he stop to think properly.

The Haymarket. The last time he had been there had been the night that Celia had died. Not that he had known that at the time. He let himself remember, almost glorying in the pain it gave him, feeling almost as though by suffering himself he could take some of the badness that Phoebe had suffered into himself, and neutralize it that way. He could handle suffering, he told himself. He could live with it and deal with it and then Phoebe would be as she had always been to him, sweet and loving and delicate and perfect. . . .

The cab wheeled and swung as the driver pulled up the sweating horse, and he sat there for a long moment staring out of the dusty window at the familiar frontage, the pillars and the playbills, the flaring lights and the inevitable hangers-on and street sellers waiting for the audience to emerge.

'Well? Are yer stayin' in there all night, mate?' the cabby shouted down raucously. He shook his head, then climbed out awkwardly and fumbled in his pockets for the fare. With a deep breath he turned and went down the side of the theatre, towards the all too familiar stage door.

He did not go in. He remembered vividly the way the greenroom would fill up after every performance, how the crowds of young men would clutter up the dressing-rooms, and knew there would be no chance of talking to her inside this great, threatening building; and anyway, it held so many ugly memories for him, was so thick with the dust of old miseries that he would not be able to speak properly at all. He would stay outside here in the alleyway, leaning against the cold brick wall, and wait for her.

And wait he did, standing there patiently in the darkness, until at last the company came out, one by one to start with and then in a great flurry of shouts and chattering. He shrank back against the wall even more, not wanting to be seen, and craned his neck, seeking among them for the sight of Lydia, but they were milling about so, and the light was so bad, with only one shaft of dusty yellow cast over the cobblestones from the open door, that it was almost impossible to see.

It was, it appeared, someone's birthday, and there were many mocking cries and shouts as they tried to decide where they were to go at the lucky celebrator's expense and who would travel with whom. Someone had gone to call cabs, and three of them came clattering up Orange Street to be greeted by even louder shouts and cheers.

As the women began to climb into the cabs in a great rustle of braided, looped skirts and fringed shawls Jonah became anxious and stepped forwards, craning to see; could she be one of this crowd? She was the leading player, he knew, and generally leading players did not hobnob with the rank and file of the company, but Lydia was Lydia and cared nothing, he knew, for what was usual. She would perhaps be one of them, if she was in the humour for a birthday party.

The first two cabs, laden with at least three more passengers than it should have carried, went lumbering away, and Jonah, suddenly afraid that he might have missed Lydia in the *mêlée*, ran forwards as the driver of the third lifted his whip and shouted at his somnolent animal. One of the young men who was perched on the step and clinging precariously to the side of the cab shouted at the sight of him, and a bonneted head inside the cab craned forwards and a small white face peered out. Jonah could just see it as the cab began to move and then gathered speed, and he stared after it, his eyes wide.

The cab was almost at the corner and beginning to turn when what he had seen at last really registered in his mind, and he cried, 'Phoebe!' at the top of his voice, and turning clumsily began to run after it. But the stiffness that still filled his cold limbs, combined with the greasiness of the rain-splashed cobbles underfoot, defeated him, and he went sprawling. His forehead hit the stones with a sickening thump that made his head roar and his eyes dazzle. He lay there for a moment, trying to regain his shattered senses. He blinked at the hot trickle that filled his eyes, and only gradually realized it was his own blood. Painfully and slowly he tried to get to his feet, dragging himself awkwardly to all fours. And found the nausea that had hung over him all evening was no longer within his control.

'My God,' a voice said disgustedly from somewhere very far away. 'Is there nowhere we can escape these ruffians? Here's some street arab casting up his accounts right in the doorway! Someone get rid of him, for God's sake!'

The retching stopped and very slowly, as though he were moving in some sort of nightmare, he moved; lifting his head, dragging himself to his feet, wiping his hand across his mouth and trying to focus his eyes.

'I wish to see – please to seek for me – Mrs—' He tried hard to make his voice come clear, stretching his stiff painful lips with enormous effort, but nothing came out but a hoarse croak. He shook his head and put out his hand, but the person who had spoken and was standing silhouetted against the light of the open stage door took a step backwards, distaste showing in every line of her body. And as she did so the light fell on her face, and he felt the strength come back into him, and moved after her, his hand still outstretched in an unconsciously imploring gesture.

'Lydia—' His voice came a little clearer now, though it was still very husky, and the word was muffled, for his lips, he discovered with a sort of objective surprise, were swollen and becoming even harder to move. 'Lydia—'

She had moved away, had been about to go back inside the theatre, but now she turned and looked at him over her shoulder, and miserable as he was, afraid and sick and in pain from his buffeting against the wet cobbles of Orange Street, he saw the beauty of her. Her bonnet, lined with creamy silk, framed her face with a sensuous sweep that matched the curve of her cheek and the line of her long neck, and her eyes, wide and surprised, glittered softly in the gaslight. Her lips, slightly parted over her even white teeth, looked moist and sumptuous and quite extraordinarily desirable. He moved forwards again. and put both his hands on her shoulders and bent his head, as though he were about to kiss her; and in a curious way he wanted to, while at the same time his fingers wanted to curl round that long, slender neck and squeeze it and shake it till it cracked and broke and carried the pretty bonneted head away with it. But it was a tough and strong neck, he thought, framing the words in his mind with great care, a slender but much too hard neck, as tough and sinewy as the face above it was soft.

'Like a sweet pea,' he said, his voice suddenly very loud and clear, and then at last the blackness that had been trying to take hold of him rose above the edges of control, and he seemed to crumble, falling to the ground as his bloodied muddy hands slid down her gown, leaving snail-like tracks of slimy dirt behind them.

He opened his eyes to look up at the cracked ceiling, and was not at all surprised to find himself there. It was as though he had lain here for hours waiting to talk to her, and now she was here at last, sitting there beside him waiting for his words, and he turned his head, and looked at her and said, 'Lydia. I must talk to you.'

But the words came out like a croak, and she turned her head and looked at someone out of his line of vision, and there was a rustle of skirts and a woman in a black bombazine dress and wrapped in the white apron of a servant came and lifted his head with a practised hand and set a cup against his mouth. And though he tried to grimace and pull away, it was no use; so he drank, not wanting it at first, and then grateful for the hot trickle of brandy on his tongue and in his throat.

He spluttered a little and then coughed; the woman moved away and left him lying there and he again turned his head and tried to speak, but now his voice came more clearly, if still thick.

'Lydia, I had to speak to you.'

'What *were* you doing there, Jonah, behaving like some disgusting street creature? And what happened to you that you look so? If I did not know you to be at heart a man of some timidity I would suspect you of fighting with someone! Perhaps about a woman, even! But you would never do that. . . .'

At first he did not realize she was laughing at him, sitting there and looking coolly at his battered and bruised face and laughing at him, and he stared at her in some puzzlement, trying to gather his thoughts. And then he saw the way her lips were quirked, the way her head was set on one side in that maddening, self-aware posture she was so fond of, and the anger boiled up in him and gave him the strength he needed. He sat up and swung his legs over the side of the couch on which he lay and shook his head a little to clear it.

'Lydia, I had to see you. You will laugh, perhaps, but it must be done. Quickly. It is Phoebe—'

'What?' She stood up, her skirts whirling softly about her as she turned and marched away from him, and then whirled and came back. 'Phoebe! God damn all of you to hell and back, is there to be no end to all this? First the boy and then that smug-faced sister of yours and now you – I've had enough of all of you! You hear me? I've had enough! You come and gibber at me, Phoebe, Phoebe, Phoebe, till I am half sick of it. You will make me think you are trying to make me hate the very sound of her name! Well, I shall not! Your sister tried her poisonous tricks, telling me that Dickon – pah! As if I would care even if it were true! Which it is not! I will not be tormented like this! You understand me? Phoebe shall do as she pleases, for my part, and I will not meddle. She shall go or stay – it is her choice. You hear me?'

He sat there with his hands hanging between his knees, his head bent and yet looking up at her from beneath his brows watching her every move with his painful red-rimmed eyes, and now he shook his head.

'I hear you. And you must hear me. She is too – she is too good, too *precious* to be wasted so. Celia – oh, it was too late for Celia, as it is for you. Your mother had done the harm to you long before I came – but Phoebe is different. Phoebe is – you *must* tell her. Tell her to go away. Tell her she must not live this life. It will do to her as it has done to all of you. It will—'

'No, no, no!' She was shrieking now, and the shrillness of the sound seemed to slice through his aching burning forehead. He shook his head and said weakly, 'Please don't—' but she could not, would not hear him, standing there shrilling her refusal at him, and seeming almost to luxuriate in the sound.

But at last she stopped, and turned to look at him again, and now he stood up, swaying a little, but feeling less ill than he had, and looked owlishly at her for a long moment. She stared back, and then slowly, dropped her hands to her side, and after a moment began to laugh, softly at first, and then louder and louder.

'Oh, Jonah!' She managed to catch her breath at last. 'My dear Jonah, if you could but *see* yourself! You are a complete guy, I do assure you! I do not know what happened out there in the alley, and I think it better, perhaps, if I don't ask! Please, my dear man, go home and mend your head! You are making a great pother over nothing, you know! Your precious girl will do well enough here with me. Mary—' She turned her head, looking for her dresser. 'Tell whoever remains at the stage door to fetch a cab for Mr. Lackland at once, and see him home. He clearly needs his bed – and you, Jonah, come here while I clean your head again. You made yourself so agitated that you have set the cut to bleeding again.'

He let her, because there was nothing else he could do. The weakness had come back now, and though he tried to make her listen to him, opening his mouth to speak, she chattered on and on, mopping at his bruised forehead, applying a salve and then urging him towards the door when the dresser came back and said a cab had been found and was waiting outside for him.

'There, my dear man! Do go away, and forget all this silly fuss you and your sister have got yourselves into! Phoebe is well enough, I tell you. She has more common sense than the rest of you put together, I suspect. No, not another word! Away with you! I shall come to see you in a day or so, and see how you are. For the present, goodnight to you.'

She was still standing there in the middle of the dressing-room when her dresser came back, and told her the 'poor man has been sat in the cab, and was away to his home, and looking shocking ill, to tell the truth,' and she sighed and then laughed and said ruefully, 'I tell you, Mary, if the wretched man had said another *word* about his precious daughter, dear child as she is, I would have had to send her packing. There is a limit to what even I can take in the way of anxious relatives! I tell you, if there is another word from anyone on the matter, I shall tell the child straightly that she will have to go. I am quite worn out with it all. Ah well! Call me a cab to go home, will you? I am too late, I think, to go to that birthday party after all! And too put about. . . .'

# CHAPTER TWENTY-EIGHT

PHOEBE was not really enjoying herself very much any more.
She had agreed to come to the party for so many reasons but
none of them had really been enough to guarantee her any
pleasure in the entertainment. Had she known it would involve
coming to quite so noisy and sawdust-strewn an eating-house
as Rules and quite so much drinking of porter, that nasty thick
black beer she had only had before to aid her recovery after the
putrid sore throats she had been used to suffer when she was
little, she would certainly not have come. Had she known that
her Aunt Lydia was not to be among the guests while Dickon
O'Hare, so studiously ignoring her across the table, was, she
would have refused. But it had seemed so charming an idea
when the girls in the dressing-room had casually mentioned it
and anyway it was gratifying to be treated like one entitled to
share the easy camaraderie of the company.

And also, she could not deny, even to herself, that it had
been so clearly a way of showing them, all of them, that she was
a free person, a woman in her own right, and surely allowed to
make her own decisions about what she would do or not do.

First Freddy and then her Aunt Abby and Uncle Gideon, all
telling her she should leave the theatre. It was too much! At
first she had feared that Freddy had betrayed her confidence
and told his mother and stepfather why he was so concerned,
but she was able to acquit him of that, and indeed felt some
guilt at having entertained the idea at all. He cared truly for
her, she knew, and would do nothing to harm her if he could
help it, though he would have to learn to stop his meddling.
But still he had had some influence on his parents and had used
it, for why else had they lectured her so? And then to tell Papa
that they disliked her acting ambitions – it was the outside of

enough! They must have told Papa, she thought bleakly, sitting there alone and lonely in the midst of the noisy singing company, for why else should he have appeared at the stage door tonight like that?

She stared into her glass of untouched porter and pondered, remembering his face, the look of anxiety on it, the whiteness and tightness of the skin as it had appeared in the feeble light thrown from the stage door, and a faint uneasiness moved through her. She had been less than honest with Papa; the time had surely come to tell him truly that she was not merely playing at play-acting; that she was determined upon the life. That he would object was undoubted, but she could persuade him, she was sure, as she always had on other matters.

Better to tell him the truth than to go on feeling as disagreeable as she did now. And the feelings she had were, surely, due only to the nagging she was receiving at Stanhope Terrace and to her concern for Papa. It had nothing to do with anything else at all; because nothing else at all had happened. That was a fact to be kept closely before her eyes. Nothing untoward had happened. Just some dreams bad enough to be nightmares, no more than that.

Across the big room, full of groups of men eating as heartily as though there was to be no tomorrow, where waiters bearing aloft great trays of meat pies and fried fish and boiled potatoes ran sweating from table to table, she could see the curtain that led to the street door, and she tried to imagine herself getting to her feet, bidding her companions a cheerful 'Goodnight', and then walking easily past those leering men and their sprawling legs, asking a waiter to call a cab for her, going out and telling the driver where to take her, going home to bed. She wanted to do that more than she wanted anything else in the whole world; for it was very late – well past half after eleven; but even as she thought of it, she knew she could not manage to get away from there without help.

If only Freddy were here to take her hand and tuck it safely into the crook of his elbow and lead her away; if only Freddy would come with that scolding face of his and tell her she was a silly madam to get herself so embroiled with so shifty a crew of ne'er-do-wells (and looking sideways at the flushed faces and too-bright eyes of her companions, the girls as well as the men, she had to admit they looked very unlike the people she usually regarded as her friends). If only. . . .

The curtain shifted and she saw a man come in, waving his hat before his face with an exaggerated gesture of breathlessness. He said something urgent to the men sitting at the table nearest the door, who listened eagerly; and one of them leaned back in his chair, and told the people at the next table something and they in their turn displayed great interest and passed the tale, whatever it might be, onwards. She watched, herself so separate from the party of which she was a member. Having something in which to take an interest helped her to be less worried about getting home, and who might take her there.

That something of considerable interest indeed was toward was undoubted; the whole room swayed with it, like a cornfield in a sudden gust of breeze, and people began to get up and go to the door to stare out into the street and the confused sound of many voices increased so that even the party of actors became aware of it.

'Wha's happenin'?' the middle-aged woman sitting next to Phoebe said thickly. 'Where're they all goin'?'

'I don't know,' Phoebe said, frowning a little as more and more diners went to peer over each other's shoulders at the door. 'Something in the street outside, I imagine.'

'We'll go and look!' someone at the far side of the table shouted, and at once the rest of them took up the cry, and they were all on their feet, reaching for coats and shawls and pushing their way through the crowd. And they were not the only ones who had made the same decision; more and more people were pushing their way out, and Phoebe felt herself carried along with them, a little alarmed, but grateful for whatever it was. Once they were all outside maybe she would be able to slip away and find a cab to take her home.

Freddy stretched, yawned and shook his head to clear it, and looked down at his notes again with the first sense of satisfaction he had experienced for some time. He had decided to work late at the hospital tonight because in all honesty he did not feel able to face an evening at home. The talking and fussing there had been about Phoebe was more than he could bear. Both Gideon and Abby had been more than gentle, more than understanding, making no attempt to force him to say more to them than he wanted, but still he feared his own tongue. To have to watch every word he said for fear some hint of what had really happened to Phoebe would be let slip was exhausting and made him very nervous. So he had thrown himself into writing up his notes on anaesthesia with all the energy he had, and had been rewarded not only with as elegant a set of pages as any student could show but also with a curious peace of mind. It was as though in being wholly the medical student for so many hours – and it was now close to a quarter to twelve and the wards had long ago had their lights extinguished and the night nurses had even longer since settled themselves in their little cubbyholes with their bottles of beer and plates of bread and cheese to sustain their nightwatches – he had ceased to be the rejected, unhappy lover.

Perhaps, he told himself with a sudden surge of optimism, perhaps I will be able to accept her decision as a final one? Perhaps I will find that there are other joys, other interests to sustain me, apart from Phoebe? She has been too much a part of my life for far too long, that is the trouble. I will have to be like the patients who have their legs amputated – those who survive, that is! I must learn to walk again on one leg, rather than mourn for two, and come to be glad I did not die of my loss. And surely I shall not die of it? There is more to life than love, after all. . . .

He sighed again, and folded up his notes, carefully corked his ink bottle and cleaned his pen. Home and bed, now. He must be at the hospital again early tomorrow morning, for Abel had said that he was to hold a special demonstration on the use of the lithotomy operation, using a new technique for going straight into the bladder from the abdomen instead of the perineum. And he would brook no latecoming, however much virtuous midnight oil that latecomer had burned.

But before leaving the hospital he made a silent round of the wards, peering in at the open doors at the humped blankets on the narrow beds, listening to the faint moans and snuffles of those who lay half awake as well as those who slept. There was something about the hospital at night that he found curiously satisfying. It was as though this was the only time when he could see the patients as real people. All day they were like animals, dumb yet vulnerable and imploring animals, clamouring for help, for treatment, for relief from their pain, a collection only of reaching hands and hungry faces, not human beings sharing the same dignity and needs and feelings and fears that he and others like him had. But looking at them in the helplessness of their sleep he could see them as like himself, and he needed that sense of oneness with them, for without it, he knew, the days would make him into the sort of harsh, domineering and even cruel man so many of the surgeons seemed to be. As, he had to admit, his grandfather usually was.

He had reached the front door, and was waiting for it to be unbolted for him by the man who acted as night watchman for the whole of Nellie's, shrugging on his coat, when the noise made him look up and then curtly tell the man to 'put a move on – there's something afoot'; and when the big door swung wide the urchin on the step outside darted in, and after one swift look round seized on the skirts of Freddy's coats and said breathlessly with a huge and excited relish, 'You one o' the surgeons, mister? Come on, then over to King Street – it's goin' ter be the wust we've 'ad in years an' years, an' they wants yer urgent – come *on*!'

And he came on, running as fast as he could after the ragged figure that went scampering ahead of him, smelling it long before he could see it, and feeling his heart sink.

Gideon looked at his watch for the third time in ten minutes and reached upwards to tap on the flap; when the man lifted it and his face appeared he said fretfully, 'Can you go no faster, man? I am much later than I intended to be, and there will be much anxiety – please to whip up the nag rather more! There's a half-sovereign in it for you if you do. . . .'

'She's doin' 'er best,' the driver said surlily, and banged the

327

flap shut, but the promise of a half-sovereign seemed to help and the rhythm of the hoofs speeded up. He leaned back in his seat to stare moodily out of the window at the passing darkened streets.

She had not been fair, he thought. She came to me and asked my advice, and I behaved as I thought best. What else could I have done? He is a father, damn it! However weak and tender a creature he may be in his character – and who knows better than I just how weak the poor wretch is? – he is still a father, and to shield him from true knowledge of his daughter's state is to deny him his rights. I could not do it to him – to lie to him would not have been my way.

But had she been right? Was it more because of my own bad feelings about my father and the way he had refused to accept our marriage that I behaved so? How could it be? Papa is Papa, and Jonah is Jonah. Why should what I do in my dealings with the one affect the other? Abby must have some maggot in her brain to think so. She had always been most distressed about Papa's behaviour to us, and especially to her. That is why she spoke so. And of course she was anxious for her poor brother. Oh, damn all relations to hell! If only it could be just us, just Abby and me, and Isabel and Sarah, of course. No anxieties about stepsons and nieces and brothers-in-law and parents. Just peace and quietness in the comfort of Stanhope Terrace and leave the world outside.

He smiled wryly at himself in the darkness at the absurdity of that thought. It was but an index of his anxiety about them all that he should think so. He, the most devoted of family men even to consider jettisoning that family! And Freddy and Phoebe were as much his family as were the daughters of his own body. Just as Jonah was part of him because Abby was.

And whatever Abby said, he thought, returning to his silent argument with her, I have done right in telling Jonah the bald truth, even though she would have preferred me to tell the lie she had chosen, that the theatre was full of fever and cholera was feared. No doubt that would have been enough to make Jonah exert his fatherly authority and make the girl give up her madcap notion; but it was a lie, damn it all! And lies have ways of making themselves known and causing more trouble than they ever prevent.

He looked at his watch yet again, and once more swore under his breath. All that talking and arguing and then reconciliation with Abby had taken so much longer than it should have done – it was now close on twelve, and although he had no doubt Mrs. Mohun would still be up and about willing to receive callers, Jonah must now be in a sorry stew. He could imagine him marching up and down and blurting out those unfinished sentences of his, and worrying himself sick. If only the wretched cab driver would *hurry*.

But at last the cab wheeled and turned and went clattering along Bedford Street towards New Row and the opening that led to King Street. Suddenly he lifted his head and sniffed, and pulled down the window and leaned out to stare into the wheeling darkness. And felt a sudden sureness that the glow that filled the sky ahead and the sickening smell of charred wood and soot was coming from his own destination.

# CHAPTER TWENTY-NINE

THE light was lurid, and immensely exciting. It lifted the faces of the crowd pressing up against the three big engines that filled the street into a sweating red eagerness that made even the least of them look hugely ferocious, and it made the curvetting, whinnying horses seem like creatures straight from hell rather than the hardworking and thoroughly reliable London Fire Engine Establishment stable they were. The whole road seemed to be alight and Gideon, pushing his way through the mob, thought for one lilting, hopeful moment that it was not the Celia Supper Rooms that were blazing, sending great sheets of flame and showers of sparks into the heavy night sky, but one of its neighbours.

But even as he thought it he knew it was not true. As he reached the far side of one of the engines, and shoved his way past its great mahogany and brass sides, he saw one of the firemen trying to dodge back as the glass window beside the front door exploded with a great ringing crash, sending dagger-sharp splinters in all directions. The crowd seemed to hiss as everyone drew a breath of shock, and then roared as a stocky man, his tall, crested, black leather helmet firmly clamped to the back of his head, went thrusting forwards to pull the injured man out of further harm's way.

'Braider! It's Braider—' and there was a ragged cheer, and then another indrawn hiss as part of the wall collapsed on top of the broken glass, leaving a great gaping hole at the front of the building.

'Did everyone get out?' Gideon tried to shout it above the noise to one of the sweating men who was pumping furiously at the huge Bramah engine, but the man went on doggedly with his heaving movements, simply shaking his head but not looking up, and Gideon pushed past him impatiently towards the tight knot of people on the far side, almost under the jets of water being thrown by the leather hoses snaking away from the pump. There was little resistance to his pushing, for few of the bystanders, eager to see all there was to see though they were, wanted to get near the engines where the heat was so intense. It brought the sweat out on to Gideon's face with a suddenness that made him blink and shake his head to clear his vision, as he stared about him angrily.

It was the man who had pulled the injured fireman out of danger who turned towards him when he repeated his shouted question, staring at him sharply from beneath heavy ridged brows. 'Wha' d'ye ask, man?' he cried. 'We've nae time t'be wastin' on ye newspaper fellars, an' so I tell ye! This is too big an' too—'

'My brother-in-law,' Gideon roared back, and pulled his hat from his head to wipe his forehead on his sleeve, for the heat was getting worse and worse. 'He's the owner of the building, damn it! Where is he? Is he safe?'

At once the man seized his arm and pulled him away from the crowd, back towards the engines. 'Come on – I want words wi' ye – but ye'll have to wait a wee moment – these men are tirin' too fast – hi! You – go call me up some volunteers! The pumps need new hands. A shillin' an hour, remember, an' all the free beer they can tak' – aye – tha's the way – come on, now, move it—'

The crowd had shifted and swayed, and men had come pushing forwards, costers and thieves and householders and young aristocrats caught up in an exciting end to a night's entertainment, and they pushed aside the almost prostrated firemen and took over the pumping lustily, and a chorus began, unevenly at first, and then gathering rhythm and momentum; 'Beer, oh! Beer, oh! Beer, oh!' they were chanting and the crowd picked it up, shouting the words with enormous gusto, and Gideon felt a sudden surge of sick rage at them, for somewhere in all this dreadful *mêlée* that they were treating as a free side show was Jonah, and behind him lay the wreck of Jonah's home and enterprise. And he shouted hoarsely,

331

'God Almighty, where is he: My brother-in-law – where is he?'

Once again it was the stocky man who had been organizing the volunteer pumpers who heard him first and he turned back and seized Gideon's elbow and pulled him away, back past the sweating shouting crowds to the side of the road, where people were lying outstretched on the pavements, and others were crouching beside them, trying to comfort them.

'Listen, mon, there's some talk among this lot as there was a matter o' purpose in this fire. Now, I've no way o' saying one way or the other yet whether this be so, but from all my experience in Edinburgh I can tell ye I soon will know whether this was arson or not – when I get the chance to look round after the fire's out. It takes a lot to pull any wool over Jimmy Braidwood's eyes, I can tell ye – now, d'ye see yon brother o' yours among this lot?'

Gideon stared at him for a moment and then, bewildered and full of a sudden new sort of fear, turned and looked at the figures at his feet and began to walk slowly along the row with his head bent, staring at each face with a kind of hungry eagerness.

Customers, most of them, he thought, customers. But not the jovial, shouting, drinking, happy men they usually were. Blackened faces, charred and torn clothes, and singed beards and whiskers which would have made them all look ludicrous if it had not been so obvious that many of them were in dreadful pain, rolling about and moaning in their agony.

But bad as they were, the women seemed in worse state. The men had been in some part protected by their tight clothes, but the serving maids whose full cotton skirts had caught fire lay there with their blackened legs and bare, dreadfully singed arms held outstretched pitifully, and he tried to look away, but could not, feeling himself forced to stare at them, and at the tattered burnt silk of the singers' and dancers' costumes. He suddenly sickened at the sight and swallowed hard.

One of the crouching figures looked up at him, and he peered at the upturned face, puzzled; then Freddy's voice said matter-of-factly, 'Gideon. Thank God you're here. Settle this matter, will you? There's some mad talk going on – they're saying this was deliberate.'

There was a sudden cry from the end of the row of injured people and he scrambled to his feet. 'I must get these people to Nellie's. Sort it out, Gideon, for God's sake – I'll see you at the hospital when you can get there. Find Uncle Jonah—' and he was gone, pushing through the crowd, and then bending to pick up and carry away one of the injured women. Gideon watched him go, looking at the way the girl's head rolled back helplessly against the strong young arms that held her, and he shook his head, again trying to clear it, and turned and hurried back to Braidwood.

'He's not here,' he said hoarsely. 'That was his nephew – he told you too, didn't he? He's not here. And what do you mean, deliberate? I don't understand—'

'This man—' Braidwood said, and turned and beckoned. A figure detached itself from a cluster of people sitting on the kerb and limped towards them. Peering, Gideon recognized him as Jonah's head waiter, and he said wonderingly, 'What is he talking about, Davey – deliberate?'

'Mr. Jonah, sir,' the man said, and his teeth looked horribly white against his blackened skin, and his eyes glinted even whiter and more threatening in the flickering yellowness that still lit the scene from the blaze beyond them. 'Come in in a dreadful state, took 'isself up the stairs wiv 'is candle, said no one was to disturb 'im not no'ow. I said as it was all wrong, an' I should send for a surgeon, 'e looked so pitiful, all beat about an' all, but 'e got right nasty wi' me, which was never Mr. Jonah's way, as well you know, sir, an' took 'is candle and said to send up an extra bucket o' coals, on account 'e was cold. And I took 'em up meself, an' there 'e was, a'sitting beside 'is fire which was built so 'igh it was fit to burn yer eyebrows orf, and shiverin', an' 'e gives me this letter and says as no one is to disturb 'im and sends me away.'

He took a deep breath then, and shook his head. 'It was so sudden then, Mr. Gideon! One minute there I was a'servin' o' me dinners an' the next there's this screamin' and the girl rushin' 'n' shoutin' as there's fire up above, an' comin' dahn the stairs, and I goes ter see an' tells the girl to shut up and get aht quiet, but it's too late, ain't it? I mean, there's the customers 'eard 'er and they're a'shovin' an' a'pushin' an' the doors get jammed and no one can get aht one way or the other, an' the 'ole place starts to go up like a tinderbox, and then—' he shook his head again. 'An' then I 'eard the noise of the 'orses, and someone's seen, an' they get us aht. Yer a great man, Mr. B, an' I'm that grateful to yer—'

'The letter!' Gideon said urgently. 'The letter! Who was it for? Do you still have it?'

'Eh? Oh yerss – shoved it in me pocket, di'n't I? Well I reckoned as I'd give it you when you arrived like 'e said, and never give it another thought. It's fer you, Mr. Gideon, see – I was told by Mr. Jonah as to give it yer the minute you arrived.'

He was digging into his pockets, pulling aside the charred remains of his coat, and then, with a satisfied grunt, he found it and held it out to Gideon, who stood there staring down at the square of sooty paper, not wanting to touch it. Braidwood said sharply, 'Well, man, tak' it, tak' it! I've t'know the contents, ye understand! If this is arson for insurance, ye see—'

Gideon's head snapped up. 'Insurance? Don't be a fool!'

'Why? Was he no' insured?' Braidwood said sharply.

'Well, of course he was! He'd be no sort of businessman if he were not – but to suggest—'

There was a sudden hoarse shout from the engines, and at once Braidwood turned and shouted back. At the reply he got, unintelligible though it was to Gideon, he hurried away, and Gideon stood and stared at the man in front of him, and then at the letter in his hand, and felt too numb to think anything at all.

'Braidwood seems to think as Mr. Jonah done 'isself in this way, Mr. Gideon,' Davey said, moving closer and staring up into Gideon's face. 'An' I cannot deny, sir, as 'e was in a right takin'. But that ain't Mr. Jonah's way, is it? It can't be – but it did 'appen so sudden an' all. Read the letter, Mr. G, and put me aht o' me misery. An' show Jimmy Braidwood as 'e's wrong. 'E may be a great fireman, but 'e don't know our Mr. Jonah, do 'e?'

334

Gideon closed his eyes for a moment, and there framed against the glow of redness that even his tight-shut lids could not exclude he saw Jonah's face with its look of dumb helpless misery, the way he had thanked him so courteously for his good offices, and then turned away. He could almost hear his voice as he had agreed so quietly to wait until Gideon had gone home and explained to Abby that together they would call upon Lydia that night, and seen him into his cab. And now—

He opened his eyes sharply, and with one crisp movement opened the letter.

*My dear Gideon, I could wait for you no longer. I am sorry to have behaved so but my perturbation was too great to permit of any delay. I went to see my sister-in-law alone and I must tell you that I obtained no success whatsoever with my errand, however hard I tried to convince her of its importance. I cannot write much now, since I suffered some injury during this visit – not, I must haste to tell you, through any fault but my own – and I feel unwell. I can only tell you now that I see no answer to my poor Phoebe's difficulty, short of Phoebe herself seeing the foolishness of her ways. And I feel such a fear that she will not – her grandmother and her mother and now her aunt are so strong in her – Forgive me, I can write no more now. Please do not try to see me tonight, I am so distraught. I will see you tomorrow perhaps, and we will see what we can contrive. – Yours always, Jonah.*

The wave of relief that came over him was so enormous that he felt suddenly weak. His knees seemed to bend under him and he put out one hand and Davey peered up at him and said anxiously, 'Mr. Gideon? What does 'e say, Mr. Gideon? 'E never fired the 'ouse, did 'e, sir? Do say 'e never—'

'No, Davey, he didn't,' Gideon said shakily. 'Thank God, he didn't. He said he would see me tomorrow – it was an accident, because he felt ill, that is all, a dreadful, dreadful accident. But, thank God, an accident. Braidwood – Braidwood!'

He whirled, and pushing, tried to make his way to the centre of the fire fighters, waving the letter above his head.

And was stopped in his tracks as, suddenly, a hand pulled on his coat from behind. He turned in fury, needing desperately to reach that suspicious Scotsman's side and convince him that Jonah had not tried some sort of bizarre suicide, that he was still in that building and could be alive and had to be searched for and brought out.

'Uncle Gideon – oh, Uncle Gideon, thank God you are here! Thank God – Papa – where is Papa: I came with the others – I did not know till we were here – oh, Papa, where is he? Where is he?'

She was weeping, the tears running down her soot-stained face, and he put a hand out to touch her shoulder and said urgently, 'Phoebe, for the love of God, go away! I am trying – I must speak to the man – wait—' and he turned again and pushed towards the centre of the crowd with Phoebe still holding on to his coat and running behind him as he tried to shake her off, but she clung harder, and at last he was there, himself pulling on Braidwood's coat, and he knew how absurd it must look, and almost wanted to laugh. It was just as though he and the children were in the garden playing trains.

'Braidwood – read it, for God's sake!' he shouted. 'He's still in there, isn't he? And he could be alive. Send someone in for him – he's there and alive somewhere – hurry, man!'

Braidwood took the letter and read it with what seemed to Gideon to be an agonizing slowness, and he tugged again on the heavy grey coat, and Braidwood lifted his head and said simply, 'Aye. I believe ye. 'Tis not arson, on this showin' – though we'll still have to check, ye understand—'

'Get him out!' Gideon screamed at him, and now Phoebe was beside him and pulling equally urgently on the other side of the uniform coat. 'Papa – is he still in there? Please – where is Papa?'

Braidwood looked down at her and back at Gideon and then over his shoulder at the building where now the roof was blazing, great flames shooting up into the sky, and he stared for a long moment, and then looked back at them and said almost abstractedly, 'He was in the upstairs front room?'

336

'Yes,' Gideon said urgently. 'Yes! That was his private room—'

'Then he'll no' be there the now. That part o' the house is fair gutted. If he's alive at all, he'll have to be on the floor below, I'm thinkin'. Would have fallen through, do you see—'

Gideon stared hopelessly at Braidwood. 'Couldn't he be alive, for all that? Could he not have got out of his room and—'

'Well, we'll get nowhere standin' here discussin' it, and that's a fact,' Braidwood said with a sudden air of purpose and he pulled his helmet closer down over his ears as he turned back towards the blazing house. 'I'd best go an' see for mysel' what's afoot. I'll see wha' we can manage. But there's no promises, mind—'

And he was gone, thrusting through the crowd of firemen which opened before him like a sea wave. He hesitated for one brief moment at the gaping black hole which was the doorway and a sort of rumbling silence fell, broken only by the creaking of the pumps and the grunting of the men operating them, all too breathless now to keep up their cries of 'Beer, oh!' which had been coming from them so monotonously. It was as though they had all been waiting for this climactic moment, and necks craned and eyes glittered in the fitful light as they watched.

He disappeared into the black hole, and Phoebe with a sudden whimper turned and buried her face against Gideon's coat. Automatically he put his arm about her shoulders and patted her back, murmuring, 'There, there,' very softly. But he didn't take his eyes from the building and the gap into which the square, helmeted figure had gone.

It seemed to go on for an eternity. He was aware of movement around him, of people moving closer to the building as the flames in the lower part of it became less urgent, cowering down now almost as though they were afraid of the man who had marched so coolly through them.

And then there was a great roar and the jets of water from the hoses seemed to bow and falter as the men on the pumps stopped to join in the cry, for Braidwood had reappeared and over his shoulder was bearing the figure of a man. He paused there, framed blackly against the light and then came stumping forwards and Gideon and Phoebe moved towards him together as he reached the open space in front of the engines and bent and laid his burden on the ground. They all stood there for a long moment, staring downwards at the travesty of a human face which lay there, at the tattered charred fragments of clothing which clung to the upper chest and shoulders and stirred a little in the movement of hot air that the fire was sending out, almost as though they were dancing.

And then the face seemed to move, to shape itself anew, and the eyes opened and the tight black lips stretched, and as Phoebe crouched down beside him Jonah said very softly, 'Phoebe—' and she put her head down on his burned chest and clung to him and wept and the arms, torn and blackened and scarecrow-like in the yellow light, came up and went round her shoulders.

# CHAPTER THIRTY

THEY sat with their chairs set very close together as though being so near each other would somehow help not only themselves but him. Gideon and Abby, and Ellie sitting grimly facing them, and never taking her eyes from Abby's face. Only Phoebe sat a little apart, her hands crossed on her lap, seemingly unaware of the dirt that streaked her face and the stains of water and soot that bedraggled her gown. Her eyes were wide and the shadows beneath them made her look older than any of them. From time to time Abby looked across at her, and wanted to reach out her arms as she had been used to do when Phoebe was a child. But she did not, for Phoebe was no longer a child, and all of them knew it.

Beyond the waiting-room with its rows of silent wooden chairs and its tall narrow windows they could see the noonday light in the street outside, could hear the children shouting and playing, and the raised indignant voices of those who were being turned away from the out-patient doors. It mattered not a whit to them that close on thirty people had been badly injured in last night's disaster in King Street, where the Celia Supper Rooms stood, a dead and blackened gap among its neighbours. That was last night's disaster. Now it was another day, and they had disasters of their own, wounds and pains and dying relations in need of treatment just as much as last night's lot. So the shrill voices shouted and were answered by the sharper deeper tones of Nellie's doorman, and still the family sat on, waiting.

Abel had been sent for as soon as the size of the disaster had been realized. He had come to find Freddy had managed to alert Nancy, who had in turn called out all of the hospital's doctors and students that she could, sending local children scampering all over London with her terse messages. But even though the hospital had been working at full strength ever since three o'clock in the morning, the results weren't what they would have hoped.

Three of the customers of the Supper Rooms had been found to be dead as soon as they arrived; and of the others only five had injuries superficial enough to require little attention. The rest had demanded much care, for not only were they severely burnt; many had great cuts and gashes from the broken glass that had strewn the ground like apple blossom in April, and broken bones from the urgent struggle to escape the burning building. Jonah was one such with one leg virtually shattered and his hip on the other side crushed out of shape by the fall that had taken him from his cinder of a room to the stone-flagged floor below.

The operating theatre had been occupied all night with sweating surgeons and screaming patients as legs were amputated and such stitching that could be done was attempted and bones were set in splints. But as the night wore on the number of dead mounted, and more and more shrouded figures were carried laboriously down to the anatomy rooms in the basement of the hospital.

From time to time Freddy came to the waiting-room to tell them of Jonah's progress, for he had set himself the task of watching him himself, as well as doing all the other work that was required of him. And there was much, for in such an emergency the difference between students and fully trained surgeons became more and more blurred, and Freddy found himself operating on minor injuries, gritting his teeth against the shrieks of agony – for there was not enough chloroform to give to all the people needing his attentions – and getting on with it. But the strain showed on his face, as he became ever more pale and his eyes seemed to sink ever more deeply into his head.

He had tried hard to persuade them all to return to Stanhope Terrace.

'There is nothing you can do, being here,' he had said earnestly, standing beside Phoebe sitting still and upright. 'We will

do all we can, I promise you. Phoebe, please to go home.
Mamma – Gideon, can you not persuade her?'

'She has a right to stay, Freddy,' Abby said softly. 'She
needs to stay, I think. And if she does, she will need me. . . .'

'And I cannot leave the two of them, can I, Freddy?' Gideon
said reasonably. 'No, my boy, you return to your work. We will
take care of matters here. Do not worry about Phoebe. We will
take care of her for you.'

And Freddy had looked at him gratefully and gone away to
work again, and still Phoebe sat there silently as the before-
dawn darkness melted into morning normality and the streets
outside filled with the bustle of traffic, stirring herself only
once to ask whether a message had been sent to Oliver, and
when he might be expected to arrive. Gideon had told her
quietly of the telegraph message he had sent, and the times of
trains from York. She had nodded listlessly, accepting that her
brother could not be looked for much earlier than six o'clock in
the evening, and then subsided back into her silence.

It was at two o'clock that Abel came to them and stood there
in the door looking at them all.

'Abby,' he said, and his voice was low. 'I would speak with
you, my dear, if you please.' And she had gone to him, throwing one anxious look over her shoulder at Phoebe who gazed
back at her with eyes wide and dark with fear.

Abel drew her outside the door, and stood with his hand on
her sleeve. 'He is dying, Abby. I – he could not have survived,
for his injuries are very dreadful. I wanted you to know that
we have made our peace, he and I—'

She looked up at him in the dimness of the hallway, at the
lined face and the tired green eyes and for the first time since
the horror had started, her eyes smarted with tears and she
lifted her hand to brush them away. For so many years now she
had hoped that the old rift that had lain between Abel and his
eldest son would be healed, and to find it had been now was so
painful and so cruel that she felt herself filled with anger as
well as distress, and said sharply, 'It should have been years
ago, Papa!'

He looked down at her and said heavily, 'I know. We – it is

greatly to be regretted.' And at once at the sound of pain in his voice she regretted her sharpness and reached up and put her arms about his neck and kissed his cheek, and he held her tightly for a moment and then almost roughly pushed her away.

'The question now is his daughter,' he said, and his voice was its customary dry self again. 'I hardly know the girl, and no doubt you will be at pains to tell me it is my own fault. Well, I daresay it is. But I must ask you now what we should do. Is she able to deal with herself sensibly do you think? Or is she the no more than flibberty miss I have observed her to be?'

'She can deal with herself,' Abby said quietly. 'More than you could imagine, Papa. She is more your granddaughter than perhaps you realized. She is very – stubborn – about what she wants.'

'Is she? I am glad to hear it. Well, you had best tell her the time is short. I do not think he can live more than an hour or two. If she can comport herself well, she should go and see him now. He remains conscious yet.'

He turned to go, and then stopped, and spoke carefully, not looking at her. 'He looks very – bad, Abby. His face is much damaged. Warn her of that. It – it is hard to recall how pretty a baby he was.' And he was gone, hurrying up the stairs back to the wards. She watched him go and took out her handkerchief and rubbed her eyes and blew her nose and then, with all the composure she could muster, went back into the waiting-room.

Phoebe was standing up and facing the door, and she looked very directly at Abby and said calmly, 'He is dead.'

'No, my love. Not yet.' Abby said as gently as she could. 'But he – your grandfather says it cannot be long. He – if you wish to see him, darling, you may. But he looks dreadfully injured and perhaps—'

'I will see him,' Phoebe said, her voice still filled with that curious flat calm, and she pulled her pelisse closely about her shoulders and put up her hand to tidy her bedraggled hair in a gesture that was as pitiful as it was unconscious. Abby swallowed, and nodded, not trusting herself to speak, and stood aside at the door, to let her go.

She walked out quietly and up the stairs, not even trying to recall which ward they had taken him to, but letting her own feet take her there, and as she reached the door to the big room it opened, and she stopped, to see Freddy looking at her with his fatigue-darkened eyes and a face as pale as her own.

'I have come to see Papa,' she said, and he nodded, and put out his hand but she shook her head. So he stood aside, exactly as his mother had done downstairs, and held the door for her. And with her head high and her steps quite steady she walked in, past the rows of narrow beds and the moaning, tossing patients, down to the far corner.

It was not until she reached the foot of the bed that her step faltered, and then only momentarily. And then she was beside him and on her knees, her hands over both of his on the coverlet, and looking down into his face.

It took all the strength she had not to show the horror that filled her at the sight of him, for the burns extended across his mouth and cheeks so widely that he seemed to be grinning at some dreadful private joke of his own, and his eyes were staring open, lacking the lids any more to close them. But she kept her face quite still and said gently, 'Papa?'

He moved very slightly, letting his eyes make the painful journey in his skull, until he could see her, and then it was as though that dreadful grimace deepened, becoming even more villainous, and she knew he was smiling at her, that tender, gentle, deeply caring smile that had been part of her life for as long as she could remember, and she smiled back, putting all of her skill as well as her pain and love into it, wanting him to see her as he always had, sparkling and laughing and teasing.

'Dear Papa! Such a thing to happen!' she said softly. 'To fall asleep beside the fire and singe your whiskers! You will have to hide away until they grow again, and restore your beauty!'

His lips moved as though he wanted to speak, but she set her fingertips on the tightly stretched skin, so fragile and broken now, and shook her head.

'No, my love. Not a word. You must save your strength to get well again.' But he moved his lips again, and this time she

343

could not prevent him, and the words came out, cracked and husky.

'Li – Li–' he said, almost like a baby speaking for the first time, and she bent closer to hear him better and said softly, 'Are you asking for Aunt Lydia, Papa?'

Again the eyes moved restlessly and she knew his mind was wandering, that he did not really know her, and again that husky croak came, 'Li – Li – Lill–'

'I shall fetch her, Papa,' she said and once more his eyes moved, but she knew now that he was trying to close them, as the remnants of the lids moved painfully, and again she gave him the sparkling loving smile and said, 'Shall I find a bandage for you, Papa?'

She felt rather than heard or saw his acceptance, and turned her head to find Freddy standing behind her and he nodded and reached to the little table beside the bed and picked up a narrow bandage and soaked it in soothing oil and set it gently over those staring eyes, and Jonah seemed to relax a little, as his hands moved under Phoebe's and she bent and kissed one of them.

'Sleep well, dear Papa,' she said. 'I will bring her. And I will return to see you again soon.'

She stood up, and for a long moment remained very still, looking down on him. 'I shall come back soon,' she said again, and then turned and moved away, back down that long ward with its rows of beds and staring eyes, back to the door and the emptiness of the corridor outside.

'Will you go home now, Phoebe?' Freddy said gently, standing there staring at her with his eyes looking more darkly shadowed than ever, and swaying a little with fatigue. 'There is no more you can do. I fear he will soon be in a coma and will not awake again.'

She looked up at him very calmly and shook her head. 'He asked me to fetch Aunt Lydia,' she said, 'so of course I must. Tell them downstairs, will you, Freddy? I must go immediately, for it is a matinée day and I will only just catch her at Soho Square.'

She was already halfway down the stairs before he realized

she had gone and he pulled his wits about him and ran after her.

'Phoebe, for God's sake! There is no use in your going there. There will not be time, believe me—'

'I promised,' she said stubbornly. 'You heard me. Tell them, remember to tell them or they will fret – I will not be long, Freddy.'

He stood there for a long time after she had run the rest of the way down the long staircase and out of the door into the sunlit street beyond and then, moving heavily, went back to Jonah's side.

The figure under the coverlet moved a little as he touched that thready failing pulse, and Freddy bent and moved the bandage protecting his eyes and Jonah looked up at him and again that grimace came as he tried to speak. But now his voice came more clearly. 'Lilith,' he said, 'Lilith.'

Freddy frowned, and shook his head. 'What, Uncle Jonah? What is it?'

'Li – Li—' This time the word did not come so easily, and wearily Freddy nodded, trying hard to make sense of it all. He was dreadfully tired and it was becoming ever more difficult to keep sleep at bay.

'Yes, Uncle. Phoebe has gone to fetch her,' he said softly, and sat down beside the bed to hold the wasted hands and watch as Jonah slipped deeper and deeper into the last sleep of his life.


'You cannot have understood,' Phoebe said urgently. 'You surely cannot have understood! He is dying, I tell you! It was a dreadful fire and his injuries – oh, Aunt Lydia, please, do not waste any more time! He asked for you, and Freddy says it cannot be much longer!'

She was standing in the hall of the house in Soho Square, the door wide open behind her and panting a little, for she had seen her aunt's phaeton with the tiger up behind come into the Square from the mews on one side as her own cab came racketing much less swiftly round from the other, and for a dreadful moment had feared that her aunt would be up in her

carriage and away before she could speak to her. But she had
caught her, running up the steps in time to meet her in the very
act of stepping out of the house.

And now she stared at her, standing there in her elegant blue
carriage-dress, her new bonnet set most rakishly on her head,
and could not believe she had heard her properly. But she
repeated it, looking back at Phoebe with her eyebrows raised
and her hands outstretched on each side of her in a perfect
gesture of supplication.

'But my child, what can I do? You must understand that this
is a matinée day! I cannot just go rushing off to a hospital with
you, whatever the reason! I will barely have enough time as it
is to get my make-up on properly and my costumes ready – if I
were to come with you now, even for a few minutes, the performance would be late! It is inconceivable I delay for a
moment longer. As it is I shall need extra time to tell them you
will be away, and they will not be best pleased, I must warn
you. One is never away, you know, when there is a play in
performance, unless there is some very good cause—'

'A good cause!' Phoebe said, and shook her head. 'I knew
you had not heard me right! I tell you, Papa—'

'My dear child, I understand perfectly, and I am prostrate
with grief, I do assure you, for he is a dear good man, I know,
and of course – your papa. But *you* are not ill, are you? That is
what is regarded as good cause, you see, and even then – why,
last year I played a matinée and an evening performance with a
fever of such severity I near died after, and as a girl you know,
once played for a week with a broken ankle! But I daresay they
will realize that for you, it is necessary to miss the performance
because of your papa, and since it is a matinée and your part is
small, we will manage well enough. I will tell them that you will
be there tonight – and better still, I shall come straight to the
hospital between the performances and see poor Jonah, and
then bring you back to the theatre with me. There! Then there
can be no worries. . . .'

She moved forwards, pulling her skirt up to give her freedom
of movement, and went out of the door to the steps outside.

'My love, I must go – I shall be so dreadfully late! I shall tell

346

them, never fear and I shall see you at the hospital immediately after the performance, I promise you – now I must go fast as a bird – be sure you are ready when I get to you, won't you? Queen Eleanor's hospital, you say? Well, we shall find it . . .'

And she was gone, running down the steps and catching the reins as the tiger threw them and on up into the driving seat in one smooth sustained movement. She raised her whip in a salute as the phaeton went rattling at a great pace up Greek Street, and then she was gone, leaving Phoebe standing at the top of the steps and staring after her.

She could not catch her breath for a moment. She pushed the words she had used round and round in her head, trying to see where she had gone wrong, how it was that she had not conveyed the urgency of it all, the imminence of Jonah's death, and above all the fact that he had asked for Lydia and no one else.

But her own fatigue and distress were more than she could handle, and she stood there in the afternoon sunshine in her bedraggled gown and let the tears begin to run down her still sooty face, watching her past happiness dissolve as her father lay ending his life in a bed in the corner of a hospital ward, just as her girlhood had dissolved under a tree in Hyde Park and finally died in an attic in Panton Street. And she saw, also, her new longed-for and dreamed-of joyous future shrivel and curl and die in her hands like an autumn leaf that lets its flaming glory crumble into brown and dusty uselessness; for where was the pleasure in working at a career that demanded such total dedication that an actress could not even go to see a dying man who had asked for her? Where was the satisfaction in living in a world where the most that could be allowed a grieving daughter was one missed matinée?

She tried to imagine herself going to the theatre tonight, tried to see herself dressing up and painting her face and going out on to that gaudy, glittering stage while Papa lay there with his staring lidless eyes, and could not imagine it at all. There was nothing left her mind could take hold of, nothing of yesterday and still less of tomorrow.

She stood there for a long time, letting her rage and her grief and her mourning for herself fill her and overflow her, and then, her tears stopped quite suddenly and she raised her head and looked about her at the sleepy sunny afternoon, at the babies crawling at their heedless nurses' feet on the sooty grass round King Charles's plinth, at the gossiping women and lazing chattering urchins, and knew, almost as though she had been told, what had happened. She wiped her wet cheeks with shaking hands, hailed a cab and went back to the hospital to be given confirmation of the knowledge that had come to her so certainly there on the steps of twenty-two Soho Square.

She saw Abby crying softly and clinging to Gideon, while Ellie stood awkwardly and watchfully behind her patting her gently on the back, when she looked at them through the waiting-room door, and she closed it silently and went wearily away up the stairs to seek her own comfort.

And found Freddy where she had known she would, waiting for her beside her dead father, sitting there on a stool beside the bed with his hands drooping between his knees, his head bent, and his eyes closed. She stood looking down on him, trying to see him clearly as a man and not as the child she had played with, the boy she had tormented, the tiresome meddler whose attentions she had found so irksome, the young doctor who had helped her so painfully.

And saw all four, and more besides, and sighed softly, and touched him on the shoulder, so that he awoke and sat there staring up at her in the bewilderment of exhaustion, blinking and confused.

'Come, Freddy,' she said gently. 'It is time you went home. I will look after you. Come along, now. It is time we both went home.'

THE END

*Other Arrow Books of interest:*

## THE RUNNING YEARS

## Claire Rayner

She was born in 1893, in the slums of London. The daughter of immigrants, the descendants of exiles, she was part of a people doomed to wander, forever strangers in the lands they had chosen as home.

But Hannah Lazar was different. She was born and bred a Londoner, and London was where she belonged. As Strong-willed as she was beautiful, Hannah would uproot herself from the gloomy poverty of her parents' lives to enter a world of elegance and wealth. As her ancestors had journeyed from land to land, with only their own resilience and determination to help them survive, Hannah would move from the slums of the East End to the salons of Mayfair, to a life that she could call her own.

*The Running Years* is Claire Rayner's most powerful and spectacular novel to date, a breathtaking testament to the human spirit – a richly dramatic and intricately woven story that traces the fortunes of two Jewish families from the razing of Jerusalem in 70 AD through two thousand years of violence, love and change.

'A huge canvas, this, with powerful characters and a gripping story' *Woman's own*

'A feast' *Yorkshire Post*

# HESTER DARK

## Emma Blair

Even to a girl from the slums of Bristol, the streets of Glasgow were inhospitable and grey; the wealth and splendour of its mansions cold and heartless. But for Hester there could be no turning back – she would make this cruel city the home of her dreams.

Everyone said that Hester was lucky. Lucky to have a wealthy uncle in Scotland who was willing to take her in. Lucky to have all the advantages that his money could buy. But Hester's new, bright world held dark secrets, jealousies and fears. And no one had spoken of the woman who would despise her for her beauty and her independence – and the men who would buy her soul and call it love.

# BESTSELLING FICTION FROM ARROW

All these books are available from your bookshop or news-agent or you can order them direct. Just tick the titles you want and complete the form below.

| | | | |
|---|---|---|---|
| ☐ | ALBATROSS | Evelyn Anthony | £1.75 |
| ☐ | 1985 | Anthony Burgess | £1.75 |
| ☐ | THE BILLION DOLLAR KILLING | Paul Erdman | £1.75 |
| ☐ | THE YEAR OF THE FRENCH | Thomas Flanagan | £2.50 |
| ☐ | EMMA SPARROW | Marie Joseph | £1.75 |
| ☐ | COCKPIT | Jerzy Kosinski | £1.60 |
| ☐ | CITY OF THE DEAD | Herbert Lieberman | £1.75 |
| ☐ | STRUMPET CITY | James Plunkett | £2.50 |
| ☐ | TO GLORY WE STEER | Alexander Kent | £1.95 |
| ☐ | TORPEDO RUN | Douglas Reeman | £1.95 |
| ☐ | THE BEST MAN TO DIE | Ruth Rendell | £1.75 |
| ☐ | SCENT OF FEAR | Margaret Yorke | £1.25 |
| ☐ | 2001: A SPACE ODYSSEY | Arthur C. Clarke | £1.75 |
| ☐ | THE RUNNING YEARS | Claire Rayner | £2.75 |
| ☐ | HESTER DARK | Emma Blair | £1.95 |

Postage ————

Total ————

ARROW BOOKS, BOOKSERVICE BY POST, PO BOX 29, DOUGLAS, ISLE OF MAN, BRITISH ISLES

Please enclose a cheque or postal order made out to Arrow Books Limited for the amount due including 15p per book for postage and packing for orders both within the UK and overseas.

*Please print clearly*

NAME ....................................................................................

ADDRESS ..............................................................................

..............................................................................................

Whilst every effort is made to keep prices down and to keep popular books in print, Arrow Books cannot guarantee that prices will be the same as those advertised here or that the books will be available.